ALPHA

K.D. Marchesi

Alpha

Cover Art and Design by - https://miblart.com/

Developmental Editing by - https://livhofer.com/

Copy Editing and Proofreading by - https://www.bardandbutter.co/

ISBN: 978-1-7641816-0-0 (eBook)

ISBN: 978-1-7641816-1-7 (Paperback)

Contents

In Loving Memory of Grandpa Ian Smith
Your simple gesture changed my life.

Party of a Lifetime

Chapter One

"You need to go," Caleb said. His apathetic tone clearly insulted the young woman he had lured to his bed. She sighed in frustration, pulling the sheets across her body, hesitating before letting him see her naked again. Caleb sighed back at her, irritated by her lack of urgency. He struggled to remember her name. A pretty lass who thought she could change him, not satisfied with a one-time fling. Then again, he could be persuaded, he thought, contemplating another round as her long legs swung over the lavish raised bed.

Pausing briefly to admire the dishevelled beauty, Caleb commended himself on his exquisite taste. The girl huffed and shuffled into the form-fitting dress that had been unceremoniously tossed to the floor an hour earlier.

"Quickly now," Caleb chided, impatient.

Father dearest was hosting a party this evening, and he'd be called down to make an appearance at any second. Not that he wanted to go. It was just another excuse for his well-off, very clever yet good-for-nothing father to show off one of his far-fetched schemes, the kind that attracted investors old and new with endless wads of cash to throw at his feet. Caleb had stopped caring about his father's ventures a long time ago. Their relationship had become strained after his mother's death twelve years prior – not that John had given him the time of day even before that. His father preferred to spend his time holed up in one lab or another, working tirelessly. "To enhance the lives of the masses," Caleb muttered under his breath. He didn't really care. Since the flood of investors, his life had become more and more privileged, and he intended to soak up the riches while he was young and hot enough to enjoy it. The rules were simple: stay out of Daddy-O's way. Unless, of course, he was needed as a show pony.

Caleb bent to retrieve a pair of ridiculously overpriced shoes to complete the outfit. He buckled his pants, throwing his shirt on over his broad shoulders, and stopped to look at himself in the floor-length mirror.

Shirt untucked, he admired his muscular shape, a shape that he maintained vigorously in lieu of friendships. And if he was honest, he much preferred friends on his own terms anyway, deciding if and when he wanted them. He smirked as he buttoned the off-white shirt over his lean torso, knowing full well he could pull another lover before the night was through.

Congratulating himself on his stamina, he took a moment to appreciate how he had filled out over the last twelve months. Girl gone, now dressed, he turned his attention to his dark hair. Not much he could do about the scruffy mane that would not be tamed no matter how many times he visited a barber.

Destined for a charming mop for the remainder of his days, he supposed.

Running his hand over his light, neat stubble, Caleb contemplated shaving, but he liked the way it shaped his jaw. He would leave it, if for nothing other than his father's displeasure. Satisfied with his look, he turned to leave. Soft, lilting music had started to flow through the air. *Showtime*, he thought. Pressing the bell on the side of his door, he called in the maid to clean up his mess.

***

As much as Caleb liked how he fit into these large, unnecessary gatherings, he didn't particularly enjoy attending them. He reminisced about the nights he was able to stay home or sneak out in his early teens. So much had changed since the night he had walked in on his mother, her eyes lifeless and his father weeping desperately on the floor. After that, he could no longer avoid these soirees.

These events were not for him. They were about John, proving he could have it all: a family, money and officials on his doorstep begging for his latest ideas.

Caleb became an accessory, his talents exaggerated to the point that investors started eyeing him for their own organisations. He hated them all.

This evening seemed particularly heinous. He had already spotted a few people his own age who he had very little in common with, uninterested in whatever they would have to say.

His hand caught the banister as he descended the curved marble stairs slowly, scanning the bustling scene below, searching for someone that might be of interest. The double doors, white with gold trim, opened to let in the glory that was the golden hour, and a pleasant warmth flowed across his skin as the soft light filled the room. This brief moment of simple pleasure was rudely interrupted by the young man who had just walked into his house.

Argo, he thought with disdain.

The ex-best friend was named after some mythological ship and wouldn't let you forget it. Slightly older, taller, broader – not to mention dumber – than Caleb, Argo had the size and brute strength to intimidate.

"A ship built with the hands of the Gods. Don't forget it next time you want to play with the big boys," he had once said.

God, his chuckle was grating.

Caleb shuddered at the memories of the few times Argo had handed him his ass. His dislike for the other man was seemingly one-sided. The giant oaf always acted like they were still best mates, like he hadn't been continually fucking up Caleb's life up in unexpected ways. If Caleb had any sort of competition in life or love, it was that giant lump. *Ass.*

"Caleb!" Argo shouted up at him, a big, stupid smile on his face.

Dammit.

"Just the man I wanted to see!"

Argo's cropped, sandy hair met with neat stubble of the same colour accentuating his annoyingly square jaw. At six foot four, Argo was impossible not to notice. It was bad enough Caleb had had to look up at him as a child, let alone now they were both in their early twenties. Caleb tried not to make eye contact as Argo made his way towards him, his eyes locked on to his target.

"Hey, Caleb. Come on, bro! I need to talk to you."

Caleb couldn't remember the last time he needed to talk to anyone. The last few times Argo had tried to corner him at these things, he had actively avoided the lout.

"We don't need to talk ... ever," Caleb muttered under his breath.

"This time we do," Argo said, his tone losing its playful edge. He stopped at the foot of the staircase, waiting for Caleb to make his way down. Six years of cadet training had almost doubled Argo in breadth, his shoulders and arms now practically begging for release from a tight-fitted polo. His sun-kissed skin made him glisten like a fucking Adonis. *Cocky son of a—*

A nervous giggle escaped one of the girls Caleb had been eyeing earlier as her gaze washed over Argo.

Markus, Argo's father, had long been in league with Caleb's own, working on one top secret project or another. As children, Caleb and Argo had been inseparable. Their mothers had taken them on play dates immediately after meeting. For four years, they did everything together.

Then Caleb's mother died.

After that, Caleb couldn't stand being around Argo's mother, Lisa, anymore. He was blinded by jealousy each time she had reached out to John to have him over. He couldn't stand the love she held for her son, the love he would never receive again.

When Argo's mother died in childbirth a few years later, they briefly reunited over shared loss. But Argo had grown up and moved on, enlisting with the military at eighteen, putting his anger and sorrow into something useful. He had left Caleb behind.

"Uh, ya comin' down those stairs, buddy, or you just gonna tease me all night?" Argo chuckled, immediately getting distracted by a woman walking by with a tray of champagne flutes. His meaty hands reached out, catching the waitress with a smile and a wink. Caleb struggled not to stare at the veins straining against the man's skin, suggesting he'd worked out before coming over.

"Got you a drink, big lad." Argo beamed, offering one of the two flutes he had swiped.

Fuck my life. Caleb finally remembered his legs and the manners he was meant to use at events. He made his way down the last few stairs and took the offered flute with a roll of his eyes.

"Why are you here, Argo?" Caleb grumbled, disguising his disgust with a swig of the overpriced bubbles, the sharp tang fizzing down his throat. Argo was usually excused from these events to attend base camp or field exercises. At least, that's what Markus had said the few times Caleb had asked about him. He pretended to care on occasion.

"Mate, haven't you heard?" Argo's playful tone returned now that he had what he wanted.

"Don't 'mate' me. Heard what?"

"Well ..." Argo paused for dramatic effect as he gestured to the room.

"Spit it out." Caleb could barely keep the growl out of his voice, patience waning.

"Simmer down, sport. Wouldn't want to have to put you in the ring hold again, now, would I?"

"You know what they say, third time's a charm."

Argo grinned. "Of getting your ass handed to you? Sure."

Caleb clenched his jaw. He could feel the vein on his forehead protruding. "Again, why are you here?"

"Dad said it was important. And it's hot outside. Better to be in here than in khakis." He smiled unconvincingly.

Caleb raised an eyebrow.

"Like I said, I need to talk to you."

The doors opened behind them, letting in a rush of warm air, dying sunlight and a handful of guests. Both men paused to inspect the new arrivals. There were more people their age than usual. Some even younger.

Interesting.

Argo grabbed his arm, leaning down to whisper in his ear. "Not here."

Caleb yanked his arm away, horrified at the fluttering sensation that ran through his body at the touch. He opened his mouth to yell at him but hesitated, his curiosity winning out. Usually, Argo would give up trying to make nice by now.

As they made their way through the grand lower level, passing large, open living spaces on either side, Caleb noticed a handful of children selecting canapés. *Weird. Since when does Dad allow children at these things?* At some point during their short-lived journey, Argo's hand had found its way to his shoulder, guiding him through his own damn house.

Fuck this.

Caleb broke free, deciding to find his father and see exactly what was expected of him tonight.

"Wait up," Argo called, reaching for him again.

"Quit it." Caleb waved him away, irritated. "What do you want?"

"Don't you see it?" Argo asked, dropping his voice low like he was revealing a big secret.

"All I see is you, in my way, like you have been for the last decade."

"Open your eyes, Caleb, just this once, and notice something beyond who you bed. Something is off here."

"What?" Caleb grumbled.

"The kids."

"What about them?" Caleb paused, taking another look around. "Maybe it's a kid-friendly night."

"You know as well as I do, the money flows freer when the little ones are left at home. More booze and less immediate responsibility. Come on, let's find somewhere to talk," Argo insisted, reaching for his arm again.

***

The house was full, fuller than Caleb had seen it in years. Come to think of it, the parties had gotten progressively more obnoxious since he had left high school. For the first year after graduating, Caleb's father had insisted he pick a career path – anything with a seven-figure income would do. To honour the family name. By the time he turned nineteen, the demands to attend college had lessened.

Caleb assumed he would pick a school at some point, but the notion of interacting with a bunch of other rich kids who didn't really need to be there was unpleasant. He would rather wait until he knew what he actually wanted out of life. His eyes flicked up to Argo as they made their way through the back of the house. *Argo never had Markus on his back; always knew what he was going to do.* The thought irritated Caleb.

The lavishly large pool John insisted on maintaining was decorated with tea lights and lilies, inviting an intimate dip. The sweetness of the pollen tickled his nose as they passed.

Argo sneezed suddenly, jerking Caleb from his thoughts. Getting increasingly frustrated, Caleb rolled his eyes at the lack of space. He pulled a set of keys from his pocket and ushered Argo into the guest house, which had been locked up for the evening.

"When I said I wanted to talk, it wasn't an invitation for you to have your way with me," Argo quipped, a stupid smirk plastered on his face.

"If I was going to bat the other way, I would at least choose someone with a brain cell," Caleb retorted.

"Funny, I didn't know you liked that quality in anyone other than yourself."

Caleb grumbled, unable to come up with a response.

"Just tell me what you want."

Argo's demeanour changed quickly. The smiles vanished as his back straightened, shoulders flexing as if he were bracing for a fight.

"Let's sit," he suggested, pointing to a decanter placed carefully on a drinks cart by the window overlooking the scenic valleys below. Unsure of where this was headed, but also needing a drink, Caleb made his way to the cart and directed Argo to the settee.

Voices outside stirred and Argo lifted his head, listening to the noise before letting himself relax into his seat.

Odd.

Caleb poured them both a measure of caramel-coloured liquor, notes of oak and vanilla permeating the air. He had forgotten his father liked his whisky sweet and strong. He carefully placed the crystal stopper back into the bottle and made his way to the plush emerald chairs John had insisted belonged in the guest house. He handed Argo a glass and sat.

For all of his earlier bravado, Argo had gone quiet, and for once, Caleb didn't push. Whatever he wanted to say had to be important enough to lure him away from the main house. Caleb watched Argo's large hands twirl the delicate glass, his eyes focused on the liquid inside. Taking a sip, Caleb let the slight burn work its way down his throat. The sweetness eventually overpowered the alcohol, settling on his tongue. Argo sighed and downed his in one gulp.

"Argo?" Caleb tested.

"Something big is happening, Cay."

The last time he called me Cay, we were boys. And friends.

"'Cay'?"

"Yeah. Sorry." Argo's voice was quiet as he stared into the empty glass, nostalgia flickering in his eyes.

"Argo, please."

"Our dads are going into business together."

"That's it?"

Argo looked up at him, his dark brown eyes full of worry. He bit his lip, moving his gaze back to his empty glass.

"They have been working together for years. Why the song and dance?"

Argo sighed again. "Because you're an ignorant douche who has become reliant on your trust fund over the last decade. Somehow, you've lost sight of the fact you could do something with your life instead of wallowing in a bed of righteous self-pity disguised as happiness."

"Hey—" Caleb started, ready to tell the big idiot just how happy he was.

Argo raised a hand to cut him off. "Shut up for a second. Think about what they both do."

Caleb really had to rack his brain. He knew his father worked in genetics, splicing genes to seek perfection, or save lives, or something. He had tried to learn about it as a kid, but John had shut him out repeatedly. Argo's father worked in ... poison? Snakes, maybe. Caleb had never really thought about it. Both men made a lot of money nowadays and knew a lot of important people. If he was honest, he never paid much attention anymore. Once his mother had died, he was largely raised by nannies, and Caleb had given up trying for a relationship with his father. He suppressed a shudder at the memories. For as long as he could remember, there had been food on the table and money in the bank, and that was all he really cared about.

Caleb's fingers gripped the glass harder. He didn't need his father's attention. Never had. Why should he care now?

Argo must have gathered that Caleb was still searching for the answer because a low grunt rumbled in his throat before he stood, walked over and handed him his phone.

Glancing down at the military-grade piece of tech, Caleb saw a news article depicting their fathers shaking hands in front of a hospital-like structure. White building, white teeth, pleasing to the camera and the world. The article had already racked up fourteen million reads worldwide, since – he paused to look at the date – twelve hours ago.

"Woah. The old fellas seem to be doing well with whatever it is," Caleb said, begrudgingly impressed.

"Just read it." Argo pointedly looked towards the device before turning and helping himself to another glass of whisky, his hand shaking slightly as he poured.

Caleb felt a twinge of panic. He hadn't seen Argo this way since his mother had died. The brute was scared.

Furrowing his brow, he glanced at the article's title.

Animal Enhancements to Support Genetic Testing.

Why was Argo so upset? It wasn't like playing with genetics was new. People had been experimenting for years, with varying degrees of success.

Industry powerhouses John Murilo and Markus Kan have joined forces to prolong human life. Both parties have spent the past twenty years working independently to enhance the human condition. Kan's research into the healing properties of venoms, blood and saliva, combined with Murilo's genetic studies, may bring about drastic change within the next decade. The University of Newell and the board of directors from several local hospitals have committed funding and research space for this project. Talks surrounding the first set of clinical trials are scheduled for later this year.

Caleb handed the phone back to Argo and stood to pour himself another drink.

"So, they are working together," Caleb said, still not seeing the relevance and secrecy, although the heaviness in his stomach told him something was off. The party tonight was very likely in celebration of this merger, yet he hadn't seen the infamous Markus Kan since it started.

Argo ran a hand over his buzz cut, jaw clenched. "There's more. This article is the beginning. The kids out there; I've seen them before. In files. In my father's fucking basement."

Shit.

Caleb frowned as Argo started pacing. The sharp tang of sweat lingered in the air. He tried to remain focused on the words coming out of Argo's mouth.

"Cabinets full of files. Most of them kids. Some around our age. Reports, brain scans; you name it and it's there. Pages and pages dedicated to people we don't even know. This shit dates back years, Caleb." The man was losing steam, the adrenaline visibly leaving his body as he spoke.

"Argo," Caleb said, his own voice shaking slightly, a feeling of dread creeping along his skin.

Argo raised a hand again. Annoyed, Caleb let the words die on his tongue.

"We're in there too ..." Argo's voice trailed off as he looked out into the night.

Breaking and Entering

Chapter Two

The noise of the soiree had reached a crescendo as Argo and Caleb worked their way to John's office.

Caleb tried the door. Locked.

Of course it was.

"Hang on," Caleb muttered. "I have a key, stay here." He slipped back into the sea of well-dressed strangers. He needed to get to his room. A thousand thoughts were running through his head. Why would their names be in those files? It didn't occur to him that Argo could have made his revelation up. Every time he had pushed the man away, he had always been there when it counted. It was Caleb who couldn't seem to let go of his resentments.

Get a grip, he chided himself.

Caleb did his best to smile politely at passers-by, grabbing a fresh glass of champagne from a waitress before glancing back at Argo. The big oaf was leaning lazily against the office door like he'd had one too many. Caleb hoped he wouldn't look too suspicious. Even casual guests at these events knew the office was off limits.

Once inside his room, he threw open the closet, reaching for the heavy safe tucked into the corner, and tapped in the code. He'd had the key made up years ago, tired of the secrets his father was keeping. There was never anything of note in there, not the part he could get into anyway. *Why would my father keep a file on me?* he wondered as his fingers closed around cool metal.

***

"Anyone come by yet?" Caleb asked as he returned, making Argo jump.

Caleb moved past him and pressed his ear to the door.

"Cover me."

"What?"

"Use your giant body for something useful and block the view," Caleb said, already losing his patience.

"Oh. Right." Argo shifted to shield him from sight. The lock clicked open and Caleb let out a breath as the door gave way. He reached behind him, tugged on Argo's shirt and ushered him inside.

"Close the door," Caleb ordered.

The door slid shut, cloaking them both in shadows. Caleb felt for the key-hole, locking it from the inside.

"This is a little more intimate than I planned for tonight," Argo teased.

"Can you be serious for one second?" Caleb chided.

A gentle blue glow pulsed under the door to the right of his father's main office. The lab. He'd never been down there. For as many times as he had been able to sneak into the oversized room full of research and musty-smelling books, that door had always remained locked tight, the swipe access much harder to replicate than the key rattling around in his pocket. He shivered involuntarily; this place gave him the creeps.

Caleb flicked open the torch on his phone, unsure what they were looking for. The office was straight out of a movie set. Lush velvet armchairs, red as blood, complemented a large mahogany desk that spanned a third of the room. Floor-to-ceiling shelves towered behind it, filled with books on every imaginable topic. He had tried to read a few but ended up getting lost in the equations his father had scribbled in the margins over the course of his studies. What little wall space remained was covered in framed portraits, doctorates and articles, artfully placed to make the space appear full but not cluttered.

"Look at this," Argo called, waving him over to a round table in the opposite corner stacked with neat piles of papers. Caleb reached for the top file and fumbled, spilling its contents across the desk and onto the floor. Names and numbers blurred together as he knelt to pick up the mess. Photos of vaguely familiar faces flashed before him. He stood and shoved them back into the folder.

"I thought you said we were in here?" Caleb asked Argo, who had gone tense beside him. "What?"

Argo shushed him.

The light from under the lab's door kept vying for his attention. Could whatever they were looking for be down there?

"See her?" Argo whispered, pointing to one of the sheets. "She's one of the women from my dad's files. She's here tonight."

"You literally just got here."

"What?" Argo shrugged playfully. "She was pretty."

"How can you be sure?" Caleb asked, taking Argo's outstretched phone, a pixelated file of the same woman amongst a handful of others on the screen.

Sweat broke out on Caleb's brow as his pulse quickened. Something was definitely off.

"There are others. Here. Tonight." The words were clipped. Argo met his gaze, pupils blown wide.

Caleb's breath caught in his throat. "Where?"

Argo swiped through a series of images on his phone, pointing each of them out to Caleb. He had seen some of the faces briefly downstairs.

"What does it mean?"

"It means something is happening ... maybe tonight."

"How do you figure?" Caleb asked.

"Why else would they all be in the one place?" Argo shot back. He had a point.

"Hurry up, man. Dad is going to notice if I'm not out there soon. Do you even know what we are looking for?"

Argo shook his head, his breath hitching as he inhaled. "I didn't get much from my dad's lab."

Caleb felt a familiar twinge of jealousy. He bet Markus didn't even lock his door.

"Where does your dad keep his files?" Argo asked. "I am guessing we will find more matches like this one."

"Take photos of these," Caleb ordered, crossing the room to the lab door. Something about the light nagged at him, pulling him in that direction. Goosebumps raised on his flesh. Maybe the real answers were in there.

"Wait!" Argo called to him in a hurried whisper.

"What?" Caleb hissed.

Argo stayed firmly in place, his head bent over the articles he'd found. Caleb could hear the soft clicking of the phone's camera stop as Argo frowned at the papers. From where Caleb stood, it looked as if each page was filled with multiple photos, more and more people who they had seen briefly in the main house.

A shadow flickered under the office door.

Caleb froze.

Argo looked up, eyes wide as they met his. Caleb pressed a finger to his lips, willing him to be silent. Slowly, he backed against the wall, straining his ears to see if he could pick out voices.

The lock clicked.

Caleb's heart dropped as the breath caught in his throat. He motioned for Argo to move. Despite his size, Argo leapt gracefully to the other end of the room, trying his luck with the lab door.

It opened.

Why was it open? Caleb lunged with far less grace, gripping Argo's arm to stifle a fall. His heart was racing as they moved into the light. His father's voice cut through the silence. *Shit.* The sound of a key sliding into the office lock cracked like thunder.

Caleb panicked, his breath shuddering. A childhood fear clawed at his mind — his old nightmare of waking up to his father standing over him, a needle in hand.

"Go," Argo hissed, sweeping Caleb through the open space. Caleb stumbled through and shut the door behind them, hoping like hell that whatever his father was showing off this evening wasn't in his lab.

***

With his ear pressed against the door, Caleb could feel Argo's warmth against his back, his breath caressing his neck. Bristling, he tried to move away, cursing the man's height. Without making a sound, he pushed back against Argo, attempting to give himself more space. Argo didn't budge. Caleb could hear his heavy breathing as he held him in place.

"Hear anything?" Argo whispered, eyes fixed on the closed door.

Caleb strained his ears but couldn't pick up anything from the other side. He shook his head.

"Must be soundproof," Argo said.

"If they come in here, we're screwed. And we won't even hear them coming."

"We may as well have a look around. Right?"

"Fine, just get off me."

Argo backed off and pulled Caleb up from the wall, a smirk playing on his lips. "Forgot you're a top."

"Piss off, Argo," Caleb snapped. Argo clamped his hand over Caleb's mouth.

A crash sounded below the stairs. Caleb grabbed Argo's arm again, cursing under his breath.

Get a grip.

"Let's go?" Caleb nodded towards the stairs, urging Argo to follow. As they descended the short flight, automated fluorescent lights flickered on, bathing the room in an intense brightness. The room opened before them and filled with high-pitched squeals.

Caleb's pulse quickened, fight or flight instincts battling within him. He stared at the lab in front of him, his jaw slack. Argo tensed, stock-still by his side. The two stood in silence, staring at the image before them for what felt like an eternity.

He had once tried to understand what his father did. His mother had tried, too. When she died, John had disengaged, burying himself in work. Caleb had eventually stopped caring, giving his father the same indifference he'd been shown. But what if his mother had known something all along? She had tried to strengthen the father-son bond, suggested they work on projects together, that he be let into his private space. Was it all a desperate ploy to pull John back from the screams they were witnessing?

Caleb forced himself to focus as the lights dimmed to a more tolerable level.

"Holy fuck," Argo muttered, his voice barely above a whisper.

"What is this?" Caleb asked, not quite believing the lines and lines of cages holding a range of rodents in various stages of distress. Their cries were piercing, and it stunk like death mixed with bleach.

He approached one of the cages, holding his arm over his nose. The clump of blackened fur inside was no longer screeching. It stared at him, one beady, red, glowing eye pulsating within its skull.

"You see anything like this in your father's lab?" Caleb asked, trying to keep his voice from shaking.

"N ... No," Argo said quietly.

Caleb turned his attention back to the rodent. Half of its face had been eaten away by chemicals, bone showing through its tiny snout. Rotting teeth littered the cage floor, probably fallen out as its skin melted away. He couldn't help but watch, mesmerised as its laboured breathing slowed. A soft cry escaped, a final gasp for life before the light in its eye dimmed.

"Fuck," Caleb mumbled under his breath. What had this pathetic, hopeless creature done to deserve such a death? "What is happening down here?"

Caleb struggled to remember what they had come here for in the first place; the rat wouldn't leave his mind. What had Argo said about the children?

"We're in there too."

Right. The files. Information on the guests upstairs. Or on themselves.

Caleb scanned the cage, looking for a label, a report, anything that might explain what had been done here. There was nothing. He looked up at the rows of cages. At the animals screaming. Some were barley clinging to life, others already long gone.

At the centre of the room stood a pristine desk, as meticulously kept as the one in John's office, but this one was surrounded by medical monitors. The cages formed a grim theatre with his father at its fucked-up stage. The desktop caught his eye. It would be password-protected, but it could be their best bet for information. Caleb absentmindedly tapped the code to his own safe, his mother's birthday, into the screen, hoping the old man had a sentimental streak. A red warning flashed as he hit enter.

Access Denied.

He tried his name. His mother's. His birthday. Their anniversary. Each time, the same red warning flashed before him.

Would too many failed attempts lock the system? He half expected alarms to blare or a cage to descend from the ceiling, trapping them in this shitshow. A vibration in his pocket tore his attention away from the screen. He jumped at the sudden sensation, pulling out his phone when he caught his breath. It was his father.

"Where are you? People are asking. Don't keep me waiting."

Crap! They needed to get out of here and make an appearance. He scanned the room for Argo, who was making his way along the line of cages. He caught his old friend looking up at him and waved him over. Argo huffed as he stood to full height, an audible crack sounding as he stretched out his neck. *Dramatic, but okay.*

"We need to go up. Soon," Caleb said, flashing Argo the message on his phone.

"Any luck on the password?"

Caleb shook his head and quickly cancelled the last attempt before potentially dooming them both. He took one final look at the clean shelves lining the right of the desk, filled haphazardly with various coloured files. No names or titles to indicate what each of them held. They could spend hours down here and still not know what exactly their fathers were working on.

"Are we going?" Argo said.

Caleb hesitated, his eyes glued to a red document wallet wedged between two stacks. This folder looked different, thin, off colour. There was potentially nothing in it, but it looked like it had been recently placed.

"One sec," Caleb said, reaching for the file.

A single page fluttered to the floor. He picked it up.

A list of names.

"Look familiar?" he asked Argo.

Argo stared down at the piece of paper, his brow furrowed. "Maybe. The one I've seen didn't have as many names."

Caleb's heart skipped a beat. There were close to thirty on the piece of paper. "It probably means nothing," he said, going to place it back into the folder.

"Wait," Argo urged, taking the list from him and turning it over. He paled, a sweat breaking out across his perfectly tanned forehead.

"Argo ... fucking say something."

The underside of the page held two more names that hadn't made the main document. Theirs. Caleb felt his heartbeat quicken and turned over the folder in his hand. Numbers had been scrawled and re-printed a dozen times, leaving one scratched into the top left-hand side.

"It's a date," Argo said softly.

"It's today's date," Caleb responded, feeling faint. They both jumped as the forgotten phone buzzed repeatedly against the metal of the table.

"Fuck," they said together.

Hot bile crept up Caleb's throat. Nothing about this felt right. He was scared. Scared of reading further, scared of going upstairs. His feet refused to move, glued to the messy penmanship that didn't fit the rest of the space. His father's patience wouldn't last much longer.

"We have to go," he said unconvincingly.

He grabbed Argo's forearm and pulled him towards the exit, forcing himself to move. The list of names lay still on the floor, staring up at them, having slipped from Argo's hands. At the last second, Caleb stopped, scuttling back to grab it. He crumpled the paper and shoved it into his back pocket. It was their only clue.

The door at the top of the stairs opened.

They froze.

"Step outside, boys," John's voice called down, laced with venom.

Caleb winced and pulled Argo up the stairs. They stepped into the office and Caleb did his best to meet his father's gaze with defiance.

"I was just showing Argo the lab."

John smiled, his teeth flashing in the dim light. He turned to Argo. "Glad to see you could make it, son."

Caleb snarled at the word rarely offered to the man's actual child. His father smirked, placing a firm hand on each of their shoulders. Caleb flinched as John squeezed. A warning.

"See, I told you he was here," John said towards Markus and several guests dressed in crisp green uniforms, their pockets adorned with official badges. Caleb's stomach twisted. Why were his father's military contacts here? They were usually reserved for luncheons and fundraisers. He tried to catch Argo's eye, but John's grip held them both firmly in place. He flicked his eyes to Argo's father, who averted his gaze to the floor.

"Shall we go back to the party then?" John asked. "The best is yet to come."

Caleb slumped under the weight of his father's hand, resigned to the controlling grasp.

"Sorry," Argo muttered, lowering his head.

"Sure, Dad," Caleb said, voice hollow. Another squeeze sent a shiver down his spine before they were turned out into the hallway. The procession of uniforms followed them out in single file.

"Good boys," said John.

We're Just Getting Started

Chapter Three

The hallway seemed overly bright after the darkness of the office. Caleb tried his best to move normally even as every instinct told him to run. His father's strong hand steered him towards one of the living areas dotted throughout the lower levels. Argo had been moved in another direction, the uniformed bodies following behind him and Markus down the opposite hall. Panic tingled underneath his skin as he lost sight of his co-conspirator.

"I'll need you soon, boy. Stay nearby," John said, his voice firm, before he turned to make his way through the gathering crowd.

"Fine." Caleb shrugged his father off. He stood on tiptoes, trying to get a view of Argo, catching the top of his head as he was ushered out of sight.

"Caleb!"

The overly enthusiastic voice sounded vaguely familiar, belonging to someone he certainly hadn't cared to learn the name of. Turning, he feigned recognition although the smile he forced onto his face wavered.

"Uh ... hello?"

The stout, rotund man beamed, thrusting his hand out for a shake.

"Ho-ho! You haven't changed a bit, young man. No doubt you have positively no idea who I am." He chuckled, unoffended. "No matter. I wanted to introduce you to my daughter! Lucia! Dear?" A slight accent crept in as he said her name.

Caleb scanned the room. A handful of teenagers moved into the party. He frowned at their presence and tried to remember if any of their faces had been in his brief glimpse of the files or saved on Argo's phone.

"There she is!"

Caleb felt his hand being tugged downward by the shorter man and followed his line of sight. His jaw nearly dropped to the floor, the problem of the strange guests momentarily forgotten.

"That's Lucia?"

"Indeed it is, my boy! My pride and joy, you see!" He beamed up at his daughter. "Lucia, this interesting young man is Caleb, Dr John's only son. Play nice, now, dear. I believe he would make an excellent addition to the household." He turned to look at Caleb. "Getting her here was the hardest thing I have had to do in years!" The older man chuckled, his whole body bouncing with the movement. "As you can imagine, the life of a socialite and whatnot. I'll leave you to get acquainted."

Caleb watched the eccentric man bouncing joyfully back into the party, swiping a glass of champagne from a passing tray and nearly taking out the server in the process. He would have laughed if he wasn't psyching himself up to meet what could be the most beautiful human being he had ever laid eyes on.

Lucia leant lazily against the marble, and she was nothing short of stunning. Caleb took in her statuesque figure all but wrapped around the solid white support and matching its elegance perfectly. Her white dress flowed gracefully to the floor, allowing the slits to be wildly distracting as she moved, showing enough skin to draw the eye but not enough to be called immodest. His eyes trailed up her long, olive-skinned legs.

Swallowing the excess of saliva that had gathered in his throat, Caleb took a step forward, nearly forgetting how to walk. Lucia crossed her slender arms in front of her, creating a clear barrier between them. The gold trim along her sleeves was accentuated by her subtle jewellery and yellow-flecked eyes. He admired her gently angled face, framed by raven-black curls. She smirked, the movement of her mouth making his pulse weak.

"So, you're Caleb," she purred, her voice direct yet melodic, simple words that drew him in and held him under. If she kept talking, he would happily drown. Caleb couldn't help but notice others had stopped to stare at her as well.

"To be honest, the way my father talks about you, I thought you were the other boy. Argo, was it?"

Caleb's shoulders tensed as a coy smile touched the edges of her lips.

"Now, now." There was a hint of condescension in her voice. "You can show me your more redeeming qualities in time, but let's start with this."

She turned to face him fully. Standing a few inches taller than his five-foot-nine frame, she looked down at him, her gaze locking him in place. He was ready to worship her, if she let him.

"Why am I here, Caleb?"

The question caught him off guard. "Sorry?" he sputtered.

"You must know. The way my father was going on about John and this ... grand presentation." She hesitated slightly, the first sign of uncertainty slipping through her bravado. "He has never insisted I accompany him, but he wanted me to meet the great Caleb Murilo – the boy he was sure would steal my heart. I assumed this was about your father's money, or my father's career, no offence. This is not at all what I expected ..." Her eyes flicked to the crowd around them before returning to him. She gestured vaguely to the room. "So, I ask again, Caleb. Why am I here?"

Caleb was having trouble paying attention to her words. His name sounded so good coming from her mouth. He met her narrowed eyes, considering her question. *Does she know something? Is her name in my pocket right now?* His mind drifted to his father's lab, the sound of the squealing rodents still echoing in his ears.

"I honestly don't know. But your father seems to think we would be good together?"

Lucia scoffed before she made to turn away.

Caleb wanted to pull the list of names from his pocket and study it with her, but he remained unmoved. Lucia must have sensed him holding back. She stopped mid-turn, then straightened, looking down at him with an intensity he couldn't bear. She touched her hand to his arm, the warmth making his skin tingle. He tried desperately to hide a gulp, looking up at her, his eyes fixated on her lips. Her mouth twitched again, a tiny dimple playing at the corner.

"If you find out, come and find me. If you don't, don't bother." Her eyes met his, flashing in the light of the chandelier above them.

"Sure," Caleb said. It was all he could manage as he watched her walk away.

He needed to find Argo.

Caleb snagged a glass from a nearby tray and downed it. He'd had enough. His father's demand to stay put ran through his head briefly. *Screw this*, he thought, moving his way through the crowd in search of the only other person who might be able to help him figure out what was going on.

If his father wasn't going to be upfront, at least he could theorise with his old friend. It was comforting to be around Argo again, working together rather than against one another. Not that he'd ever admit it to his face. Maybe they could wait for the speeches to start then slip back into the lab. His father hadn't locked it behind them.

Caleb's heart leapt as he caught sight of Argo, the big man looking downward, held in place by one of the officers that had followed him earlier. *Why is he being held?* Argo lifted his head, finding him in the crowd. Caleb swore he saw him mouth the word "run" just before an officer yanked him back in line. He jolted, his eyes now snapping forward as Markus made his way towards John at the centre of the room.

Ding, ding, ding! Caleb winced at the call to attention. He looked around the room as strangers made their way towards the noise. He didn't recognise anyone outside of Argo, Lucia, and the girl from the photos and lab reports. More strangers piled into the room, most similar to his own age.

Lucia stood apart, her body tense as she watched the growing audience crowd the makeshift stage. He wanted to go to her, and to Argo, to see if either of them knew more than they initially let on.

The chime rang out again, and more bodies piled into the room.

What are you playing at, Pops?

John's voice boomed, authoritative and practised. A man used to commanding an audience at the drop of a hat.

"Ladies, gentlemen and all those in between." This elicited some chuckles from the older guests while the younger ones smiled at the greeting. Caleb rolled his eyes, but his pulse quickened as the words carried through the crowd.

"This has been a long time coming," his father continued.

Caleb tensed, reaching into his back pocket to make sure the list was still there; his fingers brushed the paper briefly. How many of those names were here tonight? The guests turned towards the projector wall where images of a sleek, state-of-the-art research centre flashed across the screen. John beamed with pride as he and Markus played off each other, working the room. Caleb's hand itched as he pulled the paper out, hoping no one would notice.

The paper crackled as he undid each fold, and he froze. He scanned the list of names. *Shit.*

Lucia De La Courte.

Caleb turned towards the girl, only to be seized from behind before he could move. A uniformed officer locked him in place with one hand, the other hovering near the base of his skull.

"Pay attention," the officer demanded in a gruff tone. Caleb gasped, eyeing his father in the centre of the stage.

What the hell is happening here tonight?

"For years, Markus and I have devoted ourselves to the study of DNA particles, genetically modified molecules, patents and, yes, even living subjects. I'm sure going into too much detail would have you all heading out the door faster than the champagne is pouring tonight." More chuckles from the regulars. "But at the end of the day, our goal has remained the same: to enhance the human condition."

Caleb's fingers twitched.

"Our home laboratories have been operating at full capacity for months, and now we are ready to take our findings to trial."

Trial? Who is he kidding? Had he forgotten about the rejection letters piled up on his desk? Not to mention the mutilated rat downstairs.

What if Argo *had* told him to run? John's only piece of fatherly advice was now ringing in his ears like a warning.

"Think big."

What if John was thinking big? Too big?

The names on the list.

We're about to be those fucking rats.

Caleb thrashed in the officer's grip. Pain shot through his skull as a hand pressed against the back of his neck.

"Get off me," he growled, but the words were drowned out by applause. *No!* He tried to break free once more, but the officer held him steady.

More uniforms were moving into the room. Standing behind people just like him.

"This is my house," Caleb said indignantly. "You will remove yourself right now."

His father coughed and looked over at them.

"All alright?" John's voice was softer now, almost casual. Those who knew him well could hear the underlying menace. Caleb tensed, the hairs along his arms raising.

"Yes, sir," the man with a vice-like grip on his neck confirmed. Pain raced up towards Caleb's skull as the officer's finger pressed into him. He whimpered, his vision fading momentarily. The intense stabbing left as quickly as it had been brought on. He couldn't help but feel that that was just a warning.

Caleb scanned the room, spying Lucia and Argo, both now shadowed by their own guards. Sweat beaded on his brow, adrenaline pulsing through his system.

"Unfortunately, the powers that be believe the process is too dangerous for the general public at this time, so we have taken matters into our own hands."

Own hands? He doesn't mean ...

The article Argo had shown him said they had been granted funding. Who were all these fucking suits?

We need to get out. Now.

Caleb forced himself to relax, hoping to throw his captor off. But the larger man was ready, his hands finding the pressure points with ease. Agony shot down his spine, forcing his knees to buckle. A scream caught in his throat as a hand clamped over his mouth.

"We thank you all for your service in this experiment and wish you the very best."

As John stopped speaking, the uniformed figures simultaneously reached into their breast pockets, withdrawing glowing syringes. They were filled with a sickly yellow-green liquid laced with spots of brown and red.

"Motherfucker," Caleb whispered, almost silent, desperately seeking his father's eyes.

They could work this out. He'd be better. He'd stop spending recklessly. He'd try harder, care more. Desperate, he struggled, but the grip holding him only tightened.

"Dad!" Caleb yelled, sweat breaking out across his body.

John watched him. His expression was unreadable. Then, his face softened in a way Caleb had rarely seen. Only his mother used to be able to make him look like that.

Maybe there was hope.

"Dad?" he tried again, but the word came out as a pathetic whimper. He thought of his mother's body. The sick pooling around her. A mix of blood and bile.

Was the same going to happen to him?

"Dad ... please." Tears streaked his face.

But John ignored him. His father gave a sharp nod to the uniformed officers.

He was going to end up like his mother.

They all would.

A sharp sting pricked his neck. *The needle.* Caleb bucked, trying again to get loose, his efforts awarding him a slight turn. His eyes widened as he saw Lucia. The room was full of screams now. He felt sick; dizziness would have overtaken him if he wasn't still being held in place.

"C ... Caleb." Lucia's voice, weak. The officer holding her plunged a vial into her throat. He watched in horror as its contents descended slowly into her veins.

"Lucia," he choked out.

Her eyes lost focus. The hand on Caleb's own neck tightened, and he winced as his blood turned to ice.

Caleb's body weakened and he collapsed, but he stayed conscious just long enough to see Lucia crumple to the floor.

She shook.

Caleb willed his hands to move. His mouth to scream. Anything. But he couldn't. Paralysis had taken him.

Lucia convulsed, her mouth frozen in a half-grimace, foamy blood coating her lips and trickling down her chin.

She was dying. Just like the rat. Just like his mother.

And soon, so would he.

Lucia's eyes closed, her body still twitching.

Caleb's breathing hitched. His vision blurred.

Then, darkness.

Captive

Chapter Four

Darkness enveloped Caleb completely. He wasn't convinced that he hadn't woken up in some version of hell where all he could see was black and all he could smell was his own sweat. His heart thumped rapidly inside of his chest, the sound reverberating in the shadows.

Focusing on slowing his breath, he ran his hands over his body, checking he was intact. Then he stretched out his arms, feeling for his surroundings, trying not to give in to the desire to thrash and scream inside of what felt very much like a prison cell.

The scent of lacquered wood was heavy in the dark. Arms wide, he didn't feel a thing. He would have to move from his position. He let out a groan and shuffled to his side, feeling for anything solid that might give him a clue.

"Ow," he hissed as a rough splinter embedded itself into his finger. He sucked at his injury, the rusted copper taste of blood coating his tongue. It was sharp, raw, the flavour so strong it made his head spin. A growl rumbled in his throat as the metallic scent hit his nostrils, his stomach tightening in hunger. The need for bloodied meat filled his thoughts.

What is happening to me?

He placed his palm flat on the wall of his confines. *Am I in a ... box?* He thought of the rats in his father's lab. *Am I in a box in a fucking lab!* Snarling, he clenched his fist and hit the side of the wall. The floor underneath him shifted. He stumbled, his heart pumping.

How long had he been in this thing? His head grazed the roof, giving him just enough room to fit. Tentatively, he extended his arms again, testing the limitations of the space. *I don't even know what I am looking for*, he thought, feeling anger well up inside of him. He continued searching the space for a crack of light, a weakened plank, anything to get him out.

Huffing, he kicked out with his foot. Nothing gave. The structure was strong. Caleb growled in frustration, and the roll of it reverberating through his throat took him by surprise. Guttural and deep, it felt like it had come from his toes and poured out of his mouth. The hair along his arms raised and he hit the wall again, unable to control his anger. He was in a goddamn fucking crate. Contained like an animal.

He needed to get out; this couldn't be the end. He was too young. He was too pretty. Caleb gritted his teeth, allowing more splinters to dig into his skin, using the pain to centre himself.

Okay. Breathe. Damn.

Slower, he stood again, his bones cracking into the darkness as he rose to his full height.

A shaky breath escaped him as he found the edge of the crate and pushed. It tilted. Wherever he was, it wasn't stable. Maybe he could knock this thing over. With a deep breath, he shoved. The crate tipped further before rocking back into place.

Carefully, he stepped backwards, letting his back settle against the opposite side of the crate. He counted to three before throwing himself against the wall. The crate teetered and felt light, like he was suspended in mid-air. He barely had time to register his idiocy before he was falling.

The crate slammed into the ground and rolled.

Caleb wasn't a praying man. In fact, he'd never put much stock in faith as a concept, but he would pray to whatever deity would let him see daylight before he plummeted to his death.

Getting his hands on his father wouldn't be a bad outcome either, but he doubted whoever answered prayers would be inclined to grant them for vengeance.

Eventually, the crate stopped rolling. Bruises and small cuts burned along his skin. He would be lucky if he wasn't black and blue by the time he got out of this mess. *If* he got out of this mess. Regaining his bearings, he crouched inside the confines, searching for any sign of light. Surely the impact would have broken something enough for him to see where he was.

"Yes!"

A tiny glint of brightness flickered in and out of view. He followed the reflection of waves across the wall of his crate. He fumbled about, eyes widening in horror as he felt the bobbing of water beneath him pulling the box. Any relief he had felt evaporated in an instant.

He'd landed in water.

You have got to be kidding.

I'm about to fucking drown.

He could hear his heart pound, the thumps echoing in the small space. *Fuck. Fuck. Fuck.* He fought the urge to throw his weight against the sides of the crate again – he had to do something.

Focus.

He inhaled; an onslaught of dirt, clay and rotting fish invaded his nose. He gagged at the overwhelming affront to his senses.

His tomb began to sway.

With a frantic lurch, he realised water was trickling into the crate by his feet. The flow was slow, but it would still be fatal in a matter of hours if he couldn't break out of the damn thing. His mind turned to visions of him drowning, eventually falling over the edge of a waterfall. His body would be found days later, broken and bloated, impaled by jagged rocks.

The crate reeled, the sudden jerk knocking him on all fours.

He turned onto his back, kicking out at the side panels. The thick wood wouldn't budge. He was swaying, the crate moving as the current took him.

A violent crunch made him wince. The crate had slammed into something heavy. Maybe he could use that. Moving to the edge of the box, he anchored himself as best he could and kicked with everything he had.

This was either going to free him, or he'd drown. He screamed as he pushed out with his legs and the wood splintered under the impact.

"Yes!"

Again. Once, twice, each kick giving him a little more light and a lot more water. Blurs of greens and browns flashed before him as he took in more of the river he was caught in. "Let's fucking go!" he yelled.

Pain lanced up his leg as it broke out of the wood, the side of the crate crunching under his heel. He gasped. Freezing cold water rushed in. He pulled his bloodied leg back inside, the limb losing feeling.

"Move, damn you!" he swore. "We're not out yet."

The wood was giving way to him now. He hissed, dragging his leg toward him. The water lashed out, pushing him back into the death trap.

I will not die in a cage. Not like those rats.

Gritting his teeth, Caleb pushed with his good leg, hitting the water head-on. His mouth filled with water and sediment. Desperately, he fought the current, his muscles seizing as he struggled against the force.

Everything hurt. His entire body was on fire. He was tired. So tired.

The water had filled in to chest height, the weight of it pulling his crate into its depths. The hole he had made was almost big enough for him to swim out of. Groaning, he stuck his hand outside, the promise of seeing the sun fuelling his survival instincts. If he didn't make a hole big enough to swim through when the crate went under, he would never see it again.

He tore at the crate, wood burying itself under his nails. Tears were streaming down his face with the pain, only to be washed away in seconds. A plank gave way with a snap. The water rushed through, but he would have enough room. Caleb moved on instinct with an agility he didn't remember possessing. Stones flew inward, missing him by an inch only to bury themselves into the far wall. He would have to swim through the threat of that to break free.

Argo could do it.

Fuck Argo.

He lunged for the opening, hoping like hell there was something to hang onto on the other side.

He met the rushing water, flailing to grip anything solid. It was too fast. He gasped as he was pulled under.

No!

He kicked against the downward pull, determined to surface. Adrenaline fought against his consciousness. His feet slipped against the riverbed. He pushed, throwing himself upward toward freedom.

Breaking the surface, he gasped, pulling as much oxygen into his lungs as he could. The shore blurred in his vision, glorious, eroded dirt rushing before his eyes.

His body felt like dead weight, exhaustion pulling at him. The top of the crate caught his eye. He had been pulled away from it, but it was headed straight towards him. If he didn't move, it would catch him in its maw and drag him down with it forever.

Caleb's body slammed into rocks. Winded, he desperately tried to anchor himself on the slippery rocks buried along the edge of the bank. His fingers caught, a boulder steady against the unforgiving current, and he heaved his torso over the top, the edges of his counterweight pushing into his stomach as he moved. He felt the wind of the crate breeze past him. He was safe.

He crawled up the bank, the muscles in his legs useless as they vied for purchase on solid ground.

God, I'm so tired.

With one final effort, Caleb moved another arm's length away from the water. His stomach scraped against the soil, pain bursting across his ribs as he settled onto the land. Water lapped at the shore as he gave in to the need for sleep.

If the tide comes in, I won't survive the night.

***

Caleb awoke shivering in darkness, bitter earth filling his mouth. Everything ached and everything was wet. He wasn't even sure he could move.

He let out a groan as he willed his forearms under his chest and pushed. He held himself up on his arms, staring at the overgrown trees in disbelief.

This doesn't look like the building in the photos. False advertising, Daddy-O.

His arms gave way, his muscles spasming at his sides as his face hit the ground. He rolled himself over and spat mud out of his mouth. He could sure use a nice, clean building about now. Head spinning, he closed his eyes, seeing the image of his father watching him as the needle went into his neck.

How long had the bastard planned to do away with him?

Caleb cried out, punching his fist into the ground, hot tears welling in his eyes.

"How could you?" he whispered.

The tide had risen while he slept, the water submerging his shoe. He couldn't feel it; the rest of his legs were numb, pins and needles climbing up to his waist. He lifted his neck, trying to make out the area surrounding him in the moonlight.

Groaning, he tried his arms again. They protested but held as he dragged himself away from the water painstakingly slowly. Each movement brought more pain; he couldn't get his father's eyes out of his mind.

Come on, he thought, shaking his head.

Finally, he hit something solid. Bark crumbled against the top of his head. The trunk of the tree held his weight. It would have to do. He rubbed at his legs, the stubborn numbness fading. Squinting against the dark, all he saw were shadows playing in the moonlight. He would have to wait until morning to try and move again.

He let his chin fall.

Wait.

It wasn't just him that had been struck that night. But there was nothing here except for a thousand trees.

He had to try.

Caleb raised his head and screamed.

"Argo!"

He was greeted with nothing but silence.

***

Sunlight broke on the horizon, its light creating a haven of the woodlands around him. The dull ache of his muscles and inability to see his future held him as captive as the crate.

What the hell do I do now?

He hadn't moved. He had sat and he had cried for what felt like hours. He called for Argo and Lucia, too sore and sorry for himself to move. Remembering the list, Caleb reached into his back pocket and took out the soaked paper. The ink had faded but could be salvaged. Carefully, he spread the page over his outstretched leg to dry.

The first day passed in a blur of hazy consciousness; he'd fallen asleep on and off, unsure of how much time had passed since he'd first landed on the riverbank. Dazed, he watched birds flit among the branches, fish hop and dart in the body of water that had almost killed him.

Flies had started to take interest in his open wound, their incessant buzzing a constant companion.

He needed to get up.

There was a hollow ache in his stomach, begging him to move, to find something that would provide strength. He could remember the taste of his own blood upon his tongue. A growling erupted from his belly, but it wasn't enough to lure him away from the safety of the trunk.

He wasn't sure what would finally rouse him enough to move, but he hoped it would come soon. Testing his legs, he stretched out the left, then the right, pointing his toes toward the rapids.

Sore, but functioning. A hell of a lot better than they had been the night before.

Great. Now let's use them.

A rustle in the undergrowth snapped his attention to the side. He inhaled sharply, catching the smell of dense rot coming from old leaves. The earth had been disturbed, creating a pungent mix with fresh greenery. Flickering movements attracted his gaze. There were small creatures moving through the brush.

A low rumble vibrated around him.

Shit. His head whipped towards the sound. It was coming from everywhere. A hint of blood hit his nose, making his stomach grumble.

Meat.

Caleb's lips pulled back into a snarl. Something was close. Something edible. The odour pulled at him, a strange urge rising in his chest. Whatever it was, it was injured. The smell was faint. The flow of the creature's blood had slowed to a trickle, the coppery stench mingling with fresh air. The image of dying prey ready to be put out of its misery flashed through his mind.

"Where are you?"

The rumbling stopped as he spoke, and Caleb's eyes widened.

Am I ... growling?

"What is happening to me?" he cried out into silent trees. They stood un-moved, offering no answers. He shook his head and turned away from the need for blood. He would find a damn fish like everyone else did in the movies.

Instinct tugged at him. His mind was unable to ignore the animal bleeding out in the distance – it was prime for capture. He flipped to all fours, his knees pressing into the dirt. Caleb tilted his nose to the air, sucking in the scent.

A branch snapped. He lifted his head, turning toward the direction of the sound. Another growl rumbled in his throat.

There.

He zeroed in on a slow-moving tuft of brown fur no more than a metre in front of him.

Gotcha.

Caleb crouched, his legs straining as tension coiled through him, the ache in his muscles almost forgotten as he watched the small rabbit hopping along the forest floor. It hadn't seen him. Hadn't sensed him.

The creature moved directly in front of him and Caleb's stomach clenched. He could feel it now, the dust on the creature's fur faintly tickling his nose. He pressed his foot into the ground, ready to pounce.

The rabbit's large ears shot up at the sound. Alert, leaning on its haunches, preparing to flee.

It leapt—

So did he.

Caleb was faster, catching the animal mid-air. He pinned the squealing critter, feeling it squirm beneath his hands.

Agony ran through his jaw. Caleb grunted. His grip tightened on the beast, leaning his mouth down against its pulsing throat. He could feel the frantic vibration of its breath against his lips.

He bit down, needing to feel its blood hot on his tongue. He groaned in pleasure, the rabbit's acidic, coppery tang sliding down his throat.

Another bite, his teeth held firmly onto the creature's fur. He lifted his head and shook its struggling form side to side, a wild, uncontrollable instinct taking over.

And then the desire vanished.

The rabbit dropped, its battered body landing at his feet.

Caleb lifted his hands to his mouth, the slick blood coating his fingers. He shivered, bile creeping up his throat.

What the fuck?

He doubled over, vomiting blood and fur into the dust.

Dead End

Chapter Five

His stomach empty and pained, Caleb realised he would have to eat if he had any hopes of getting stronger and learning more about where he had been dropped. He walked back to the rabbit and ate it raw. He could still feel its slimy flesh making its way to his stomach. The thought made his stomach grumble. He shuddered, remembering the animal helpless in his grasp.

This time he would cook his meal. If he could find one. The little buggers had avoided walking past him since the massacre. Not that he could blame them.

Caleb frowned down at his hands, striking stones together, urging a spark to take to the kindling he'd gathered during the day. Feeling had worked into his legs the more he moved, but he wasn't quite sure what to do next. His only thought was on food. It was too dangerous to fish with the rapids being so fast, and the instinct to hunt and kill wasn't as forthcoming as it had been earlier.

Orange sparks flew from the rock, teasing the edges of dried grass before fading back into the dirt.

"Fucking damn it!" he yelled, throwing the rocks to the ground. "Grow up."

Great. Now I'm arguing with myself. Just ... great.

The fluttering of wings caught his attention. Above him, resting in the trees, was a small spotted owl. The bird had visited him twice now, flying in to call down to him.

"Thanks for stopping by," he said, returning to the rocks.

***

A circle of heat engulfed Caleb as firelight illuminated a pile of small carcasses. Every bone had been licked clean, and they gleamed against the orange haze. He had finally succeeded in his mission and found himself at the entrance of a burrow. The hares hopping out to investigate the flame fell straight into his lap.

Between sleeping and gathering sticks for his fire, Caleb had watched the rapids and waited, hoping another crate would turn up along the shore. Nothing came. There were at least thirty names on that list – someone else had to be here. He just didn't know where to start.

Caleb watched the flames, not bothering to stop the tears that had been a constant companion since he was able to move again. He hated his father, and he hated Argo for not coming to him sooner. Closing his eyes, he leaned back against a tree and watched the moon rise. It shone like a beacon through the deep green canopy, casting light and shadows over his new home.

Absentmindedly, he ran his tongue over his new tooth, an elongated canine that had descended when he tore into his first rabbit. He'd stared at himself in the water's reflection after first noticing it. The sharp fang protruded out from the top of his mouth, hanging over the side of his lip, preventing him from closing it completely. He had tried to push it back in, almost chipping the damn thing in the process. Nothing worked. In the night since, he had used it to tear the throats from his kills, letting them bleed out quickly. His squeamishness over their blood dissipated a little more each time.

He reached his arms out in front of him, catching the heat in the underside of his palms. The hair on his arms had thickened, changing colour seemingly by the hour. Soft black and grey tufts had started to sprout at strange intervals along his body. The patterns didn't make sense, but there were more of them every time he checked his reflection.

When he slept, his dreams were filled with the night of the party. It seemed so long ago now. Only days had passed. He couldn't shake the memory of the syringe plunging into his neck; Lucia convulsing, bloody foam forming at her mouth. Flashes of his mother, her pale flesh flecked with the same spittle as she died. His subconscious would show him images of his father sitting with him, reading, not long after his mother's death, trying to make amends. He had never been able to love him after that. They tried, over and over again.

And then he sent me to the forest to die.

"Can't handle your good-for-nothing kid? Hey, I know what will do the trick. The weirdest boot camp imaginable. Here, have this handy crate to pack them up in." Caleb scoffed out loud, his tooth catching on his lip.

A branch snapped in the distance. Caleb whipped around at the unwelcome sound. Hair raised against his neck, and he sniffed at the air.

"Who's there?" he called.

He tensed, trying to hear through the cacophony of insects chirping to each other and the harsh crackle of the flames as they licked leaves too ripe for the fire. There was something in the distance. A sound he couldn't quite place, like rusted spokes in an old bike wheel, or a zip caught in a dryer. The clicking was slow, soft and repetitive. Whatever it was, it stunk. Pungent death hung in the air.

Caleb kicked at the fire, dousing the light in dirt, pitching him into the dark of the night. He swore he saw a flash of eyes before the shadows turned from him.

"Holy … shit," he panted out, dropping onto his ass and hiding against a thick trunk.

His nightly visitor fluttered to the tree above him, the owl tilting its head toward the shadow. Could it sense it out there? His breathing eventually returned to normal, and he lay back, the bird still watching over him.

He felt no animosity towards the owl. Nothing inside him urged him to capture or kill his night-time companion. Its gentle calls were welcome after whatever they had just witnessed.

"How are you doing, bird?" he asked the creature, half expecting a reply. He coughed at the roughness of his voice. It felt like he constantly had a tickle in his throat when he spoke.

Caleb shook it off and stood. The owl hooted, ruffling its dotted feathers, the whites and browns shimmering in the low light. They locked eyes before it lifted from its perch and flew deeper into the canopy. This wasn't the first time it had done that.

"Do you really want me to follow you with that thing out there?"

The owl chirped in response.

Fine.

He just hoped that whatever made that noise wasn't looking for a fight.

***

Dense earth and loose leaves crunched under his feet. Moonlight filtered through the tall, ominous trees either side of him as he moved. They were much more approachable by daylight.

The further he walked into the foliage, the more the forest came alive. Insects sung, bright nocturnal eyes glowed, and the small creatures he had hunted for the last few days hurried out of his path.

Caleb's mind wandered as he followed the owl flying overhead. It stopped occasionally to preen itself on a branch, as if waiting for him to catch up. He was stronger now, but that didn't take away the fear of being in an unfamiliar place. Maybe he was being led to another crate. Maybe the owl was some sort of guardian, collecting lost fuck-ups whose dads had too much money and influence and could apparently rid the world of actual human beings without repercussions.

The bird called down to him, breaking him from his thoughts.

Should I talk to it?

"Have you ... uh ... seen any others?"

It stared blankly, turning its head upside down.

"Of course not; you're a bloody bird." He scoffed under his breath. "Look, I know you can't make sense of what I'm saying, but I just need a minute to think." He started to pace.

There were so many of them that night. He could see the uniformed guards like they were still behind him. Him and a bunch of others just like him. The bastards seemingly came out of the walls. They were there the whole time, ready to plunge ... what? Poison? From animals? Into their necks. And, what, Lucia got froth and he got a fang? *Luck of the draw at its finest.* Caleb reached up to touch his neck, feeling for a raised bump, a scab, anything to tell him he hadn't made it up.

If you had made it up, you probably wouldn't be roasting a rabbit over a fire in the middle of nowhere. Right.

He had no idea if there were more of them than those on the list. Caleb hit his head against a trunk gently, trying to force his brain to make sense of the limited information. If they were illegal experiments, they couldn't be kept in their homes. Not if his father was expecting the changes to cause disfigurement or death like the rat in the lab.

But it wasn't just John, was it?

Every parent with a child in that room had to have known what was happening. Or else they would be in the damn forest too. Had any of them agreed?

The owl whistled in front of him, its small form perched a handful of steps ahead.

"Just—" Caleb held up his hands. "I need a minute."

His father had mentioned that the lab wasn't big enough, that they had to think bigger. It was the only thing he could really remember John saying consistently. *Think bigger.*

If he and whoever the fuck had buy-in from the government, who were investing heavily and secretively, they would have been able to find space. So, they bought a park? In the middle of nowhere? This sure as hell wasn't a lab. The number of officers that night coupled with the kidnappings suggested liberties Caleb could only imagine. *An island? Only the government would have that sort of power, right?*

Caleb dropped to the ground with a frustrated huff. The owl chittered, turning its head to clean its feathers.

"I refuse to be timekept by a bird," he said, closing his eyes, trying to make sense of it all.

There was so much noise in his head, and he swore his hearing was getting sharper by the day. He felt the vibration work its way along his throat before the low rumble escaped his mouth.

What is happening to me? There were too many things happening at once, too many needs competing for attention. He needed to find people. He needed to figure out where the hell he was, and what he was turning into.

"Hey, bird? Can you find us somewhere to sleep? I can kinda see better in the day."

The owl answered him by flying further into the trees and tucking its head into its puffed-up chest.

***

The soft glow of the early-morning sun filtered in through the thick foliage. The warmth was welcome, but Caleb knew it would soon become uncomfortable as the sun climbed higher in the sky.

The owl stayed with him, flying off occasionally, only to return and call out to him. When he asked for help finding water, it had led him back to the rapids. He had tried his luck again, asking about other humans, clinging to the hope that he hadn't completely lost his mind by putting faith in a creature that could very well be his next meal if he didn't find anything better. The water from the rapids was full of sediment and grainy against his tongue, but at least it was fresh. It would keep him alive long enough until he found another source.

You also stink, he thought absentmindedly.

Leaning down towards the torrent, he carefully caught handfuls of water, running them over his body as best he could. Catching his reflection, he sighed. How had his father so easily discarded him?

Had he been such a bad son?

But he'd tried, hadn't he? He'd tried for years. John had never seemed interested. Not really. A night here or there when he was still a kid didn't make up for the sheer lack of interest as he'd entered his adult years. Then again, if he'd paid more attention, maybe he wouldn't be in this mess.

Maybe I could have stopped it from happening to any of us.

He had made a key to the office ages ago. He had given up too fast. What if he followed the investigation of his mother, instead of giving in to the bullshit "underlying medical condition" explanation he had been given every time he'd asked about it?

And where the hell is Argo?

"Hey, owl, have you seen a big idiot with muscles and shit for brains?"

He couldn't see the bird ahead of him anymore. *Fantastic.*

Caleb kicked at a stone, the shoes on his feet starting to tear from the rough terrain. He frowned at the space around him. Would he have been able to stop it? He honestly didn't know. Argo would have tried to stop it. A pang of guilt and longing pulsed through his chest at the thought of his old friend. He had been an idiot, letting his jealousy get the best of him. Now he may never see the man again. *No,* he thought. *I will survive and I will find him.* Together they would survive whatever their batshit fathers had come up with. He would prove to John, and to the world, that he was worth something.

He caught movement in his peripheral vision, making him jump. Where was the owl now? He'd gotten so caught up in his head he had lost the damn bird. The trees all looked the same. Everything looked the fucking same. If only he had his phone and a signal. He had rechecked his pockets earlier to no avail. The only thing he was left with was the list. The piece of paper was safely crumpled in his back pocket.

The growl that had been sitting in the back of his throat escaped as he slammed his fist into the nearest tree. Crumbling dark wood splintered under the weight of his anger. In an instant, he was crying again. He dropped to the ground. Blood trickled from his split knuckles. He needed food, he needed to stay close to water, but he also needed to move. The sun dipped behind the trees, its dying glow moving further west, promising another night of fitful nightmares.

On the Move

Chapter Six

Caleb plunged his hands into the icy shallows, the river having calmed the further he'd travelled. He shivered, using the intense cold to wake up. He couldn't believe people actually did shit like this for their "wellbeing". He scrubbed at his skin and new patches of hair, checking the water for signs of more changes. The momentum of the water didn't scare him like it did when he was trapped inside a box. Now, it was keeping him alive. He lifted a handful to his mouth, grateful for its sharp and sweet tang. Its soothing cool was a stark contrast to the constant fire simmering beneath his skin since he'd arrived here.

The owl had returned, flying deeper into the forest and calling for him to follow. But he wasn't willing to leave the water without a way to carry any with him.

Caleb left a hand submerged, letting the cool water flow over his knuckles as he thought about the day ahead. He hadn't seen or heard any sign of a coastline. If he was on an island, it was damn big. He also hadn't seen another crate, or the shadow creature – for that, at least, he was thankful. Ripples formed where his fingers stirred the surface, the current brushing against the new fine hair along his skin. The owl was right. He would need to move inland; it just felt weird to trust something that couldn't speak. The dew that formed in the mornings might be enough clean water to sustain him for a day or two, but he would need more before too long.

Caleb pulled out the list of names. He had them memorised by now.

Isabella Knox, Ralph Mines, Darius Tekla … and over two dozen others.

His mind wandered to Argo, hoping the brute was safe. *If you're out here, I'll find you.* Then again, he was probably better off without Caleb. He was the size of a damn bear, not to mention his military training. He could probably survive just fine. The familiar heat of jealousy burned through Caleb and he wondered if his friend knew more than he had shared. *If he did, he could have tried a damn sight earlier*, he thought, bitterness creeping back in.

"Maybe he should find me instead," Caleb grumbled to himself, putting the list back in his pocket.

He turned to the rapids, surveying the trees beyond as far as he could see.

A few things were starting to fall into place. Whatever they had injected him with was some kind of enhancement. The changes happening to his body within a matter of days had given that away. Not only that, but he felt stronger, faster, and he was picking up smells and sounds further away than he thought possible for a human. His eyes were adjusting better when the night fell as well. He didn't know exactly what he had been stuck with but given his father's expertise and seemingly sane mastermind fuckery, it was something to do with animal DNA. Something that would survive in the woods. He'd been infected. *Me and all the others with needles to their throats.*

He made his way back to the water and stared down at his changing reflection. His once-dark eyes looked back at him, one now an unfamiliar, brilliant blue, the other streaked with emerald through the brown. He reached out a finger to run it along his tooth. It had come in handy, more so than his new patch of ass hair, that was for sure.

"Who are you becoming?" he asked his reflection. He ran through a list of animals in his head, checking them off one by one. Some kind of big cat, maybe? They were strong, fast and could see well at night, right?

He narrowed his gaze, trying to make out smaller details that could offer him a clue. His jaw had shifted. It was sharper, more of a point than the rounding of a feline. It was kind of like a—

Wolf.

Caleb lifted his chin, tilting his head to catch the sun's warmth. He sniffed the air, searching for something, anything that might lead him to one of the others. The forest's familiar scents filled his nose: damp earth, fresh foliage, dust and wildlife. The owl's scent was lighter, cleaner, soft and earthy, its dust mites tickling his nose.

Giving up on his reflection, he made his way to a patch of wild berries. He sniffed at the fruit before taking a step away from them. His tongue coated with saliva at the anticipation of their bitter sourness. Yuck. They were not ripe, and he had no idea if they would kill him or not.

The owl called to him, chittering its beak in an impatient whirr of noise.

"Okay, okay. It's not like there is anything new to see here anyway." Caleb rolled his eyes and took a last look at the water before walking after his companion.

He knew next to nothing about his father's research, or Markus's for that matter, but Argo said they were in this together, playing with people's lives. It might be changing him, but he had no doubt it had killed others, especially if authorities had pushed back and it was too dangerous to be conducted in the public eye.

Just how much blood is on your hands, Dad?

His body *had* changed, if that was the end goal. What had they said? "To enhance the human condition." His father had done it, at least with him. Unless he was bound to suffer the same fate as Lucia. Caleb had no idea if she had been brought to this place alive. Her glassy eyes had looked devoid of life the last time he had seen her. Just like his mother, Lydia. He took in a sharp breath, new tears filling his eyes at the thought.

His jaw clenched tighter with each new step into the woods.

"You know what, Dad? Fuck you." He hadn't been consulted. He hadn't been given a choice. And he sure as hell hadn't thought he would end up on the worst camping trip of the summer.

What if the others weren't so lucky?

The words from the party played on a loop in his mind.

"Unfortunately, the powers that be believe the process is too dangerous for the general public at this time, so we have taken matters into our own hands. We thank you all for your service..."

Caleb stopped and took a steadying breath, running his hands over his body, making sure nothing else had changed overnight. At this rate, he'd be a fucking dog by the next morning.

Turning his attention to the sky, Caleb followed the sun's movement and continued inland with the owl. He had grown used to the wildlife scuttling and hopping along the forest floor, and the calls of birds vying for the same prey he hunted each day. In turn, the hares and small land critters had grown more wary of him, knowing when to run and when it was safe to emerge from their burrows.

Wait. Was that salt?

The coast? Maybe he *was* on an island? Lifting his nose to the air, he inhaled. The owl was leading him towards a shore. Maybe there were more crates there. He quickened his step in the direction he hoped would lead him to more answers.

***

The faded glow of the moon flickered through the leaves, casting shifting shadows across the undergrowth. The jittery, darting creatures of daylight had given way to the steady glowing eyes of nocturnal hunters.

Exhausted, Caleb watched as predator and prey continued their endless cycle, unchanged across species and time. His limbs ached, shallow cuts patterned across any available skin, he was hungry and he stunk. The smell of salt had dissipated over the course of the day. He wasn't even sure it had been there in the first place. He wanted so badly to find another human being, even if that person had ended up with some other animal parts.

They had turned back to the rapids at dusk, Caleb drinking deeply from the grainy water. He would continue to follow its path, hoping to find another crate. His stomach twisted. Panic gnawed at the edges of his thoughts. What if he never found another living soul? What if he was the only one left here? He gripped at his arms; his nails had grown and thickened. The sharpened edges broke his skin but he didn't care. The pain was good. It reminded him he was alive.

"Do you even know where the hell we're going?" he called to the bird, yelling hoarsely as loud as his voice would allow. It seemed like it changed every time he talked.

"I'm losing it," he whispered when the bird didn't react to his outburst.

He needed to eat, but the thought made him feel sick.

Lazily, he pursued a rabbit. The small creature didn't seem to be in a rush, hopping slowly towards its burrow as the darkness of the forest engulfed the trees. It was an easy kill. He lunged toward it. The pathetic thing whined and squirmed beneath his hands. It nipped at him as he held its tiny thrashing body in place, its heartbeat thumping rapidly under its fur. Its teeth couldn't reach him. It would be so easy. He could steal this life as easily as his father had stolen his. He shook his head at the thought. He should eat. It was the circle of life. The rabbit had stilled some, resigned to its fate, the fight or flight instinct no longer an option. Its beady black eye watched him, waiting for him to lean down and tear its head from its body.

Monster.

He removed his hold on his prey. Not quite believing it had been let go, the rabbit took a second before darting off into the night with everything it had.

"Run, rabbit, run," Caleb said, choking back more tears.

***

Dawn came again and he continued his journey along the bank, the owl calling to him occasionally with what he hoped were words of encouragement. Each step was more and more of the same wilderness with varying degrees of greenery. Risking moving away from the rapids, he walked deeper into the woods towards a peak on the horizon. He hoped a higher vantage point would award him with a better view of his surroundings. Maybe he could see other crates, a campsite or a way out.

Moisture beaded against the underside of his hands the further he walked, then sweat broke out across the rest of his skin. By the time he reached the edge, the sun had started to dip behind the trees, but not before Caleb was able to see an endless forest before him. Not a crate in sight. Instead, he was met with a vast nothingness.

His heart dropped with the sun, the shadows of night creeping upwards across the hills. "How do I get out of this mess?" he said aloud. Finding a bunch of trees growing close together, Caleb settled in for the night.

A heavy thud jolted him awake. He sat bolt upright, stretching his neck, his back arching, muscles coiled.

But there was nothing. Just his nerves.

He let his hackles drop.

The sound came again, forcing its way through the trees.

What is that?

Caleb shook his head and turned towards the rhythm of the thuds. He frowned, focusing on his hearing, trying to pinpoint where it was coming from. It was different to the chirps and growls he had grown used to. It didn't sound overly close, but it was consistent. Closing his eyes, he tried to open his mind to follow his senses. Inhaling deeply, he let his breathing slow, images of the terrain he had covered flashing through his mind.

Running water filled his ears coupled with the thudding of something heavy against the stone. Was it coming from the rapids? He had come across another fast-moving body of water as he walked. *Shit.* Whatever was making the noise was caught, thumping against rocks. Whatever it was was caught. Excitement replaced his fear; nervous energy bubbled up his stomach and stuck in his throat. This was new. He winced as a harsh scrape played inside his ears. *Ugh.*

He had heard that sound before. He had heard it from the inside.

That was a fucking crate.

Adrenaline surged through him, burning away his fatigue. He was on his feet in an instant, ears tuned to the drumbeat of wood against rock. His breath came hard and fast as he sprinted towards the sound, desperation clawing at him. The sound was a promise. A sign of another human dropped into this hellscape. The pounding grew louder.

Almost there.

Sweat slicked his skin, trickling down his face. Sticky dampness clung to the soles of his feet. He could see it now, trapped against the rocks on the opposite bank. The crate was in bad shape, much worse than the one that had been holding him. A bitter tang flooded his nose.

Acid.

He stopped dead.

No.

The rapids raged against the side of the wood, battering the box with a deadly barrage of water. He would be putting his life in danger if he crossed, but he had to know. Whoever was in there was sick and wouldn't be able to escape alone.

"Hey?" Caleb called, hoping for a response, a word, a cry – any sound that would tell him if someone in there was still alive. Maybe they'd already gotten free? Maybe they were in the forest, watching him.

There was no reply.

His feet felt like lead. His mind ran through possibilities, each worse than the last.

"Hello?"

Still nothing.

Shit. He was going to have to get into the rapids.

The flapping of gentle feathers fluttered above him. It was the owl calling to him.

"What?" he asked, his voice shaking. Glaring at the bird, his eyes widened as he saw thick vines curled around the tree.

Clever bird.

Making his way over, he unwound the vines. He pulled at them, testing their flexibility against his strength before tying them around his waist, hoping like hell the knot would hold. The tree was a solid anchor; he should be able to get back to this side of the moving water without too much trouble. He took the list from his pocket and placed it under a rock. His only clue was already in bad shape. It didn't need another round of drowning.

Come to think of it, nor do I.

He stared at the current a moment before plunging into its freezing depths. Cold locked around him. He flailed against the force, the vines slipping further up his torso.

Fuck!

He jolted, caught by the harness now tucked under his arms. *That was close.*

The reek of decay thickened in the air; he could all but taste it.

"No," he whispered, his chest tightening.

Argo.

The thought of his friend trapped in that box was too much to bear.

He surged forward, gripping at rocks while the rapids fought to pull him under. The crate was right there, directly in front of him.

Jagged stones scraped his skin underwater. His foot hit soft, sucking mud, threatening to trap him. He fought against it, forcing himself forward, nostrils filling with earth and rot. The crate had wedged itself tight.

He needed to get inside, hoping the wedge the box had found itself in would hold long enough for him to pry open the weakened wood banging against the edge of the rocks.

His stomach churned. Faces flashed through his mind. Blood. Vomit.

Keep going. He had to know for sure.

Caleb held against the rapids, one foot unconsciously stepping towards the rushing water. If he lost control now, he invited death.

The vines pulled tight. He wouldn't make it with them holding him back.

This is the dumbest thing I have ever done.

He unwrapped the vines from his body and lunged.

He caught the corner of the box, fighting the onslaught of water. He clawed at the wood, digging deep. Caleb struggled forward, one hand over the other, using the crate as an anchor to cross the steady stream before throwing himself at the bank.

A low vibration rumbled from his throat, raw frustration escaping with his breath.

The crate had cracked. Water had battered its frame against the rocks until a hole had splintered open. Peering inside, his breath caught.

His heart dropped, eyes filling with tears as he saw the shadow of a bloated corpse. He couldn't make out much in the dark, only that whoever was inside was never coming out. The stench clawed at his throat, forcing bile up. He turned his head and vomited.

"I'm sorry," he choked, pressing a hand gently to the wet wood. A faint mark glistened beneath his palm.

DUS-GOA-023.

"What do you mean?" he whispered to the empty night.

He turned away, sinking to his knees, and screamed.

Is Anybody Out There

Chapter Seven

Death stared at Caleb. Its cold, dead eyes were accusing, taunting, hateful.

The contents of his stomach littered the leaves, a mix of half-chewed meat and bile adding to the smell of rot. Yet he couldn't stop staring.

Caleb had no idea who this person was. Who had been reduced to this bloated, bluish corpse oozing stinking, yellow-green pus? The body moved with the gases trapped inside its rotting flesh. Whoever had been in there held clues he desperately needed. His nose twitched at the stench, his brain sorting through the individual layers of decay. Blood, brain and sinew clung to the sides of the crate, pooling in the corners. It was hard to tell how it had happened, but whatever transpired had enough force to crack a hardened human skull, making them bleed out. He'd only seen one dead body so far in his life, and that had been his mother, and it had looked nothing like this.

A shallow pool of diluted, bloodied water sloshed inside the crate, human debris floating in the filth. Another wave of nausea rose, but he swallowed it down.

This could have been him.

He sighed, moving into the crate, hoping that the rocks held his added weight. Using the sides of the wood for balance, he managed to get to the head of the broken body. Their face had swollen so much it was hard to determine any features at all, let alone if was someone he had seen a few nights before. He leant down, cautiously reaching out a hand to its skull. Something bone-like was protruding from the top of its head. The solid off-white lump had broken through the skin in a bloody mess.

Fuck me, that's a horn.

Caleb searched the body for anything of use. The poor bastard didn't have so much as a pair of shoes that could be salvaged. He would need to move the body. Its decay could poison his only natural drinking source, and the idea of cannibalism didn't sit quite right.

I'm not that desperate yet.

Breathing in, he pulled the gaseous body toward the land, trying not to gag at the pungent rot it gave off. Exhausted, he dropped the corpse, its eyes staring back at him in horror. Whispering another apology, he leant down to close their eyes. He could award them that peace at the very least.

The owl found him, flapping its wings and hooting. Its eyes were wide as it squawked.

"What?"

A snarl answered him.

His stomach clenched, eyes focused on the ground, not quite able to make himself look. Cold crept up his spine as the growl deepened.

Look up, you idiot.

Slowly, he raised his head, fighting the numbness that had taken over his limbs. Bright blue eyes met his own and lips pulled back, showing rows of sharpened teeth. Caleb held his hands up, taking a step back from the wolf.

"Hey there, little guy … I'm not here to hurt you."

The owl called from across the bank. He risked turning back, the vine rolling in the rapids. Another step.

The wolf lowered its head to the corpse, sniffing at the flesh before tearing a piece off and chewing.

Caleb fought the need to be sick, moving backwards towards the water. The wolf met his gaze, still chewing on the decaying limb.

That's it. You eat them … and leave me alone.

It tilted its head to the rising moon and howled.

Caleb turned and leapt from the crate, fumbling for the vine whipping back and forth along the surface of the rapids. The chill of the water threatened to make his muscles seize.

Not now!

He thrashed his hand, securing the rope-like plant, pushing against the opposing current and pulling himself towards safety. He met the land, scrambling up the bank back to the tree and his list. Turning towards the wolf, he saw it was surrounded by several others joining in for the evening meal. The creature that had growled at him stood watching his movements, its pack gorging on flesh.

Caleb straightened, meeting its gaze. The fear dropped from his body and his breathing returning to normal. A sense of calm overtook his rapid heartbeat. The wolf broke eye contact, dipping its head as if nodding before turning back to its meal.

Weird.

Caleb made his way further inland, picking up his list of names, wondering which of them would need to be crossed off forever.

The Boy

Chapter Eight

Caleb studied the list against the glow of a fire. He had gotten a lot better at starting them in just a few days. He stared at the names which had started to fade; he would need to memorise them lest they be forgotten forever.

A familiar flutter of wings followed by a soft hoot caught his attention.

"Good to see you too," he grumbled, coughing at the scratch of his changing vocal cords.

The owl called him again. Its brown eyes flickered with a blood-orange glow. He didn't know where he'd be without the little wood owl visiting him each day, cooing and urging him forward. Its brown feathers ruffled in the gentle breeze, the moonlight catching the soft whites underneath as it preened.

"Are you trying to help me?" he asked.

The creature tilted its head, then fluttered to the ground, holding a field mouse in its beak. The bird dropped its kill at his feet.

"Oh, you shouldn't have."

Its tiny, clawed feet scratched the mulch as it cautiously hopped closer.

"I'm not going to hurt you," Caleb said gently. The owl's claws dug into his thigh, and he hissed. The bird fluttered its wings for balance, eyeing him warily before settling down on his knee. Caleb relaxed and leaned back, and his breathing slowed as they watched the night unfold together.

"Are you really a bird?" he asked.

The owl turned its head toward him, puffing out its feathers, and cooed. If Markus and his father had been working together for a decade, maybe some of their experiments had failed so badly they had completely morphed into something else entirely.

"You sure talk like a bird."

***

The owl's call jolted him from his thoughts. It fluttered down and tugged at the back of his jeans.

"What?" He swatted. "Quit it."

Persistent, it tugged again, catching the white strip of paper poking out of his pocket and tearing it slightly.

"Careful with that," he said, pulling it out of his pocket and unfolding it on a dry patch of land for the bird to see. "Can you even read?"

The owl tapped the paper lightly with its claws, tilted its head and hooted as if speaking to an old friend. Caleb stared at the bird, trying not to let his jaw drop.

Wait ... can you read?

The familiar rumble of a growl escaped his throat. He was sick of that happening without warning. The bird jumped and huffed at him, puffing up its feathers at the unexpected threat.

"Sorry," he muttered as it flew off to a branch, nestling among the leaves.

What are you trying to tell me?

Caleb stood to walk over to the owl's tree when an unfamiliar scent tickled his nose. The air was acrid and sweet – sap and wood mixed in a haze. His eyes shot open. A vision flashed before him, the sharp tang of fresh leaves thrown on a young flame.

"You found someone else! On the list? Why the fuck didn't you say that?"

Caleb jumped, holding on to the desire to hoot lest he scare off whoever was there. He forced his eyes closed, homing in on his senses, searching for the source of the smell. The owl flew inland, leading him into darkness. He squinted, hoping to make out something other than leaves as they walked.

A hint of cooking flesh drifted lazily through the air and his stomach practically begged him to find whatever animal had fallen victim to another's hunger. His heart raced. Someone had made this fire. Someone who was alive. The owl was right! He wasn't alone.

Caleb crept through the woods, cursing every crack, snap or rustle beneath his feet. Fear and excitement battled inside him. He didn't want to spook whoever was out there before he had a chance to celebrate their existence. Saliva filled his mouth, the smell of roasting meat growing stronger with every step.

Smoke curled through the air, casting shifting grey shadows in the darkness. Caleb crouched low, listening for movement.

Fat hissed as it hit the flame, a powerful waft of game tickling his nose. *Was that ... pheasant? Or turkey?*

His stomach grumbled, threatening to give him away. His lips pulled back, revealing his elongated canine.

Chill, dude, we're here to see them, not to kill them.

He stalked around a thick tree trunk, trying to stay silent as he peeked around the wood's edge. He imagined a burly hiker, a skilled hunter, someone able to take him back to a camp and eventually home. Maybe it was another survivor, like him, but he hadn't smelled the treated pine the crates were made of anywhere nearby. *What if it's Argo?* He leaned forward. A branch snapped underfoot.

"Ah crap," he hissed, ducking back behind the tree.

"Who's there?" a high, shaky voice called into the dark.

His breath caught at the sight of a hunched figure curled over the fire. A tiny body rising and falling with sobs. *Ah hell*, he thought.

"Don't eat me ... okay?" The kid's voice hitched, the sorrow catching Caleb off guard. His heart lurched.

That's ... just a kid. He wasn't ready for this. He didn't like children at the best of times, and he sure as hell didn't need one now. He was barely able to take care of himself. This was who was out here?

I could turn back. Let the woods take him. He doesn't need me. The kid's cooking a pheasant over an open flame, for heaven's sake. He's doing better than I am.

"Mum?"

Mum ... He stopped. His stomach felt like it fell out from under him. He had called for his mother like that once as a scared boy not much older than this kid.

Fuck.

Caleb dropped to the ground, anger burning through him. How old was this kid? Seven? Eight?

Were there kids this young at the party? He had expected someone fully grown, similar to his own age.

He turned back toward the fire. The kid sniffled, poking at his kill.

How long has he been here?

The owl called into the night and flew past Caleb.

"Where are you going?" he asked the owl, keeping his voice low.

"Oh, hi," the kid called up innocently once the owl had settled on a branch overlooking the fire. "Where have you been? I think someone's out there. I hope it isn't one of those yucky long dogs. Those are scary, and they make weird clicky noises. Have you seen them? I don't think I'm ready to be their dinner. I haven't even had my dinner yet. Do you think it might wait? I'm hungry."

I ... can't with this kid. He won't shut up, even with a bloody owl.

Caleb listened as the kid continued to babble at "Mrs Owl", rambling about his day. Come to think of it, Caleb wasn't even sure what gender the owl was. To him, it was just a bird.

Minutes later, the kid was crying again.

"It's not like camp. It's not like Dad said it would be."

A thud. The kid fell on his ass, knocking the bird off the spit. Embers scattered to the sides. He was lucky he didn't burn himself, or the forest around him. How the hell did this kid even know how to build a fire and a spit, anyway?

"I learned this in the Scouts, you know."

Oh. That's how.

"Yeah, my dad made sure I was a good Scout. Been there two years now. We learnt all kinds of things."

Does he ever shut up?

"My dad though ..." The kid went quiet. "Um, my dad didn't want to spend time with me a lot. He was too busy, he was always going to the labs, so I went to Scouts. I was with him when ... when ..." The crying started again.

Caleb crouched, watching as the kid tucked into the cooked meat, leaving the raw pink spots untouched. He hoped the boy would sleep soon and leave the remainder of the meal for the taking.

With a sigh, Caleb sat down and leaned back against a tree, listening to the boy talk to himself. The kid was lonely. Scared. Caleb swallowed, a lump forming in his throat. The boy's call for his mother echoed in his head. His eyes burned, tears threatening to spill for his lost childhood. He couldn't leave the boy.

He was the only other soul Caleb had found in a week.

The owl fluttered down beside him, hopping to sit at his feet, looking him in the eye.

"What?" he hissed in a whisper.

The bird nipped at his toe, chirping softly when he pulled his foot back, glaring at it.

"What the hell am I going to do with a kid?"

In This Together

Chapter Nine

"Who are you!"

Caleb startled awake, an undignified snort escaping him as he came to. He blinked, trying to adjust to the darkness in rapid time.

"Shit. I—"

"Hey! Don't swear!" the kid said, the pointed tip of a branch dangerously close to Caleb's face.

Caleb held up his hands, watching the boy to make sure he wouldn't stab him the second he tried to get up. The little guy was trembling, the weapon shaking in his grip, and Caleb could see the hint of tears in his eyes.

"I won't hurt you, kid." He flipped himself up in an instant, startling his new acquaintance.

"Don't come close!" The kid swung the stick wildly.

Caleb jumped back at the careless swipe. *If that hits me, it's not going to tickle.*

"Wait a second." He dodged another swing, his teeth bared as a snarl tore from his throat. "Kid, quit it."

The kid's mouth dropped open, the stick falling from his hands. "How did you do that?"

"Do what?"

"Your toof. Are you gonna eat me?" The boy stepped back, nearly tripping over his feet.

"What about my tooth?" Caleb ran his tongue along his mouth, feeling the sharpened canine protruding. A surprised chuckle escaped him as he considered the poor kid's first impression of him. Wild, dirty and flashing a fang. "No, I'm not going to eat you. The owl led me. I ... I don't know where we are or what's happening either, kid." Caleb dropped to one knee, hoping that being at eye level might put the boy more at ease. When the kid didn't pick up his weapon again, Caleb took a slow step forward.

"I'm as lost as you." Caleb attempted a tired smile. He didn't want to befriend the kid, but human contact felt good. He just needed to stay on the child's good side to avoid being impaled with an oversized twig.

"I'm Efan," the boy said, his small body standing tall, almost rigid as he stuck out his hand.

"E-Fan?"

"No, E-T-H-A-N."

"Ethan?" Caleb asked, offering his own hand in return. "I'm Caleb. How long have you been out here, Ethan?"

The boy hesitated. "Are you sure you're not going to hurt me?"

Caleb sighed and dropped his hand; it wouldn't do him any good to lose patience with the kid so soon after meeting him.

"No, Ethan. I'm going to try and help you. I'm going to try and help us both."

Before he could react, the boy threw himself into his arms. Caleb stood still, unsure of what to do. "Ahh." He looked for the owl to help. The bird was nowhere in sight.

Within minutes, his chest was wet with the tears of a scared child unwilling to let go. Shuddering, Caleb gently pushed him back, creating some space between them.

"It's alright, kid. We'll be alright."

"I'm keeping the stick just in case," Ethan said defiantly.

Caleb let himself laugh. The boy looked at him with a frown before letting a smile tease the corners of his lips. "Get some sleep, kid. I'll take first watch."

***

Caleb let the kid sleep longer than he had anticipated, trying to get a better look without disturbing him. He looked weak. Gaunt and pale.

Sorry, kid. He nudged Ethan with his foot, the boy grunting at the intrusion.

"Five more minutes."

Caleb rolled his eyes and nudged him again.

"Hey!" Ethan grumbled, rolling over to rub his eyes.

"We need to keep moving. Try and find the others."

"What others? There is no one here," he said, shrugging his shoulders.

"There has to be. I was taken, put here just like you. I was at a party and there were heaps of us. They must be here ... somewhere."

"Can you get me breakfast?"

Little shit.

"Come on, kid. Let's move."

They'd walked an hour before Ethan needed to rest. The boy tired quickly. Caleb wasn't sure they were making any progress at all. The kid was miserable; tears trickled down his face each time they stopped.

"You'll dehydrate," Caleb warned, but that only made the boy cry harder. By the time the sun set on their first day together, Ethan had fallen into a fitful sleep, shivering against the cold night air, something Caleb hadn't thought of himself since he arrived. *Did wolves run hot?* He took off his shirt, revealing faint tufts of new hair on his bare chest, and laid it over Ethan.

The owl had remained with them, circling above and diving for mice, occasionally calling to them to move inland.

"How long has ... Mrs Owl been visiting you?" Caleb asked the first time Ethan woke during the night. He had managed to get a fire going and cooked a rabbit he snatched from a nearby burrow. He handed the boy a leg of meat.

"Not long," Ethan muttered, picking at the flesh.

Caleb looked to the sky, willing himself the patience looking after a child in the middle of nowhere would require. "Do you think it tried to help you?"

I sound insane.

"She brought me mice." Ethan scrunched his nose up as he said it.

"Yeah. Funny. It brought me mice too."

"Did you eat them?"

"No ... did you?"

"That's gross."

"Hey, kid. I know walking all day isn't fun, but—"

"My feet hurt," Ethan whined.

"I know. Mine do too. Look, you're the first person I've found. We need to look for more. Maybe we can find help to get out of here. Mrs Owl wants us to keep moving, right?"

The kid sat upright, folding his arms over his chest, and pouted. With a sigh, Caleb knelt, fighting against the desire to grind his teeth.

"The owl helped me find you last night. I didn't know you were there. If we keep following it ..."

"I don't feel good." Ethan's arms dropped, and he stared at the ground.

"It's okay. We can rest now. Keep going in the morning." Caleb wondered if the owl's goal all along was for him to find the child. He placed the back of his hand against Ethan's forehead, his messy blonde hair stirring with the movement. *He's burning up.*

The boy finished his meal, placing the bones on the ground in front of him. His eyes were drooping.

"Try to get some more sleep, mate," Caleb said, his voice soft.. Ethan lay back down, Caleb tucking him back in. He watched as the boy's chest rose and fell, his breathing falling into an even rhythm.

"How do I look after him?" he asked the owl that was waiting patiently a few trees ahead. The bird ruffled its feathers and nestled into itself, ready to watch over them both.

They stayed put the next day; he wasn't sure if the boy would consent to being carried just yet. Ethan showed him how to build a proper fire and shared stories from the Scouts. Caleb hunted, making sure to cook everything thoroughly in an effort to put some weight on his new companion. He let Ethan eat first, encouraging him to take in as much food as his little stomach could handle before finishing the rest himself.

Together they found long planks of stripped bark, thin vines and large, thick leaves. It was enough to create a roof between a cluster of trees. Caleb vowed to stay put for a few nights. It would take weeks to get Ethan to the strength he needed to cross the forest – weeks they probably didn't have. Caleb could only hope a few days of consistent meals and rest would do the kid a world of good.

To Ethan's credit, the little guy put on a brave face, but he still tired quickly and struggled to keep food down. That morning, Caleb had caught sight of worms in the kid's stool. With no access to a doctor or medication, all he could do was hope that clean food and water would flush out the parasites.

***

Over the ensuing week, the boy gained a little weight and his stool solidified. The parasites were fewer and less frequent. Nights were getting colder, and Caleb wasn't sure how much longer their luck would last against predators; he had no desire to meet the shadow beast that clicked in the distance. Tomorrow they would continue moving into the forest. They would have to come out the other side of these woods eventually. Maybe there was a dock, sitting in the ocean, ready to take them home mere days away.

Yeah. Right.

Leaving the boy to rest, Caleb rose and made his way to the river, cursing as his foot hit a sharp stone. He searched for smooth, sharp rocks. They would gather vines and long branches before they left.

He felt like he and the boy were sitting ducks. They still didn't know who, or what, was out here, and if he was morphing into some kind of hybrid, chances were others were too. Eventually, they would need a weapon.

When Caleb returned to their makeshift camp, Ethan was gone.

A grunt to his right caught his attention, and he ran towards it, only to find Ethan drenched in sweat, retching against a tree. Cursing silently at whatever force had put him in charge of a sick child, Caleb swallowed his frustration and anger.

"Hey, kid," he said, trying to keep his voice gentle.

"Hey," Ethan croaked, doing his best to sound nonchalant and failing miserably.

The air around them smelled sweet, different than before. Ethan turned, reds and blues smeared around his mouth, the clumpy paste running down his chin. Caleb grabbed him roughly, fury rising in his chest.

"What did you eat?" he growled, unable to tame his temper. "I told you not to eat anything we haven't tested together. I thought you were a Scout, for Pete's sake!"

New tears welled in Ethan's eyes. "I thought they were okay! I tried these before, I swear it! At camp! They didn't hurt my tummy then!" He pointed to his swollen stomach and let the tears fall. Caleb turned away briefly to rub his eyes and muttered a prayer that they would make it out alive. He hadn't meant to lose his temper.

Dammit.

"I'm sorry, kid. I don't know what I'm doing here. Any of this shi— stuff" – he emphasised the bushes Ethan had stumbled across – "can kill us. We don't know." He winced as Ethan's shoulders hitched with a sob.

"Come here." Caleb opened his arms awkwardly. Neither of them moved. It was the first time he had offered to hug the kid; it looked like Ethan didn't know if he could trust the gesture. Caleb knew that feeling all too well. He had felt it every single day growing up.

"It's okay," he promised, waving the boy in. Slowly, Ethan stepped forward, pressing against him cautiously at first, then melting into his side. Caleb's breath hitched at the contact, an unfamiliar instinct to protect taking over his thoughts.

"You done puking?" He felt a wet nod against his chest. "Cool. Let's make some weapons."

"Weapons!" Ethan perked up, wiping his face.

"Yeah. Weapons."

Caleb set Ethan up against a large tree to offer insight while he worked between bouts of sleeping, puking and shitting his brains out. He worked with vines, sticks and stones, trying to come up with something useful. Spears seemed like the obvious choice given the materials surrounding them. By sundown, Caleb had collected two dozen "spearheads", half a dozen flowering vines that made him itch like crazy and a handful of sturdy branches.

While Ethan slept, Caleb returned to the bushes, collecting a handful of red and blue berries. He wasn't quite sure what the kid saw in these, but he supposed not everyone could live solely on meat like he seemed to. Cautiously, he picked up a red orb, sniffing it. His nose wrinkled at the bitter smell. He wasn't sure if this was the one that caused Ethan to hurl earlier or not.

Curiosity won over logic. *What harm can one berry do?* He popped it into his mouth.

Caleb bit down and winced as harsh flavours erupted against the inside of his cheeks. He gagged; this had to be what had caused the kid to hurl.

He had made it to the water's edge, lifting a handful to his mouth. Dead fish guts and dirt was preferable to the acidic burn. He swirled the liquid inside his mouth, spitting out on the shore. *Yuck!* He turned to check his reflection when sweat broke out across his skin. His hands and feet turned clammy as he burned up.

"Holy shit," Caleb whispered as he regained control of himself, struggling to hold onto his dinner. Glaring back at the tiny red fruits, he made a pact to never eat a berry again.

***

"Look over here!" Ethan's voice carried across the distance, jittering with excitement. Whatever he had disturbed was disgustingly earthy. Caleb's nose twitched as the smell grew stronger. He had started to pick up on Ethan's smell, able to tell if he was close by or had wandered off too far. Each day, his range seemed to increase.

They had started moving inland. Ethan showed him how to cup leaves to carry small amounts of water and use thin vines to hold the plants together. The owl flew into their view each day, its calls drawing them onward.

"Coming, Scout master!" he called out playfully, realising in horror he had started to enjoy the kid's company. When Caleb found Ethan at the mouth of an abandoned burrow, he was pointing towards a cluster of mushrooms.

"Hold up. The last thing you shoved in your mouth nearly killed you."

Ethan rolled his eyes. "These are safe. Uh ... I'm pretty sure." He paused, then grinned up at Caleb. "But we have to be careful. If we just pick them up, we could damage the spores, and then they can't grow again."

"Wait a sec, how sure are you? What are you holding in that little brain of yours?"

Ethan frowned in concentration, studying the bulbous, papery ball sticking out from the ground.

"It's a puffball!" he finally exclaimed triumphantly.

"A what?" Caleb couldn't help but snort at the name and the boy's excitement. Ethan tried to be serious but as soon as his smile broke through, they were both in fits of laughter.

"So, you eat it?" Caleb asked.

"Yeah, tastes like dirt raw, but they are good on the fire." The words came out rapidly, Ethan picking up excitement as he spoke. *Maybe he isn't so bad after all.*

"Alright, kid, I am not putting that thing in my mouth, but if you're sure about the puffball, how do we protect the spores?" Caleb gestured toward the fungus.

Ethan used the sharp edge of the spear to gently lift the bright white morsel from the soil, placing it carefully in Caleb's outstretched hand.

"Reckon there's more?" Caleb encouraged.

"Probably." Ethan shrugged. "They usually grow in clusters. We should check the hardwood trees, sometimes mushrooms grow on them too."

Caleb winced at the thought of eating something scraped off a tree, but they needed food they could carry. This was as good as anything they had found so far. Ethan chattered about the various plants he had picked up, teaching Caleb what was safe to eat and what wasn't. He wasn't about to trust the kid with berries anytime soon, but the mushrooms seemed ok.

"Caleb, look!" Ethan jumped, running towards a patch of delicate white flowers.

Caleb struggled, holding the water leaves and mushrooms in his arms while hurrying after his overstimulated companion.

"Kid … that's a flower. We have seen at least a million of them since we've been here. Come on, we need to keep moving."

"Sometimes you're a big dumb-dumb for someone so old."

Caleb felt himself growl. "Enlighten me."

"Hey. Stop that, cranky pants. Look closer."

"I dunno what you want me to see. It's dirt, dirt everywhere." A rough brown bulb caught his eye under a long stem. "Wait, is that …?"

"Onions!" Ethan laughed, picking two of the bulbs from the ground. "And these *flowers* are garlic. See!" Ethan knelt in the dirt, gently prying one of the sprigs upward, the papery-white casing glistening through the muck.

"No shit," Caleb said, smiling in awe at the aromatics.

"You said you wouldn't swear."

"Grab a bunch of this stuff, as much as we can carry. We can make stews if we find something to hold it all." Caleb's mouth watered at the thought.

"Nuh-uh," Ethan said, holding three fingers to the air.

"What? Why?"

"Scout's honour. We only take what we need."

"Really, kid?"

Ethan wouldn't budge.

By the end of the day, they had gathered a treasure trove of goodies, bulbs of wild garlic, onions, more mushrooms and some nettles. That last one had confused Caleb, but the kid insisted they could be dried, roasted and used to flavour their meat. They had also cautiously tasted some dark blue berries and were delighted to find they were sweet and didn't upset their stomachs.

Caleb stopped, hands full of the forest's offerings, tilting his nose to the wind that had gone cold.

"What is it?" Ethan asked, concern crossing his brow as he turned away from another mushroom.

Blood. Fur. Mild decay. Caleb inhaled deeply, catching the scent on the wind.

"Blood," he said quietly, lowering himself to place what he was carrying on the ground and motioning for Ethan to do the same. "Get on the ground and stay."

Ethan obeyed and dropped to the dirt, flat on his stomach. Dirt covered his skin, blending him into the forest floor. Caleb crouched, slowly following the scent, hoping the kid stayed put as the trail took him further and further away from their foraging spot. The hairs along his back and neck rose. A warning.

"I'll be back," he said, voice low.

Through the trees, he could make out a large fallen creature. A doe, killed within the last day or two. Caleb nearly jumped as a twig broke underfoot, disturbing the macabre silence. His ear twitched, picking up the sound of Ethan moving.

He crouched to stare down at light tan skin speckled with grey-white spots, its face frozen as if it had tried to scream. This was the largest kill he had seen in the forest, and it was messy. Shreds of meat and skin hung from its side. It didn't look like any part of the animal had been taken for food. Its innocence had been torn down in a moment of untamed fury.

Caleb leant down and inhaled. The musty scent of sweat mixed with the sharp copper of blood both sickened and enticed him. Closing his eyes, he tried to place the familiar notes.

Argo?

He wasn't sure. The scent on the carcass wasn't quite animal. At least not yet.

A snap sounded behind him. His head whipped around. Ethan was peering at him from behind a copse of trees.

"I told you to stay," Caleb growled, turning to face the wide-eyed boy staring at the bloody mess before him.

"What happened?" Ethan asked, not acknowledging Caleb's anger. His focus was drawn to the mutilated deer.

Caleb forced himself to stay calm and motioned for Ethan to come closer. "You've already broken the rules. Just get over here."

Ethan hesitated, then approached cautiously as Caleb resumed his inspection. Parts of the meat squirmed with maggots.

"You should use the skin," Ethan said. "Like I told you."

"You want to do it?" Caleb held out the spear. Ethan recoiled, shaking his head. Caleb sighed. "Alright then, tell me what to do."

Caleb took his spear, the solid wood sturdy in his grip, and slid the stone tip under the deer's hide. He pulled, working against muscle and sinew.

"What are you doing? You need to glide the blade along the fat – it's easier that way," Ethan said, sounding horrified at Caleb's butchery.

Caleb hung his head before letting out a frustrated scoff.

"Okay, okay. Like this ...?" He placed his hands on the body of the beast, holding it as still as possible as the sharpened stone moved between skin and flesh. *Huh, that is easier.*

"See! I'm a Scout master. You said."

Caleb rolled his eyes. The kid was going to hold onto that forever.

Intruders

Chapter Ten

"Caaaleb!"

The boy's panicked shriek pierced the air around him. Caleb snapped to attention. Ethan's screams were muffled, the sound distorted and fading. He lowered his body to the ground, the hair along his spine standing to attention, eyes darting frantically for a sign of the struggle. A deep, guttural rumble built in his throat, a mix of fear and fury pushing its way out.

Pressing his nose to the forest floor, Caleb inhaled deeply, seeking out Ethan's scent. The shuffling of large inhuman feet, too large, scraped and scratched in a steady rhythm. Ethan's much smaller body had caused the dirt to stir, the boy's struggle against whatever had taken him evident. Caleb locked on to the smell of old and bitter sweat, unwashed bodies covered in drying blood, dirt and grime.

"A-leb! Elp!"

Caleb's heart was racing as he whipped around to what he hoped was Ethan's direction. Images of the child flashed in his mind, the boy getting stronger and stronger with each day they spent together. His heart dropped at the idea of something taking Ethan from him. *He is mine.*

He wanted to run, to follow the child's sweet scent, not yet tainted by the signs of puberty. He had no idea what he was up against. The scratching in the distance indicated at least two others, their rhythm out of sync with one another. One heavy, one light, the former making the ground shudder as it moved.

What if it's a trap?

Caleb inhaled, willing a clear path to come to him, smelling a mingled tang of dirt and blood from opposing directions. The blood smelled old, the coppery notes having diluted with the healing process. He hoped that meant the kid wasn't hurt.

A sudden gust carried the familiar scent of dust and feathers. The owl swept past him, and Caleb sent a silent thanks to their companion and pushed off the ground, stumbling as instinct told him to run on all fours before righting himself. The bird whistled, the beats of its wings growing further away by the second.

His feet pounded against the forest floor, each stride kicking up dust. He raced past their camp, leaving behind the stacks of dried animal skins, the weapons they had crafted and the food they had gathered.

Rage took hold of him, the heat of it fuelling each step. Ethan was the first thing he had truly cared about in years. He had been in the forest for weeks, Ethan his only other human companion, with no sign of others. Now someone finally turned up and they had the audacity to steal his friend. He was just a boy, for fuck's sake.

The sight of white feathers turning a corner alerted him to do the same. He forced himself to move faster, the muscles in his legs protesting. Holding his nose up, Caleb searched the air for signs of his friend until he came across the owl, perched on a tree, its chest rising and falling rapidly.

The air stilled, leaving him with silence. He could feel faint pulses of bodies in the distance, lingering wisps of the intruders hanging in the air. *Where are you?* A faint breeze came from his left. Light footsteps were coming towards him at speed. He only had moments before the weight of his attacker barrelled into him.

He hit the ground, and the impact drove the air from his lungs. Caleb lashed out blindly, pain piercing his fingers as nails pushed through his skin, sharpening into tiny blades. His swipe met only empty air.

Whoever had hit him jumped back, their smile haunting as their shadow danced around him, ready for another attack. A flash of sharpened grey stone caught a flicker of moonlight to his side, his eyes latching on to the motion. *They have weapons.*

Caleb looked around wildly, hoping to pick up anything of use; he had left the spears back at their camp, foregoing the weapons for speed.

His assailant was on him again in an instant.

He kicked out, both legs thrown into a powerful swing. He connected with a satisfying "offft".

Using the time to flip to his front, he grabbed a handful of dirt and leaves, flinging them. He steadied himself, using the distraction to brace; he could feel tension build in his legs, waiting for him to pounce.

He launched forward, his body soaring over the creature before hitting the ground on the other side.

Dammit!

He skidded across the dirt.

A laugh came from his side.

Caleb crouched and readied himself. His opponent hadn't moved, seemingly content to watch him struggle. The bastard was toying with him.

This time, when he lunged, he struck true. His arm slammed down, pinning the thin figure beneath him. The hood slipped back, revealing sharp white teeth and bright, cat-like eyes.

"What are you?"

Before the stranger could answer, something massive wrenched him away. Caleb barely had time to register the size of the second attacker before he was hurled backwards. A thick, clawed hand clamped around his throat, tightening as he struggled.

The scent hit him like a tidal wave. He was right – they weren't human. He battled for purchase, struggling against the grasp behind him. Memories of the officer holding him tight before plunging a vial of animal gunk in his neck came flooding back. The trees around him blurred as he thrashed. The arm holding him looked like a furred trunk, his flails not having any effect.

Ethan! He strained against the crushing hold, gasping for breath. His chest heaved, and his vision darkened at the edges. He bucked violently, but the arm holding him didn't budge.

"Who are you?" he rasped.

No answer.

His lungs burned. His limbs were heavy.

This forest is utter bullshit, he thought, kicking backwards and hoping he struck something. The thing holding him didn't flinch as he made contact. He tried again, swinging wildly. He let his body go limp, hoping they'd loosen their grip, but the weight pressing against him didn't shift.

Bite them. Use your fang.

A voice drifted through the darkness, warm, lyrical, condescending. "That's a good boy."

The tone sent a wave of fury through him. It reminded him of his old housekeeper scolding him for stealing treats before they had cooled.

Maybe he wouldn't give up after all.

Caleb bucked hard, but his captor lifted him off the ground like he weighed nothing. The thick, furred arm held him effortlessly in place.

"Where is Ethan?" he shouted, anger fuelling him with adrenaline.

His jaw twinged and he winced as another tooth pushed through the roof of his mouth.

Finally.

He smirked. Two sharp teeth were better than one. Tilting his head back, he looked up at his captor, then slammed his teeth down. Hard.

Thick blood filled his mouth along with rancid body hair. He gagged, sputtering, but refused to let go. The beast barely reacted. A grunt was the only sign that he had done any damage.

"That was not very pack-like of you now, was it?" The lilting voice caressed the air like a song on the wind.

Caleb bared his bloody teeth.

"Little dog needs some training." The figure smiled, revealing shining, sharp teeth. "We can help with that."

"Big talk for such a little shadow." Caleb wrenched his head back and bit down again, this time harder. The response was instant. The grip on his throat tightened, cutting off his air. His vision swam.

"What are you?" he panted out. Whatever it was, it was strong. His knees buckled. His body sagged. Cool, coarse binding slipped around his wrists. His mouth barely moved as he whispered, "Ethan."

Everything went dark as the owl called from a distance.

***

Caleb's vision was hazy as his eyes adjusted to a flickering light in the distance. He grunted as he moved, and his head and throat hurt more than any hangover. He struggled to recall the events of the night. His skin prickled, the hairs on his arms raising as he sat up. He blinked in an effort to make his vision clear, hoping to get a picture of where he had ended up.

"Hey, kid," he said, inhaling sharply at the pain in his throat. "Ethan?" Nothing. *ETHAN!* his mind screamed. Memories of the last few hours rushed back in a blur. The boy had called to him, taken by something in the night. Caleb forced himself to stand, only to slam his head against the top of something.

"Son of a bitch," he rasped.

Blinking against the dim light, he looked forward, making out thick wooden stakes acting as bars.

He was back in a damn cage.

A rage-induced growl rumbled through his raw throat as he grabbed the bars and shook with everything he had. They didn't budge.

Is this actually hell?

Wherever he was, the heat was nearly unbearable, suffocating him in a fog of humidity. He panted, sweat dampening the balls of his hands and feet. This was a woodland, for heaven's sake; where was all the fresh air?

What about my teeth? His canines hadn't retracted since they had pushed through his gums. He placed his teeth against the stakes, biting down.

Nothing. Not even a dent.

How the hell have they kept these things in place? He tried to shove them again.

Unable to sit still, Caleb paced the claustrophobic space, three strides one way and three strides back, hoping the movement would force strength back into his body. His thoughts flickered to Ethan. Had the boy gotten away? Or was he caged too, waiting to be rescued? A shadow crossed in front of his cell. Caleb flinched, eyes widening as a monstrous body came into view. A sharp breath caught in his throat.

That thing must have been seven feet tall.

Wait, why didn't I smell you?

Was his fatigue dulling his senses?

The giant tilted its head, peering into the cage with an undignified "hmph".

Its broad body was covered in patches of mottled fur and skin, muscle and veins bulging at odd angles. As it straightened to its full height, Caleb noted its width doubled that of any bodybuilder he had ever seen. He couldn't stop staring. When his gaze landed on its bloodied forearm, his face twisted in a scowl. He inhaled to pick up the creature's scent. It came to him slowly, the musty, dirt-clotted fur of the night before.

"You!" Caleb growled, pushing against the bars.

The mangled mess of fur and flesh stared back. Its jaw was too large for its skull. Half of its teeth had been pulled into a malformed snout, creating a horrific overbite that looked capable of snapping human bones. One eye was sealed shut beneath a patch of misplaced hair, one ear crumpled against its head.

Caleb shuddered, hoping he never had to face that thing again.

A small, lithe creature moved beside the beast, catching Caleb off guard.

"Good. You're awake," a low yet feminine voice purred.

Caleb's eyes gawked at the feline presence in front of him. *What is this place!?* "Are you ... a ... cat?" The words left his mouth before he could stop them.

"Not quite." Her voice lilted with amusement, a mocking purr playing him like a ball of string. "But, as suspected, you are an idiot."

"Time out! What the hell is happening here? Where am I? And where is Ethan? And how do you both look like ... that!" Caleb demanded, gesturing at them.

I'm going insane.

The bear-like mutant grunted, stepping towards the cage. Caleb instinctively jumped back, not ready for a repeat of their earlier encounter.

"It's okay, Jan," the feline creature said, emphasising the "y" sound at the beginning of the mutant's name. "Stand down."

The beast tilted its mangled skull in acknowledgement and slowly stomped away, each footstep sending vibrations through the ground.

"Where were we?"

Caleb's whole body tensed, waiting for her next move.

She turned her large, sparkling eyes on Caleb and studied him. He tried to do the same, distracted by the way her animalistic features blended seamlessly into her human form. She looked ready to move at a moment's notice. Her legs were thin but powerful, the muscles standing out against her skin. She stood between four and five feet tall, her back arched slightly. Every movement carried a grace, as if she were dancing on air rather than walking. Her steps barely touched the ground, toes bouncing with each movement. Her figure was still somewhat human, but small and thin and covered in a fine, dark fur that concealed most of her skin.

As his eyes travelled up to her bust, Caleb reddened. She wasn't wearing any clothes other than a sash across her torso, holding what looked like a number of homemade throwing weapons. The fur stopped abruptly where her arms met her hands, her fingers giving way to long, sharp claws. Caleb's stomach tightened as he watched the pointed ends retract into her skin. Her angular features twitched in amusement. "Got a good look, then?"

Caleb snapped back to reality. The two creatures before him were part of the sick experiments his father was running with the approval of governing bodies. Only, they didn't look like they had arrived a week ago. He stepped towards the bars and gripped them tightly, locking eyes with her. He wondered if he could extend his own claws at will, focusing on the curved points breaking out of his skin. He felt a small prick before his hands settled back into themselves, not a claw in sight.

"Where am I?" Each word punched the air like an accusation. "And what the hell am I doing here?"

She sauntered up to the cage, looking down at him in the pit that made the base of the cell.

"You seem to be some sort of dog. And you are part of something much, much larger than your ego." Her lips curled. "I suggest you sit down, boy, and when you comply, maybe you'll get some answers."

A chill ran through Caleb's body. There was power in her words, something primal that triggered an instinct he didn't want to acknowledge: the urge to submit and tuck his non-existent tail between his legs.

No.

He shoved the thought away, throat tightening. His mind raced. He clawed for something, anything, that made sense.

Nothing.

Frustrated, he moved to the back of the cage and sat, staring up at her. His mind was so loud he barely heard her speak. He needed to know where Ethan was.

"Each year, you pathetic fools get weaker. Behave, and we can talk when I come back." Her words were sharp, accusing. She stalked off, disappearing into the night.

Caleb exhaled slowly. *Did she just say "each year"?*

The sun rose from the east, climbing higher over the trees, giving him a better view of his surrounds. Cages were arranged in a neat pattern. There were another four identical prison cells that stood empty. A man-made path cut through the rough bush and dry earth to where he was held. Standing on his tiptoes, he strained to see more, hissing out Ethan's name. If the kid had made it out, he wasn't anywhere near him, or he wasn't responding. Squinting into the distance, he thought he could make out the edge of a wall, thousands of trees used as fencing for ... what? A compound? A camp? It would have taken years to build a fortress out here.

Caleb grew frustrated as the day passed, his feet creating a track in the dirt underneath him while he paced. He had tried to call out to the guards on patrol, who had walked down the pathway to check on him before returning towards their lodgings. The owl had greeted him in a similar fashion, flying to him, calling softly and flying back. The bird didn't seem to be in any distress, but he didn't know if that meant he was safe. *What if the damn bird was working for them and this was all a trap?*

The air cooled as the sun dipped low, and dusk created a purple-orange hue across the horizon. Caleb's stomach growled. The more he changed, the more he seemed to need to eat, his metabolism working in overdrive. He strained his ears, hoping to catch some sound, any sign of his young friend. Instead, he heard others, brief snippets of conversation or movement. The scent of roasting meat and vegetables carried on the wind, not helping his increasing appetite.

Jan made his rounds periodically, checking that Caleb hadn't miraculously escaped, his one good, bulging, reddened eye trained on him during each rotation. Caleb had tried snapping the bars several times, launching himself at them, trying to recall how his legs had built up power the night before. But the bars held still.

A sharp crack against his cell caught him off guard. He'd been too focused gathering information about the fortress to pay attention to what was happening behind him. Another crack. Someone was throwing stones at him.

"Oi, quit it," he grumbled, scrambling to his feet.

Moonlight streamed through the bars, casting a pale glow. His prison looked almost serene in the quiet. Then, behind him, the bars rattled. Branches crunched. Leaves rustled.

"Hey!" he called, irritated, turning towards the sound. He sniffed the air. The sweet scent of his young friend filled him with joy. "Ethan."

"Shhh! Shut up," a small voice whispered. "Please."

Caleb turned to see the kid swinging a crude-looking axe at the bars at the back of his cage.

He lowered his voice. "What are you doing here?"

"Saving you, duh." The kid's tone was annoyingly condescending.

"How did you—" Caleb started, but then he froze. His instincts prickled. "Shh ... get down," he warned, picking up on Jan's scent and another unfamiliar one approaching. Heavy footfalls and a second set of lighter shuffles moved in the distance.

Ethan scrambled behind him, slipping into the trees. From this close, Caleb could hear the panic in the kid's breathing, each breath coming out in short gasps.

"Hey, kid."

"Yeah?" Fear made Ethan's voice shake.

"Thanks for coming back for me."

"Yeah," Ethan repeated. "You're my friend." He pressed himself flat against the bushes.

Caleb's throat tightened. He could hear the boy trying hard not to cry, his small frame hitching with silent sobs. "Ethan."

"Yeah."

Caleb softened his voice. "I need you to breathe." He strained to hear any conversation between the two patrollers. If they noticed Ethan, he'd end up in a cage too.

"I c … c … can't." A sob escaped him.

"Hey. It's okay." Caleb turned toward the heat radiating from the boy's body in the dark. "I'm right here."

"You're in a stupid cage," Ethan rebutted.

"And you're gonna get me out. Soon. But for now, you need to be quiet. Okay?"

"Okay," Ethan whispered.

Caleb refocused on the patrol outside his cage. *I wonder if they can smell him as easily as I can.* He rattled the bars, trying to draw their attention away from any new scents they might pick up.

"Hey! I've been here all day, man. At least get me some food!" he called out. Jan's eye narrowed. He lifted his mangled snout to the air. Beside him, the second figure moved, a thin, slippery thing with scales that glistened in the newly rising moonlight. A long, forked tongue flicked out of its mouth, tasting the air.

Holy … shit. It's going to pick up on the boy's scent.

"Oi! Over here, you big oaf! Can you not understand anything? I said I was hungry!"

Jan ignored him. Heavy footsteps shuffled towards the bushes.

No. He couldn't find him.

A sudden pain exploded behind Caleb's left eye. It seared through his skull, and he yelped, clutching his face. It felt like his eye was about to drop from its socket. His canines throbbed in his gums, instincts flaring before he could even process what was happening.

Footsteps quickened. The pain spread through his body, and a pathetic whine escaped his lips. He rolled across the floor, trying to shake it off.

"Caleb!" Ethan's voice came from the front of the cage. The footsteps had stopped. They were close.

"Ethan, get back!" Caleb's voice came out rough, almost a growl. The boy flinched.

"There you are, little rabbit," a new voice said. It was slimy, cocky, and made Caleb's skin crawl. "We were wondering where you'd gotten to. Jan, if you would be so kind?"

Jan's massive, wounded arm reached for Ethan.

"No!" Caleb shouted, gripping the bars. For a second, no one moved. They all stared at each other, wary of the next move.

Caleb's breathing slowed. An uncanny calm settled over him, even as pain ripped through his body. He stopped fighting it. He had to get to the boy. His bones cracked, his body expanding. His skull slammed against the top of the crate. Each new snap made him bigger, stronger, something not to be trifled with. Heat and rage fuelled him, but his focus stayed on Ethan: his brown eyes, his small frame, the smell of fear embedded into his skin. The way he stared in horror as Caleb's body changed.

Fear hit him. What the hell was happening? His spine snapped, curling, forcing him to his knees. His legs pulsed, his thighs and calves burning as they stretched and fell into shape. He lurched, catching himself as his chest expanded, ripping his clothes apart. Muscles thickened, each line defined, rigid and hard.

His teeth sharpened into neat, pointed rows. Fine grey-and-white fur covered his body.

Caleb snarled, locking eyes onto Jan and then the second guard. His throat constricted, vocal cords tightening, then expanding. One thought consumed his mind.

Rip their fucking throats out.

His skull broadened, new hairs sprouting unnaturally fast, forming a dishevelled mane. He was dangerous. He could feel it. It was time to take back control.

His vision sharpened, the night lighting up as clear as day, but he only had eyes for Ethan and the thin, scaled fingers gripping the boy.

"*Let. Him. Go.*" The words came out as a series of threatening throat gurgles.

"Is that a threat?" the creature hissed. Its green eyes flashed, its grip tightening, claws puncturing Ethan's shirt.

Let's find out.

Caleb gripped the bars of his cage with clawed fists and pulled.

Camp Chaos

Chapter Eleven

A menacing growl broke from Caleb's throat as splintered wood burst from his cage, the bars snapping inward. The lizard creature pulled Ethan to its side, holding the child away from the destruction, looking unconcerned at the changing scene.

"You alright, boss?" it called out to the bear, who was watching Caleb's shift intently. The beast huffed in response, not taking his eyes off the cage.

Caleb cried out in pain; his body was morphing, bones snapping into place, the need to protect the boy filling his thoughts. Jan huffed as he watched Caleb's body break and change, bracing for the inevitable impact. Caleb's world darkened, his vision blurring with a mix of yellows and blues, but he could still smell them, the bigger bear-like creature in stark contrast to the slick reptilian. His senses found the pair, tracking their movements as his eyes adjusted to a new way of seeing. Caleb's body heaved with the exertion, continually expanding, becoming more and more animalistic as the seconds ticked by.

Fear flickered on Ethan's horrified face as the child watched his friend become a beast. Caleb saw him step backward only to be held in place by a clawed hand, a dark patch spreading down his trouser legs.

"Caleb?" Ethan's voice was high-pitched and scared.

"That's not Caleb no more, son," the second guard said, his slimy voice almost gleeful.

Jan tensed beside him, grotesquely misshapen veins standing out against his mangled arms. He had his back leg pressed hard into the ground, ready to strike once the cage had completely shattered. The oversized mutant crossed his arms against his chest, breathing steadily as he watched Caleb.

As soon as he was free, Caleb lunged for the smaller reptilian guard holding Ethan. The boy squealed as Caleb's new claws swiped for any available flesh. The scaled humanoid stood its ground and flexed its arm, pulling Ethan closer like a shield. Its smile remained, fuelling Caleb's desire to rip into him.

Jan moved, pinning Caleb against the unbroken side of the cage. The structure rattled with their weight. Instinct took over and Caleb snapped his jaw in a flurry of saliva and teeth.

I have to get to Ethan. Caleb thrashed at the strong arm holding him tight.

"You alright, kid?" The sound of the lizard hybrid's voice speaking to Ethan pulled Caleb's focus from the fight. "Been a while since we've had one of your kind here. Delia will be thrilled."

What are they going to do to the kid?

Caleb wanted to yell, to tell the freak to back off. He saw the guard tilt its head like a bird, one slitted eye focusing on Ethan. Colour had drained from the kid's face.

Stay with me, Caleb thought, unable to speak. Ethan had gone limp, the lizard-like guard catching him before he fell to the ground in a faint.

No, dammit!

Jan tightened his grip, pulling him back into the fight. Caleb urged his legs to summon the same power from the night before, thrashing wildly, snapping his teeth again. Each new movement cost precious energy he didn't have. His limbs grew heavy as he fought for control. There would be time to freak out about the change later. Right now, all that mattered was the boy. He landed a bite and a deep groan escaped Jan, but the bear held on as Caleb's strength rapidly waned.

His head pounded again. His bones shrank and his insides twisted, morphing back into place. His vision wavered as he tried to bite at the beast holding him. He convulsed, the adrenaline draining from his body. Pausing, he waited for the brute to loosen his grip, eyeing the toothmarks along his arm. Jan relaxed slightly, ready to reapply the pressure if needed. It would have to be enough. Fire filled Caleb as he realised he had another chance at marking his captor.

He forced his failing wolf body up, launching at the bear's mangled throat, aiming for a protruding Adam's apple that looked as if it had swollen to double its original size in his mutation. Teeth met neck and he yanked with all of the strength he had in him, blood spewing from a now-gaping wound.

Jan roared, his pain echoing through the trees. His grip tightened, and he hurled Caleb into the air. Caleb's head screamed with pain, and suddenly he felt small again. The power he'd had seconds before abandoned him. Jan's massive hand clamped around his ankle mid-ascent, then he smashed him back into the dirt. The edges of Caleb's vision darkened. He tried to kick out but couldn't. He was done. He hurt. And he would likely be dead in minutes. Jan dropped him, holding a large, mangled paw to his throat, blood seeping out over his knuckles.

Caleb tried to call for Ethan, but the words strangled in his throat, and all that came out was a raspy huff.

He had tried to protect him. And failed.

Jan snarled, hot, angry air puffing from his nostrils, the blood flow slowing with the pressure. *I hope it hurts, fucker.*

Caleb's body relaxed, bones aching, shrinking and expanding as he struggled to hold onto consciousness. A chill ran across his spine, his flesh filling out while he stretched back into human form. Colour returned to his vision.

What the hell was that?

The lizard slinked his way to Jan's side and placed a slender, scaled hand on the larger hybrid's arm. Somehow, the smaller guard seemed to be calming the fury that had nearly killed him.

"May I?" The words snaked out of the second guard's mouth, a courtesy rather than permission being sought.

Jan nodded, his good eye glaring daggers at Caleb.

Caleb lifted his head, searching for Ethan. Lying naked and sore, he tried to call for the boy. No sound came out. *Where is he?* He let himself fall back, watching Jan and the lizard in fascinated horror. Jan allowed the smaller guard to inspect his wound; long-practised fingers prodded the edges of the gash. The bleeding had slowed but hadn't stopped.

"This next part could be unpleasant," the lizard creature warned.

He opened his mouth, an elongated, forked tongue darting out. Blue veins stood out as it flicked through the air, the split tips moving independently.

Caleb thought he was going to be sick.

The lizard guard rested his hands on the bear man's arm as he tensed and let out a low growl. "Easy, big fella," the lizard said, taking a step back. "Like I said, it's unpleasant, but good news!" Suddenly jovial, he announced, "No infection, no poison. Wolf boy seems to be clean, if a little boring. Personally, I thought by now they would be splicing different combinations; now I see he's just full of fleas."

Jan merely grunted again. Caleb had become smaller, more human as he lost consciousness, his hand searching for Ethan.

"Yeah, yeah, I know. Let's take them back to camp. Looks like this one needs a bigger cage anyway."

***

Twelve Years Prior

"Dad? Dad?"

Caleb was desperate now, searching for his father in their huge but empty home. His mother had died three years ago today. He missed her – he always did. He just wanted to be held, to be loved, for a moment. A moment was all John had for him these days.

He wondered briefly where his dad had gone. It was their night to read together. One night each month set aside for them to be in the same room. It was the only time he felt connected to the man who was supposed to love him unconditionally. The grand staircase and silent halls made the space even lonelier. The only sounds in the mansion were the distant movements of the cleaning and kitchen staff.

"Dad," he tried again.

Each time they read together, Caleb would fall asleep too fast, sometimes blacking out and missing the time altogether. He didn't remember much the next morning, but it was often the best sleep of the month if father could spare the time. The frequency had been dropping. Caleb wondered if it had to do with the fact his father would always take to drink during their evenings, often waking cranky and haggard the next day. Like he couldn't bear the thought of spending more time than necessary with his son. It hurt, but Caleb was growing used to it. He would take what he could get.

"I wish you were here, Mum," he said to no one in particular as he continued his search.

Caleb had tried to talk to his father after these nights, ask why he was so battered, why Caleb himself couldn't remember anything. Sometimes he would get flashes of something against his skin. He wasn't sure if he was making up the slight pain that accompanied these nights, or if he forgot to ask about it, craving the time they spent together over a potential confrontation. He thought whatever it was might be what helped him sleep. His father had shrugged it off the first time he had asked. Gotten angry the second. So, he let it go.

Caleb's twelve-year-old brain couldn't quite find the words to explain it, but after those nights, he never felt comforted. He felt strange, out of place, like he wasn't fully himself. Still. He wanted his father and missed his mother terribly.

He sighed and tried again, gripping the banister leading down to the lower level of the house, calling his father's name out into the space. Since losing his mother, nothing had been the same. John spent all his time with Argo's dad and rarely saw the light of day outside of work in his newly locked office. Caleb was told not to step foot in there if he wanted to be a good boy. A tear trickled down the side of his cheek – silent, the way everyone preferred him to be.

Orla, their kitchen hand turned gardener, walked past him in the hallway, vibrant, leafy green vegetables bobbing in her arms. She caught sight of him and called out, her accent thick but friendly.

"Ho there, little bean! Why te sniffles? 'Tis a wonderous day, wonderous. Come along wit ye, stop yer eye water and come ere, 'elp an old woman out then."

Caleb couldn't help but smile at her, tears not quite convinced to stop, but he shuffled into the kitchen, the smell of his mother's favourite meal tickling his nose. He sighed, trying to hide the fresh tears glistening in his eyes. Orla did this every year. She had loved Lydia as much as they had.

"Have you seen Dad?" he asked, trying not to look hopeful.

Orla dropped her eyes to the bunch of greenery in her hand before answering. "Nay, lad. Maybe you ain't reading tonight. Come on an' get a dish though. You'll feel better. It's ye mam's favourite." The last was said with a wink, recovering from her own disappointment.

"I miss him," Caleb sighed out, blinking back more tears.

"Aye, lad. I know."

***

Caleb woke to the rough movements of Jan's shoulder beneath him, his body bouncing up and down with the grace of a dead fish. His limbs were tied together with fresh vines, and everything ached. At least he had been dressed in a rough, itchy gown of some sort. He didn't think his nudity would have made him feel any better about being carried like a child. His head pounded, making his vision spin.

He attempted to lift his head, but it dropped back down, his neck too weak to support the weight. He groaned. Jan turned slightly, but he didn't slow his pace, only huffed before looking forward once more. They were moving up the pathway towards the fence of trunks he had seen earlier. Now, he could smell others. Many others. And fire. Something roasting. His mouth watered. Weary, he opened his eyes and spotted the second guard, Ethan's small body slung over their shoulder. His heart lurched seeing the unconscious boy, his body limp and unmoving. Frustrated, he knew that he could do nothing but wait until they made it to wherever Jan was taking them.

"Let go of him." Caleb struggled, his restraints digging into his skin. He needed to see the boy breathing. "What did you do to him!"

The slitted eyes of the second guard looked up at him, his head tilting to the side. Jan stopped suddenly, like he was waiting for an invitation to continue.

"Fascinating," the lizard-like creature murmured, its voice slow and tired, hissing slightly on the "s" sounds. It appeared that Caleb wasn't the only one exhausted.

Caleb swallowed past the dryness in his throat. "What?" His voice came out deep and croaky, as if he had to relearn how to speak as his vocal cords settled back into place.

The reptilian's eyes flicked toward him again but he didn't answer.

"What exactly is happening here? Why have we stopped? Where are you taking us?"

Jan grunted, still unmoving. The second guard reached out to touch the air with his tongue. *I don't think I am ever going to get used to that.*

Atop Jan's shoulder, he could just make out the path lined with crude makeshift torches. The canvas-wrapped tops burned with some kind of oil, though half had fizzled out, their remains crumbling into dust. He wriggled in Jan's grasp, hoping for the large guard to loosen his grip.

The air had gone still. The only sound was the quiet crackle of fire.

"Oi! Lizard breath," Caleb snapped, his patience wearing thin.

"Winson."

"What?"

"My name is Winson."

"Fine. Winson. Can someone tell me what is going on?"

"I don't know." Winson sounded genuine. He placed Ethan's unconscious form on the ground with care, the boy's floppy hair now covering most of his face. Caleb exhaled in relief as he saw the gentle rise and fall of the little guy's chest.

Winson stood beside Jan, looking up at the path before them. "It doesn't feel right, Jan. Maybe something happened while we were gone. A raid?"

Jan grunted in response.

"We should go in there," Winson said, followed by another grunt from Jan. Winson narrowed his eyes at the aggravated bear. "It's not safe to take the newies in and you know it."

Jan turned to look at the smaller guard, his eye focused on him and then Ethan.

"Look, kid. This ..." Winson gestured to the fenced path before him. "This is home. When it's quiet like this, it's rarely ever good."

Jan grumbled, putting Caleb on the ground with much less grace and care than Ethan had been shown. Pain shot through him as he hit solid ground.

Winson crouched beside him, hooking a claw into the vines around his wrists and slicing them apart with a quick flick.

"I know you want answers, and you'll get them. But right now, you need to stay put. The others ... they are wary of newcomers. That's what the cages are for. Think of them as quarantine. Especially when you try to take out our biggest threat."

"They attacked me," Caleb sulked.

Winson continued, not acknowledging his comment. "More and more experiments are being rushed these days." His tone shifted. Caleb swore he could hear sympathy in it.

So, they were experiments. Were this lot in on it?

"Come on," Winson said to Jan, who hadn't taken his eyes off Caleb and the boy. "I wouldn't try walking yet." They turned and started walking up the path. "Just stay here, alright? I expect you'll be weak for a while yet."

Caleb ignored him and began crawling toward Ethan. Every movement was agony.

Winson rolled his eyes, standing to full height again. "You shifted, lad. Actually shifted, like full-blown became something else and now you're back. Well, for the most part – we still must check you for those fleas." He chuckled to himself before the seriousness returned. "It's not something we have seen before."

"Before?" Caleb rasped, gritting his teeth through the pain. "What the hell are you talking about?"

"There is a lot you don't know. Hell, a lot *we* don't know. But that will come in time. For now, just stay down. We'll be back." Without another word, Winson turned to follow Jan. His body moved in sharp, jagged motions, swaying unnaturally as his pace quickened.

Was that a tail? Wait. I shifted into a fucking wolf!

Later.

Shaking off the thought, Caleb picked up the agonising crawl to the boy. He was breathing steadily, a soft snore playing on his lips with the rise and fall of his chest. They'd need food to regain his strength. Caleb ran through a mental list of the safe forest offerings Ethan had taught him about. Muscles on fire, skin still tender from the shift, he pulled the kid into his body with a whisper of relief puffing from his chest.

"Caleb? Are you back?" Ethan's voice was soft.

Caleb was so strained with exhaustion he couldn't do much more for him than confirm his name. "Yeah, kid, it's me. Go back to sleep." Caleb stroked the boy's dirty blonde hair. Ethan nestled closer, his breathing evening out. Winson was right, he was weak, but he could at least offer the kid some comfort after what he had been through.

***

Caleb turned at the sound of a guard approaching, narrowly avoiding a kick from the lizard hybrid.

He snarled, glaring up at Winson as he shook Ethan for a gentler approach. The boy grumbled in a groggy haze. It was still dark out, the path glowing in the light of the torches leading up to the encampment. The night was warm in the stilled air. A fluttering caught his attention. Caleb tilted his head towards the sky, waiting for it to come again. A soft spattering of dust filled his nose, earthy and light.

The owl, he thought. *What was it doing here?* A soft "hoo" called in the distance, confirming his suspicions.

"Where's the big guy?" Caleb asked, noticing Winson had come alone.

"Don't be rude," Winson said, attempting a joke, though exhaustion was clear in his voice. "Just get up. We're going home. This night's been long enough already."

"What's going on?" Caleb asked, pulling Ethan to his feet and steadying him against his side. He had no idea whether he was walking into a lion's den. The beasts he had met so far hadn't been overly friendly, but none of them had tried to kill him yet. This was his best shot at finding answers. Hell, he would settle for finding a meal at this point.

Winson's tongue flickered, pausing as the wind caught against it. Nodding, the lizard hybrid turned without a word and beckoned them to follow with a wave of his arm. Ethan moved first, more trusting and less concerned at the animal-human hybrid in front of them.

"Come on, boys, you can walk now. No more free rides." Winson chortled as he led the way.

Caleb rolled his eyes and jogged to catch up, taking Ethan's hand. At least they would face "home" together.

The path ahead was desolate and eerie, the shuffle of their feet the only thing breaking the silence. As they neared what he presumed was the compound, a small gasp escaped Caleb's lips. His body tensed, a now-familiar warning of danger. Winson flashed him a glare over his shoulder, all friendliness and joviality gone.

"Start something here and you will be killed," he warned. "Keep yourself and the kid in check, and you might just make it through the night."

Caleb could make out movement around the torn-up grounds, strange, shaped creatures moving quietly in low light. The area just inside the heavy wooden gates was littered with crates, just like the one he had arrived in. Caleb frowned, trying to take it all in. Further ahead, more crates were lined in an orderly fashion winding through paths in all directions. He strayed slightly from Winson, poking his head into one of the boxes. It had been cleaned out and sanded smooth. *Was that a bedroll?* He felt a tug on his hand urging him onwards. This place was far bigger than it looked from the outside.

How long has this been here?

"I was hoping to have more time to explain before we let you in," a velvet-smooth voice carried through the air, making the hairs on his neck stand on end.

"Argh!" Caleb flinched as the cat-like creature moved around his side, surveying the scene before them.

"Manners," she said, serious rather than teasing as she motioned towards Ethan sticking close to his side. Her eyes softened when they landed on the boy. Caleb thought he saw her pause, an almost imperceptible intake of breath, like she had been caught off guard. The moment passed too quickly to be sure.

The ground vibrated beneath them. The scent of Jan, all too familiar in his nose, mixed with a multitude of other bodies. Caleb grimaced, his senses picking up too much at once, sending him into overdrive.

"Come," she said, her long black tail curling around his leg, pulling him gently towards a row of crates. Caleb followed without a word, his hand reaching down to grab Ethan's, giving it a squeeze of reassurance when the boy hesitated.

Their feet shuffled wearily through the dirt as they made their way past lines and lines of the large wooden boxes. This wasn't a commune or a camp; this was a neighbourhood, a settlement that had existed for some time. A myriad of smells threatened to overwhelm him at every turn, not all of them human or animal – sweat and skin were mixed with everyday life. Cooking pots, fresh earth, water and vegetation came together although somewhat disturbed from recent events.

"What happened here?" he asked cautiously.

"We were attacked." Her voice had grown weary, as if this was an occurrence that had happened before. "I apologise. I missed the spectacle of the cages. Jan tells me you put on quite a show. In all my time here, I have never seen someone shift back. You must be special."

Could Jan talk?

They came across an empty crate, Jan standing guard beside it. His eye bored into Caleb with contempt before he looked down at the feline.

This is so not happening.

The tail leading Caleb unwrapped from his leg as the feline woman stepped to Jan's side. They both looked defeated but somehow still terrifying.

"You have questions, I'm sure. I did too, many years ago."

"How many years?" Caleb cut in, only to be met with a raised hand, her delicate fingers waving as if scolding a child.

"The cage you were in was never designed to hold you forever. But the arrogance rattling in your thick skull drives your temper. I needed to be sure you weren't going to upset the balance before bringing you here." She looked to Ethan and smiled; it wasn't as cruel as it was awkward on her feline features. There was no threat to the child. Her gaze held genuine warmth for the boy.

"Curious," she murmured.

"My name is Ethan," the boy said cautiously.

"Delia," she responded, catching Caleb's eye.

"Caleb," he offered awkwardly after a pause.

"Well, Ethan, Caleb ..." She pointed to the crate behind them. Caleb's eyebrows rose in question as he noticed two bedrolls topped with rough-looking blankets inside.

Where did they get bedding from?

The smell of meat and something sweet hit his nose. Winson appeared from behind the crate holding a plate of food. Breads, mushrooms, fruits and seasoned hare. Caleb's stomach growled, and his mouth filled with saliva.

Delia's voice brought him back to reality, although he couldn't quite stop the drool hanging from his jaw.

"Tomorrow, you'll get answers. Not all of them, but some. I ask you not to run. You will see no bars in the main camp. Your place here is voluntary. For now." An edge of caution crept into her voice, a warning as her eyes flickered up to Jan, who nodded down at her.

Were they communicating?

"Jan will pick you up in the morning and bring you through camp. There are others to meet." With that, the three captors left, leaving the plate of food at the entrance of the crate.

"Can we eat now?" Ethan asked, his voice hopeful.

"Yeah, kid, let's eat.

You Are Not the First

Chapter Twelve

The tip of a cold syringe pressed against the side of his neck, making him stir. Caleb mumbled a sluggish attempt to brush the feeling off as the needle pierced him. "Nnnn." He tried to move, but thick straps dug into his skin, pinning him to the bed. He urged himself to wake, to call out for his father. Forcing his eyes open, he saw his father already there, above him, holding him down as thick liquid seeped into his veins. "Dddd—" he tried, but darkness swallowed him whole.

Caleb swatted at a mosquito buzzing near his neck, shuddering at the thought of its needle-like mouth pushing into his skin, just like the nightmare he'd woken from. He sighed. Were they even nightmares? Or were they memories? Was that why he was different?

Warmth crept into the dawn as the camp started to move. Caleb strained his ears, trying to visualise hundreds of mutilated bodied going about their business. He had no idea when Delia would be back for them and didn't know how much longer he could stay still. He needed answers, they needed to see what these people – animals knew. Ethan snored gently as Caleb paced, a barrage of thoughts running through his mind.

I don't even know if Delia is going to give me answers.

He circled the crate, looking at a few others that had been turned into sleeping quarters, the insides stripped bare to create as much space as possible. The occupants eyed him with curiosity, not willing to make the first move before going about their day.

He sat heavily on one of the two stumps positioned out the front of their lodgings. A larger trunk had been carved into a makeshift table where they had eaten the night before. Caleb picked at the remains of the food, now half full of ants. He wasn't that desperate.

Maybe I could shift again. I could move faster through the camp. Make my way back before anyone noticed.

He could hear Argo's voice in his head calling him an idiot.

"You don't think these folk would question a wolf walking in their midst? Did fairy tales teach you nothing!"

He isn't even here and he's annoying.

Not listening to his better judgement, Caleb frowned in concentration, letting the memory of his shift fill his mind. He felt the hair on the back of his neck raise, but his bones remained in place. So did his muscles.

How the hell did I do it last night?

He scrunched his face, doubling over on the stool, shooting his legs out in front of him, trying to achieve ... anything.

"Caleb?"

His eyes shot open, heat rushing to his face as he met Ethan's amused gaze.

"Hey, kid. You're up."

"Caleb. Do you need the toilet?"

He dropped his heads in his hand and let out a weak laugh.

"Not quite."

***

"Bugger this," Caleb muttered after another half hour of waiting. Delia didn't mention he would have to wait all damn day for an escort. He whipped around to the path, turning to find anyone who could tell him where the hell he had ended up and when the first barge out of here was. His foot slammed into the stool, and he yelled. He balled his fists, ready to scream.

"What the fuck is happening here?" he hissed under his breath. "And why won't anyone talk to me? Hello!" Caleb said, waving to a human with an elongated neck, their head ending in tiny, rounded ears.

What the hell are they meant to be?

"Caleb?" The question was groggy and soft, the boy having gone back to sleep after Caleb assured him he wasn't going to shit the crate.

"What?" he snapped, his breath ragged, body burning with pent-up frustration.

"Um, have you heard about breakfast yet?" Ethan hesitated, fishing for words, clearly not asking what he really wanted to.

Caleb growled, his eyes flashing as he glared down at the boy who had somehow attached himself to the worst person, or wolf, imaginable.

"No, kid. I don't know where breakfast is. I don't even know where we are or why you're here, or why I'm apparently supposed to look after you. We are both fucked! And if I can turn into a damn dog, why can't you do anything? The bear, the lizard with the weird tongue and a bloody cat! Why is no one normal? Why ..." He trailed off as the boy curled against the back of the crate, tears welling in his eyes.

Caleb let his head drop and sighed.

It's not his fault.

After a moment, he glanced back at Ethan, who had turned away from him. "No one is normal, except you," Caleb said softly, his fists still clenched as he fought frustration.

"I'm sorry," Ethan murmured, his words trembling and muffled by the arm covering his face.

Caleb's shoulders slumped, wincing at the pain he had caused. "No. I'm sorry. I just ..." His voice trailed off as his gaze drifted past the crates and into the distance, scanning the pathway. There were more creatures than he'd imagined. Many more.

"Caleb?" Ethan's question was cautious, always cautious.

He looked over at the boy. His heart lurched at the sight of the kid's tear-streaked face.

Scowling, he reached into his back pocket for the list. It was weak, crumpled and at risk of tearing in several spots. He'd be surprised if it lasted another day.

Ethan shuffled over, his body warm against his legs.

"Izabella?" he asked as if unsure he had the correct pronunciation.

"Hey," Caleb said, a smile catching him off guard. "That's pretty good, kid; didn't know we had a scholar on our hands."

"What's a scholar?"

"Never mind." Caleb shook his head, smirking at the confusion on Ethan's face. "Did you know an Isabella?"

Ethan thought for a moment then shook his head.

"What about Darius?"

The kid shook his head again.

"Damn," Caleb muttered.

"Sorry," Ethan mumbled again, making a move to pull away.

Caleb hesitated before putting an arm around him, drawing him closer, carefully, in case the kid resisted. He thought about all the times a simple gesture like this from his own father might have saved them years of curt conversations and discomfort. It was the least he could do for the boy. The kid craved closeness and a sense of home, just like Caleb had at his age. His mother had been that for him. He tilted his head back against the crate, smiling, remembering her warmth. Ethan shifted closer, settling against his side.

"Not your fault, kid. I don't know them either and I don't know anyone who might."

He heard footsteps. Soft, light. Like someone walking on a cloud. *Delia.*

Finally! He congratulated himself on identifying their not-so-ferocious captor.

"Hey, Ethan?"

"Mmm?"

"I gotta be real with you, alright?"

Ethan's big eyes looked up at him with cautious admiration. Caleb winced internally. "I don't know how to be a parent. I don't even know how to be a good friend." Caleb let out a nervous laugh, squeezing Ethan's side. "But I'm sorry I snapped."

The boy placed a small hand over his bigger one, and played with the now thick, wiry hair that resided there. He tried not to grumble as Ethan plucked one by accident.

"I think my dad sent me here."

"Yeah, kid, mine too." Caleb listened for Delia's footsteps, still struggling to gauge distances with his newfound senses. "Do you remember anything?"

"About my dad?" Ethan asked.

"About him sending you here?"

Ethan tensed for a second, then continued fiddling with Caleb's hand. "I woke up here. Same as you, I think."

"In a crate?" He knocked on the one behind them. "Like this?"

"No," Ethan said softly. Caleb felt him put his walls up.

"Okay, kid. Thanks. We can talk later if you want."

"Goooooood mooorning!" Winson's loud, playful voice echoed through their crate, his smile horrifically reptilian. *Dammit*, Caleb thought. He could have sworn it was Delia. He would have to practise harder and train his senses. Caleb frowned at the lizard, whose iridescent scales flashed bluish-green in the daylight.

"Oh, come now, be polite." Winson's tongue flicked out for good measure.

"You're in a good mood," Caleb grumbled.

"Where's breakfast?" Ethan insisted.

"Patience, youngling," Winson teased. "Been a big night, it has, and morning if I'm honest, getting everyone back in their places, making sure the rascals were chased off appropriately and all that."

"Yeah, about that ..." Caleb started, wanting to know more about the attack. *Who had attacked them, and why was Winson so cool about it?*

Winson cut him off. "Looks like you two could use a bath." He flashed them a set of short, sharp teeth. "Come now, let's get you cleaned up. Can't have you walking through camp looking like a wet dog." His slitted eyes glimmered with amusement. "No offense."

***

Relief washed over Caleb as he dived into the cool water. He sighed in pleasure before realising the once-clear water rippling away from him was clouded with grime. "Gross."

"Who are you?" A tiny, demanding voice, barely audible from below the surface, startled him. Large, unblinking eyes stared up at him from the water.

"Ugh." Caleb plunged his hands into the water, covering his manhood. A chuckle bubbled up from below, sending ripples across the surface.

"I've already seen it, dear friend, and I'm not overly impressed. You're safe."

The voice was meek, buzzing around him like a bug. Caleb didn't move his hands as a bulbous head breached the surface, bobbing on the waves it had created.

"Wait, who are you?" The fire had faded from his voice; he almost felt sorry for the thing, and it's not like his world could get much weirder than it was. Beneath the head, the creature's body was slimy and elastic, moving like it had no bones. It flexed its limbs in the water, revealing two moss-covered, webbed hands.

Caleb tilted his head, trying to see more.

"That's it," the thing teased, flicking a tail up at him. Small spines covered the base.

"I ..." Caleb had no words.

"I, my dear boy, am a failed hybrid experiment, I would say. Suppose the powers that be never expected one to live this long in such a sorry state. But of course, you mustn't focus on the negative now. How else would I get to meet new, delightful creatures such as yourself and the young one down aways?"

Caleb furrowed his brow as he watched the talking aquatic blob move gracefully through the water.

It's not like this shit could get any weirder.

"Hmm, thought you would be more interesting, to be honest. I've heard that you shifted and turned back. Marvelous! First of your kind." A giggle escaped, sending small bubbles dancing across the surface of the lake.

Caleb shook off his surprise enough to speak. "What do you know about the experiments?"

"A rag-tag bunch of misfits a decade old, surviving in this … paradisío," the creature replied in a sing-song tone.

That didn't tell me anything.

The blob dipped its head beneath the water before surfacing again, wobbling from side to side to shake off excess droplets.

"Blasted thing, this head. Gets dry in seconds, but it's terribly inconvenient to have the drip, drip, drip trickle into your eyes when you try to have a conversation, now, isn't it?"

Its eyes darted to the side with such speed Caleb wasn't sure it happened. "Excuse me, would you?" it said before its long, sticky tongue thrust out of its jaw, flicking out almost a full metre to catch a nearby dragonfly. The blob crunched the defenceless insect with gusto, letting a papery wing float back down to the lake. Caleb grimaced as he tried to make eye contact again.

"You were saying … the experiments?"

"Ah yes, Delia did say you were a bit daft," the creature said with amusement.

"While we are on that, who is Delia really? And where the hell is she?"

"Don't you know, dear boy?" The creature's voice lilted at the end, pausing as if waiting for a response.

"Know what?"

"Delia is our leader." It dipped its head back beneath the water, resurfacing with a dramatic spin. "She keeps this place running, shoos away the baddies who try to raid and pillage our fine inhabitants. Of course, they stopped worrying about me a while back, you see. Too far gone to gather anything of use …" It trailed off and Caleb's attention wavered. More bodies moved through the water. A long, green, bump-covered shape glided across the surface before hauling itself onto the opposite shore.

"Is that a croc?" he blurted, turning wide-eyed to the talkative being before him.

"Who used to be human. Why yes."

"So all of the creatures in this place started out human huh? Just like us?" Caleb pointed himself and then over to where Winson was watching Ethan further down the waterfront.

"My boy, anyone and anything in this wretched place is an experiment. Some cruel joke played upon the young to achieve who knows what. I stopped trying to make sense of it long ago."

Everyone he'd encountered over the past few days had some trait that didn't fit the body they'd presumably been born into. Including himself. *So, what is so special about Ethan?*

Caleb seemed to be changing daily, and he wasn't sure how far it would go until he too became unrecognisable.

"Why do you think you were a failed experiment?"

"Well, that's just a presumption, young fellow." The face before him scrunched before it let out a grunt and launched itself onto its back, creating a scattering of ripples. It flicked up its barbed black tail and brought it down with a splash, chortling to itself.

A heavy weight dropped into Caleb's chest. "When did you ... stop being human?"

The creature sighed, letting its body fall back into the water so that only its head remained above the surface. "I arrived here almost two years ago, although it is hard to tell. That's what the calendar says, anyway. Many moons have come and gone." There was an underlying sorrow in its voice. "I've been water-bound for over half of that time. I'd say I am nearly at my end."

"What makes you say that?"

It lifted a webbed hand from the water, the slimy membrane glistening in the sun. "This happened just yesterday. The changes are happening slower, but they're still coming. Soon, my humanity will leave me, as it does with all the ferals and the failed. I only hope the latter will be my fate."

"What happens then?" The constant beat of treading water lapped against Caleb's chest, in time with the heavy drum of his heart. How long did he have before he lost his own humanity?

"It could go one of two ways, I'm afraid. I could be perfectly at peace, playing in the lakes until my body passes on to the next life. Or I could turn." Its voice dropped lower. "Turn on the people who have cared for me. Morph into something that needs to be put down. Or exiled to the wilds. But, being water-bound, I suppose it would have to be the former."

"Right," Caleb said, nodding. *What if I turn feral and they have to put me down?* His mind flashed briefly to the torn doe he and Ethan had seen not long ago, the smell of Argo on the shredded flesh. *What if Argo is already feral?* He hadn't caught his friend's scent since arriving at camp. Caleb looked towards Ethan, dread creeping in. What would happen to the boy if he turned? The owl was with him, watching over him as he splashed in the shallow water.

When did the bird arrive? No one else seemed to pay it much mind despite the blaring daylight.

The thud of Jan's feet sent pulses through the water with each step.

Across from him, the creature's eyes widened in obvious fear. "Ah, right, nice talking to you. Must go, algae to clean and all that."

It splashed, flipping itself and attempting to dive.

Caleb grabbed its arm, yanking its head above the water. "Why are you scared of Jan?"

"Can't you see it?" Its eyes darted to the sound of the footsteps. "Jan has turned completely, my boy. The humanity in that bear is long gone. I'd be surprised if he didn't turn feral before the year was out. If that thing turns, run." It shook free, sliding out of his grasp and into the lake.

Caleb made for the shore to dress, squinting as the top of Delia's head appeared beside Jan's.

About damn time she showed up.

The outfit Winson had provided wasn't a perfect fit. A too-small t-shirt clung to his newly formed muscles. If he shifted, he had to remember to take the thing off instead of tearing it apart.

If you ever figure it out, you mean.

Jan and Delia had stopped their decent to the lake, their eyes turned towards the sky. Caleb sniffed the air and followed their gaze. Smoke drifted on the wind.

The two of them started running back towards the camp. Delia was lithe and fast, pushing well in front of Jan's bulk. Caleb turned to see Winson rushing towards him with the boy. The lizard-like hybrid put Ethan's hand in his.

"Stay here," he huffed before running towards the others.

Bodies jumped out of the water in various half-human forms. His jaw dropped as he saw scaled humans racing upwards on human feet. *I really shouldn't be shocked at this point.* One of them had a hardened, rough brown exterior, their mouth twisted into a sharp beak, their beady eyes boring into him as they scuttled up the path on deformed stumps. Another burst out of the ground, balling up dirt with pincers far too large for their swimmer's build.

"Come on, we aren't staying put this time." Caleb pointed towards Ethan's pile of clothes. His body flushed with anxious excitement as he watched the rush of hybrids running towards the camp. His skin tingled but nothing inside him ached. Not like it had the night before, when he had jumped out of his cage. Right now, he only felt pure human panic.

As soon as Ethan was dressed, Caleb grabbed his hand and raced up the slopes that led away from the lake, following the assortment of oddities ready to defend their home.

The clash of manmade weapons, pained moans and grunts of fury pounded through his head as they neared the camp.

His heart was thumping, but he forced his breathing to slow, unable to take in the vastness of the camp. Rows upon rows of crates lay before them as they ran forward. Communal pits for fire and food, storehouses, herb gardens and weapons sheds lined the main camp next to a rough training ground complete with a dummy made of canvas and straw.

Bloodied bodies lay on makeshift stretchers. None of the injured looked over twenty-five. His age, or very close to it.

How long had they been here? Were they on his list?

He pulled Ethan alongside him, his weight heavy on his arm. The boy was fighting off shock, his body resisting forward movement.

I need to get him somewhere safe.

Caleb looked skyward to see the owl flying over the chaos. His skin tensed and released beneath his clothes, pain shooting through his gums as his canines made their presence known. This was what he had felt the night before. Right before his head felt like it split down the centre and his body contorted into a beast. He had to hurry. Shifting before Ethan was safe would only traumatise the child more.

Caleb stumbled upon a series of crates positioned side by side, rough arches cut out of the sides allowing the rooms to flow into one another. One held a workbench, covered with cups, plates and jars holding balms or dried herbs. The small space was overrun with plant life and clutter. There were bedrolls deep into the crates, some with bloodied bodies. *A med unit.* Caleb wrinkled his nose at the intoxicating herbs and urged Ethan inside.

Hello?" he called out hoarsely.

There were two short and stout women fussing at the far benches. Caleb counted eight beds in total, six of them currently occupied. One of the women turned, gaping at Ethan first, then meeting his stare. She held out a leathery hand to the boy, wrinkles crinkling around her face with a smile.

"Ho there, little one." Her soft Irish accent carried warmth, and Ethan relaxed against Caleb's side at the sound. Caleb tried his best to smile, his body pulsing with the need find Delia or Jan. Someone to tell him what was happening. He caught the woman's soft grey eyes; she looked far older than the others he had seen so far. She called to Ethan, motioning him over with a nod to Caleb. Ethan moved towards her, lulled by the woman's calm.

"Come now, see if you can help us out here. See those pots?" She pointed to a shelf lined with clay pottery, each vessel filled to the brim with various herbs. "Be a lamb and get those two off the top. Aye, there ye go, lad. Good, now come 'ere."

"Thank you," Caleb said, voice barely above a whisper as he turned and ran into the chaos.

Injured bodies lined the sides of the camp. Some had made it into the crates; others were battered and bleeding directly on the path. As far as he could tell, they were all still breathing, if only just. The air was thick with blood and the sounds of battle.

Fire pumped through his veins, the heat building across his skin, his hairs standing on end. Weapons and claws clashed around him as he moved through the battlefield, scanning for familiar faces. Some of the fighters were more human than others, but all bore signs of their transformations.

A body slammed into him, hard and fast, its sweat pungent. Caleb recoiled in horror. The creature's head was angular and disjointed. It looked like a hyena's – if the hyena was dirty and feral. The thing's limbs were too long and bony, making it appear as if it were walking on half stilts.

The creature clicked as it moved. Caleb's stomach dropped. Those were the clicks in the distance he had heard all those nights in the forest. The horrifying sound that had plagued his dreams. They were real. The creature's disjointed torso stretched out like an accordion, each rib elongating to stretch out its matted skin against the bone. Its movements were jerky, but it snapped down towards his face with determination.

It lifted a claw, swiping at him, catching the underside of his chin, ripping a line of skin off in the process. Caleb grasped the swinging limb but faltered, feeling the blood dripping down his front. He changed tack as its head swung wildly, moving to wrangle its jaws before it could latch onto him.

He growled, his body pulsing with raw energy.

Now would be a great time to shift!

Nothing happened. The best he could do was snarl, adjusting his grip on the creature's neck. The flesh squirmed under his hands like a bag of snakes, the horrid clicking picking up tempo with its movement. It stopped pushing against him, then opened its jaw and licked the side of his face.

"Ugh!"

Caleb let go, disgusted, nauseated by the feeling of its rough tongue. It was playing with him. The thing's mouth split into a toothy, terrifying grin, its jet-black eyes threatening to plunge directly into his soul. He ducked as it swung a wild claw at him again, missing him by an inch.

"Kajia! At ease," a new voice commanded. The figure was partially obscured by the trees.

The beast hesitated, its head swivelling toward the call. A man stepped forward, tall, broad and completely untouched by the ongoing fight around him. The creature made its way back to its master.

Caleb's mouth dropped open in horror as the animal's vertebrae disjointed with each step, only to snap back into place with another sickening click.

The man who had called the beast nodded at him as if he knew who he was, before turning around with Kajia at his heels and walking deeper into the forest. Several of the beasts turned from their fight to follow without command.

"Hey! Wait!" Caleb shouted, moving to follow. A sharp hiss stopped him in his tracks.

Delia was on the ground, her feline face spattered with blood. She had fallen beside another of the clicky creatures but moved to all fours, her hackles raised high across her spine. She glared daggers at the beast beside her. Its size easily tripled her own. She faltered, her back leg bleeding and sapping her strength. *She's hurt.*

Caleb searched the trees, desperate for a glance at the man who had called the other creature away. He had been human. How had he gotten here? He had to know.

A throaty gurgle spilled from one of the beasts still in their midst.

Shit.

Thudding footsteps rumbled behind him. Jan was coming. The owl flew before him as if directing the bear-like figure to his leader. The creature opened its jaw in a roar, line upon line of sharp teeth becoming visible as it moved its head back to strike Delia. The movement was slower than he expected, but poised, reminding him of a cobra. Jan wasn't going to make it to her in time.

SHIFT, DAMN YOU! Caleb's body tensed, coarse fur spreading across his torso as pain filled his skull. He shuddered as his bones split and grew, crying out against the pain while urging the process to speed up. The clicking creature struck. Delia barely moved her head in time. It seemed the camp leader wasn't willing to give up yet, but her eyelids flickered and strength was leaving her body.

He wouldn't let her die, not before she explained how there was a whole ass camp full of hybrid freaks.

Caleb snarled, surging forward as the beast took aim again. It caught his movement and turned to face him, leaving Delia to fall back into the dirt. He leapt, tackling the abomination to the ground. Its neck wound back and it aimed right at him.

Its body needs to click into place before it can release, he thought, watching warily as its neck moved into position.

Each click bought him time.

Caleb advanced, forcing the beast away from Delia. He rolled on top of it, disrupting its momentum. He had it pinned down, but it was still able to snap at him, its teeth coated in a filmy white goo.

"Don't let it bite you," Delia said weakly, attempting to stand. "It's poison."

Fan-fucking-tastic, Caleb thought, glancing at the snapping jaws. He jerked his head back, avoiding its bite, then slammed his forehead against its skull. Stars danced before his eyes, but the beast's body dropped, its tongue lolling out of the side of its mouth. An unfamiliar burning lingered on the air. He turned towards the trees.

Gunpowder?

The figure stood watching from a distance.

Caleb turned to run towards him, but a small claw settled on his back.

"Leave it," Delia rasped.

Her touch jolted his awareness. She was bleeding and needed medical attention. He stole one last look at the shadow of a man in the distance before he folded in on himself, his bones moving back into place.

Panting on all fours, he wanted to scream at Delia, at any of them. He needed to know what the hell was happening.

Jan scooped Delia into his arms, not bothering to look at him.

"Hang on," Caleb said. "I'm coming with you." Jan grunted and tilted his head, waiting for something.

"What?"

The bear huffed. *Was that a smirk?* Caleb looked down at himself in horror. His clothes had ripped during his shift. He was naked ... again. He looked around frantically for something to cover himself, but Jan wasn't waiting. He carried Delia off towards the medical unit where Caleb had left Ethan.

Stupid bear.

Checking himself, he was surprised to see his small cuts already starting to heal, the larger ones crusting over with dried blood. He grabbed a brown canvas sack from a stack of crates and tied it around his waist before hobbling after the bear and his little cat.

Dozens of hybrids, weary and worn, were scattered throughout the campgrounds with various injuries. Those still standing worked to restore order, picking up debris and tending to the wounded. As Jan and Delia passed, each of them turned, offering silent nods of acknowledgement and looking at their leader with sympathy. Caleb caught snippets of conversation as they walked.

"She always fights for us."

"She's hurt again. How long do you think she can keep this up?"

"Who's the new hunk in the sack?" The last comment caught him off guard, making him adjust the canvas to cover more of himself.

"Hey, kid." Delia's weak voice called him forward.

He jogged to catch up, but Jan didn't slow down.

"Delia ... I—"

Her eyes fluttered closed before she could hear whatever he was going to say. A long, nasty cut ran along her side, blistering where fur met skin.

They reached the medical bay. The number of injured bodies had increased since he had been here last. Ethan waved at him, his expression shifting to concern when he saw his friend bloodied and half-naked. "Caleb, what happened?"

"Long story, kid," Caleb said warily. "Who's in charge here?"

"Oh! Ava! I'll get her. You'll see." Caleb couldn't help but smile as the boy ran off. Jan grunted at him and held Delia out.

"Me?" he asked, awarded with another gruff grunt. There was no way Jan would fit inside the crates.

"Oh. Right." He fumbled, holding out his arms, the canvas sack slipping from his waist.

"Heavens," a mousy woman gasped from inside the crate. Caleb felt heat rush to his face.

"I ... I ... I'm—"

"Delia!" she exclaimed, saving him the explanation.

"You know her?" Caleb asked, trying to fish for as much information as he could, feeling stupider by the second.

"She's our leader, dear. Hadn't you heard? Put her down and help yourself to some pants." The slight woman tutted, pointing to a spare bedroll in the corner. "Please." Her voice was meek. He appreciated her trying not to laugh at him as he followed her instructions.

Delia's long lashes fluttered open briefly as he set her down, closing again almost instantly.

"What happened here today?" Caleb asked as the aide with soft rounded ears shuffled him aside and directed him to a stack of clothing. He pulled on a pair of worn jeans and a cotton shirt while she pressed wet gauze to Delia's wounds. Delia's face contorted in pain as each movement exposed fragile flesh and sinew beneath her matted fur.

"Grab a cloth and set ta helpin' if ye gonna stand there," the woman he had handed Ethan to said from behind him, the boy close on her heels. Ava, he presumed.

Caleb eyed a pile of clean cloths, taking one for himself. The material was rough, handmade, and itched the second it touched his skin. He squirmed against it, trying not to scratch.

Kneeling beside Delia, Caleb was instructed to hold a clean bandage against the weeping wound, allowing Ava and another woman of similar build to potter about the bench full of herbs and the smaller aide to tend to other patients. They had Ethan take crude clay pitchers of water to the injured.

"So, you're the leader of this place, huh?" Caleb said to no one in particular. Delia looked the most at peace he had seen her since she told him he didn't have to stay in a cage.

"Aye, lad." The woman's voice was soft. She brushed against him as she made her way through the room, a bowl of cream-coloured paste in her hands. "Put this on her when you're done with your tea." She bustled away again.

"Tea?"

"Ava said you should drink this," Ethan said, carrying a steaming mug towards him.

Caleb smiled up at the boy. The warmth from the cup spread through his hands, the smell of peppermint and lemon drifting upwards. He sipped cautiously, pleasantly surprised by the taste.

"Tell her I said thanks. You're doing a good job, Scout." He winked. Ethan beamed and hurried back to help Ava and the other helper in the supply crate.

"He's a good kid," the woman who was working beside Ava said, turning towards him.

"He is," Caleb agreed, his heart swelling with pride as he watched Ethan talking to the medics about forest herbs.

Ava let out a soft chuckle, excusing herself from the boy. The other woman eyed her with slight exasperation at being left with the nattering child, a feeling he had come to know all too well.

"Here," she said, reaching out for the sweet-smelling paste, leaning down to apply it to Delia's exposed flesh.

"You remind me of someone," Caleb said after a pause, staring into his cup. "Same accent." His chest ached. Memories of Orla in the kitchen filled his thoughts.

She nodded. "I get that all the time," she said with a wink.

He got control of himself, taking another sip. "So, it's Ava and ...?" He left the question hanging in the air.

"Aiel," the other woman said, trying to keep up with both Ethan and the conversation he and Ava were having. "That there is Jane." She nodded towards the third woman. "She helps when te raids come."

"How did you end up ..." He gestured around them. "Here?"

"Now, that's a story for another time. For now, you should rest. Can ye make your way back to your crate? Not eenuf beds in 'ere for ye."

"Yeah," he replied, nodding. "Is she going to be okay?"

"Aye. It's not the first time one of the nasty beasties got to us. Go now. Come back in the mornin' if ye so please. She ain't going anywhere, lad," Aiel offered.

Caleb nodded before calling Ethan over to join him. They made their way back to their crate and were welcomed by a plate of flatbreads and nuts. He was grateful this one didn't seem to have attracted any critters just yet.

"Eat, then sleep," Caleb instructed Ethan. The boy's eyes had started to droop on their way back. He lay on his own bedroll, closing his eyes, frustrated at another day with more questions than answers.

Friend or Foe

Chapter Thirteen

S weat beaded on his brow as the pale light of dawn uncovered quiet activity among the crates. Caleb had waved to a few of the hybrids as they had stirred. No one waved back. Rolling his eyes, he focused on his shifts again, trying and failing to force the movements from his body. Not even a measly claw.

Ethan woke and ran off. The boy seemed to be settling in well. Merely a couple of days and he had a handful of acquaintances to talk about.

I've never been much good with other humans, though, have I?

Giving up on the shift, he walked towards the medical unit, hoping to pry more out of Ava and Aiel. The two of them had given him more time of day than anyone else. Delia hadn't stirred by the time he arrived.

The two women were whispering softly to one another when he arrived, the faint grinding of herb and stone flitting through their chatter. Caleb smiled at the pair, wondering absently if they were more than friends as he observed their comfortable familiarity. He made his way over to them; Jane didn't seem to be in attendance. Maybe if he offered to help with the morning chores, he could pry more information from the medics. A bitter, earthy aroma hit his nose, his mouth instantly watering at the prospect.

"Coffee, dear?" the older woman asked, turning to offer him a steaming clay mug.

"Oh hell yeah," he said, reaching out greedily. The warmth of the cup shot up his arms as he inhaled deeply. "How?"

Ava chuckled. "It's a plant, ain't it? We grow it, dry it, roast it an' brew it."

"Don't suppose you have any cream?" he asked.

"Yer outta luck on cream, laddie, but I can offer you some oat milk."

"Oat … milk?"

"It don' keep too well if it ain't cool, but this is from this mornin'; it should be right." She leant over Aiel and offered him a small pitcher, the watery, white liquid riddled with chalky oats.

"Cannae strain them all. Sorry, lad."

"I'll, uh, stick to black, thanks."

A sudden voice broke the quiet.

"Ava! Aiel!" Ethan's shout made them all wince.

"Shhhhh, quiet, lad. You'll wake the dead."

They all stopped and looked at each other before trying to contain their giggles. Ethan frowned, annoyed he had missed the joke.

"Whatta ya got there, kid?" Caleb asked, eyeing the plate of warm breads and fruits he carried, a mix of sweet honey and sharp herbs now mixing with the coffee.

He beamed, proudly offering the food and setting the plate on the bench, scattering bunches of herbs in the process. Ava opened her mouth to scold him gently, but he was already bounding happily down the path back to the main camp.

"Kid's taken to this place way better than I have."

"Give it time. We aren't all bad."

"I would find that a lot easier to believe if someone would tell me what exactly we're all doing here. As of a few days ago, I thought my group was the first."

"Hardly," Aiel scoffed before reaching up to the shelves for a handful of plates, made from the same clay as the mugs. Carefully, she divided the food over the crockery and paired them with a mug of tea or water for those still in their bedrolls.

"Give me a hand, would ye?" she asked Caleb.

"Sure," he spluttered, wiping coffee that had dribbled down his chin. Aiel shooed him away to help and set to cleaning up the mess Ethan had made before putting more water from their rapidly emptying bucket on their small fire pit.

Delia was the last to receive a plate of food. Ava had given him the honeyed bread and a handful of raw nuts to place beside her. He almost jumped out of his skin when he noticed she was watching him.

"Tea?" she asked, her voice raspy.

"Water first," he said, bringing the small cup to her lips and lifting her head. She tensed against his hand, resistance fading as quickly as it had come. He wiped her mouth with the blanket she had been under.

"Uh, do you mind if I help you sit?" He pointed to her arms; she was slumped awkwardly against the edge of the crate. She nodded, letting him place his hands under her arms and lift, easing her into a sitting position.

"Sit down, Caleb," she told him, her voice firm. He obeyed without thinking, barely realising it had been a direct command before she continued. "What do you know?"

"I ..." he started, falling flat.

Ava toddled over with Delia's tea, handing it to her without a word. Caleb didn't miss the wink she gave him before moving on to tend to the others. Delia winced as she sipped, her tail flicking in agitation. She handed him the mug without a word and took a pained breath.

"Obviously, things here aren't normal," she said. "You've spoken to some of our hybrids; almost everyone has an addition of some sort to their bodies. I simply wish to gauge what you have deduced for yourself."

Caleb's skin tingled. He was finally going to get some answers. It had taken a series of attacks and some freak-of-nature beasts to get her to open up, but now she was here, ready to talk to him. The words tumbled out of him in a flurry. "We're experiments," he stated, trying not to flinch as Delia's tail swished outside of the blanket, stiff with agitation.

"There are lots of us, more than I could have imagined. I had barely scratched the surface of what my father was up to before I landed in here with you all. It seems like this has been going on for a really, really long time. The blob ... thing in the lake said you've been here years – it has been here at least two.

"Somehow, I'm different. I shift then turn back. No one else does that. But I think this shit has been injected into me since I was a kid. I keep dreaming about it. Memories? I dunno. I have a list. Of people probably here with me." Caleb couldn't stop. He felt like he had been holding the pieces for days and he needed help putting them together. He didn't trust Delia, and she certainly didn't seem to trust him. But she and the creatures here knew a hell of a lot more than he did.

Delia flexed her claws around the mug, her lips pulled into a tight line as she listened.

"Before I woke up here, I was at a party. My dad and my friend Argo's dad were announcing another business together." Caleb stopped to take a breath. Delia was now rigid before him, her thin, sharp teeth poking out of her mouth like she was going to snarl at him.

"We were there, and Lucia, I don't know what happened to her, but she foamed at the mouth, she was shaking as the soldiers jabbed me with a syringe. Next thing I know, I am here. Looking for others, like you. And you have a whole damn camp!"

Delia raised a hand to silence him. His chest was rising and falling too fast. She was still as stone.

"Your father?" she asked, letting the words hang in the air, an accusation on her lips.

Caleb frowned. "Yeah," he said, taking a breath. "He did this to me. He sent me here, him and those military assholes. There must be at least twenty of us! Did you see anyone else around the same time you found me? Do you know about the feral ..."

Delia's eyes had gone cold.

"Who is your father?"

"What?" He met her stern gaze. "John Murilo," he said, his voice lifting slightly. "Why?"

"Dr John Murilo," Delia repeated, each word slow and deliberate.

"Yeah."

Delia's back pressed into the wall and the fur along her body stood to attention. Her eyes narrowed at him as she clutched her mug.

"Get out," she hissed, her fur bristling. She twisted in an attempt to get up. A line of red bloomed beneath the canvas blanket.

"Shit, Delia, your wound—"

"GET. OUT!" she screamed.

Aiel came rushing over. "What happened?"

Caleb stared at Delia in shock. He hadn't thought anyone else could be as mad at his father as he was. Her anger pulsed through her small body before she went rigid. Her eyes rolled back into her head, and she collapsed.

He caught her before she fell, Aiel helping him to lay the patient's body back down. She took a moment to inspect the new blood before carefully removing the bandage to wipe Delia down with a pot of salve and redress the wound.

Caleb stood, stepping back from the bodies. "She knows my dad," he said softly.

"Aye, lad, we all do," Ava said, moving in beside him.

"Sorry. This is all so new. Whatever these experiments are, they've been going on for years. Ethan and I ... we're just the latest batch. And I think my friend is out there too."

He winced at the thought of Argo, pausing to pull out the almost destroyed piece of paper from his pocket, the names barely visible.

He offered it to Ava, and she took it, squinting at the text.

"I was hoping these people would be here. Do you know any of these names?"

"Nay, laddie," Ava said, handing the note back. Empathy shone in her warm eyes.

Caleb swallowed hard and glanced toward Delia's frail form.

"How do you know my father?" he asked, willing his voice not to shake.

"His name has been on crates. Reports. Sometimes, after the raids, our scouting parties find old camps. Some knew him before they were dropped here. Most of us have made peace with it."

"What happened yesterday and the night before. Those are raids?"

Ava nodded, pausing to look back at Aiel who was busying herself at the herb-filled bench.

"What are they looking for?"

"Us. To find out what we've become. To take from us more than they already have."

"Why don't you fight back, try to leave this place?"

"Now that is a story for another time—"

"Oh, come on!" Caleb threw his hands up, exasperated. "I've been here two days, and no one will talk to me. What is Delia so afraid of me knowing, huh? And you all know my dad? You know a damn sight more than I do!"

"Be still, child," Ava cooed, her leathered hand resting on his shoulder. "There is more going on than we have time to explain right now. Give the others time. Aiel and I will talk to Delia, when she wakes."

"Aye," Aiel said. She had watched his outburst without saying a word. "Grab the little 'un, and get some rest. You've only been here a day or two and already experienced a raid. I am sure you will be put to work soon enough."

Caleb rose to leave. "I want to help. I just don't know what the hell I'm helping. Or if you even want it."

Aiel had moved to Ava's side, their pinkies wrapping around each other.

"We know, love," Aiel offered.

"Come by tomorrow. Bring Ethan."

"She likes him," Ava added.

Caleb's shoulders sank. He had never felt more alone.

Apologies

Chapter Fourteen

That night, Ethan had fallen asleep as soon as he lay down in his bedroll. Caleb watched him for a while, unable to settle. He hadn't stopped to really look at him, to take in the intricate features of his little face since the owl had brought them together in the woods. His skin was sun-kissed, face dotted with light freckles. He was so innocent. His hair had fallen across his eyes, his exhales blowing a few blonde strands away from his face. Caleb moved to kneel beside him and hesitated before reaching out and gently moving it from his eyes. Ethan stirred at his touch, scrunching his eyes before groaning and turning over.

What kind of a monster sends something this beautiful to die?

Caleb crept out of the crate, walking on his tiptoes, hoping not to disturb the child. Sporadic lanterns gave the space a warm glow. He tilted his nose in the air, testing his senses. Nothing seemed to be stirring in the night. Their human and animal odours settled in their sleeping quarters. He let his eyes adjust and made his way slowly towards the entrance gate, hoping to see if he could suss more information out before dawn broke.

A central fire pit sat burning. Two hybrids had curled around each other in front of the heat. He thought he could see patches of fur like his own poking out of their arms. Their faces were angular, their jaws and nose pointed into a snout. The two of them had long, white whiskers that twitched in their sleep.

Weird, he thought, spying the opening behind the fire. Thinking it was as good a place as any to start snooping, he stepped towards the flames.

"Halt," a voice from behind called.

Caleb jumped. "I was just ..." The words died on his lips as he took in the creature that had startled him. They stood slightly taller than him, legs squared, holding a spear they looked ready to use. They had a long neck, the back of which was covered in dirty white fur that travelled the whole way to the top of their skull, settling in two long, pointy ears standing at attention. One ear turned towards him and the other focused at the gate.

"Come on, now, I didn't mean to scare ya. It's my watch, is all." The hybrid smiled at him. Friendly, but not enough to let him pass without question.

"What are you watching for?"

"Scouting parties. We have one due back any day now. And you, I suppose."

"Me?"

"You're Caleb, aren't ya?"

"Hush! Stop talking to him and tell the wolf to get back to bed," a firm voice called to the watch guard. Caleb poked his head through the gate to see another similar hybrid posted on the other side. This one's fur covered the front of their torso as well. They both wore a wooden chest plate. He looked the second guard over, her legs ending in sturdy hoofs.

"That there's Missy; I'm Edgar. Pleased to meet you and all that. You aren't 'xactly what I espected. But she's right. We aren't supposed to let you leave."

"Delia said it was voluntary."

"That was before word got out about your daddy. Word travels quick here. She wants information from you as bad as you want it from her," Missy said, her southern American accent more pronounced with her annoyance.

"So, I'm trapped?" Caleb huffed.

"Not exactly. But it won't do to get caught where you're not supposed to be just yet. My advice, hear the cat out. She's done a hell of a lot for this place, includin' getting herself beat up for these here folk."

"Stop causin' a fuss and go back to bed. I won't ask you again," Missy chastised.

"Fine. One more night. If I don't get anything worthwhile by then, I'm out."

"Good luck with that," Missy said, facing back towards her post.

"Go on now." Edgar shooed him off.

Caleb stifled a growl and made to sit by the fire, refusing to go back to his bed just yet. Closing his eyes, he focused on channelling his frustration. The heat of it made his body pulse. He tried to channel his will across his back, feeling the hairs raise against his shirt. Then he thought of his hands, his fingernails tingling with the promise of claws. Nothing stuck. He kicked at the dirt, the dust falling into the fire with an angry hiss, causing the other hybrids to stir.

"Dammit."

****

He woke Ethan early. The boy grumbled but he had spent time learning about the camp, talking to other hybrids, gathering information Caleb desperately needed.

"Psst." He rocked Ethan harder this time.

"Five more minutes," Ethan muttered under the thin blanket.

"We need to go see Delia. I thought we could get the breakfast trays for Ava and Aiel."

Ethan stirred at that. He had talked about the medics incessantly on their journey back to their crate the day before. Caleb had to give him credit – the boy retained a lot more information about healing herbs, oils and plants than he would have thought possible.

"Do you think Delia is okay today?" Ethan asked, his voice thick with sleep.

"Let's find out." Caleb tried not to laugh as Ethan woke in a confused daze, his wild hair sticking out at all angles. "Come on." He shoved Ethan playfully and made to leave, tilting his head to the sky and inhaling the scents of the awakened camp. He hoped Ava and Aiel would have more coffee.

They made their way through the winding path lined with several sleeping crates. Ethan waved and smiled to a number of hybrids along the way. Caleb was amazed at how many smiled back and said good morning to the kid as they made their way to the central gathering area of the camp.

There was more to see in the daylight: benches, huts made of dirt and leaves and off-path areas that led into open spaces.

"... and that's Michael. He thinks he's been spliced with a *horse*! Can you believe that?" Ethan nattered.

Caleb could believe it. Michael's face had elongated uncomfortably, large teeth protruding from his jaw at odd angles. His legs were long and powerful, ending in a broad torso covered in a light brown coat. Caleb greeted Michael and his roommate, who looked as if they had been mixed with a border collie, their angular head jerking at the sounds of life around them, teeth jittering in puffs of long black-and-white fur.

"That's just Ralph," Ethan said with no further explanation when Caleb asked if they were alright.

They made it to the fire pit he had visited last night. Caleb noticed two new guards were on duty. This pair looked to be spliced with something different again. Around the edge of the pit lay a central kitchen. Ethan tugged at his hand, pulling him towards the food. Old metal benches were lined with plates of fruits, nuts and breads. Bowls of sloppy grains topped with fresh berries took up another section alongside jugs of water and juice. It looked like an elementary school camp kitchen, with the addition of animal-enhanced servers.

"Has anything been sent to Ava and Aiel yet?" Ethan asked, breaking off from his side. Caleb looked up from the plates of food and caught up to the boy.

"Yes, sorry. Hi," Caleb started.

"Hello, Caleb," a quivering voice answered.

Caleb met the creature's large, rounded eyes, trying to hide his shock at being named. There were three of them, fussing over the food, calling others over and handing out crockery to passing hybrids. Another of similar size and features moved quickly to collect dirty cups and plates from the area, rushing back to wash them in large basins. Behind the benches, another hybrid was busy with a water pump, each pull sloshing clean water into buckets. All five of them had small horns pushing through their skulls and stood slightly hunched on hoofed feet. Each had a relatively human torso that morphed into a goatlike head, complete with a human mouth.

Caleb wrinkled his nose as the dry smell of straw hit him.

"*Caaa*n I help you?" the one who had spoken his name asked.

"Yes, sorry," Caleb said, nodding.

"Come on, slow poke!" Ethan called, a large plate of food balanced in his arms.

"Young Ethan has told us all about you, young m*aaa*n." Their speech was formal and clipped. "Best get on to the medics, then. See Gulia at the end of the line. She will make sure you have pitchers of what you need for the patients." They bowed their head slightly before moving on to the next hybrid along the bench.

"Don't mind Charles," a much lighter voice chimed in before placing two large pitchers of water before him. "Throw this over your shoulder, dear." They handed him a hessian tote full of clattering cups.

"Thank you," he said, slinging the bag over himself and picking up the jugs and following Ethan down yet another path.

***

Caleb placed the pitchers down on a wooden bench to the side of the medic crate, fighting for space amongst the various dried herbs and half-filled pots. Ethan busied himself sharing out plates of food amongst the patients starting to stir from sleep, dividing the portions equally.

Ava offered him a smile as he started to fill the cups.

"She any better today?"

"Aye, lad, seems quite taken with your boy at the minute. We spoke to 'er but tread carefully, hey?" she said, touching his arm.

"Where's Aiel?"

"Speaking to the birds." Ava's lips curved into a smile, her eyes glazing over momentarily before refocusing. "She does it every morning."

Caleb wondered if one bird in particular was out there with her. He handed out cups of water, stopping at Delia's bedroll. She was already leaning against the side of the crate, her wound freshly bandaged, holding her hand out for the cup.

"I'm sorry," she started, flicking her eyes up to him briefly before returning her gaze to Ethan as he moved through the crates. "Sit."

He held his own cup, watching the coarse fur move on the back of his hand as he fidgeted.

"I knew your father. Knew *of* him, at least." It sounded like she was forcing herself to speak, pushing the words out through her teeth.

"How?"

"I worked for his laboratory. Years ago. Testing samples, extracting bloods from mice, proofreading reports. That sort of thing. Met my husband there."

Husband?

"I quit. Or I thought I did. My husband stayed on. The experiments were getting too big, too dangerous. Even then. They had decided to start testing on living human subjects. I thought it was premature. The rats weren't lasting nearly long enough for them to be ready. I found out some things I wished I hadn't."

A lump caught in his throat. "What things?"

Delia looked at him sadly before sipping her water and putting the cup down. "Help me up."

"What?"

"I can't show you them here."

"Uh ... Ava? Aiel?" he called, unsure what to do. The desire for information was at odds with the need for their so-called leader to heal.

"I can't walk yet. You, child, will have to be my legs."

"Where is Jan? Wouldn't he ... carry you?"

"Help me before I lose my nerve," she said, lifting her arms up to him.

"Yes, ma'am," he said, not quite sure how to lift her safely.

The wound on her side had crusted over while another gash in her leg still looked angry and raw. Slipping one arm under her knees, the other supporting her back, he lifted her off the ground. The fine black fur tickled the back of his neck as she moved her arms around him. She hissed in a breath as he held her against his body.

"Sorry," he muttered.

"Take a right immediately outside the crate."

"Stay here and help Ava and Aiel, okay?" Caleb called to Ethan.

"Uh huh!" the boy called back, not bothering to look at him.

Delia guided him through the camp. More and more creatures were coming out of the trees and crates. Eyes turned towards them as Caleb held Delia against his body before quickly turning away. Others looked on in shock at the display, wide "O"s forming on their faces. Some simply continued their work – cooking, cleaning and repairing their homes. There were half-breeds and hybrids of all shapes and sizes filling the camp as they walked. A few tended to the wounded who hadn't made their way to Ava and Aiel while others worked together to upright crates.

There are so many of them.

"Tell me about the raids," he said, having built up the courage to speak while carrying the camp leader through the twists and turns of the grounds. "Ava said they happen periodically?" Delia grunted in his arms and pointed him towards the next turn.

"My home is right through there," she said, not answering the question. They entered a secluded section off a well-worn track. Caleb followed the dirt path, noting how the trees had been either cut back or allowed to grow in a way that gave her privacy not found in the central areas. Her space had been decorated to feel more like a home than the simple bedrolls littering most of the crates he had seen. Delia's house was painted a woody red, the outsides reinforced with logs to delay decay. The walls of four crates had been removed to create a much larger living space appropriate for a leader.

Caleb was amazed to see she even had a door: a collection of fabric and leaves woven into a shawl that he had to move aside before stepping in. He placed Delia on a bedroll in the far-right corner and whistled. It was almost homey in here. Rough homemade cushions lined the wall beside the bed, and a well-preserved oil lantern gave the promise of light.

Oh, how the other cat lives.

Caleb stood watching as Delia struck her claw against the metal frame, sparking a flame.

Handy trick.

The flickering light illuminated a makeshift desk and trunk used as a stool. Paper bark and charcoal were strewn across the surface, while the wall behind her was filled with pieces of paper, just like his, with lists of names.

"Woah." He moved to the wall and scanned the names for anything familiar. Finding none, he shook his head in disappointment. He reached into his back pocket and drew out his own list.

"How many of these people are here?" he asked, his eyes stopping on a photo hidden behind several faded sheets. Frowning, he moved the paper out of the way. Caleb held in a gasp, looking back at Delia in shock.

"Is this ... you?"

"It was," Delia acknowledged, tiredness seeping into her voice.

Caleb stole a glance at her, making sure she wouldn't fall asleep before she could tell him about her findings. She lay her head against the back wall, eyes closed, inhaling deeply as if steeling herself. Gently, he took the photo from the wall. The yellowed, glossy paper showed a short, slender woman with her arms around two small children, a boy and a girl, no older than Ethan. The woman beamed at the camera, while the children looked as if they had been arguing moments before, their faces slightly scrunched. The wall held a few more photos. One of a tall, broad man Caleb suspected was Jan, his arms around another man of equal build, their smiles warm in each other's embrace.

What had they all been taken from? Tears welled in his eyes. These photos were real memories of loved ones. He wished he had a photo of his mother to add to the wall; he could barely see her face in his mind anymore.

He placed the photos back. "Should I add this one?" Caleb asked, holding his list in the air.

"Please," she said, her voice distant. Delia's eyes had closed. He focused on the sounds around him, trying to extend the reach of his hearing towards the main camp. He picked up on signs of life but nothing approaching them.

May as well see what I can find out.

He made his way towards the desk. Sketches of the camp lay scattered across the surface. There were more rough bark pages filled with names, numbers and what looked like character sheets. Caleb tilted one toward the light of Delia's lamp. It was a charcoal portrait of the man from the photo staring back at him, the name "Jan Davies" written underneath.

Caleb flipped the page over. The writing was jumbled and hard to read, but it seemed to be a report divided into years, detailing symptoms and developments.

A large pile of smoothed-out bark caught his eye, a rock weighing it down. He lifted the stone, and his stomach dropped.

Deceased.

A wave of sadness rolled over him. How many had died for his father's sins? How many more would there be before they could find a way out of here? He replaced the weight.

"Delia?" He hesitated, torn between waking her and continuing his search. When he looked back, she was watching him, her tired eyes taking in his every move.

"No more hiding," he said. "What is this place?"

"This is your new home."

"Where are we?"

Delia grimaced as she pushed herself further up against the wall. She reached for a pitcher of water to her side, pouring a cup before holding it out to him.

"I don't know exactly. An island off the coast of the United States is my best guess."

"So, it *is* an island!"

"We are surrounded by water. Yes."

"How big is it?"

"Caleb, please." She held a hand up.

"I've been here for weeks; I never found a damn coastline."

"I don't know exactly. The shore is just over a week's trek." She cut him off before he opened his mouth. "When I worked for your father, the average lab assistant knew less and less about what was going on, and there was secrecy and hushed whispers, and whole facilities with restricted access."

"So why haven't you escaped? If you've been here long enough to build this place, surely you've had time to find a way out." Caleb tried to keep the frustration from creeping into his voice. It was all he'd been thinking about since realising how many hybrids were here. They could build an army and get the hell out.

"We've tried. There is no point. There isn't a world for us out there," Delia said. It sounded rehearsed, like something she'd said many times before to newcomers who asked too many questions.

"That's bullshit, Delia. How many do you have here? A hundred? Two? I've been in this forest for fucking weeks and in this freak show of a camp for days! If you aren't willing to talk to me, then point me in the direction of someone who is."

Delia raised her eyebrows. The look made him want to put his non-existent tail between his legs. He took a breath, trying a different approach.

"These names ... where did they all come from? Are they all here?"

"Some are. Some have moved on, passed or turned. Some tried to escape only to be destroyed by the clickers."

"The clickers? Are those the beasts that attacked us? Who was that guy with them?"

She kept quiet. Every answer just led to more questions. He wanted to go home, to take Ethan somewhere safe. He sighed, watching Delia's eyes close again.

"Delia, please."

"We have been here longer than anyone initially thought. Those names, the photos" – Delia nodded at the wall – "are clues we've collected from the new arrivals. You're not the first person to bring a list, but a lot of the time we rely on people arriving together or being picked up in counterraids. The drops—"

Caleb frowned. "The drops?"

"It's what we call it when new hybrids get dropped. They usually fall along the rapids. At first, it happened once a year. Only a handful at a time. Now it happens every few months. Less and less of the new hybrids are well enough to be brought back here."

"What do you mean?"

"The experiments are getting reckless. Human bodies aren't mean to shift, let alone shift this quickly. You yourself aren't immune to the change, or haven't you looked in a mirror lately?"

Note to self. Find a mirror.

"Myself and Jan, we changed gradually. Some of the latest batches have turned feral or died by the time we got to them." She paused, watching his reaction. Caleb sat, unblinking, waiting for her to continue. "I have been here about six years now, according to the charts."

Caleb looked down towards a rough map of an island, a key of seasons and timings at its side.

"I've been running this camp for the last four."

Four years. Caleb couldn't believe it. They'd built this place over four years. There was even a map. Surely, with the right team, they could make it to the mainland.

"Delia, what if we—"

She raised her hand, cutting him off. "Jan has been here for ten. He was one of the first. He wasn't always mute, you know. He and I might not have many years left. Jan is at risk of turning as we speak."

"Feral?" Caleb asked.

Delia nodded at the table. "See for yourself," she said, indicating a file in front of him.

The bark felt fragile in his hands, but it held the charcoal well. Whoever had written this had taken great care to minimise the bleeding. There was an artist in the group. A rough sketch of Jan's bearish form filled the top page, the animal traits mixing in with his human features. Caleb could see how the animal side had gradually taken over, replacing a soft, square jaw with a harder, more bestial look. The eyes that had once smiled in the photo were now hard and black.

Name: Jan Delamere

Age: ~~33 34 35 36 37 38~~ 39

Hybrid Species: Bear

Location: Upper Woods, near Calming Rapids

Survival: Fish, berries, mushrooms, plants

Physique: Broad, strong
Personality: Gentle, disciplined, helpful

As Caleb flipped through the pages, he saw a timeline of Jan's deterioration into the animal he seemed destined to become. By the latest entry, Jan had lost his voice, and his nature had become more menacing. Loyal to those he trusted, but dangerous to newcomers.

"I thought you said he had been here ten years. This only marks the last six."

"I guess your listening skills haven't advanced as much as your hearing."

Caleb let that slide.

"I have only been here six. I found him when I arrived. He was the first person I came across. He was a wild man then." She smiled to herself. "The larger hybrids seem to resist the animal side longer."

"So?"

"Eventually, Jan will die. With the loss of his voice and change in demeanour, he may not have much time left. I'm barely human myself, these days. We've seen dozens come and go. Eventually, whatever they injected us with wins. We can only hope we don't turn feral first."

"Do you know what we were injected with?"

"They've mixed our DNA, from what we've gathered, by trying to pinpoint those animals with something more to offer. Something mere mortals can't obtain for themselves."

"And Ethan?"

A soft smile broke Delia's features, her eyes twinkling with fondness for the boy. She placed a hand over her heart.

"I don't think the boy has had the pleasure," she said, looking grateful.

Caleb's ear twitched as he caught footsteps coming up the pathway. They would have visitors soon, but he still had more questions.

"What are the clickers? Where do they come from?"

"Clickers," she answered shortly, her voice laced with disgust. "Another experiment, bred to keep us in line while they run their observations. They patrol the island's perimeter, and sometimes they break into the camps, as you saw."

"The man in the shadows ... He called the beasts away. He named one of them. Who is he?"

Caleb toyed with the file, trying to stay calm. He was surprised to see Winson's face on the paper bark below. The lizard hybrid was a relatively new addition. His changes were happening much faster than Jan's.

Life expectancy: two years.

Ava and Aiel were next. He couldn't help a small chuckle reading that they were suspected to be spliced with elephant DNA. Their weathered skin and kind eyes made more sense seeing his suspicions confirmed. His father seemed to have a twisted obsession with splicing genetic make-up that didn't belong together but suited their human hosts. This had Dr John Murilo written all over it.

A cough filled the air, and Caleb's head shot up just in time to see a clump of fur spill from Delia's mouth. He grimaced. "A furball, really?"

"Down, boy. Don't think I didn't notice the fleas."

"What?" He whipped his head around, checking himself for the little critters, catching her smirk. The footsteps he'd heard earlier stopped as Winson appeared in the doorway.

"Hey boss, you wanted to see me?" *Had she called him here?* Caleb wondered as Delia squared her shoulders, sitting up straight and directing her full attention to Winson.

"Have scout party number three follow the clickers' trail. Their keeper was spotted in the recent attack, so they may be keeping them in a holding camp nearby. I want to know where. Check for supplies. Take three of the hunters in case they haven't retreated to the shores. And Winson?"

"What is it? Wolf giving you trouble?"

"He saw Caleb. He knows he's in our midst."

Winson eyed him. "Right."

"You're going to follow them?" Caleb asked, incredulous.

Winson glanced at Delia before looking back at Caleb.

"Believe it or not, those attacks don't happen often. We think it's when the big science folk want to check up on us, see how their experiments are doing. Sometimes we find supplies. Needles, cutlery, blankets. And it helps us figure out where they might come from next. Sometimes they follow a pattern. Their holding cells have been found all over, usually a day or two in any direction."

"Put a watch in the known locations. The last two raids happened in short succession. I want to find out if they have another up their sleeve."

"Hold on," Caleb said, his voice tight with anger. "You're telling me the outside world comes to check on us? Why haven't we captured one of them? Stolen their boat or whatever they're using!?!"

Delia's voice firmed. "That's how we end up dead."

He fell silent.

When he spoke again, it was with caution and a touch of fear. "They're killing us?"

"One way or another. Some get taken in the raids. Others try to escape but are chased back by clickers or lost at sea. No one's ever come back. Better to die here among friends than—"

"I will not die here," Caleb snapped. "I will find my father and put an end to this savagery. We're not a damn experiment. We're human, or at least we used to be. Whatever you have left is worth fighting for!"

The coarse hair stiffened along his body, his muscles flexing under his skin. His body ached with the increased flow of his blood.

The anger I need to shift. Remember this.

"Breathe," Delia said calmly. The uncanny need to obey filled him. "We don't know what each shift is doing to you yet, Caleb. They could be your downfall. Each time, it seems a part of you doesn't shift back, or haven't you noticed?"

"We need to go. These guys never stay put for long after a raid," Winson said, his eyes focused on Caleb.

Delia nodded. "Go. Be careful."

"Always am, boss." Winson was oddly joyful to be sent into obvious danger.

Caleb turned to leave.

"And where do you think you're going?" Delia called after him.

"To see more of this damn island for myself."

Clickers

Chapter Fifteen

Winson introduced him briefly to his scouting party before they headed into the forest. He was met with scowls and looks of disdain from the group. Tilon, the scout leader, gave him a firm once-over before taking position at the head and motioning for the rest to move out using hand signals. Argo had told him about similar commands used in combat drills to maintain quiet order.

Tilon's second in command, a younger but similar hybrid named Sythe, kept the group in line. His sharp eyes scanned everywhere at once, hands hovering at his sides, ready to draw the spears strapped to his back at a moment's notice. There were three others who looked to be spliced with the same animal as each other; Caleb couldn't quite pick which creature they looked like. Their bodies held a feminine curve. Each of them stood tall and agile, towering over the group, and paid him no attention, obviously unimpressed with their new addition. The party moved quickly and quietly through the brush.

Caleb hadn't missed traversing these dense trees. It was hard to believe that only days ago, he and Ethan had made their own little nest in alcoves and shrubbery just like this. He smiled to himself at the sight of the berries, mushrooms and leaves the boy had pointed out on their travels.

"So, you're the reason we are here, huh?" Winson asked ten minutes into the walk. The break in silence and loaded question caused the rest of the scouting party to tense.

"Shut up, man," Caleb spat, aware of how tenuous his acceptance was.

"What do you mean?" Sythe turned his sharp catlike eyes on them, his orange-and-white furred torso taut with tension.

"Dr John," Winson said with a shrug, oblivious to the rapidly quieting group.

"Winson, I'm serious. Shut. Up."

"Let him speak," Sythe said. The group halted, turning to listen. Tilon let out a low grunt but didn't object.

"The rumours are true then?" one of the other scouts asked, stepping in front of him. Their voice was high and grating, like it hadn't quite broken.

"He's John's son," Winson said, shrugging again. "It doesn't mean anything."

The three taller scouts rounded on Caleb, pushing him into their circle, each of them towering above him. Their long noses huffed down in accusation. Caleb held his ground, glaring up at them defiantly.

"You!" one of them said, shoving Caleb with what looked like a mangled stump at the end of their arm.

"Hey!" Caleb yelled. "He put me here too!" He snarled, pulling his lips back to reveal his new teeth.

"Back off!" Winson confirmed, worming his way between them. "Who knows? Having him here might help!" The lizard motioned for the group to take a backwards step.

"Leave him," Tilon said, his deep, smooth voice carrying the same authority as Delia's. Caleb shuddered as the group moved back into formation and resumed their march.

"You're an ass," Caleb muttered to Winson.

"For what it's worth, I'm sorry you're here." Winson's eyes softened. "Your old man, putting you in here? That sucks." He stuck by Caleb's side as they pressed deeper into the forest.

Caleb couldn't hate Winson as much as he wanted to. He doubted the lizard hybrid had meant anything by the comment, but clearly, he didn't understand that the others, who had been trapped here much longer, would take issue with a Murilo in their midst.

Tilon's fist shot into the air, signalling for them to stop and take stock of their surroundings. The leader stood broad and imposing. His thick, powerful legs looked built to run down nearly anything. Bright orange fur dappled with black and white stripes covered his entire body. He hardly spoke during their trek, communicating instead with grunts and hand gestures, which Sythe repeated. The second in command was his spitting image aside from being shorter and leaner. The two worked without speaking, their looks and throaty growls the basis of their communication.

"They been doing this a while, huh?" Caleb asked Winson, trying again to make nice.

Winson followed Caleb's gaze to the two feline hybrids. "Tilon and Sythe? Yeah, long as I've been here."

"Hush," Sythe scolded, his spear pointing towards a break in the trees.

Caleb went to retort before catching a faint clicking in the distance. He shuddered, recalling the creatures he had fought two days ago and the way their plated necks elongated and contracted, each vertebra clicking in and out of place as they moved. The memory of their black-beaded eyes set in hyena-like faces and their wiry, matted fur caked in filth made his stomach turn. He hated to imagine what those poisonous fangs could do to him after seeing what they'd done to Delia.

He inhaled, trying to catch its stench. The smell of decay was muted but moving. *One of the patrols*, he thought. Caleb let his eyes adjust to the darkening forest, scanning the shadows for movement. A shape flitted between the trees. It looked to be alone. Longer than he expected. Caleb tracked its movements, watching its thin back legs tremble under its weight. It turned towards him, eyes glowing.

"Hey, guys—" Caleb said, turning to the others.

The collective shushing of the group put him on edge, and his breathing quickened as he turned back to face the creature. Its neck twisted separately from its body. Its eyes finding his.

"Shit."

The group burst into action, grabbing the weapons from their backs with practised speed. They arranged themselves into a star formation around Caleb, holding him in the centre. He stood stunned as they braced, the defensive positioning rehearsed, the scouts nodding to each other to communicate. The clicker growled, and every muscle in Caleb's body tensed.

The beast moved fast. Its light feet barely made a sound as it bounded towards them in long strides. The clicking grew louder with each movement. Unable to move, Caleb watched in horror as it advanced, its stained, jagged teeth gnashing in its gaping maw. A piercing scream tore from its throat, grating against his ears as thick globs of saliva dripped from its jaw.

Winson grunted as the group shifted, pivoting all the while to keep their eyes on the beast. Caleb stood frozen. The clicker lunged. One of their group drove a spear into its side; the beast yowled in pain but its gaze remained fixed on him. He was the weakest of the group. Three rows of jagged teeth, bloody with old flesh and bone, snapped inches from his face. Tilon and Sythe crossed their spears to push it back.

"Move!" Sythe hissed at him as the group continued to strike at the beast.

Caleb heard another yelp, this one more pained than before. Hot, black blood splashed onto the ground, sizzling before hardening like tar. The smell was sickening, and he doubled over trying not to hurl. One of the scouts bumped into him as they lunged at the clicker, toppling him over. They swore as they broke formation to move around him.

If I could turn, maybe they'd have a better chance. He closed his eyes, trying to harness his fear and anger.

"Come on, Caleb, move!"

"He's trying to shift!" Winson yelled.

A scream tore through the air. One of them had fallen, the clicker's jaws latched onto their leg. Caleb could smell the coppery blood – human, not beast.

Now, dammit! Caleb forced the hot, prickling sensation of a shift through his body, using the fury at his father to fuel the ripples across his skin. One of the scouts lunged, pushing the clicker closer towards him. Sythe darted in, two spears ready, covering gaps the taller scouts left.

The clicker's neck elongated to full length, the cries of a scout dissipating into desperate wails. The formation broke. The clicker had one of them in its teeth. Tilon shouted for Sythe and Winson to cut it down.

A violent crack stole their focus. The clicker had slammed the head of the warrior against a stone, dropping the limp body without a second thought. The beast met Caleb's eyes, its own flashing red before settling back into inky blackness.

"Strike!" Tilon's voice was faint.

All four of the group lunged forward with their spears. The creature snarled and evaded the strikes with incredible speed. Its eyes remained locked onto his. Caleb scrambled to his feet; the clicker was coming for him. His muscles tensed, his skull splitting with agony.

"Don't fight it!" Winson called.

The clicker was closing the distance between the warriors and his shifting body. There was no time.

Pain ripped through him as his bones broke and reformed. Caleb screamed, fur rapidly forming across his limbs. Smooth, pointed teeth pushed through his gums. His vision greyed, but the clicker's red eyes were burned into his mind. The shapes of the group melted into the trees. It was between the two beasts now. Caleb braced himself to launch, huffing and snarling. His hind legs tensed, the lean muscle pulsing with untapped power, each limb trembling. His fear felt more controlled, compelling him to survive. He could beat this thing. He was strong enough. The clicker stared back at him as if stunned. *Haven't seen this before, have you?*

The creature braced, flashing its teeth. Caleb lunged.

The clicker's movements were so fast they became a blur. It dodged, whipped around and snapped at him. Caleb rolled, his new body matching the agility of his foe. They circled each other, growling and ready for the other to make the first move.

He feinted a pounce. The clicker took the bait and jumped.

Caleb dug his opposite leg into the ground and pushed hard, using the momentum to change direction. He crashed into the clicker. His teeth found its armoured neck and plunged into any weakness he could find.

A squeal rang out as his teeth met the soft flesh between the creature's plates. Black blood oozed into his mouth.

It burned.

Caleb dropped the clicker, hacking out what he could. The creature wheezed, blood spilling from the wound, its plate unable to shift back into place. Caleb took a moment to breathe, but the clicker growled and jumped towards him.

He tried to dodge but wasn't fast enough. The weight threw him off balance. They rolled through the dirt before the clicker pinned Caleb underneath its hefty bulk and lifted its neck, blood still dripping. The beast unlatched its jaw, striking down.

He didn't have time to move.

Fuck.

A yelp followed as the body on top of him collapsed, two spears jutting out of its side. The beast snapped in a panic, its head lolling around as more and more blood poured free.

Caleb staggered to his feet and stared down at the dying beast. All four scouts had pinned the clicker to the ground. The heat from their bodies vibrated around him. Pain lanced up his leg. He had taken a hit or a bite; the wound looked swollen and angry. Using his snout, he nudged the dying creature. Its struggle was slowing, its breathing now ragged, before finally stopping altogether.

A wave of sorrow washed over him as the adrenaline started to fade. His body thrummed, fear and anger taken over by melancholy. A pathetic whimper escaped him while his bones reshaped and moved into place.

Caleb looked up to assess the group. It looked like the tall hunter was their only casualty. Tilon, Sythe, Winson and the other two were intact. The two hunters were busy wrapping the body in thick canvas.

Winson handed him a pair of khaki pants. "We didn't know what to expect with your abilities. Figured it was safe to bring a spare set."

Tilon grunted, helping the hunters with their dead. He watched Caleb with caution as he knelt. "You did well."

"We are going to need the weavers working double time with you around, aren't we?" Winson mused. "Thanks for your help." His scaled head dipped in a respectful nod.

"Thanks for the pants." Caleb put them on before inspecting the underside of the clicker.

The plates didn't go all the way around. Underneath its head lay soft, off-white fur, dotted with flecks of rust. Caleb cradled its head in his hands. In death, the beast looked almost peaceful.

"I'm sorry," Caleb whispered.

"Whatta ya sorry for?" Winson watched him cautiously, breath still heavy from the fight.

"Whatever this thing ... this clicker is, or was ..." He patted its fur like a long-lost pet. "It's an experiment. Just like us. None of us chose this. These beasts included."

The realisation hit him like a sledgehammer.

These things were powerful enough to hold hundreds of hybrids back. One of them had taken on six trained fighters and one amateur shifter. It was little wonder some of them had given up. But Caleb couldn't let that stop them from trying again.

"Aye," Winson said sadly, before shaking it off and turning to the group. "But it did try to kill us. And I bet there's more up ahead. Plus, they're delicious!"

"Please tell me you're kidding."

"We cook the poison right out of them! This stuff, with chef's gravy and wild rice? It's a camp treat."

Caleb resented that his stomach grumbled at the thought. The two tall surviving hunters grunted impatiently.

He hadn't paid them much attention during the fight. Their spears looked natural in their hands. He had no idea what they were spliced with, but their height had to be an addition. They looked like wind, tackling thrashing beasts with more ease than the rest of them.

Caleb let the clicker's head drop and tried to stand. Pain flared in his left leg, and he hissed. The wound hadn't healed when he'd shifted back. One of the hunters planted their spear firmly in the ground, offering support as he stood.

"Thanks."

"Hey, kid ..." Winson cautioned.

"What?"

"Your ear."

"What about my ear?"

"It, ahh ..."

Caleb reached up. His fingers met fur. His eyes widened as they traced the soft, triangular shape twitching under his touch.

"Holy shit."

Experiments

Chapter Sixteen

The group fell into a melancholy silence as they continued their journey. Their footsteps echoed through the forest and a soft flutter of wings accompanied the group. Caleb's wolven ear picked up the crunching of twigs and stones as if they were snapping directly next to his skull. It twitched constantly. Caleb tried to focus on using the enhanced ability to listen for clickers up ahead but grew frustrated when it homed in on minute details instead.

What good is being able to hear so well if I can't even use it properly?

The two hunters dragged the dead bodies behind them. Caleb wanted to study the clicker more before they hung it over the cooking fire. He wanted search for more weaknesses to be ready for the next fight. His skin itched where new, thicker body hair caught every passing breeze. More than once, he shook himself off in irritation. Winson tried – and failed – not to laugh when it happened.

Tilon's fist raised in the air, stopping the group in its tracks. A soft thud sounded behind him as the canvas-wrapped bodies were dropped. Sythe moved to stand alongside their leader, their strong, furred bodies ending in khaki pants and steel-capped boots. They were mirror images of one another. Tilon's fist dropped and the hunters glided forward, their bodies contorting around thick trunks to scout ahead.

Ethan could have done that with ease, he thought.

Winson jerked his head, gesturing for Caleb to follow.

"Wait a minute," Caleb said, concentrating on the faint sound he had picked up. Excitement flared. Finally, something other than their own movements. The group stopped to look at him. "It's nothing ... sorry," he said sheepishly, shaking his head. Tilon let a low growl rumble from his throat, his hand pointing directly in front of them.

"What's happening?" Caleb whispered to Winson, who was ushering him around the trees.

"This is what Delia sent us to find. Holding areas. Like day camps for the raiders. They change position all the time, but they tend to leave stuff behind. Trees can't grow fast enough to hide their tracks."

"I don't see anything."

"They hide in plain sight. You probably walked past a few of these before Delia picked you up. Come on."

They pushed through the trees, shadows giving way to a dishevelled camp. It looked like someone had left in a hurry.

"What the ...?" Caleb whispered under his breath. A large metal bench sat in the middle. A shelter of canvas and rope was haphazardly strewn amongst the trees on the far side. It looked like someone had tried tearing it down but thought better of it. *The dude with the clickers?* He seemed too well dressed to camp out in the mud. *Is this where they take us?*

Tilon urged them to spread out, searching for anything of use. Caleb tried his ears once more, frustrated that it was another thing he couldn't just switch on and off at will. At least his nose worked. The air held a whiff of bodies and chemicals he couldn't quite place.

The owl had followed them, flittering from tree to tree, tilting its head to watch them as they worked.

One of the hunters called him over. "Check this out." A thick piece of beige canvas had caught on one of the branches during the evacuation. Caleb nodded towards another further on, still held in place with a tightly woven rope slotted through a drilled-in peg. Whoever had been here had planned to stay a while; their lodgings had been secured too tightly for a quick getaway.

"How often do you find stuff like this?" Caleb asked as he and Winson pulled the rope through its loop and stored it in the pack.

"More often than I'd like," one of the hunters mumbled. "Spaces like this mean they have been watching us. Learning when best to strike. It sometimes happens around the same time as a drop. New hybrids mean Delia is busy. Easier to take us when she isn't watching." She left him to work on another piece of fabric tied to the trees.

"Get that, will you?" The other hunter pointed to a second rope.

The owl flew down to the bench and started tapping.

"Hey?" the hunter called out.

"Hang on a sec. What are you trying to say?" Caleb tilted his head at the owl attempting to drill into a solid bench. The owl clicked its beak, hopping to the edge of the metal table. He followed its path. The bird dropped to the dirt. He bent, seeing faint tracks in the path, the dirt disturbed and hurriedly swept to hide the movement.

"No shit." *I'm getting good at this*, he congratulated himself.

"Hey!" Caleb called out to no avail.

Dirt coated Caleb's hands as he knelt and put his nose to the ground, hoping he could find the direction whoever it was had come from. He wasn't sure he'd ever get used to the instinct to shove his nose into everything. A familiar chemical smell hit him as he leaned down. *Where have I smelt that before?*

Caleb forced his head lower. He needed to know if he could pick up the scent of a body, fuel, anything. The more he found out, the more he hoped he could fight back.

Whoever had been here was alone; he could only detect a single thread of skin and soap. It was as clear as the pungent smell of the clicker they'd dragged behind them. *This is where they've come from.*

Bits of torn blueprints littered the tracks, the paper smudged with dirt and mud. It looked like whoever had orchestrated the attack had left in a hurry, careless enough to leave evidence behind. The owl picked up tiny fragments, one by one, placing them in a pile.

"Good idea."

"Oi, Wolfy," Winson's annoying voice rang out.

Caleb stifled an eyeroll at the nickname. "Over here," he said, picking up the pieces and placing them on the bench.

Winson's long, slender body twisted around several trees, grunting and hissing as bark scraped against his sensitive skin. Sun glinted off metal, the gleam catching the edge of a scalpel lying carelessly tossed on the ground. Winson picked it up before turning to him.

"Delia said you find helpful titbits in these camps. Ever find any people?" Caleb asked.

"A few times," Winson said with a shrug, continuing his search.

"And? Has anyone actually tried—"

"Tried to what?" Winson's tone had sharpened.

"To capture them? Find out where they are coming from, how they are getting home?"

"Delia said to leave them alone. Besides, they usually have clickers with them, and they aren't afraid to unleash the beasts on us."

"Why do you follow her, man? What has she done for you?"

Winson went rigid, his voice dropping in a warning. "She's done more for us than you will ever know."

"Then tell me. Help me understand. Because to me, it looks like she is just keeping you here and has no interest in getting any of you out."

"She's built a life for us here. More than you or any of the new hybrids have done. She's earnt her place. Now drop it."

"Come on! We're basically fucking hostages here. She hasn't even tried."

Tilon broke into the space, moving to stand in front of the two of them. "There are things at play you do not understand." His deep baritone held Caleb in place. His head was wide at the top, angling down into a strong feline jaw, much broader than Delia's and filled with sharp teeth.

"Don't you want to go home?"

"We are home. You need to accept that," Winson said defensively.

"But—"

"No." Winson turned from him to kick at the ground.

"Finish up," Tilon said, walking back towards the edge of the trees where the rest of the group were packing their findings in bags and canvas.

A soft hoot drew Caleb's attention. The owl tapped at his foot. Looking down, he saw it clutching a much larger piece of paper than the scattered fragments near the exit. It was crumpled, but a thin sheen of plastic had protected it from most damage.

"Winson!"

"What?"

"Just look."

Caleb placed the partial map on the metal bench. He pointed to the circular area depicting their current location. To the left, several ovals clustered together. They were not too far away if he was reading the map correctly.

"Where did you find that?" A sense of wonder crept into Winson's voice.

"I didn't. The owl did."

Winson tilted his head at the bird and gave it a nod.

That is so fucking weird.

The bird copied the gesture until they were both looking at each other side-on.

"Yeah, cool," Caleb said dryly, "you can both tilt your heads further than the average person, but can we focus?"

Winson approached the owl, offering his hand. Light caught his scales, casting a greenish hue over the silver. The bird hesitated, then hopped onto his fingers.

"What are you doing?"

"Just—" Winson raised his other hand to silence Caleb, staring intently into the owl's eyes. A soft gasp escaped his lips. "Well, I'll be damned."

The owl hooted softly in response.

"What?" Caleb asked.

"You *are* one of us," Winson said, staring intently at the bird.

"What?" Caleb repeated more forcefully.

"I always suspected," Winson said to the bird softly. "Its eyes, they're human."

The owl puffed its feathers. Butterflies stirred in Caleb's stomach as he extended his hand. The tiny weight of the bird settled onto his skin.

"So, you *have* been leading me this whole time?" Caleb asked, confirming his suspicion.

The owl cooed in response.

"You've been ...?" Caleb looked back down at the map. "It's trying to tell us something," he said, beckoning Winson over.

Seemingly annoyed at the attention, the owl twitched its nose, sneezed and hopped off his hand in a huff.

Winson and Caleb looked at one another before bursting into laughter. The owl glared at them – at least, it looked like a glare – before tapping at the map again.

"Right, sorry," Caleb and Winson said together.

"There really isn't much here," Winson said to the bird.

"Maybe not, but there is more than I've seen so far." Caleb pointed down at the page. "We're here, and I'm guessing that torn bit is where we walked through to get to this point, right?" He paused to check Winson was following along.

"So, what's all this then?" The drawing revealed a set of other closed-off areas, each surrounded by a wall of trees.

"I don't know. This doesn't match the maps Delia keeps in her office," Winson said, leaning closer to the ripped document.

"Why are you putting up with these damn raids if they happen so often? Not capturing one of your captors? That just seems insane. Do you just take it lying down? What the hell aren't you all telling me?"

Winson looked pained. "Delia wasn't kidding when she said this is how we die, kid. It's no use—"

"There are so many of you!"

"You saw how powerful that clicker was against an entire group. We've tried; it's not worth it." Winson's voice grew soft. "Now we do our best to protect the camp, protect our own. Hide the most vulnerable and get on with the lives we have left."

Caleb wasn't convinced. "Have you at least tried to get them back? The ones who are taken?"

Winson shook his head. "Not anymore. Before my time."

"What does that even mean?"

"Those that made it back were ... changed."

"What about that guy? He was here a couple days ago, when the raid happened. Big dude, black uniform, hiding in the shadows. He had a pet clicker. He looked pretty fucking normal to me."

Winson's body went rigid.

"Who is he, Winson?"

"You need to leave that man alone," Winson warned.

Caleb felt a scream build in his throat. "WHY?"

"The Shepherd is dangerous. He doesn't just work with the clickers, he controls them and he's damn near untouchable."

"How the hell do they get on the island, huh? Helicopter? Wouldn't you have heard it?" Caleb said, his mind going a million miles a minute.

Tilon entered back through the trees, the remainder of the group following close behind. The hunters placed an armful of goods on the ground before standing to the side, waiting for their next order. Tilon and Sythe walked over to them, not interrupting the exchange.

Winson wouldn't budge.

Caleb slammed his fist on the table. The owl startled, flapping to a nearby branch. The sharp sound echoed through the space, ringing in his ears.

"Enough." Tilon's deep voice sent a warning through Caleb's body, making him flinch.

Struggling to contain his anger, Caleb turned to the group's leader. The hybrid stood unmoving, tall and broad, his well-trained muscles creating rounded pecs. His boulder-like shoulders and strong chest tapered into a lean, muscled stomach and waist. Each deep and controlled breath he took made his furred skin contract against his abdomen, the dull oranges and browns shifting with the breeze. Sythe stood next to him, his spitting image on a smaller scale. Caleb's hackles rose in retaliation to their stillness.

"At least tell me how you got here. Crates?"

"It's time to move out," Tilon said, ignoring him. "You ready?" he asked Winson, who tilted his head in affirmation. Caleb stood still as Winson gathered their findings. Tilon watched, unmoving, as the group divided the loot.

"I understand your frustration, young man, but you've only been here a handful of days. You don't understand yet. But you will. The Shepherd is never alone. He either brings a pack of clickers that obey him like vicious, well-trained dogs, or he orders armed soldiers who take us from our home."

"You've been here for a decade!"

Tilon met his gaze, remaining calm. "I shared your thoughts when I first arrived. You must understand that they not only take what they want, but they slaughter those who try to escape. Fear is a powerful motivator."

"There has to be a way out?"

Sythe had moved beside his commander. Arms crossed, watching, his expression grim. "We've searched the perimeter of the island, losing allies and our friends with every mission. Clickers patrol the shores, and who knows what these bastards have for us inside the water."

"You have claws and spears, you've built houses. Why not a raft?"

"Our spears are no match for guns and soldiers," Sythe offered matter-of-factly, the fire falling out of his retort.

"Come on, guys—"

"Caleb, enough," Tilon said with finality. The group had gathered at the edge of the camp now, waiting for instruction. One of the hunter's lips had curled.

"They are obviously leaving this shit here to help us survive long enough for the next intake of their sick game!"

Winson hissed, moving forward to get in his face. "You've been here five seconds, and you think you know better. You. Know. Nothing."

Sythe's arm shot out, stopping the lizard's advance.

Caleb squared his shoulders, hackles rising. He snarled. "You have a fucking life out there, you know. You won't even try to get it back?"

"What would we be going back to, kid? Look at us. You think we would be welcomed back with open arms?" one of the hunters said, looking down at their nails.

Sythe placed a hand on Caleb's chest. "At ease," he said, his voice softer than Tilon's but demanding the same attention.

Winson took a breath, stepping back. "We'll fight if they come for us, but we're dying here anyway. Let us live in peace."

"Caleb," Tilon started. "Every so often, someone new comes along, like you, full of big ideas. You're not lasting as long as you used to. The experiments are growing bolder, the drops are coming more often, and the animals you're being spliced with don't fit the bodies they're assigned to. Your father and whoever he is working for are getting desperate. And that means he's dangerous."

Caleb's shoulders dropped at the mention of his father, the fight falling out of him.

Tilon rested a hand on his shoulder. "Most of you are dead before we find your crates." Images of the dead body he'd found flashed through Caleb's mind, bile rising in his throat at the memory of the stench.

"You said it yourself," Caleb continued to argue. "I'm something new. Maybe that's what we need." He looked at Winson. "What *we* all need."

"No," Tilon said. He looked up at the sun, turning to the others. "It's time to move."

"Where are you going?"

"Back. We have the supplies, the map," Winson said, his voice softer now. He nodded at the sheet Caleb clutched. "There is nothing else here."

"Wait!" Caleb called. "One second." He smoothed the partial map the owl had found on the bench, gesturing the group over, his eyes silently pleading with Tilon. The leader hesitated, then moved towards him. The hunters joined them first. Caleb pointed to an area of interconnected circles on the map.

"What is this?" Caleb asked.

"Not our business," Sythe quipped, his voice rough and husky.

"Come on," Caleb tried. "This looks like your prison set-up. What if these guys have the same idea? What if they are holding others? We could save them! Ten minutes, tops."

"No," Winson said.

"Why not?" One of the hunters shrugged. "Not like we don't have a few minutes to spare. Kid's just had his whole life torn from him."

Caleb was shocked they were siding with him after their friend was so brutally murdered. Tilon and Sythe sighed then relented with a nod.

"Ten minutes," Tilon said, his eyes glinting.

He wants to believe me.

"Five against one. Let's go," Caleb urged.

Winson scowled. "No. I'll see you back at camp." He turned and made his way back out of the trees.

The owl called from the treetops. Caleb glanced up, then at Winson. "Watch over him? We won't be long."

The small bird ruffled its feathers and followed Winson into the trees.

"And drag that clicker back with you!" one of the hunters called out.

***

Humidity rose as the trees grew denser. Overgrown branches reached out to others, closing them off to the breeze. Caleb stared at the map, doing his best not to pant with the cloying heat. The hunters were the only ones that looked comfortable with the change in air pressure. They had walked at least a mile – his timing was way off.

"Thought you said this was going to take ten minutes," Sythe complained.

"I don't understand. It didn't look this far on the map."

Tilon grunted, wiping his brow, and pressed forward, hacking through vines and weeds with his spear. Whoever had designed this place ensured people would give up before exploring too far. Each location on the map was hidden behind enough foliage to blend into the rest of the forest.

"Hey, what do you do for power supply?" Caleb asked.

"Fire," one of the hunters remarked, not offering any more information.

Caleb absentmindedly swatted at a bug, its body making a crunching sound against his arm as he crushed it.

"Oh shit." He stared at the insect in horror. His companions chuckled.

"Don't worry, we've never fully turned into a mosquito," Sythe said dryly.

The sweet, earthy scent of decaying wood filled the air. Ethan would probably tell him it wasn't the tree that smelled but the things living inside it or growing on it. Rolling his eyes at the thought, Caleb caught sight of the biggest, brightest mushroom-like growth he had ever seen.

"Woah," he said in awe, unable to help himself.

"You find something?" the same hunter asked.

"Look at that!"

"You really are a city boy, aren't you?" the smaller of the two said.

"Hey!" Caleb protested, mildly insulted. "What is it?" He moved closer to the dying tree, examining the thick layers of orange and gold fungus. It looked heavier than the puffballs he'd eaten since arriving in the woods. He reached out to touch it.

"Are you sure you want to do that, big fella?" Sythe said. A teasing note hung in the air.

Caleb yanked his hand back, eyes widening at the thought of the potential poisons that could seep into his skin.

"Tha—" He stopped as the hunters broke into childish giggles. "It's not poison, is it?"

Sythe let out a laugh, the two hunters joining in.

"You lot are dicks, you know that? Hand me your spear."

The two tall guards looked at each other, concern furrowing their brows at his request.

"What?" Caleb asked.

"Delia had you in a cage for a reason," the taller one said bluntly.

"And John Murilo *is* your father," the other added.

"I think he's proved himself enough," Sythe said, handing over his weapon. "Go ahead."

Caleb placed the sharpened edge against the base of the mushroom, prying as gently as he could to avoid damaging the tree. The rippled fungus made it hard to find where it ended and the tree began. He knelt and lifted the lower layers, the soft flesh peeling away with ease. He was surprised by the raw, meaty smell that hit his nose and made his stomach grumble. The thing was huge, and weighty, but if it was edible, it would feed a bunch of them back at camp.

"Looks like your pack mentality is settling in."

"What?"

"Nothing." The hunters smirked.

"It's called 'chicken of the woods'," one of them said. "Good find. They grow occasionally out here. We've not seen one in quite a while. Bring it with you, it will be good in a stew or two."

A raised fist from the smaller guard silenced them. Caleb flexed his new ear. The hunters tensed.

"Wait," Caleb hissed, swearing he could hear something in the distance. "I ... I think I know what those other ovals are on the map."

A faint click echoed through the trees, followed by several more.

"RUN!"

You're Not Going Anywhere

Chapter Seventeen

Their feet pounded against the earth, dirt and debris flinging up around the group as they ran. Whether real or imagined, the clicking hadn't stopped, its insistent rhythm hammering in Caleb's skull.

Sweat coated his body, his palms and feet slick with unwanted moisture. He was lagging and he knew it. Tilon and Sythe were almost a league ahead keeping a steady pace. His tongue slipped out, desperate for cool air. Horrified, he forced it back into his mouth and hoped no one had seen.

I really am turning into a damn dog.

Winson was dawdling up ahead, dragging the body bags behind him. The owl flitted from tree to tree, hovering over his slow movements. Winson's head whipped around at the commotion.

"No, time! Clickers! Run!" Caleb yelled.

Winson hesitated. Tilon stopped his run and raised a hand for the group to follow suit. Caleb protested before Sythe touched him gently and shook his head. Winson dropped the body and rope holding the dead clicker, flicking his tongue out and tasting the air. Caleb scrunched his nose. He really wished Winson wouldn't do that quite as often as he did.

"No live clickers around here. But I'm glad you lot have seen the danger of sticking your noses where they don't belong."

Caleb slumped against a tree, sniffing the air, certain the clickers were still on their trail. Fighting to steady his breath, he couldn't pick up on their odd, sweet decay pursuing them through the trees. Sythe, Tilon and the two remaining hunters panted beside him. Maybe he wasn't as pathetic as he initially thought.

"There were definitely clickers," Caleb insisted, crossing his arms over his chest. He couldn't help the petulance creeping into his voice.

"Yes, there were," Winson admitted. "Those rings we saw were probably holding cages either from the raid just gone, or the next one if they are going to continue the onslaught. Which means the Shepherd will be back for them. And when he comes, we need to be far, far away, unless you want a repeat of our friend here." He indicated the second canvas bag.

"Would they send them back so soon? I thought you said this didn't happen all that often? That the last time was an anomaly."

"If they think we're a threat, or that we are attempting to flee, the clickers will be sent to keep us in line. Or weren't you listening?"

"If we all worked together, we could capture the—"

"Drop it." Tilon raised an eyebrow at Caleb.

You want to believe me, don't you? "Okay, okay."

Winson knelt to grab the bag holding the clicker, hoisting it upwards, the rope tangling at his feet. "Help me with this, would ya?"

Sythe moved quickly, untangling the cord before tying it around the corpse. Winson tilted his head, beckoning Caleb to join him at the front of the pack.

They made their way back in silence. Caleb struggled not to plead his case with Winson once more. They had almost made it back when he blurted, "We really should go back. With a team. We could build an army, take the Shepherd on for good! We have a map, we know where he is. Think about it, Winson! We could wipe out the clickers, force the Shepherd to tell us how to get off this island. We could get out of here!"

"I need you to drop this," Winson warned, still refusing to look at him.

Caleb stopped, gripping the slippery, slightly scaled arm and forcing Winson to face him. "Just ... give me a good reason?"

"Because the more we dig, the more of us they take. This is my family now. Don't you get that? Just because all you can see is yourself doesn't mean you get to come here and destroy the only sanctuary these people have known for years.

This is bigger than you, bigger than your ideas. We have tried, and we've failed. Let us die here in peace." Winson's foot struck the ground on the last word, and he yanked his arm out of Caleb's grip.

"Then why did you let me take the clicker?"

"I told you; we eat them." Winson's voice faded as he walked away. "Think of it as revenge."

***

Dozens of faces poked out from their homes as the group walked back into the camp. Edgar and Missy were back at the front gate ready to wave them in. Caleb caught a few of the hybrids turn his way, their fear and disdain giving way to curiosity. The camp was looking much better than when they had left that morning, although there were several hybrids visibly injured from the raid. One of the bodies lying on a stretcher let out a scream, curling in on themselves in pain only to have their skin redden and detach from their body. New pink skin bubbled under the surface of their settling carapace, free of the previous scrapes and bruises.

"Fucking hell," Caleb murmured.

"We're home." Winson smiled at him, looking genuinely pleased to be back.

Caleb let his eyes wander over the sea of hybrids coming together to right the mess of the raids. There was a rhythm to their actions, different bodies working as one to rebuild and repurpose broken wares. They way they worked with the strengths and weaknesses of the collective – he hadn't seen it in action yet. Everyone here had a place. Even he could admit there was a homely quality to that. But he still couldn't understand why they would just let these attacks happen.

"Caleb!" an excited voice trilled down the path before Ethan slammed into him at full force.

"Oof." Caleb grunted, instinctively wrapping an arm around the boy. "Good to see you too, kid."

"Ew, what's that?" Ethan pointed to the furry leg that had escaped the canvas.

"Ah, that's a long story. Where's Delia?"

"Oh, she is in her lab."

"You have a lab?" Caleb turned to Winson. *Of course they do.*

Winson's clawed hand clamped around his bicep, sharp edges pressing just shy of breaking skin. "Not here," the lizard hissed, raising his other hand to the onlookers, urging them back inside.

"I'll take you!" Ethan offered excitedly. "Come on!" Caleb felt a tug on his hand as Winson let him go, allowing the child to take over.

The lab looked more like a cabin. Several crates had been pushed together to form a series of rooms and like Delia's house, they had been cut out and manipulated to give the occupants room. The building had been enhanced with wooden logs protecting the inner panels. Two thirds of the main room housed a large metal bench, much like the one they'd found on their mission, while the remainder contained an odd array of medical, scientific and household tools.

The storeroom was the most intriguing with its collection of hammers, scalpels and syringes. Along the floor were several baskets, made from drying vines and pieces of cardboard. Strips of bark, rope and canvas spilled over the top of each. Two boxes tucked into the back of the room were overflowing with used clothing that had been cleaned and folded.

How many of their people have died to leave behind so much clothing?

Delia was in the last room, hunched over a stack of papers, a medical ring light bathing the room in a too-white glow. A familiar tingling curiosity crawled under his skin. *How the hell does she have a light in here?* He stalked around the side of the crate, feeling eyes on him as he searched for the source of power.

As he moved, he noted the cane Delia was leaning on – her wound still hadn't healed. Her torso was also tightly wrapped in a yellowing bandage, crimson spots marking where her stitches had burst.

The low, repetitive hum led him to the generator behind the structure. An old but functioning piece of equipment. *That explains the light.* It buzzed away merrily, connected to a series of worn solar panels soaking up the sunlight. The trees around the building had been cut back, allowing more light to hit the panels just right.

The advanced equipment made him uneasy. For a population a military group wanted vulnerable, that was a handy novelty to leave behind. It had to have been planted. He wasn't as convinced that the items left behind after a raid were as random as some of the other hybrids seemed to. Caleb returned to the front of the lab, taking a moment to watch Delia before opening his mouth.

"You found a generator?"

She raised her head. "We've found lots of things."

He frowned. "Evidently. But what else are you hiding away from the others?"

"We don't hide anything." Her response was clipped. "The resources, when found, are simply placed where they can do the most good."

"You don't think these resources are a little convenient?" The hair along Caleb's arms raised; nervousness made his skin crawl.

"Careful," Delia warned.

"You can't see it, can you?" Caleb desperately met Winson's glare. The lizard was standing behind him, leaning against the crate opening.

"If they wanted us helpless, why the fuck would they leave behind something as useful as a generator? Maybe ... they don't want us helpless."

Delia stiffened.

Every tool, every scrap, every spare part was intentionally left behind.

It was all part of the experiment.

Caleb wanted to scream. A strangled noise caught in his throat as he made his way back to the group waiting outside to deliver their reports, his shoulders heaving in frustration. "I can't be the only one seeing this!"

Delia and Winson followed him outside. Ethan looked up from drawing in the dirt near the entryway to the grounds.

Tilon motioned for the child to stay where he was, leaving his side and walking over to the group. "What's wrong?"

Delia cut him off before he had the chance to open his mouth. "Nothing is wrong. Tell me what you found out there."

"No!" Caleb yelled.

All eyes were on him. Two of the hunters moved their hands to their spears. It was clear their loyalty was to Delia.

Deep vibrations worked up Caleb's throat, tearing out of his mouth in a rabid growl. His muscles pulsed and pain seared through his skull. He shook his head. Spittle flew as his facial features started to morph. He screamed, new teeth pushing through his gums, his temper boiling over.

"Caleb." Delia placed a hand on one of her guards' forearms. They straightened at her touch, though their hands never strayed far from their weapons. Delia and Caleb stared at each other for a long moment. His chest heaved with effort. Delia looked at him coolly, waiting for him to speak.

"What is it?" Delia said, moving towards him. "At ease, Tali, Jules. Please." It was the first time he'd heard the hunters' names spoken aloud.

"Are you sure, ma'am?" one of them asked, their well-trained eyes never leaving Caleb.

"He isn't feral. He is angry."

"Delia." Caleb's voice was clipped, jaw locked, the veins in his neck taut with the effort of controlling the fury boiling in his blood.

"Just breathe."

How could she be so patient? Surely, she had put these pieces together already. *Of course she has. She's running the place. She knows exactly what's happening.*

Caleb snapped his eyes shut, forcing himself to focus on the scent of the woods, trying desperately to stop the mingling of fear and fury that made him turn into a beast. He could pick up the fires and sweet grass, the compost that helped the crops grow, Ethan disturbing the ground within a couple of steps. He could do this. For him. His body relaxed with the exhale.

"They're playing with you." The words fell from his lips, slow and deliberate.

Delia's gaze sharpened. "Who? Who is playing with me?"

You fucking know who, he thought, biting his tongue.

"The scientists. The soldiers. The sick bastards who put you here. I don't know. But this ..." He gestured to the generator, the light, the crates full of instruments. "They're leaving it for you. On purpose."

"I'm not sure I follow." Her tone was wary.

"Don't play dumb with me, Delia, it doesn't suit you."

She raised a thin eyebrow and leant further onto her cane. Jules pulled in a breath.

Caleb ignored the hunter. "Why would they leave you a power source? Why, every time they raid you and take your friends, your family, would they leave little pieces of their experiments behind? Unless it's a way to spy on you, to see how you use them, to see if you even can. How often do these raids occur, really? Your recruits seem to have different stories. So fess up."

"Excuse me?"

"The raids, how frequent? Months, weeks? Days? How often are you being taken from your homes and paraded in front of rich assholes before you're killed?"

Tilon braced, his gaze concentrated on Caleb. The hybrid's movements were controlled and disciplined, head tilting from him to Delia as they spoke. The rumble of his voice came from deep within his chest as he joined the conversation. "Every three to four moons." His arms dropped, and his shoulders came forward as he listened more intently than the others.

He knows I'm right and he wants to do something about it.

"What are you getting at?" Delia's voice was tense, the veins in her hands taut as she gripped the walking stick. Caleb couldn't tell whether she truly didn't know this was happening or had chosen to ignore it and was now being found out.

He dropped his voice, willing himself to stay patient despite the pressure building inside him.

"Look ..." Caleb paused and caught Tilon's eye. The man gave him a slight nod as if encouraging him to go on. "The raids happen periodically. They take your people, your ... hybrids."

Delia's jaw clenched, but she didn't interject. Winson and Sythe had moved in behind her, while Ethan prodded at the dead clicker on the ground, apparently finding their conversation too dull to follow.

"When they leave, they leave some injured but never dead; the ones they take, they move around to these camps ..." Caleb reached for the map in his pocket to wave it in front of him. "And you never see them again, at least not the same."

A call from the owl followed by a series of taps caught his attention. It had made its way into the lab, seemingly working out the puzzle of the ripped paper it had collected.

Even the bird wants to help.

"You scout, you follow their tracks, but you never catch up with them. Or is that just your orders, Delia? Meanwhile, they leave convenient little bits and pieces, but my guess? Trackable."

"Trackable?" Tilon dropped his poise, the question accusatory. He shot Delia a heated look.

"How would that work?" Winson asked, curiosity getting the better of him as he took a step towards Caleb. Delia remained silent, gripping her cane, the white of her knuckles shining through the black fur covering her hands.

Gotcha.

"What year are you from?" Caleb threw his hands up, exasperated, before walking over to the generator.

"Don't," Delia commanded.

Tilon ignored her and, together with Winson, followed Caleb around the corner to where the machine hummed.

"These things have serial numbers that can be traced. Six years in the forest wouldn't have made you forget that." He spat the words at the cat. "Right now, this generator is probably listed as belonging to whatever company bought it. But the solar panels? Convenient, don't you think? A self-powering source, perfect for—" He ran his fingers over the back of the device, feeling along the ridges until he found a small nub that didn't belong.

His heart sank. A part of him didn't want to be right.

Taking a deep breath, he wiggled the object free and held up a small tracker, its ripped cord dangling. The last of its power flickered in a slow, red flash before dying.

"A tracking device."

Caleb turned to look at them expectantly. Delia's chin had sunk to her chest. Winson looked like he was trying to decide whether to comfort her or not. Tilon was glaring at the device still in Caleb's hand. There was a simmering tension hanging around the disciplined hybrid. His chest rose in a slow and steady rhythm, his mouth half turned up into a snarl, showing two curled fangs larger than his own. Up close, Caleb could see how powerful he was. In the light, Tilon's tri-coloured fur didn't quite match any one animal. He was something different again. Maybe he had been spliced with different genes, along with Sythe. There seemed to be groupings of like-spliced creatures spattered throughout the camp. *How often does Dad try to modify us?*

"What are you thinking?" Tilon asked, finally looking at him.

"I think we need to prepare for another raid."

"We just had one – two, really," Winson said, not catching on.

Tilon didn't look away from Caleb. "If that was the device tracking the camp's location and it's now been disconnected, they'll want to confirm we're still here. That we haven't figured them out." He spoke slowly, piecing the thoughts together as he said them.

"It may not be the only device," Winson interjected. "We might be alright if there are others."

Delia had gone rigid, her jaw clenched.

"Alright?" Caleb spat. "None of this is fucking alright. This is sick! If there are others, we need to find them and destroy them, then move camp so they don't know where we are! From there we can build a—"

Delia's hand shot up.

She winced as she moved to stand in the centre of the group, taking a moment to make sure she had their attention before speaking. "We do nothing."

"What?" Tilon and Caleb said in unison.

"We – we can fight! We can be free! We can get off this damn island and fight my father and this whole damned operation together!" Caleb objected.

Delia stood tall and unwavering. "The world doesn't want us. We're no good out there. All we can do is live out our lives in whatever peace we can find and keep our people safe."

This was the message the leader of their operation was spreading to the hybrids. It was no wonder Winson felt so strongly about giving up. Caleb admitted he hadn't been the most accepting of differences in his own life, but he was beginning to see this was so much bigger than that.

"Delia. We could stop this shit from happening to anyone else. We could get these people home to see their loved ones. We could get Ethan home." His voice dropped on the last part. He saw Delia flinch, though she quickly masked it. It was no secret she had taken to the boy.

She stood up straight, recovering quickly, and looked him dead in the eye. "So what? So they can be shamed, gawked at, put on display? What is the point, Caleb? You may be learning, but you're only thinking about yourself right now. Do you really want what's best for everyone here, or just for you? To run home to Daddy so he can tell you how proud he is that you didn't die out here?"

"Fuck you, Delia!" Spittle flew from his mouth as he lunged forward, only to be stopped by strong hands gripping him in place.

"Do you not think the people who did this to you deserve to face justice?" he growled up at Tilon, struggling against his hold.

"It's time we revisited escape, Delia," Tilon said, hand on his spear.

"Yes!" Caleb pushed against the restraint, trying to break free.

"I said no!" Delia's command made them all jump. Ethan looked up from the clicker and scuttled to Caleb's side, poking at the hybrid holding him. Tilon stepped back, letting the child get closer, though his gaze carried a warning. Caleb wrapped an arm around the boy, using him as an anchor for his anger.

"You're right," Caleb started, squeezing the child's arm gently. "I want to go home. But not to my old life. Right now, I want to see my father and try not to kill him. To get to the bottom of what's happening here, to me, to you, to all of us. We're not going to find any answers on this damn island.

"You said it yourself, things have changed, right? You've almost completely turned. So has Jan. How many others? How long before it takes over, Delia? And what about the ferals? Are they still out there? How do we know that isn't where it ends for us? Why hasn't Ethan changed at all? Why can I shift back? And what the hell is Tilon?"

"Tiger lion," the mission leader interjected.

"Oh ... Ti-lon. Real original, man."

Tilon shrugged, waiting for Caleb to continue.

"My point is this has been happening for a damn decade. How many have you lost in that time? How many more are you willing to lose? How many are you willing to watch die because you refused to try again?"

"I told you," Winson said, now standing closer to Delia. "It wasn't worth it."

"Says who, you and the cat who supposedly leads the group?" Caleb shot back.

Thunderous footsteps shook the lab. Caleb looked up to see Jan striding towards them, his massive form moving with grim determination. Delia's eyes widened as the mutated bear reached her. He shot a glare at Caleb before offering his leader a paw for support. Only now did Caleb notice thick, black claws at the end of Jan's hairy stump. Caleb's heart rate quickened. He never wanted to fight that thing again.

"This discussion ends here," Delia said. "You have a choice: join us and contribute, or leave. The same choice will be given to all the others. Your life as you knew it is over. Accept it. I won't stop you from leaving, but no one here will join you on a suicide mission. The people in this camp will remain as safe as humanly possible until the end of their days, with or without your help."

"You'd actually let me leave?"

"It's your choice, and if you need a meal and a bed, we will provide it. This camp will be open to you so long as you choose to remain in it."

With that, she turned and made her way towards the main camp, stopping to inspect the clicker briefly, instructing Winson and Sythe to take it to the kitchens. She offered Ethan a smile, who looked to Caleb before smiling back. The group dispersed, the hunters following after Winson and Sythe. Tilon remained by his side, watching the others leave. Ethan was torn; he looked after the clicker then back to Caleb.

"Go on, kid. It's alright," Caleb said gently, wanting to speak to Tilon alone. "We'll follow soon. They are going to cook the clicker, you know."

"Really? Cool!" Ethan exclaimed, scampering after the group.

"You said it's time we thought about escape again?" Caleb said, still watching the boy.

"I have a plan," Tilon responded.

***

Tilon jerked his head towards the owl. Its tiny claws scraped softly against the metal bench as it hopped, placing pieces of the paper together. Without a word, he and Caleb stepped closer, inspecting what looked to be a faded piece of map, not unlike the ones in Delia's rooms.

Rough, hand-drawn sketches of the woods and marked-out areas were laid out before them. Caleb placed his map down to see if any part of their blueprints matched.

It was unclear whether this was a replica, an extension or the same map. The patterns of circles looked similar, but the two drawings differed slightly. Tilon leaned in to pick up a piece of shredded paper. The owl shrieked. He dropped it and jumped back. A laugh caught in Caleb's throat, and the big hybrid grumbled.

"Don't take it personally," Caleb offered.

"Can I see that?" Tilon asked, not acknowledging his embarrassment. "It looks like an extension," he muttered, frowning down at the broken pieces.

The tapping stopped. A hoot signalled the owl's task was complete. Tilon eyed the owl cautiously while examining its work. The owl raised its feathers as if preparing to strike. Tilon flinched and the small bird puffed up, letting out a rough, bark-like noise.

"Are you laughing at me?" Tilon grumbled.

"We both are." Caleb snickered.

"I'm your only ally here right now," Tilon reminded him.

"Right." Caleb straightened. "Back on the mission. You believed me. I could see it. Why?"

Tilon nodded down at the maps and pulled a third piece of paper from his cargo pants pocket. He unrolled the scroll of bark. Soft and flexible, it revealed another variation of the space he had wanted to explore.

"Because you're right. I've suspected for a while. Explored these areas with small, trusted scouting groups." He tapped the map.

"Delia has the camp brainwashed, but she really is trying to keep the people here safe. She's scared for them, and for herself. But I know she came here with insider knowledge. Probably why she reacted so poorly to hearing who your father was."

"You heard about that?"

"I did. There isn't much I don't hear one way or another, Caleb. You'd be wise to remember that." It was the most Tilon had said since Caleb had known him. He admired the man's ability to observe and remain quiet. It seemed he had been piecing things together long before the new hybrids arrived.

"The soldiers I know wouldn't stand for this," Tilon continued.

Caleb's ear twitched in his direction. "Did you know a cadet named Argo?" he asked without thinking.

Tilon frowned and shook his head. "Look, Caleb. Some of us have been talking about leaving. The plans aren't solid. The dangers out there are very real, the clickers and the soldiers. They are out there on the coasts, and sporadically in the woods. What you propose to do – and what I've been doing in my own time – isn't safe. We don't have a boat, we don't have a compass and there is no guarantee we will find anything more. Perhaps Delia is right. But I don't know for certain. If we do this, I doubt we'd be welcomed back."

"What about the ferals?"

"It's a risk. One I am willing to take to see if we can make it. Many of us gave up on our own lives long ago, but you're onto something. The experiments are changing ... again. Your father sent his child into the mix, and the number of dead we have found in the last year makes me suspect something in the background isn't working as well as he would like."

"You said he was desperate?"

"Do you remember issues he had, disgruntled contributors? Other young people like yourself who had a stake in his findings?"

Caleb looked at the ground, scuffing his heels. "I never paid attention. I just ... I wanted to be left alone. We ... never really cared much for each other. Not since my mum passed. I was a trophy to him. The job paid well." Caleb pinched the bridge of his nose with a sigh. "Before I came here, I saw his lab. There was a rat; I watched its body mutate and bend, its bones expand and snap out of its body. Whatever he tried down there didn't work. It could be the same shit he put inside of all of us that night."

"And did you see anything out there, before Delia found you?" Tilon's voice was steady.

"I only found one other, dead when I got into their crate. Along the rapids. That was before I found Ethan."

Tilon met his gaze. "We found two others. Same drop, I presume. You're the only one we found alive from the latest drop."

Caleb tried not to panic about this revelation, swallowing the lump that tried to catch in his throat. He couldn't help whoever it was they'd found – he just hoped neither of them was Argo. "We need to stop it."

"I agree. The trouble lies with convincing others without them going to Delia or Jan first. Whether we like it or not, she holds the loyalty of the majority, and my small scouting party isn't big enough for what we want to achieve ..." Tilon frowned, studying the maps again.

"You're ex-military, right?" Caleb asked.

Tilon gave him a single nod, then continued. "Sythe and I were in a unit together. We rarely complied with things we didn't believe in. There were rumours of a splicing program filtering through the fighting forces. People enhanced with better senses like smell and eyesight. Things like you're dealing with right now. We were asked to take part in the experimentation. We refused; there is a reason humans and animals were separated by nature. We never believed the promises others fell prey to."

"It was just the two of you fighting back?"

"Far from it. Others from our unit were discharged, not an honour to their name. Some simply went missing. Sythe and I stayed; we wanted to sniff it out from the inside. Try and stop it at the source. Find out where the genes were coming from, who was responsible for the funding. Like it or not, your father isn't alone in this. It got too big for us. I suppose they got to us before we got to them."

A breath caught in Caleb's throat. "What happened?"

"Went out for drinks one night with the unit who remained behind. Next day, Sythe and I woke up together in a crate, covered in fur and fucking furious. Ended up out here."

"Why haven't you said anything?" Caleb was too tired to feel angry again, and Tilon would have him on his ass in seconds if he tried something.

"We have, kid. Same response. 'Simmer down or leave.' Delia has been giving everyone here the same message for years. She built this sanctuary from the ground up. She is a beacon of hope for so many who are scared."

"She's keeping them caged," Caleb huffed.

"Sometimes a cage isn't a prison, Caleb. There is a reason so many find comfort behind a safety barrier. It takes courage to break through and take charge of your own destiny. It's not something you can force others to see. But we can be the change. We can create a path for others to follow should they choose to."

"What's the plan then? How can I help?" Caleb's shoulders slumped. His voice softened. The determination from minutes ago drained as fatigue hit him.

"Lay low for a few days. Try not to rile anyone else up."

"What are you going to do?"

Tilon placed a hand on his back. The touch was almost fatherly. Caleb's body naturally tensed at the touch while his mind scolded him for not being able to lean into the comfort it offered. He felt the big man squeeze gently before turning back to his normal, hardened self. "We aren't the only ones who feel this way. But I need some time."

Caleb nodded slowly, resisting the urge to ask more questions.

"Hang tight. Gather supplies without raising suspicion. Wait for my signal."

"Fine." Caleb reached down to collect the maps, the owl tilting its head as if it were still studying the paper.

Tilon shook his head. "You will have to leave that too."

"I found this!" Caleb's voice rose in protest.

"If you take it, Delia will know you're still thinking about leaving. I suggest you commit it to memory. We'll need it." Tilon turned and walked away, leaving him alone with the owl and the map.

Caleb stayed until he couldn't look at the blueprint anymore. The owl sat patiently, head continuing to turn at odd angles as they studied together.

"You ready to go?" Caleb held out a hand for the small creature, noticing the hair growing ever thicker on his skin. The small creature hopped on, trusting. He lifted it to his shoulder, earning a sharp nip on his softened, furry ear.

"Ow! Okay, okay, not a shoulder bird. Got it." His stomach grumbled, and he sighed. *Lay low*, he thought. *How the hell am I going to do that?*

Patience

Chapter Eighteen

The next few days felt like torture. Caleb kept searching for Tilon, desperate to know when and where the next stage of the plan would happen. Hell, he would settle for knowing what the next stage of the plan was. But the big hybrid was nowhere to be found. Every time Caleb thought he had caught sight of his broad torso or orange, dotted fur, another hybrid would turn the corner.

Each morning, Caleb woke to Ethan's incessant chatter about the people and hybrids he had met. A steady pile of thinned bark covered in rough charcoal drawings had begun stacking up in the corner of their crate. Ava and Aiel had taken a real liking to the boy, keeping a stack of the drawing supplies to gift him on nearly every visit. Even Delia had made her fondness known, inviting Ethan to different sections of the camp every other day and encouraging him to get involved.

Caleb had heard her name one too many times over breakfast for comfort. He had to stop himself from glaring whenever he saw her with her arm draped over Ethan's shoulder or handing him the first bowl of the evening meal with a smile before stalking off to her own lodgings.

Each morning followed a familiar pattern: Ethan talking, then Sythe poking his head in to ask if Caleb wanted to go for a run or lift something heavy to help expand the camp. The smaller of the two tiger-lion hybrids made a clear effort to get close. He found out Sythe had been chomping at the bit for an escape attempt nearly as much as he was, but asked Caleb to put his trust in Tilon, assuring him the larger hybrid knew what he was doing.

The more time they spent together, the more Sythe shared about his own experiences. Most of his changes had occurred in the first six months. At first, he thought he was going to die, that the beast would eventually take over and there would be nothing of him left, but the changes stopped as suddenly as they had begun. Caleb wasn't sure if Sythe genuinely wanted to be friends or if someone had told him to keep an eye on him. Jan tended to hover nearby, always within the same space as Caleb, and Delia wasn't far behind.

Still, the physical exertion made him feel better, more alive. The exertion of trying to keep up with Sythe while not stumbling over forest debris was the most fun he'd had since waking up in a box.

After this morning's run – several laps around the lake while waving at the water-dwelling hybrids – Caleb practically salivated at the scent of salted meat wafting through the camp. Another scouting party had managed to capture two clickers on their rounds. Caleb wasn't sure he was ready to eat the disgusting beasts but the temptation for something other than tubers, forest greens and the occasional hare was growing. Caleb let out a low, involuntary groan, lips curling into a snarl at the sight of one of the designated cooks turning the spit.

"Hold up, sport. Meat's not done." Sythe smirked and patted him on the back.

Caleb forced himself to ignore the instinct screaming that everything belonged to him, that it was his right to distribute food as he saw fit.

Pack mentality. That's what this was about, wasn't it? He wanted to be in charge, to make sure the people who had looked out for him were fed and watered. His father must have known that when he put him here. No matter how little they interacted, he'd always been shown to be the best, whether he possessed the skills being sold or not.

Caleb shuddered as the body of the clicker turned, fat sizzling as it dripped onto the hot stones below. As disgusted as he was, it smelt delicious, the mix of natural oils and foraged herbs filling the air. Maybe today was the day he gave in.

Most of the hybrids abstained from meat, focusing solely on harvested foods; even some of the predatory hybrids were weirded out at the prospect of eating the deer, rabbits and birds their friends could have been spliced with. A rumble from his stomach told him he wasn't quite there yet, and he didn't know if he would ever be.

Sythe gave him another pat and moved on to help elsewhere, leaving Caleb to fend for himself. He'd been meaning to talk to more of the hybrids, to find common ground and hear their stories. Communal spaces were always crowded, dozens of different species in various stages of transformation chatting as they worked. There were small areas sectioned off for nearly everything you could think of to do in the woods.

Ethan waved at him while flitting between groups, eagerly seeking anyone willing to teach him something new or simply pay him attention. Caleb felt himself smile, watching the boy thrive despite their situation. His heart swelled with pride; Ethan didn't have trouble talking to any of the hybrids. Caleb imagined some of them had likely been parents before they became experiments. Most of them took to Ethan instantly, laughing at his childlike wonder and scolding him when he got into things he shouldn't.

Caleb's chest felt full each time he saw the boy happy. The little guy had gotten under his skin in such a short span of time. *Little brother*, he thought, watching him shake off a gentle shooing from the group attempting to soften and cut the canvas from the last scouting mission into strips of cloth. He would do everything in his power to get him back to safety, somewhere he could live a normal life.

He had asked Ava and Aiel to give Ethan a full examination, hoping they could determine if he was anything other than human. The boy squirmed and complained while being poked and prodded, but nothing had seemed out of the ordinary. Not long after, Delia had asked about it too, though she kept her interest in him at arm's length. Caleb thought he saw a yearning in her when she talked to the kid. A desire to be close but not allowing herself to cross the line. Each time Caleb saw them together, jealousy twisted in his gut.

I could have been like him if I wasn't kept under strict guard as a boy. Maybe I wouldn't even be here.

Blinking back the tears that threatened to fall, Caleb watched as Ethan settled in for the day, sitting cross-legged and frowning in concentration while stripping nettles for cloth. Back home, the kid would have racked up several Scout badges. Here, there were no other children. The youngest was still six years older than Ethan and sick besides.

Ethan had told him about the adolescent boy in the medical unit. From the sounds of it, the kid didn't have much longer. His gangly body couldn't keep up with the changes, his bones too weak to sustain the transformation.

Caleb made a mental note to check in on the medics later, maybe take them some of the stew Gulia and Charles were busy preparing.

Tilon's head emerged from behind the flames, a rough clay plate of steaming meat in his hands.

Finally!

Caleb rushed forward, only to be stopped by a massive paw to the head. He stood impatiently as Tilon removed his hand from his face, skewered a large chunk of burnt clicker flesh on a claw, and to Caleb's horror, swallowed it whole. A deep groan of pleasure filled the air. Caleb hesitated. Maybe the big guard needed a minute.

Tilon didn't break eye contact as he picked up another piece and offered it to him. Caleb couldn't suppress his grimace, drawing a hearty laugh from the hybrid.

"Remember beef? Tastes just like it."

Once again, Caleb was taken aback by how deep and commanding Tilon's voice was. Some part of him resisted the instinct to blindly obey, but the saliva pooling in his mouth was winning the battle. The meat glistened with natural oil, the scent of wild rosemary and garlic hitting his nose. He placed it in his mouth. The saltiness of the flesh combined with the herbs made his knees weak. A groan escaped before he could stop it.

"See?" Tilon teased, handing him the rest of his plate. "Relax a little. Start gathering what you can. I'll find you in a few days."

"Oh, come on, Tilon. You said that days ago," Caleb protested.

Tilon's large paw was over his mouth before he could alert others. His ears twitched at the sound of Jan's footsteps, followed by the lighter patter of Delia's. They both froze, watching in the direction of their movement. Jan broke through the bushes first, not paying attention to them as he continued down the winding path. It looked as if they were heading away from the camp. Delia followed shortly after with Tali, Jules and several other hunters of similar build. Delia caught sight of the two of them and frowned before walking out of sight.

Caleb picked up another piece of clicker meat and held it out to Tilon, who had gone tense beside him. "This really came from a clicker?" he asked, trying to sound nonchalant.

"Yup." Tilon grabbed another bite.

Caleb listened, waiting until both sets of footsteps faded. "Where do you think they are going?" he asked, voice barely above a whisper.

"I don't know, but it isn't the first time they have been spotted walking away from camp together," Tilon replied.

"You ever follow 'em?"

"Didn't think much of it before you came along."

"Why?"

Tilon's gaze darkened. "Because I couldn't prove she was hiding anything. Life here gets comfortable, even with the raids. When you found the tracker ... well, that was damning." He turned his full attention to Caleb. "Spend some time with the boy. He won't be coming where we're going."

"What? Why? He has to come. What if we find a way out? I need to get him out, Tilon." Caleb's words tumbled out in rapid succession. He couldn't protect Ethan if they were separated.

Tilon softened, sympathy clear in his dark eyes. "It's too dangerous. The boy doesn't have the strength and stamina of the pack." The words hit Caleb like a punch. The pack. He had begun to think of those around him as family, one he wanted to save.

Tilon let the words settle before continuing. "It is very likely that we will find things out there we aren't prepared for. Are you ready to put him in that kind of danger?"

Caleb hadn't thought he could be leaving Ethan behind for good. His heart clenched, eyes searching wildly for the boy. What if he never saw him again?

"I can't leave him, Tilon." The words came out shakier than he intended.

"If he comes, he'll die." Tilon's voice held no room for argument. "If we find a way out, we'll come back for him. I promise. Remember who you're doing this for."

Panic rolled through Caleb in waves. He fought the urge to run to Ethan, to wrap his arms around his small frame. He knew Tilon was right, even if he didn't want to admit it. The boy would be a distraction. He was doing this for Ethan, to get him out. To get anyone out who could still live a normal life. To stop this once and for all. Caleb nodded as he turned towards the other hybrid. "Okay."

"Be ready," Tilon said, handing him the plate and leaving him by the fire.

***

Ava and Aiel were pottering around a quiet medical bay, exchanging soft words as they tended to their private gardens and plucked herbs for various salves, pastes and brews.

Tilon had told him to gather some things. What things? For ex-military, Tilon had been annoyingly vague on what they would need to escape into a clicker-infested wilderness. Caleb thought about all the things he wished he had had when he was dropped unceremoniously into the woods. Non-perishable food, something to carry it in, hiking boots, not to mention his phone complete with GPS signal and anything that could ease the thousand cuts and bruises he had obtained.

His eyes scanned the homemade shelves, searching for anything useful. Guilt pricked him at the thought of stealing from the two women who had been nothing but lovely to him since he had shown up on their doorstep. He smiled as he watched them work in unison until a sharp, bitter scent hit his nose.

"Ugh." He gagged as the acrid smell of fermenting fruit seemed to burn the back of his throat.

"Why is it spicy?" he whined, clamping a hand over his nose.

The ladies jumped at the intrusion, staring at him wide-eyed before breaking into laughter. Their chuckling turned into the kind of uncensored joy that made eyes water. Doubling over in amusement, Caleb continued to hold his nose as they recovered from the outburst. Aiel held her knees as she got herself under control, and Ava placed a hand on the small of her back to steady herself.

"It's just vinegar," Ava said. "Surely you used it back home."

Caleb frowned at them, then rolled his eyes with a grin. He noticed how the lines around their eyes crinkled when they smiled. They were beautiful together. Ava's hand moved down to Aiel's, like she wasn't quite ready to stop the connection. His heart ached for Argo. As much as they had drifted apart, they had laughed like that as boys.

"*That* was not vinegar," Caleb said. The smell clung to his nose hairs, making him want to sneeze. Aiel couldn't keep her chuckle from escaping.

"Well, it's not like the vinegar you have at home, sure, but a bit of fruit scrap, some sugar and water will help create a cleaning solution you won't find anywhere else," Aiel explained, squeezing Ava's hand.

"For good reason," Caleb huffed.

Aiel eyed him suspiciously. "What brings you here, laddie?"

Bugger. He hadn't thought of an excuse.

"Ethan!" he blurted.

Ava's eyebrows lifted. "What about 'im? We saw him not long ago, headed down to the water. Looked like he was with the nettlin' crew to wash."

Aiel stepped closer to him, placing a hand on her hip.

"Right, yes. I was with him. He, uh ... fell. Scraped his knee. I was wondering if you had anything that might help."

How am I so bad at this?

Aiel jumped to action, her fondness outweighing her suspicions. Ava, however, kept her eyes on Caleb, watchful but not unkind. Aiel returned in an instant, pressing a small pot of rough purple paste into his hand.

"Thanks. What is it?" Caleb sniffed it tentatively. Floral and peppery, not nearly as unpleasant as the vinegar.

"Anti-inflammatory. The mint should help cool a scrape," Aiel said like she was talking to a naughty schoolboy. She handed him another pot; this one was smoother with a greenish tinge.

"Where did you learn all this stuff?"

The women shared a look, eyes softening as the corners of their lips lifted slightly. "We were in nursing school together, back in the day. Somehow, we ended up here so many years later."

Caleb felt a soft breath escape him as the warmth passed between them. "Do you remember? How you got here, that is." He couldn't hold the question in.

Aiel smiled sadly. "I don't remember much. It was a few years ago now."

"Ironic, ya know." Ava met her partner's smile with tenderness.

"How so?" Caleb asked.

"An elephant never forgets." Ava beamed while Aiel rolled her eyes.

"Well, thank you, ladies. Appreciate it. Must get these to Ethan! See ya!" He spun on his heel, making a show of heading toward the lake before circling back toward the main camp.

***

Each part of the compound held something new. Over the long days of waiting for Tilon to give the signal to move out, Caleb discovered dozens of different areas inhabited and run by hybrids who had brought their real-world skills into their new home. Through these interactions, he also learned that several members of the group recognised him as his father's son and were wary of his presence. Word spread among the hybrids; some were willing to talk but most remained standoffish.

He had asked about Argo and anyone else who had been found or seen recently. A few had been picked up on scouting trips, but none he recognised. The young boy found weeks ago wasn't doing well enough to talk. He had been sent to the medic crates for observation as soon as he arrived. Caleb had tried asking Ava about him, but she didn't have much to say, only that his body wasn't coping with whatever he'd been spliced with.

Ethan had friends all over the place who waved and called him over through their daily ventures into the compound. Tilon had sought him out once more, telling him to find a job of use.

"Speak to Delia, see what needs doing. The longer you delay getting involved, the more suspicious she becomes. Contribute and keep your ear to the ground," he had said.

Delia seemed pleased when he asked for a job. "The cooks could use someone to sort and store the compost," she said, flicking through files on her desk while he waited at the door.

"Surely there is a spot on a scouting team," he responded, eager to map more of the woods in his head.

"Even scouts have other jobs when they are home," she replied without looking up. He had seen Winson and Sythe both hauling in trees and stones and repairing fencing.

"What about building up defences? Get ready for the next raid, somewhere we can hide when the bloody Shepherd comes. We could get him, you know."

Delia scoffed. "You can't control your shifts, and you need training before I let you join my defences."

He shrugged. "Then let me train."

Jan appeared in Delia's doorway, huffing down at him as he crouched to see him inside.

"Feeling is mutual, buddy," Caleb muttered.

"Go to the kitchens, see if you can stay put for a while. Then we'll talk about training," she said, clipped and final.

"What about—"

She cut him off. Two hunters approached, their scent like clean earth. These two had long, curled horns atop their heads. Their angular faces were narrow and watchful. They knocked. He had barely heard them over the bear's heavy breathing.

"That will be all, Caleb," Delia said. Jan shoved him toward the door.

"Fine," he muttered, making his way back to the kitchens.

***

The population wasn't as large as he initially thought, most of the hybrids occupying several of the dozen or so communal locations throughout the day. It gave the compound a well-lived-in feeling, but Caleb was starting to recognise their familiar faces. He watched groups form and disband each day as he sorted seeds in the kitchens, the goat-like hybrids seeming thrilled to have someone with more nimble hands for the task. On his trips to the storerooms, he was able to palm dried meats, mushrooms and fruit.

As Caleb carried the unusable compost to the worm farms, he noticed several activities he would never have thought of. There were hybrids pressing paper and sharpening old bits of coal for sketching and documentation. Some worked to the side of the gardens, grinding soybeans to extract the oil, and others worked out new spice mixes to flavour their food. Caleb was stunned at the amount of thought that went into each task. He observed basket weaving, clay moulding, and fibre extracting, which was used to make very scratchy items of clothing. Regular activities that were more standard of a survival operation were also evident: scouting parties came and went, often bringing small game back for the predator-based hybrids or fish from the streams.

Caleb longed to go out with one of those parties, looking for anything that might help his escape, his frustration growing at having to stay put. Gatherers and gardeners sought wild food or tended to the crops they had managed to grow; these were Ethan's favourite. Two small creatures with thin arms and stubby legs swung through the trees, dropping hard-to-reach fruit into Ethan's basket. The poor boy managed to get hit on the head with some dates when he misjudged their fall, but his laughter told Caleb he didn't mind.

The cooks then worked hard to make mother nature's offerings edible and delicious. Even Ava and Aiel had an apprentice who would go out to gather herbs and carry things back and forth to the medical units. Caleb concluded that life in the camp was boringly normal.

His kitchen duties didn't last long. Delia reassigned him as a runner when a hybrid fell ill. "It'll build strength and resistance," she told him. "If you can keep up, you'll get your shot at training."

Within a week, Caleb understood why people stayed. Without the threat of raids, life was easy. Their system worked, and they just wanted to live. The hybrids seemed genuinely happy together, accepting each other for their differences and working as one to live peacefully. What did the real world hold for them? More experimentation? Still, they should be given the option, and they should want it to stop happening to others.

It wasn't until the tenth day of no progress that there was any sort of commotion amongst the group.

A bloodcurdling scream filled the air, coming from the direction of the medical unit. Caleb dropped the wood he was carrying and ran. As he neared the doorway, Jane whipped past him, her face ashen. The young boy Ethan had told him about was curled over himself in a grotesque shift. Black feathers, mottled with blood, burst from his body. The teenager's shrieks echoed off the walls as he thrashed against his own transformation. Caleb couldn't look away as Ava and Aiel struggled to keep him still.

Bones snapped and broke with loud cracks, pushing through skin that split and bled. Feathers pushed their way out in sharp barbs. The noise stopped suddenly, turning into suffocating gurgles as his jaw dislocated with a sickening crunch. A disfigured bone-white beak broke through the middle of the boy's throat. His eyes rolled back. He lost consciousness. Human teeth, now sharpened to jagged points, jutted out at odd angles. Aiel sobbed as the boy went still, his mangled body falling to the ground. Ava wrapped her arms around her, both women pale with disbelief.

Caleb wanted to be sick, the bile hot in his throat. Ethan's voice carried down the path, his chatter growing louder.

No. He couldn't let the kid see this.

Caleb stepped outside, trying to compose himself before calling out, "Hey kid, the adults need some space, okay? The cooks might need help chopping."

Ethan narrowed his eyes sceptically; there was no way he didn't hear the screams. The colour had drained from the child's face, but he nodded and turned back the way he had come. Caleb took a moment to breathe before going back inside.

"What can I do?" His voice came out as a rasp, as if sandpaper clogged his throat.

He looked around for something to bundle the child up in. The kid's once long and gangly features were reduced to a bloody pulp of feather and bone. Caleb swallowed down the sick that threatened to spill all over the floor, and he found a rough woven blanket.

"Where do you take them?" He winced, moving the dead weight of the boy into a bundle, praying that no blood would seep out on his trek.

Ava's voice shook. "There's a burial ground." She swallowed hard, trying to hold back tears. "The cart is around the side."

"We need to tell Delia," Aiel whispered, unable to look away from the bloodied remains.

"Aye," Ava murmured.

Caleb's ears twitched at her tone. There was anger beneath the grief.

Would she come with me?

He nudged Aiel gently. "I got him," he said softly.

She was like stone, unmoving, eyes fixed on the shrinking body.

Slowly, she shifted toward Ava, leaning into her partner. Silent tears streaked her face.

"It's okay, love," Ava cooed while Caleb placed the broken boy into the blanket, tying the ends together as best he could. The body felt so light in his arms, now more bird than boy.

"This has to end," he muttered.

"Aye," Ava said, gently moving Aiel away from her body, helping her to lean on their supply bench. Ava looked the other woman over, leaning in to press her lips to Aiel's cheek, cupping her face in her hand.

"Rest," she said quietly before leading Caleb outside.

***

The burial ground was kept well away from the main camp. Ava and Caleb had to venture outside of the perimeter to bury the boy. It took close to an hour, moving through the campgrounds and back into the forest where a dimly lit path guided them towards the graveyard. Light struggled through the trees; Ava stopped to light the lanterns along the path as they walked. The smell of moss and dying earth grew pungent the further they walked.

Caleb had to resort to covering his nose to combat the smell, his other hand dragging a rough wooden cart behind them. Ava walked silently, breaking off to light their way, her breath hitching on occasion.

The trees turned into open space, trunks cut away to make way for lines of graves in the darkness.

Caleb shivered as a slight breeze ruffled his new fur.

Ava made her way to a sconce close to the edge of the trees, lighting a thick candle that had been melted to its bark with wax. The flickering glow cast eerie shadows as she moved to light another. It was just enough to see the rows of graves stretched before them. Another line of empty plots waited for new bodies.

Caleb clenched his fists. The sight of the secluded, forgotten burial ground sent a low growl up his throat.

"Get the boy," Ava said, her voice thick with sorrow and defeat. Her tears had been close to silent, but her steps had grown heavier the further they walked.

Caleb swallowed his anger and lifted the fragile body wrapped in canvas and carried it to an open grave. It was one of six neatly dug rectangles, all waiting for the next casualties of his father's experiment.

"How many are in here?" Caleb asked, his voice as soft as he could make it.

"Too many," Ava said sadly as he placed the bundle into the earth. She gripped a crude shovel, made from smoothed stone. She nodded to another lying at the edge of the trees. They worked in silence, the squelch of mud and sharp taps of the shovels filling the air.

"Ava, stop," Caleb said, his hands shaking. He dropped to his knees, staring at the cloth that had fallen from the boy's face. His mess of a beaked jaw poked out. Ava pulled in a breath, letting her shovel drop, walking away from the two of them. Caleb hunched over, holding a hand over his mouth while his own tears welled hot and heavy. The first of them struck the blanket. He reached down, pulling the material up, making sure the boy was covered. Protected from the dirt they still needed to throw into his grave. He stared at the body, half buried, unable to make himself get up.

Ava dried her eyes and offered him her hand.

"Let's finish this and go home."

Caleb shook his head. "We shouldn't be dying like this."

Ava studied him for a long moment. He wasn't sure if she would speak. He forced himself to stand and grip his shovel. It was getting cold. At least the earth would keep the child warm.

He caught the woman's eye as he finished patting the earth down. A final tear slipped down her cheek. Then, she repeated the single word that had given him hope earlier in the day. "Aye."

***

Their walk back to the camp was slow and mournful. Caleb stole glances at Ava, trying to read her expression. She kept her eyes straight ahead, her brow furrowed. She looked angry. The more time they spent together, the more he recognised her moods.

He desperately wanted to tell her about his plan to leave with Tilon. If Aiel could manage without her, maybe she would come. It would make sense to have a medic with them when they left. *What if she never sees Aiel again?* Caleb frowned, conversing with himself in his head. *She will. She has to. We'll make it work.*

"Ava?"

"Yes, child?"

The words poured out of him then. There was something about this kind-hearted woman that made him need to tell her about the pain he had been carrying for years. He wept freely as he babbled about losing his mother, the distance from his father, years of doing nothing with his life while money poured in. His breath hitched with guilt. If he had paid more attention, maybe none of them would be here. He spoke of the crushing shame he felt with every new hybrid he met. How Delia was supposed to be a leader but did nothing to help.

Ava listened patiently. When his words finally slowed and he had said everything that had weighed on his mind, she stopped in front of him, pressing a broad, leathery hand against his chest. She looked him in the eye, then reached around the back of his neck, pulling him to her. Her arms wrapped around him, holding him as his tears came again.

"It's okay, lad," she said gently, urging him closer to her body.

He stayed there for a few minutes, breathing in a mother's embrace. He let her hold his weight, melting into her arms, soaking her sleeves with his grief. Ava held him with a patience and kindness he so desperately needed. The type of unquestioned love that he couldn't give to anyone else. Her hand stroked his hair, her words soft in his ear. His body let go of its tension, allowing himself to be soothed. That made his heart ache. When he pulled away, he saw determination and anger in her eyes.

"That boy should never have been here," she said, standing up to her full height again, stretching out her back.

"Neither should Ethan," Caleb said, worried about the boy suddenly changing in the same way as the child they had just buried.

Ava pulled him up tall, motioning for him to grab the cart before moving back onto the path.

"Delia is wrong," she said.

Caleb raised his eyebrow but stayed silent.

"I don't trust her. These raids, they seem ... planned. We never should have stopped looking. I ... Aiel."

"I understand." Caleb reached out, clasping her shoulder. "We're going to try again."

"To get off this island?" she asked.

"Yes. Tilon is gathering more people willing to leave. That's why I was in your crates the other day. Not because Ethan fell and scraped his knee."

Ava nodded, not looking at him. They walked the rest of the way without a word, stepping back into the glow of the main camp. Hybrids gathered around fires, settling in for the night. Ava reached for the cart, her hand lingering on his for a second too long.

"I'll gather some supplies, lad. Tell Tilon I'm in."

***

Night fell. The main fire crackled and hissed as the camp gathered for a meal. Over a hundred faces crowded into the space. Delia had called the communal meal to mourn the losses of the last few weeks. The smell of the gathered bodies drifted on the breeze, the flames casting flickering light on their faces. They had never been together in one place before.

Enough for an army.

A few of them spoke kind words for a child they hadn't really known, others for a hunter who had died in their recent scouting mission. Sniffles broke through the crowd, some taking the losses harder than others.

Caleb looked over the crowd, searching for faces similar to his own age. Playing with his meal, his mind drifted to Argo again. *Was he still out there?*

Winson appeared beside him, the owl perched nearby, preening. The lizard hybrid tilted his head, glancing at Caleb's bowl of stew.

"Good, isn't it?"

"Better than I expected. Where did you pick up another clicker?" Caleb kept his tone cautious.

Winson shrugged, the owl flying to sit next to them on their chosen log. Winson had taken to the bird, who was happy enough to follow him on scouting missions. "We went hunting. It was trying to attack a deer. Managed to get them both."

Caleb nodded, staring into the fire.

Winson started cautiously. "I'm sorry about the boy. Aiel told me. Sounds like a bad shift."

They both looked up as Delia moved through the crowd, touching shoulders, whispering to hybrids he didn't recognise. Jan shadowed her.

"Did you find any new arrivals?" Caleb asked Winson.

"Two. Worse off than we were. Whatever your dad's cooking up, it's ramped up. Very few survive the trip back, even if we reach them before they change."

"Why am I different?" He said it aloud without thinking.

Winson sighed. "My guess? He loves you. In his way."

Caleb fidgeted, unsettled by the idea that his father had given him some unfair advantage. That he was something ... other.

Winson nodded. "I know about the plan." He glanced at Delia, now sitting between two almost fully shifted hybrids, their long snouts and beady eyes making it difficult to tell what they had been spliced with. "Tilon told me."

Caleb fought the urge to look at him. "You're coming?"

"Yeah, kid. I'm comin'."

"What changed?"

"You did." Winson sighed, resting a clawed hand on Caleb's arm before standing. "Doing nothing won't help that boy you buried today." He looked Caleb in the eyes. "You've stopped thinking about yourself. Took me a minute to realise that."

Caleb stared into the fire as Winson walked away. Delia stood, offering Jan her hand before they disappeared in the direction of the graveyard.

What are you up to?

A firm hand patted his back, the pressure causing him to wince. "Don't turn around." A deep purr rumbled through his whole body. Tilon.

He waited, forcing himself to sit still.

"Tonight," Tilon said, pausing as mourners passed. "We move. Get ready. Bring anything you have to the back gate."

The pressure eased. Caleb exhaled, giddy excitement and adrenaline working its way through his bones.

He nodded to no one in particular, then glanced at Ava. Their eyes met. He tilted his head towards the exit. He had mentioned to Tilon that she wanted to be involved when they returned from the burial only a few hours before. Had she even had time to gather her supplies? It didn't matter now. They would both have to be ready to move.

Caleb searched for Ethan and saw his little friend being held by Aiel, watching the fire, a distant expression on his face. He was safe.

It was finally time.

Moving Out

Chapter Nineteen

Caleb stood at the front of the camp, his palms damp with perspiration. Every movement made him jump, worrying at who might be around the corner. He glared at the flickering torches inviting unwanted eyes to his location. Delia had said she wouldn't stop him from leaving, but a group of people who had started to question her decision-making? He doubted that would go down quite so well.

Come on, Tilon! Where are you?

Caleb had started to pace when he caught the sound of shuffling feet. The scrape of dirt and stone made him cringe.

Hurrying out of sight, he flattened himself against the rough fencing, hoping whoever it was moved along without poking their head outside the gates. The watch had been called off for the night of mourning. This really was their only chance. What if one of the guards poked their head outside? What excuse could he give?

Caleb racked his brain, hurriedly thinking up reasons he would be outside the camp, alone, at pre-dawn. The shuffling moved closer with each second.

"There ye are, lad." Ava's voice was too loud for comfort. Caleb jumped at the intrusion.

"Shhhhh." He moved his hands downward, emphasising the need for discretion, trying to contain his rapidly beating heart.

"Alright, alright." Ava could hardly keep the amusement from her voice. "You're at the wrong entrance, though. If you'd be so kind as to follow me." She let the words hang before gesturing back inside.

Caleb deflated, annoyed at her amusement and ready to defend his actions. What other entrance?

They said back entrance, idiot, he chided himself.

Swallowing his pride, he picked up his canvas pack full of his measly offerings of salves and stolen dried goods, then followed her quietly through to the other side of the compound leading to the lakes.

This does make more sense. He recalled the maps showing a number of circular areas beyond the large body of water and cursed himself again.

Caleb's mood lifted seeing a handful of people huddled in the darkness. The crisp early morning air drove them closer together for warmth. Tilon had done it. He'd gotten a group together. As Caleb's eyes adjusted to the dark, he made out the outlines of Winson and Sythe leaning against a rock, deep in conversation. Sythe was frowning, his mouth moving, but Caleb couldn't quite make out the words. He met Tilon's gaze, and the other man nodded, waiting for Caleb to reach the party before alerting them to his presence.

Several pairs of eyes turned towards him and Ava as they joined the group. He exhaled. They were really doing this. There was no going back now. He had a real pack. Eight willing and able bodies, ready to take a chance for a better future. Not too many to be slowed down but still too few to take on any big battles. They would have to be careful, and fast.

Three of their crew were small and nimble. Caleb had only seen them briefly during his time at camp. Their movements seemed restless and twitchy, their small, blackened eyes unable to focus on one thing at a time, each pair darting in different directions, their noses scrunching up as they took in the surroundings. *Odd*, he thought, wondering if they were related.

Caleb sniffed the air. As his vision sharpened, more of the night came into focus.

"Woah," Sythe said, staring at him.

"What?"

"Your eyes. They're glowing."

"Aye, lad," Ava agreed. "They are."

He shrugged. "Wouldn't be the weirdest thing that's happened to me since I've been here."

"Wolves have night vision, much better than the average human," Tilon offered. "Can you see better?"

Caleb nodded.

"Good. Now, let's move," he said, his deep rumble not leaving room for question. Standing at least a head taller than everyone else, Tilon's strong form looked formidable in the moonlight. He was a vision of power, discipline and determination. Caleb was glad it was Tilon leading them into the forest, trusting the man's map and plan more than his own. He was in awe of how much respect the hybrid commanded with few words. He wanted to learn how to lead others like that, so they would trust him and put their lives in his hands. Caleb couldn't help but picture his father's face when they met again, his now-glowing eyes boring into his old man's soul. Then he would get his answers, for him and everyone here.

Caleb stood to attention, tuning into Tilon's briefing. Sythe had moved to his side, the second in command standing tall and proud beside their leader.

"Thank you for your patience," Tilon started. The rest of the group looked up to him, hanging off his every word.

"The hybrids are changing. The experiments are getting more extreme. Fewer of our kind reach the camp without turning feral or dying alone. If we make it, we're herded like sheep while our leader hides the truth. It is time for it to stop."

He paused to look at Caleb. "We may not have been placed here by choice. But we can choose to fight for those who might suffer the same fate. You've joined us for the chance at a better life, not just for yourself, but for your fellow hybrid. We may not make it out alive. I don't know how far Delia's connections will go to stop us, but I refuse to sit back and watch history repeat itself time and time again. These experiments won't stop unless we stop them. This ends with us."

A low growl rumbled in Tilon's chest as he emphasised the last word. Caleb's hackles rose in response. He was ready to leap and follow Tilon wherever he went.

"We start here." Tilon held up a map, the crude replica of the area they had run from over a week ago. "Winson thinks they're caging the clickers there, which means the Shepherd won't be far. Let's get to them before they get to us. This time, we won't be the ones being taken away. These are your supplies." He gestured to small canvas packs with rough handles made from thick vines. "Grace, if you would, please." A smaller female member of their group handed the makeshift backpacks out, followed by a spear. "Grab one and move out."

A gentle hoot called to them overhead as the owl moved up and landed on a branch to observe the path before them.

Tilon held his furred fist into the air, all eyes watching him intently. He looked at each one of them in turn, never blinking, meeting Caleb's eyes last before putting his fist in the middle of the group.

Caleb almost laughed. After all that, a childish teamwork gesture? Instead, he inhaled deeply and placed his hand on top. One by one, six more hands followed in a silent show of companionship, some covered in fur, some leathery, some still human. Together, they raised their hands to the sky, slung their packs over their shoulders, and followed Tilon into the trees.

Caleb hesitated briefly, frowning into the darkness. His ear twitched.

What was that?

The others moved ahead, Ava glancing back to hurry him along. His ears perked up, unsure if he was picking up the padding of little feet as they moved away from the camp.

***

Beads of sweat broke out on Caleb's skin with the dawn, the rays of light catching those leading the pack. A precursor to the heat that was about to hit them. They had walked the rest of the night, not daring to stop, it and was likely they would not rest for another twelve hours. Caleb noted Ava tiring, unsure if she was able to power through, her face showing fierce determination.

Tilon had placed Caleb at the rear, challenging him to focus on his hearing abilities and raise the alarm if they were being followed. Sythe and Winson positioned themselves a few steps behind their leader, tense and ready to fight or run. Caleb was surprised to see how well they moved together. Tilon's military experience and disciplined charisma had them all falling in line without hesitation.

Caleb was slowly introduced to the rest of the group. Each member took a turn to fall back and give him their names. Lilah, Berrum and Grace were natural scouts. They were each of slight and nimble build, their voices high-pitched yet soft. The three of them stuck together, heads always jerking in one direction or another. Under the moonlight, they looked eerily possessed. Ava had explained they suspected that the three of them had been injected with a small rodent, a squirrel or chipmunk. They were hoarders by nature and always ready to flee at the first sign of danger. But they were fast, quiet and ready to be part of something bigger. Caleb hoped these three had better luck than the rats in his father's lab.

He watched them as they walked, their bodies reacting instinctively to the smallest disturbances. They took turns running ahead or to the sides, gathering intel on the terrain. They often returned with food – offerings from the forest they could cook once they were at a safe distance from the camp. *Foragers, not fighters*, Caleb thought, holding out his hand to Grace who offered him a handful of mushrooms for his pack. At close range, he noticed the fine grey whiskers sprouting from her nose. She giggled when she met his eyes, button nose twitching before she scurried off to find the others.

"I think she likes you," Ava teased.

Caleb's mind continued to wander as they walked, his ability to focus on sound slipping with each stray thought. He wanted to ask Tilon how many fellow hybrids had refused to join them and if there were any who might alert Delia. A group of them leaving with the intention of escape put her plans of subservience guised as peace at risk.

How long until she sends Jan after us?

Caleb stumbled into Ava's back, knocking one of their scouts in turn. He gripped onto Ava's shoulders to steady himself. Grace let out a high-pitched yelp and staggered towards him. Caleb's arm shot out to catch her before she fell face first into the dirt.

Tilon scowled. He had told them to make as little noise as possible, reminding Caleb that he wasn't the only one out here with good hearing. Caleb frowned as he righted the twitchy hybrid, her nose wiggling like she was about to sneeze. He mouthed an apology, but she had already turned, letting out a series of short barking noises toward the others. The three of them scattered into the trees, each taking a different angle. Tilon signalled the group to halt.

"Wha—?" Caleb started, but Ava silenced him with a look.

He breathed deep, trying to pick up a scent, his ears pricking. Silence stretched. The rustle of the leaves and beating of their chests thudding in the huge, open forest reminded him that they were only a speck in an experiment that had run for so long. The scouts scurried back through the trees, holding a squirming new member of their group by the scruff of his neck.

"Let go of me! I can help! I am a Scout! Didn't you—" The boy froze at Caleb's scowl before breaking into a beaming grin.

Ethan struggled free. Berrum chuckled, letting him go. Ethan flung himself at Caleb, who barely caught him in time, grunting at the weight.

How did I miss him? he thought before catching a whiff of dried mud and damp foliage the boy had used to mask his scent. *Damn Scout.*

Relief and frustration warred inside him. He wasn't sure whether to scold Ethan or lean into the comfort of knowing the boy was safe. Tilon's furrowed brow suggested anger was the better choice, but Caleb simply held the small boy tighter, relishing in the warmth of his growing frame.

Ethan's dirty hair tickled his nose, and Caleb sighed. "We'll talk later."

The boy just grinned at him, unbothered.

Sythe and Winson watched, awaiting orders.

"This is Ethan," Caleb told the three nearest to him.

"Oh, we know," Berrum said, not unkindly, his voice high and amused.

"He causes mischief in the camp and now he causes mischief outside the camp," Ava teased, smiling as she reached for Ethan's hand. The boy slipped from his grasp and ran to Ava.

Caleb approached Tilon for advice. "What do we do about the kid?" he asked.

"If we go back, we'll be locked up. Or worse." Tilon's voice was firm.

"Worse?"

"Exiled. Killed."

"Delia said—?" Caleb tried.

"This is different, kid." Tilon turned to look down at him. "We aren't here looking for scraps we've been ordered to find this time. We are looking to find a way out, to take her and my former bosses down. We don't know how many powerful people are now involved, but she is scared – of them, and of us finding them. Delia's interests don't align with ours anymore. We're a threat to her now."

Caleb swallowed a lump in his throat as the words hit home.

"We need to keep moving," Tilon scolded. "The kid's your responsibility. We are less than a day away from camp, and some of Delia's allies are much faster than us. Our best chance is that the wake for our lost last night and subsequent mourning period buys us some time. If we can find solid evidence of clicker holding cells, or a well-set-up camp to prove the hybrids are being messed with, that she knows about it, maybe, just maybe she will stop fighting us. That or we bring more of her loyal subjects into our fold. It's worth a shot, if we ever want to get off this island and stop this from happening again."

"How long do we have?"

"A day at best. She's been watching you, Caleb. And the boy. Or haven't you noticed?"

"I'd noticed."

"Take the rear with him," Tilon ordered. "And do better with your ears." He tapped Caleb's twitching wolf ear. "Your instincts are there. You need to stop falling back into human habits. It's not who you are anymore."

Caleb opened his mouth to argue but snapped it shut just as quickly. He was one of them now, whether he liked it or not. Sullen, he nodded. Tilon gave his shoulder a reassuring squeeze before nudging him toward the rear. Then, raising his fist once more, he signalled the group to move out.

They walked in rhythm for hours, the scouts occasionally dropping tubers, nuts, herbs and mushrooms into Caleb's pack. Ethan kept pace in between him and Ava, struggling to remain quiet. After one too many shushes and a glare from Sythe, he fell into a sulk. Caleb focused as hard as he could on hearing the world around him. Gradually, the forest came alive to his senses – leaves rustling, rabbits scurrying, Tilon's steady breathing, Ethan's little huffs.

A sudden roar split the air, and Caleb jumped. The scouts stiffened, their bodies tense at his reaction to the sound. There were no clicks to be heard nearby. Caleb's pulse quickened as he searched for the cause of the commotion.

"What is it?" Tilon asked pointedly.

"Give me a minute." Caleb closed his eyes. "Dammit."

"Caleb," Tilon pressed. "Concentrate. Now."

"A roar. Something I've never heard before. Guttural and—"

"Pissed off?"

"Exactly."

"Coming from that direction?" Tilon pointed back towards the camp.

Caleb swallowed. "You think ...?"

"Grab the boy. Let's move. If that was Jan, Delia is on her way."

Just Keep Walking

Chapter Twenty

Darkness wove through the fading daylight, shadows dancing and flickering among the trees. The group's progress slowed as the hours wore on. Caleb's feet ached, his body protesting with each step. He was surprised they hadn't started bleeding yet. Listening for Delia and Jan's approach became impossible; he could only focus on putting one foot in front of the other.

The clicker camp from the map stood bare in front of them. Caleb was right – the five ovals looked set up like the prison back at the compound, each with a cell at its centre. These cells had metal bars rather than wooden stakes. If this was where the Shepherd and his soldiers kept the trained beasts for the raids, they had moved on.

"Do you think they let them loose?" Caleb asked Winson, who had flicked his tongue out at each of the cages.

"Hard to say. They haven't been gone long though. I can still taste their fur."

"That's disgusting."

"Hush," Tilon ordered before asking the rodent hybrids to examine the area. "We need to keep moving. Search for other holding cells, a campsite. An active one if we want to find one of their recruits alive."

"And if we can't?" Caleb asked.

"We make our way to the coast. Look for an entry point."

"Aren't there clickers patrolling the border?"

"What did you think was going to be in here?" Sythe asked with a scoff.

Caleb caught Ava leaning against a solid trunk, holding a tired Ethan against her. The owl perched above them, preening its feathers.

"They need rest," Caleb said to Tilon, tipping his head toward the trees.

"No time. Not yet."

Tilon kept them moving, gathering scraps of material and food before pressing toward the shoreline. Their scouts scanned for crates, other camps or ferals as they advanced. They had stopped briefly to study the maps, still convinced they were heading in the right direction. The reprieve brought a collective sigh of relief, though it didn't last long.

Ethan's gentle snoring caught him off guard, and he turned to see the kid bouncing on Ava's back, a soft smile on her lips. Warmth surged through Caleb's chest at the sight. She was a good mother figure for Ethan. For them both.

The owl took off, calling out as it flew. Sythe tilted his head, touching Berrum on the shoulder to run ahead. Both the scout and the owl were back within minutes.

"It's safe," Berrum said in his high-pitched squeak. They moved into a new clearing and Tilon signalled the group to halt.

"Caleb?" Tilon asked.

"What?"

"Use your senses, boy. Tell us if it's safe."

"Berrum literally just did that."

"I wasn't asking Berrum, was I? What can you smell? What can you hear? Let your senses guide you and confirm Berrum's assessment."

Caleb closed his eyes and took a breath, letting the wood and leaves fill his senses. The air was clean, aside from the bodies in the group. "I think we're good."

"You're sure?" Caleb saw Tilon look quickly to Sythe to confirm.

Caleb rolled his eyes. "Yes, I'm sure."

A smile broke out on Tilon's face. "Good. You've done well today," he addressed the group. "Rest."

Caleb motioned to Ava and took Ethan from her back. The boy grumbled sleepily. Winson unrolled a mat and placed it on the ground.

"Don't take it personally," Winson offered as Caleb laid the boy on the mat, placing his pack beneath his head.

Caleb grunted in response.

"You're learning. Sythe has been with him years." Winson paused and turned to their leader who was leaning against a tree, eyes fixed on the way they had come.

"He sees something in you, kid. We all do."

Caleb walked to where Tilon was perched. He opened his mouth to speak but hesitated as he noticed the concentration on their leader's face. Instead, he stood awkwardly, waiting for Tilon's focus to shift.

"You should rest." Tilon's lips barely moved with the suggestion.

Caleb ignored him. "What are you looking for?"

"Delia is smart, and Jan deceptively fast for his size. I fear ..." Tilon's head snapped toward the sound of breaking twigs and shuffling leaves.

"It's the scouts," Caleb said, recognising their jerky movements. "What are you afraid of?"

Tilon met his gaze, his body squaring up as if bracing for a fight. "Jan has been with us a long time. Longer than I have."

"You think he's feral?" The question slipped out before Caleb could stop it.

Tilon's jaw clenched.

"Why does she keep him around if he's dangerous?" Caleb pressed.

"She loves him."

"She ... what?"

"Not like that. It's not romantic. It's primal. She can't see the danger, even if she knows it's there. So, she keeps him close. He's also a hell of a bodyguard."

"Did you know him? Before he changed?"

"Not well. He'd lost his voice by the time I got here. The changes have slowed, but his fur keeps thickening, his body growing more mutated. If he turns ..."

"We're screwed," Caleb finished.

"To put it bluntly."

"What happens? When we turn, I mean."

Tilon exhaled, letting his shoulders fall. "It isn't pretty." He hesitated, waiting for Caleb to push further before repeating his earlier advice. "Get some rest."

"What about that kid the other day? He didn't turn feral, right?"

"That child is why we need to stop this. He shifted, like you do, only too fast for his body to handle. Your father may not know if you are alive or dead right now, not unless the Shepherd really is in his pocket." Tilon paused. "It's likely. From what I can tell, Dr Murilo and his buddies are throwing new genetic splices at this place, hoping for something to stick. If you prove to be a success, it is only a matter of time before he tries to turn others the same way."

The blood drained from Caleb's face. Nausea twisted his stomach. "Holy shit," he whispered.

"Caleb?"

"My dad … the kid." Memories crashed into him. The itching beneath his skin after nights with his father. John's sunken, regretful eyes. His gaze dropped to his arm, to the always-tender vein inside his elbow.

"Caleb, talk to me," Tilon said.

"I – what if the—" His airway closed. A lump of stone was lodged in his throat.

"Breathe, boy." But Caleb couldn't. Flashes of the past blurred together in his mind. He swatted at his neck; phantom needles plunged into him from every angle. He was falling, drowning, the weight of the past threatening to pull him under the cold, dark surface of the rapids, just like his crate had.

All this time.

Caleb gasped, clawing at his throat, breaking from Tilon's grasp. Ava's footsteps approached, her hands soft and warm. He couldn't accept her love, her need to care for him. He had been such an idiot.

"Look at me," she said gently. His eyes met hers as he struggled to pull air into his lungs. "You're having a panic attack, child. Breathe with me." She placed his hand on her chest, over her heart. The rhythm guided his breathing until it matched hers.

"I knew he was never reading to me."

Tilon and Ava exchanged concerned glances, neither of them speaking, letting Caleb come to his own conclusions. His body tensed. The hairs along his neck and spine thickened, pressing against his clothes.

"He was injecting me. He has been injecting me with this shit. For years." He spat the words out. "The difference between me and the kid who caved in on himself is that I had a batshit crazy father making sure his kid would be the best."

"Why hadn't you changed before coming here?" Ava asked, concerned.

"The party. You said that boy came in not long after me, right? He was probably in the same drop. Whatever we got injected with was new, a catalyst. Maybe for a new wave of hybrids. My shifts ... they're triggered by anger and fear. That boy must have been so damn scared." Caleb choked out a sob. "You said they wanted soldiers, right?" He looked at Tilon, dropping his hands from Ava. "Weapons? What better than enhancing your fighters with skills that would give them a genetic, controllable advantage? He's trying to make shifters. You all changed slowly; I am guessing one injection, for the most part. Slow release, making you change over time. If Argo is out here, I am guessing he was primed just like me. Maybe there are more of us. Shifters that haven't died yet. There were a lot of wealthy investors, maybe they—"

"Who's Argo, Caleb? You've mentioned him before."

Caleb stopped before he could speak, arms dropping to his sides.

"Caleb – who's Argo?"

"A friend." He swallowed, struggling to get the words out. "He tried to warn me, tell me something was going on. That me and a bunch of others were in my father's files. His dad's in on it too. Working closely with mine. It would make sense they wanted their sons to be the best. To show the world the experiments were finally working."

Caleb took a deep breath and shook his head, trying to fight the panic from coming back. "I think we might have been primed without our knowing. And you're right. If they think I'm a success—"

"There'll be more," Tilon finished.

"Yeah."

"Try to rest," Tilon said. "If we have any chance of getting off this island, we're going to need our strength."

"Why don't I take first watch?" Caleb replied.

"What?"

"I'm too wired. And if we are going to need to move, it won't be for the next couple of hours, right? If we get attacked, we are going to need you. My shifts are still too unpredictable. Besides, I could use some practice with my senses."

Tilon grunted, unsure but not dismissive. "Sythe, you and Caleb take first watch."

The smaller of the two feline hybrids stepped forward. Tilon patted Caleb's arm before lying next to Ethan and closing his eyes.

"Big move, kid," Sythe teased approvingly.

"Hey, Sythe?"

"Yeah?"

"Can you teach me how to use my nose?"

A Bigger Playing Field

Chapter Twenty-One

Caleb's foot connected with a tree, a huff falling from his mouth. All he could smell was dirt and the people around him.

"Breathe," Sythe offered.

"What the hell have I been doing this whole time?"

"Okay, fine. Come sit," Sythe said, his whiskers twitching as he smirked. "Besides, if you keep kicking the trees, you'll wake the others."

Caleb flopped to the ground, frustrated.

"Now, breathe. And close your eyes."

"That's how I hear, not how I smell," Caleb argued.

"You need to learn to use your senses together. Stop focusing on them as being different. Allow them to create a vision. What you hear and smell paints a picture. When you heard the roar, you could basically see Jan, right?"

"Yeah."

"It's easier with him because you've seen him in the flesh before, but the concept is similar. Your senses expand your surroundings. Hearing the wind through the trees helps you visualise them. Smelling a new body or fur helps you sense where they are coming from."

Caleb did as he was told, battling his natural instincts to focus on his hearing.

"Your sense of smell has been getting better this whole time. With or without you noticing it. Now. What can you pick up?"

"You lot," Caleb retorted.

"Focus on the picture you know to be in front of you, but don't open your eyes. Let your nose be your guide."

"What are you talking ab—" A vision of Ava and Ethan filled his head. He could sense their breathing, the sweet tang of the dates on Ethan's tongue as he snored softly. His ear twitched, sensitive to the child's exhale.

"I think it's working," Caleb said, the vision disappearing as he spoke. "Dang it!"

Sythe chuckled at the outburst. "That was good; keep at it."

***

Tilon moved them at first light, concerned that Delia and Jan were on their way.

Their leader wanted to spread out and search the surrounding areas as they worked their way to the shore. They were all to be on the lookout for the clickers and alert the group for a potential fight. Caleb tried to focus on his senses with each passing step. They hadn't walked far before the stench of death hit them with full force. A pungent, sweet yet sour aroma stung their nostrils, making Caleb regret asking how to use his heightened senses.

He led the group to the kill, fighting back nausea at the sight. Bloodied, mangled fur stuck out at odd angles. Its glazed eyes remained open, frozen in fear. Maggots writhed in the rotting flesh and flies buzzed around the decomposing carcass. Sythe crouched to examine the body while Tilon and the scouts searched for who or what may have done it. Standing watch beside Winson, Caleb flexed his ears, trying to separate the sounds of his friends, the forest and anything that might wish them harm. But all he could focus on was the reek.

"It's not a normal kill," Sythe remarked unhelpfully, breaking Caleb out of his concentration.

"Obviously." Sarcasm dripped from Caleb's voice. "It looks like it's been shredded by an oversized grater."

Sythe's face contorted. "What I mean is," he said slowly, "this wasn't for food. It doesn't even look like a kill for defence. It looks like ... a kill for fun. Training, maybe. It's too messy."

"Ferals?" Caleb let the question hang in the air. Winson and Sythe shared a look.

"Ferals would have eaten it whole." Sythe shook his head. "There'd be nothing left but bones."

"And there would be more bodies," Winson added.

"True," Sythe agreed. He must have seen the confusion on Caleb's face because he sighed, dropping his frustration. "From what we've seen, they hunt in packs, but they don't understand the dynamic. Not a lot going on up there." He tapped his temple. "Even the clickers work together. Ferals? Not a chance."

"There is a reason we steer clear," Winson agreed.

And a reason you're all so worried about Jan.

"Once they kill, the bloodlust takes over, and more often than not, they turn on their own. It's why we don't see a lot of them. They tend to take each other out, but they are dangerous." Sythe's voice tapered off as he looked sadly into the never-ending trees.

The three of them turned to the sound of the scouts approaching.

Tilon's heavy footsteps gave their location away.

"Once you're done inspecting this one, there are more up ahead," Lilah said, pointing deeper into the trees.

Caleb breathed like Sythe had shown him, catching smoke on the scout's skin. His jaw clenched as he forced his mind to see the little hybrid without opening his eyes. It was there. In the air. He could almost see it in his head. A shudder ran through him, the hairs on his arms standing on end.

"Come," Tilon commanded. "This is new. We haven't seen an attack like this one; if whatever did this isn't feral, we should find out what it is. Could be from your drop. Stay close and be ready." Tilon, Winson and Sythe took the spears from their backs and moved in the direction Lilah had come from.

Sythe handed him his second spear. "Just in case," he said.

The scouts ran ahead while Caleb and the others walked slowly through destruction. Burnt and blackened branches littered the ground and darkness crept up the spindly trunks, painting a horrific scene of death. Twisted trees reached out to each other, their tangled limbs creating a suffocating humidity that only accentuated the stench of the clickers lying dead in their path. Caleb struggled not to gag and yanked his shirt over his nose. Several of the beasts lay in front of them. Each body looked to have met a similar fate to the one they had found earlier.

Caleb's ear perked up, a low grumble reverberating in his mind. He whipped around, trying to focus his vision to sharpen on command.

"Did you—?" Caleb started.

"I heard it too," Tilon confirmed.

"Fly up ahead, see if we're in danger," Winson said to the owl. The bird spread its wings and left them in the stagnant air.

The noise sounded again, a threatening rumble echoing through the damaged trees.

Caleb turned to Ava and Ethan, who had moved in behind him. "Hold him," he said, moving forward with the scouts.

"Stay here." Tilon stretched out an arm to force him back. Grace, Berrum and Lilah stopped immediately in their tracks.

The owl called them forward.

"Sythe, with me." Tilon gripped his spear, and they moved as one into the trees.

Caleb wouldn't let them go alone. Fear be damned. "Tilon, wait!" he called in alarm. His vision sharpened. Cold grey eyes stared back at him. It held his gaze for a second, then snarled, entrails dripping from its jaws.

Feral.

It hadn't fully changed yet. Its mangled head kept watch as the rest of its body contorted. Red saliva dripped from its mouth onto a solid human torso. Mottled fur covered well-developed muscle. The crazed hybrid cried out in pain, growing agitated as bones cracked and limbs snapped into place.

Caleb's body reacted instinctively, his muscles tensing, hackles rising.

"Get back!" Tilon barked, stepping in front of Caleb.

Caleb shoved him aside. "What are you doing?"

"We don't know what this shift will do to them or us," Tilon shot back. "And judging by those dead clickers, it won't be good. You have no combat training,

Caleb." His words weren't unkind, but they hit him like a ton of bricks. "Get to Ava and the boy." Tilon forced Caleb behind him, bracing himself with one leg forward, spear ready.

Caleb watched in horror as a mutated wolf-form dropped to the ground. Its legs grew longer, leaner, ready to run at them. Caleb's instincts battled against logic. He was scared and angry – shifting should be a breeze. But there was more at stake here than just him. The creature morphed back and forth between its human and wolf form. Cries of pain escaped its body with each convulsive change.

"It's trying to control it," Ava said in awe.

"It's losing," Sythe said flatly. He stood beside Tilon, spear held out, while Winson watched from behind. Light footsteps picking up speed caught Caleb's attention, and he whipped around just in time to see Lilah sprint towards the beast. A panicked scream escaping her.

"No!" Winson yelled, lunging to grab her as she ran past. "It's too strong!"

"Stay back," Tilon commanded, halting Winson before he could follow.

"Why would she ...?" Caleb asked.

"Fear," Tilon answered. "Take it before it takes you."

"She'll die," Winson protested.

"As will you if you run out there." Tilon's words were final.

Lilah appeared beside the beast, her eyes wide with fear. She looked back to the group, a squeak issuing from her throat as the creature lifted its head. Caleb's heart caught in his throat as she turned. *No.* She'd lost her nerve and was headed back toward them. Tilon and Sythe held their spears low, bracing for the shifted body to turn on them.

The creature's massive, distorted head whipped towards her. It stopped fighting itself, its body rapidly changing into its wolven form. Terror stabbed at Caleb's heart. He suddenly regretted leaving the relative safety of the camp two days ago. His muscles tensed, his breath coming shallow and fast. Yet, he couldn't look away. The beast, now fully formed, stood on its hind legs, swiping at Lilah as she darted around it. She was damn lucky she was fast.

She's trying to disorient it. Caleb barely had time to register the thought before the beast's paw caught her. Its head flashed to the side, catching Lilah mid-stride. Its jaws snapped shut around her tiny body as if she were nothing more than a rabbit to be hunted.

She cried out in pain, squirming, clawing at its sharp, bloody teeth as they sank into her.

"We need to move!" Winson yelled, but Sythe's arm held him in place.

"On Tilon's command," he said, arm straining against Winson's scaled body.

"We need to save her!"

"Listen," Tilon hissed, his eyes not moving from the bloody scene in front of them. "Lilah is gone. This beast is stronger than any clicker we have come across. You saw the bodies as well as I did. Our best bet is to use the distraction her death gives us. She doesn't have to die in vain."

Lilah had gone limp in the giant wolf's jaws. If she wasn't dead yet, it wouldn't be long.

Caleb stood frozen, his fear stealing any desire to fight. If this was a feral, how the hell were they going to get past its berserker-like rage? Ethan whimpered beside him, clutching his leg. Ava hovered close, tense and silent, unable to look away.

Something was wrong with this creature.

Blood vessels had burst in its eyes, giving them a dangerous red glow. It let out a muffled howl through Lilah's bloody and beaten body, its last shred of control crumbling. Its jaws clamped down.

A sickening crunch echoed through the clearing. Lilah's scream turned to a gurgle. Blood dribbled onto the forest floor as the beast shook her side to side, slamming her against the ground.

Ethan sobbed while Ava tried to shield his eyes.

"Now!" Tilon shouted.

Winson and Sythe moved in with their spears, unable to get a clear shot at the thrashing beast.

Then, suddenly – silence.

Lilah had stopped moving. The beast dropped her, no longer interested.

Its massive head turned on the group slowly, its chest heaving with exertion.

Caleb swore he saw recognition in its eyes before they paused on Ethan. It snarled at him, Lilah's blood dripping from its maw.

Tilon and Sythe charged, thrusting their spears into its side, one from the left, the other from the right. The beast snapped, its attention on the boy. Winson darted around, searching for an opening, desperately trying to cause a diversion from the front.

It broke out of its trance and roared.

"Ava, run," Caleb said, turning back to her and the boy.

"I can't."

"You have to."

"Caleb, I can't." She looked terrified, frozen in place and holding the boy against her leg. Grace and Berrum were not far behind them.

Caleb turned back to the fight.

Shit.

The three warriors fell into rhythm. Jab, pull back, jab, pull back. Light on their feet, they forced the creature to divide its attention by keeping all three in its vision at once.

I should be helping, dammit.

The beast swiped with claws too large for its body, nearly catching Sythe as he thrust his weapon forward. One of the spears pierced its side. Dark blood oozed from the wound, but the rabid hybrid twisted, knocking the weapon away in an instant.

There was something about the wolf that felt familiar. The way it fought. Its eyes.

And Caleb's fear mixed with the desire to know who or what this thing was.

He stepped forward.

Ethan clutched his leg, sobbing. "Don't go," he whispered.

Caleb took his hand. Ethan's grip trembled in his own.

"Hold him," Caleb said to Ava, his voice unsteady. He turned to Ethan. "I won't let it get you." He tried to sound braver than he felt.

Get out there. Now.

Caleb forced his eyes closed, allowing a rush of adrenaline to add fuel to his fear. His muscles strained then pulled tighter underneath his skin. He held the tension in his body, focusing on filling each limb. He felt the veins harden across his arms, hair pushing through his skin.

Come on.

His breathing slowed, heavy but controlled. He could feel the pressure building as he focused on the shift, not quite able to make it happen.

It's you or the boy.

Another cry sounded, louder this time, pained. The echo made Caleb flinch, breaking his concentration. Tilon's voice joined in the cry of suffering. A claw had ripped across his stomach. The feline hybrid was struggling to stay upright, leaning against his spear, which was now buried in the beast's side. Tilon and the mangled wolf slumped together, panting.

Winson and Sythe stayed on alert, circling behind the fallen foe to strike from behind. Caleb winced at the sight of blood seeping through Tilon's fingers as he pressed his hand against his abdomen. Their leader still clutched his weapon.

A yelp escaped the beast and its body shrank, collapsing in on itself as its human form took over. Their muscles rippled, limbs reshaping, skin marred with scratches and blood streaking across bruised flesh. Patches of fur refused to fade.

Just like me.

The body collapsed, breath haggard. The beast was gone, replaced by a battered, unconscious man.

No one moved.

Caleb lifted his nose, inhaling deeply. The scent of sweat and blood made his skin tingle. His stomach dropped as he stared at the two hybrids before him.

Tilon grunted, yanking the spear from the body. He swayed and dropped to the ground. The fur on his face was damp with sweat; his breathing had turned rapid. Ava ran to him, having found her feet, satchel in hand, already pulling out thick thread and a rough needle.

"Stay back," Tilon whispered weakly.

"He ain't gonna hurt me, he's in worse shape than you." She knelt, clearing away blood as best she could. It was still pouring out of him too fast. If she couldn't stop it, he would be dead by nightfall.

Not taking any chances, Winson picked up Tilon's spear, aiming it at the unconscious man.

Caleb stepped forward as a groan escaped the body.

"Stay with Grace and Berrum," Caleb told Ethan, holding his hand up toward the boy. He sniffed the air again, unable to place the scent coming off the body. The man moved slightly, his body folding in on itself. He would have looked peaceful if not for the blood and fur. His limbs twisted at odd angles, partially deformed by the uncontrolled shift.

"What are you doing?" Sythe asked as a sharp intake of breath and cursing escaped Tilon's lips.

"Hush your whining," Ava scolded. "Go on, lad," she urged Caleb forward.

Tilon grumbled but obeyed, pressing a hand against his stomach to slow the bleeding.

"Stay still," Ava muttered.

Caleb reached the body, staring down at the familiar curve of muscle.

Is it really you?

Placing a foot against the man's side, he pushed, the dead weight offering mild resistance to the nudge before falling back into place.

He gulped, crouching. His hands shook. "Please," he mumbled quietly.

Ava lifted the gauze she was holding to the body, stepping back to give him room. "Hurry, child. He doesn't have long for me to close that wound."

The others watched in silence. He heard the soft clunk of the spearhead hitting the dirt, no longer pointed at their fallen foe.

He pushed again, this time with both hands. The body rolled over, revealing a deformed six-foot figure he had known most of his life.

Caleb's breath hitched.

His knuckles turned white as he grasped at the ruined flesh, nails digging into unscarred patches. Shuffling forward, he pulled him against his chest. His friend's face was torn by shifts and scars.

A strangled cry tore from Caleb's throat.

"Argo."

Old Friends

Chapter Twenty-Two

Caleb refused to leave the body, watching the slow rise and fall of the man's chest as he struggled for air, grimacing at every wheeze. He had begged Ava to stitch up his wounds. Blood covered almost every inch of visible skin. Tilon and the others hesitated, reluctant to aid a creature that had killed one of their own in a frenzied bloodlust.

"I know. I know. Just, please." Caleb had never begged for anything in his life; he'd never had to. This was different. He wasn't even sure he liked the brute before they were trapped in this hellscape together, but Argo was the first sign of his old life, the first sign of his own world, he'd seen in weeks.

"Can you hear Jan?" Tilon asked weakly after Caleb pleaded for Argo to be spared. Caleb shook his head in response.

He needed to talk to his friend, questions bubbling on the edge of his tongue, waiting to burst out of him the second Argo woke. Maybe he'd found others like them; perhaps he had a plan to get off this damn island. Tilon agreed reluctantly, placing Caleb in charge of watching over the healing hybrid. If there was any sign of him shifting again, Caleb was to call out. He knew they wouldn't hesitate to run his old friend through at the first hint of transformation.

The group risked a fire, Ava insisting Tilon rest for the evening. The heady scent of clicker meat filled the space, making Caleb's mouth water and his nerves race with fear of being found. Winson, Sythe, Berrum and Grace had done their best to move the dead animals to the outskirts of the tree-filled space, salvaging what flesh could still be cooked and dried through the night. The cooling gloom of the brush had slowed their decay, but it wouldn't last another day.

Caleb traced Argo's hand with his own, lifting it to examine the similarities of the thickened hairs along its side. His skin felt tougher now, harder to penetrate. He glanced down at the two crudely stitched wounds at his side. Blood had pooled then dried underneath him.

"Is this your friend?" Ethan's voice startled him. Caleb spun around to find the boy watching him intently, holding a large leaf piled with steaming clicker meat.

Caleb placed Argo's hand gently back on the ground and waved Ethan over, patting the ground next to him.

He had pulled a spare shirt from his pack, draping it over Argo's broad frame. It didn't cover much, but enough to shield the worst of the blood and bruises from Ethan's view. The boy sat and leaned into him, seeking comfort in the uncertainty. Caleb draped an arm over him, shifting slightly and giving the boy permission to move closer. It didn't take long for the familiar warmth of Ethan's body to press against his side.

"This is Argo." The words came out choked, surprising both of them.

"Ar-go?"

"Yeah. I knew him before … all this." Caleb gestured at the trees, at their friends around the fire. His eyes met Tilon's, the leader watching them as intently as ever. Caleb sighed, wishing he would trust him.

"He killed Lilah," Ethan said matter-of-factly.

"He did, yes, but not this Argo." Caleb pointed to his friend. Perspiration had broken out on his skin, his face drained of colour.

"He doesn't look so good."

Caleb lifted his chin, trying to stop new tears welling in his eyes. He didn't want Ethan to see just how scared he was. "He'll be alright," he said, unable to stop his voice from shaking. He covered his mouth with his free hand. Breathing into the small, hot space, he resisted the urge to rock back and forth.

Argo looked awful.

What if he doesn't make it?

"I need to check him." Caleb reached out, placing his palm against Argo's forehead. He tore his hand back. He was burning.

"No, no, no!" He sat bolt upright, leaving the child staring up at him, concerned. He ripped at his hair, pacing around the still body.

"Wake up, damn you." Caleb pushed at Argo's side.

He didn't move.

Shit. Panic tightened his chest and he reached for Ethan, gripping him too tightly.

"Ow."

"I'm sorry. I'm so sorry." His tears fell.

Ethan stepped away from him, his own fear and sorrow filling his little face. "I'll get Ava."

Caleb's eyes widened at the boy's intuition but nodded gratefully. He caught Winson pacing the perimeter, spear gripped tightly in his hands. He wasn't impressed they hadn't avenged Lilah by killing the "feral beast". Caleb wanted to talk to him, to try and explain, but he couldn't bear to leave Argo's side.

Ethan returned with Ava, who carried a cup of clean water. Her eyes held a wary sadness as she looked between Caleb and Argo. Ethan followed, clutching a small pot of salve.

"Caleb," she started, her voice gentle, motherly.

"It's not good. I know," he said, placing the food aside before reaching for the shirt covering Argo.

"He killed one of us, you know. He won't be forgiven any time soon. I'm surprised Tilon has let him live," Ava said, taking a clean bandage from her pocket and dipping it into the water.

"It wasn't him ... at least not this version of him." Caleb reached out for the cloth. "Let me help."

Ava handed over the dampened rag, instructing him to dab off the sweat and cool his body as best they could. She moved around Argo, checking his pulse, then his temperature. They worked together, applying salve and tree oils on the cuts and bruises. His friend's body felt wrong, muscles bunched in places they shouldn't, skin twisting unnaturally beneath his fingers. Argo occasionally let out a soft grunt at their efforts.

Would this happen to him if he shifted too many times?

Caleb fought to keep his emotions in check, instead asking what came next. There was little else they could do. Argo's survival depended on him now.

Caleb wondered if Argo had been injured like this before. Given the number of fur patches and the misplaced muscle on his body, he suspected this was not his first time in a frenzied shift. Caleb hoped his old friend could pull through to tell him what he'd found out. Right now, he'd be content if he just opened his eyes.

***

Daylight struggled through the canopy, giving it an eerie glow. One by one, the group stirred, rubbing sleep from their eyes. Tilon instructed them all to collect their possessions and get ready to move out.

"How's he doing?" Sythe asked, looking down at Argo.

"I don't know," Caleb admitted. Not much had changed overnight. He had stayed with him, wiping him down each time he covered in sweat.

"He's breathing better," Sythe offered. "Did you eat?"

Caleb shook his head, the plate of clicker dried and discarded. "You're ready to move on?"

"Yes. Once Lilah has been buried," Tilon said, his powerful presence joining them. He was leaning on his spear, his midsection home to a tight bandage. "We'll move towards the coast. The map indicates another camp, not far from here, then we are in unknown territory. If we're serious about exposing the truth and finding a way out, we'll need to venture beyond what these documents tell us." He took a moment to look down at Argo's unmoving body. "Delia won't stop just because we have, and she knows this forest better than anyone. The scouts have been running through the night, hoping to throw her hunters off the scent."

"Tilon, I can't leave him," Caleb said, almost pleading. "What if he wakes up?"

Tilon studied them both for what felt like an eternity before he sighed. "I understand, boy. I do. But we don't know whether this man is friend or foe.

The only information we have is that he murdered Lilah, and it took three of us to put him down. He nearly got me too."

Caleb placed a hand on Argo's arm, turning from Tilon to watch the rise and fall of his friend's chest.

"He was your friend; I don't want to take away from that. But this isn't just about him, or any of us for that matter. You heard Jan the day before last, and I've never known Delia to send him out without her troops. Stopping last night could well have been a mistake."

"It was necessary," Ava chided.

Tilon raised an eyebrow, ignoring her. "If the bear is on our trail, they won't be far off."

"And what's she going to do, huh?" Caleb challenged. "She doesn't want violence against her own."

"She doesn't want progress either, and that may as well be the same thing," Tilon started sternly. "We wouldn't be the first group not welcome back after defying her one too many times. She keeps those she has sway over close. Protects them with an open arm while pushing out those who fight her."

"She's sent her troops against rogue hybrid groups before," Winson said, he and the owl sidling up to Tilon. "We're ready, boss."

"Caleb. Her warriors are well trained and largely kept away from the group. There is a reason we fear them. I am not looking to start a war, but I am looking for answers. The same as you."

"Exactly why we need Argo!" Caleb said, exasperated.

Tilon pressed on. "The group can't stay. If you need to, I won't fault you for it. But we're leaving."

"Wait." The voice was weak, rough, like words pushed through sandpaper.

"Argo!"

Air rushed past Caleb as Winson appeared, spear pointed directly towards Argo's throat.

"Winson!" Sythe yelled.

"He killed one of us, or have you forgotten?" Winson hissed, touching the blade to Argo's neck.

"Of course I haven't." Sythe knocked Winson's spear down with his own.

"Then why are we letting the bastard live?"

"It wasn't him," Caleb said, dropping to Argo's side.

"Take a walk," Sythe said to Winson. The lizard hybrid let his spear fall with a huff but didn't move.

Caleb gripped Argo's hand, fighting the urge to shake him fully awake. Instead, his hand trembled as he guided Argo's fingers to his jaw, hoping his friend would recognise him by touch.

"Argo," he whispered.

Argo's fingers twitched, tracing Caleb's jaw before moving to his hairline. With Caleb's help, his weak grip cupped his face.

"It's Caleb." He wasn't sure how much prompting Argo would need.

Ava hovered nearby. Tilon grunted and stepped back, returning to the others. His voice drifted in and out of Caleb's awareness, but Caleb stayed fixated on the man before him. Argo's eyelids fluttered. He managed to open them once before exhaustion and grime forced them shut again.

"My Caleb?" The words came easier than before but still pained.

"Aye. Didn't leave your side all night. Guess that makes him your Caleb, alright," Ava said warmly.

Argo flinched under his hands as Ava spoke, a pathetic attempt to shuffle his partial nudity out of her eyesight, barely managing more than rustling damp leaves underneath him.

Caleb pressed a firm but gentle hand against his bare chest, keeping him still. "You're hurt, Argo. Ava's helping you."

"Ava?"

"Yes, lad. Now open that big mouth of yours and take a sip. You need water."

Argo tried to chuckle, but it turned into a coughing fit. He finally opened his mouth, and Ava placed a cup against his lips.

"The monster's awake! The monster's awake!" Ethan's excited voice cut through the trees. Moments later, the boy came sprinting toward them. Sythe intercepted him like a thrown ball, lifting him awkwardly off the ground.

"Hey! I wanna see. Put me down!"

"Shush, kid. We still don't know what's out here and you would wake an army of clickers with that gob of yours," Winson scolded.

The boy huffed and tried to break from Sythe's grasp. "Kid, stop squirming!"

Caleb laughed as Sythe struggled to hold onto the wriggling child. "Let him through."

Ethan rewarded him with a beaming face.

"Argo's not a monster."

"Last night, he was a monster. He killed Lilah."

The words made them all flinch. Argo's face dropped, his body going stiff under Caleb's hand. Tilon shot Caleb a look that made it clear he needed to make a decision. Now.

"I don't know what happened to him last night," Caleb admitted, "but I'd like to find out."

A rush of wings stirred the air behind Caleb's ear as the owl swooped in, settling on Argo's chest. Tiny claws padded up his torso before the bird hooted directly at Caleb.

Argo swallowed the last sip of water and managed a weak smile. "Hey, little guy."

"You know it too?" Caleb asked.

"Sure. It's been hanging around a bit. Never wanted to eat it though," Argo said.

"Caleb," Tilon said firmly, not introducing himself to Argo.

You know he's right. We have to move.

The owl cooed, and both Caleb and Argo turned towards it. It looked like it was trying to tell them something. He focused, letting his ears tune into the sounds of the forest. Footsteps crunched against the ground. One person, moving alone. Large. Trying to stay quiet.

"Can you stand?" Caleb asked Argo.

"I don't know," Argo stammered honestly.

"Let's try," Ava said, placing her hands under his arms, pulling him into a sitting position with Caleb's help. Winson gripped his spear at the movement.

"Easy," Caleb tried, holding his palms up.

"What if he shifts again?" Winson asked, eyes not leaving Argo.

"It only happens when I'm scared. Really scared. Or pissed," Argo muttered.

"Doesn't change the fact you killed one of us," Winson spat out bitterly.

Caleb's ears twitched. The footsteps were closer.

"Something is coming."

Tilon glared down at him, using his spear for support. "How far away is it?" He crossed his arms over his strong chest, the dark circles under his eyes giving away his weakened condition.

"I dunno. I'm sorry."

"Go," Winson said to the owl. The little bird took off from Argo's chest and flew into the trees.

"Grace, Berrum. See what you can find. Be careful," Tilon commanded. The scouts moved in opposite directions. "Get him up," he said to Sythe, who moved to take Argo's weight from Ava.

"One, two, three."

Caleb left Argo to dust himself off and pull on the clothes he had slept under. He turned to Tilon, cringing under his scrutinising gaze.

"You need to concentrate." The weight of Tilon's gaze made Caleb stiffen. "You're part of this team now. You have abilities that can help. Start pulling your weight and listen. How long do we have?"

Each word hit Caleb like a punch. It was obvious Tilon's patience was wearing thin. This wasn't just a demand; it was another lesson. He hadn't given up on him.

"How do I—"

Tilon pushed off the tree, cutting him off. "Use your fear. Let your survival instinct take over. Not just for yourself but for your pack. Be the protector. If you don't, they will die. And it'll be on your watch."

"I'm not anyone's protector. I'm a—"

Tilon's hand shot up, claws at the ready. Caleb shut his mouth.

"We are out here because of you. You've given us hope for something more. You've made us see that we might have a chance out here. Now – concentrate, and be the damn alpha I know you can be."

"I've never wanted to—"

Tilon growled, upper lip curling into a snarl. He launched forward, gripping Caleb's shoulders with his massive paws. His claws bit into Caleb's skin. "Concentrate, or the two boys you saved will die."

Caleb wanted to fight back. He wanted to cry in frustration. Neither option would help. He sucked in a breath, filling his lungs, and closed his eyes like Sythe had taught him. Tilon's grip loosened but didn't let go.

The footsteps had stopped approaching. Instead, they were shuffling over dense foliage in slow, deliberate movements, unlike the quick, light steps of the scouts just outside of their periphery. Whoever it was was cautious. Following their steps.

"It's not Jan."

"You have no idea what Jan is capable of," Sythe said from where he and Argo stood.

"If Jan had found us, he wouldn't hesitate. Nor would Delia if she had him with her. What can you see?" Tilon asked.

Caleb pushed himself to see past the darkness behind his eyes. To feel the forest around him. The terrain was familiar now. The trees stood thick and dense, providing enough space to hide someone as big as Jan. He could sense his pack, Tilon at the centre, his heat radiating like a fire. Caleb's brow furrowed as he concentrated on his instincts.

There. It clicked. The image of a creature about Sythe's size but lacking his finesse, sniffing around the last place they had stopped. *That was only yesterday.* Caleb couldn't gauge how fast this thing could move or determine specifics about its body or the species it was mixed with, but it had given itself over to animal instincts.

"Half a day, maybe. It's not far." Caleb opened his eyes. Tilon's gaze bored into him, his eyes light with pride before his expression hardened into a determined nod.

Tilon turned to Winson, Ava and Sythe. "Call the scouts. Be ready to move as soon as possible." Tilon pulled out the map, squinting at the set of oval cages they had passed not long ago. "We're headed here." He indicated what looked to be the last documented campsite on the map. "We should reach it through the line of trees left of where we came in."

"You think it's a path?"

"I'm hoping for all our sakes it is."

"Is it safe?" Ava asked from behind them, Argo now able to stand on his own. Sythe returned with the scouts, the two of them doubling over and panting with physical exertion. The owl flew in after them.

"I don't know. Just because there are no clickers left here doesn't mean they aren't up ahead." Tilon frowned at Argo while he spoke. He nodded to Winson and Sythe, who gripped their spears, their focus shifting to the trail.

"What about him?" Caleb gestured towards his friend, confused to see colour returning to Argo's face.

"I'm fine." The strength in Argo's voice made Caleb jump. The weakness from only minutes ago had vanished.

"How?" Caleb frowned in confusion.

Argo shrugged, chest flexing. His nonchalance irritated Caleb almost immediately.

"No, seriously. You were close to death seconds ago, and now you are fine. What the hell, man?"

Argo held up his hands in mock surrender. "I'm still hurt, and my head is killing me, but I can walk." Taking three large strides, he closed the distance between himself and Tilon and extended a hand.

"Hey, big fella. I'm Argo. Thanks for not killing me. Much appreciated." Argo dropped his hand at Tilon's unwavering stance. "And, hey. I'm really sorry. About Lilah. I – I can't control it. Not an excuse, I know. But I'm trying. Really trying."

"I still don't trust him!" The last words were said with disgust.

"Winson, please," Tilon started. "We need to move. You and Sythe watch him. If he shifts again, we may need to put him down for good."

"I'm right here," Argo said.

"You're a murderer. Forgive me if trust isn't forthcoming."

Pain and confusion worked its way through Argo's features.

"I – I'm sorry. Usually, I just take out the clicky bastards." His body slumped forward as he looked to Caleb to reconfirm the news.

"Could you feel me? Before you turned?" Caleb asked quietly. "It looked like you were trying to stop it."

Argo looked at the ground, furrowing his brows before answering. "Sort of. But … I didn't know it was you. More like a sense that I had to stop. Something was there I shouldn't go after, ya know?"

Caleb swallowed, his tongue sticking to the roof of his mouth. He didn't want to believe his friend would really tear him apart. "Tilon's right. We need to move before whoever is tailing us catches up."

"I know a place," Argo said.

"We have a place," Tilon countered, standing tall, arms crossed, biceps flexing as if waiting for a fight.

"Oh yeah? Where?" Argo smirked, oblivious to the tension.

"Don't be smart with me. If you're coming, get yourselves up." Tilon's teeth flashed white, showing Argo just how sharp they were.

"You're looking for a camp, right? I've been staying in one. I … sort of killed the woman who was there. One of the ones spying on you, I assume. I'm guessing if you're out here, you've figured that much out, right?"

"What do you know?" Caleb asked, trying to hide his desperation for answers.

"I've been living there for weeks. The hyena-looking things show up every so often to find their leaders and I, well, you saw."

"Have you seen the Shepherd?"

"The who?"

"Big dude in a cloak, walks around with a couple of trained clickers. One of them is named Kajia. We saw him once, back at camp."

"Hold up," Winson scoffed. "You killed another woman? Who was she?"

"I don't know, man. I didn't question why you're a damn lizard and this guy looks like a giant cat. Can you lower the spear? Please."

"The woman?" Winson asked again, not taking his hands off his weapon.

"She was in a camp, not all that far from here. Holding a couple of the mangy bastards. Training them, I guess. She was talking to someone on a walkie-talkie. I got close. Too close. She spooked, sent her rabid pets my way and then I ..."

"Shifted," Caleb said.

"So, you can do it too, huh? Turn back, that is?"

"Move this along," Tilon ordered. "Ava, get the boy and the scouts."

"Are there more like us?" Caleb asked hopefully.

"We don't have time for this now," Tilon interjected. "Let's go."

Argo grinned, revealing sharp canines. "Mi casa es su casa!"

Dead Scientists

Chapter Twenty-Three

"What happened here?" Caleb asked, struggling to believe the sight in front of him. They had walked for half a day before reaching Argo's lodgings. Tilon was curious enough that he wanted to map out the area but not so much that he committed to rest at the new location. The creature Caleb sensed that morning still hovered in the periphery of his awareness.

Clean, solid structures of corrugated iron had been fitted together to house working electronics; another served as a sleeping quarter, complete with actual camp cots. The thin foam mattresses looked like pure luxury after nights spent sleeping on the ground.

Caleb stared in disbelief. Weeks had passed since he'd last seen a fridge, yet there it was, stocked with an assortment of food he never thought he'd see again. His stomach growled at the sight of hard cheeses and cold cuts. Was that cola? Without thinking, he reached in, grabbed a can and popped the tab. The ring pull hissed as it plunged into carbonated sugary goodness.

"I want some! I want some!" Ethan sang, the promise of a sugar high worth giving up an out-of-date sandwich. The only thing of importance right now was sweet, processed sugar. Caleb laughed and handed him the can. Within seconds, sticky brown liquid was dribbling down Ethan's face.

"Oh man, Dad never let me drink this at home. This is the stuff," Ethan said melodramatically.

"Alright, easy, kid." Caleb took the can back and wiped off Ethan's spit before taking another sip.

"Little tyke, isn't he?" Argo remarked offhandedly before tilting his head, motioning for Caleb to follow him toward a structure emitting an ungodly noise.

Caleb looked for the others. Tilon and Sythe were scouting the perimeter, mapping out the new area in relation to where they had come from. Their brows furrowed as they talked hurriedly and did their best to sketch the new location.

Ava had taken Ethan to lie on one of the cots. Her efforts to keep a newly caffeinated, squirming child still were in vain. The scouts had passed out for a quick nap on the remaining beds. Winson and the owl were out of sight. Caleb listened for them; the lizard's scratchy steps were not far ahead. It sounded like he was collecting wood.

Caleb and Argo rounded the corner of a second structure, and what he saw nearly made Caleb drop the cola. He grappled for the beverage before it spilled all over the pristine floor of the building they were now entering. It was a solid demountable, one with flecks of wear and rust. Caleb reached out to the sheets of cool metal fit together to create a workable space. This place had been right under their noses ... unmapped.

Delia must have known about this.

Caleb recoiled as a high electrical buzzing niggled in his permanently shifted ear, the noise worming into his skull. He clenched his jaw, trying to force himself to focus on the sounds of the group and threats outside. The room held neat rows of equipment – working equipment. Two rough but clean hospital-grade beds stood against one wall, coupled with a bench holding a set of computer monitors plugged into a solar-powered generator in much better condition than the one at Delia's camp. Bright white text blinked across blackened screens. The machines looked to be at least a decade old, the large backing still holding the cables intact. Nothing like the new-age hardware he had back home.

Caleb approached one of the whirring machines, its fan struggling to keep it from overheating. He frowned at the endless lines of numbers displayed on the screen. He found it hard to believe this area hadn't been found or documented before. They had only been moving a couple of days, and already more information lay at their feet than Delia had told him in weeks. *How much more is being hidden from us?* A dull throbbing started behind his eyes, worsened by the relentless beeping of a heart rate monitor. It pushed his frustration closer to the edge.

"Can we turn that off?" he asked.

Argo flicked the side of the device, and the screen turned black.

"How long have you been here?" Caleb asked. He felt like he would burst, his brain working at rapid speed to piece together the facts he knew, the things he suspected and the new information in front of him.

"A couple of weeks." Argo pointed to a wall etched with rough tally marks. Caleb slumped down on a plastic chair leaning against the wall. *Weeks.* He knew they didn't have time to dwell. Tilon wanted to keep moving, but Caleb needed to stop for a damn minute. He wanted to figure out what was being researched here. He held his head in his hands, feeling the tension in his jaw.

"How the hell have we not heard them? They are barely three days from the main compound." Caleb was talking to the floor.

"My guess is they are travelling on foot. There was no transport when I got here. It's how we were taught back in the academy. You get dropped off a long distance away from your destination and travel as quietly as you can for an ambush."

Caleb raised his head. Argo was leaning over the desk, looking at him intently. "If I had known you were this close ..."

"I could have killed you. You think I was out of control a day ago?" Argo paused. "Nah, man. That was nothing. The only thing I've been good at is killing those fucked-up dogs that would have taken you out if you had ventured out here sooner."

"We knew they were patrolling the forests; I didn't realise how many or how close."

"The buggers are everywhere."

"They're called clickers."

Argo raised his eyebrows and let out a surprised snort. "That tracks. They're loud enough."

Maybe Tilon could help. He and Argo shared tactical training that might make sense of it all. Caleb's ear twitched, picking up on their leader ordering the others to collect whatever food and gear they could carry. Tilon's breathing was heavy. He wasn't moving himself, leaning against his crutch or a tree. *I hope he doesn't take long to heal.* Another ring pull hissed. *Please don't let that be Ethan.*

"Argo," Caleb started, struggling to find the words.

"Here." Argo gestured to a cot beside him.

"That night, I ..." Caleb hesitated.

Argo's arm draped over his shoulder. Caleb felt small next to the giant of a man his friend had become.

"I'm sorry too," Argo said. "If I had come to you sooner ..." He gave Caleb a squeeze before letting go.

Caleb leant forward, putting his head in his hands, inhaling deeply before he spoke. "Where did you wake up? How did you get out?"

"On a coast, probably a week or so from here. When I woke up ..." He sighed. "I wasn't human."

"You woke up as a wolf?"

"I guess." Argo shrugged. "I woke up angry, scared, unable to control what I had become. I didn't know who I was. I don't remember getting out of the crate, only that when I came to, there was a wooden box torn to shreds, and a rotting corpse beside me. I was covered in something else's blood." He stared into the distance. "I thought I was dead."

"You can't control it," Caleb offered.

"I'm getting better, at least with the shifting part. But after that, no. Not really."

"Have you seen anyone else?"

"Yes." Argo didn't offer any more than that; he looked pained.

"Feral?"

"Is that what you call them? Their eyes were red, manic. Came at me with ungodly speed, ready to tear me limb from limb. I fought ..."

"You killed them all."

Argo didn't say anything to that.

"What have you found out? With all this?" Caleb asked, standing.

"That it's been going on for years."

Caleb nodded. "A decade, from what I've been told."

"The Australian and U.S. militaries are working with our fathers to create an army of hybrid soldiers, but the science behind it isn't quite there yet. My guess? They're running out of time. There were final notices pasted all over my dad's workboards. The world is changing. Wars are breaking out everywhere. The people in charge want to be ready with something no one's seen before. They want something they can use to control nations, not destroy them."

"You think that's why we're different?"

"How do you mean?" Argo asked.

"You and I shift back. Tilon, Sythe and Winson, they all changed over time. A slow-release injection that turns them almost completely. Some of them have been here for years. Delia said—"

"Delia?"

"You know her?"

"If that's who I think it is, there's something you need to see." Argo stood and moved to the bench, pointing at the monitor.

"Let me get Tilon. You both have a way better grip on this than I do."

As if summoned, Tilon appeared at the entrance. He didn't trust Argo, that much was clear, but he also knew this was more information than they had found in years.

Caleb waved him into the room. "How are the others?"

"Fine. Resting. We can't stay long. I'd like to put some more ground between us and whoever is tailing us before sundown."

"Do you have your map?" Argo asked.

Caleb was surprised to see a rough sketch of the surrounding area scratched into the surface of the bench. It displayed the terrain surrounding the clicker cages, showing where they had come from earlier.

"You did this?" Caleb asked.

"Yeah. Do you mind if I see that?" Argo held out a hand for Tilon's canvas map and unfolded it next to his own.

"Delia's name has come up in here before." He pointed towards the computer. "This isn't the first research site I have come across since I've been here. I've tried to map out as much as I can. If your Delia is the same one, she's been working with them."

"What?" Tilon's voice dropped dangerously low.

Argo ignored him, focused on the maps.

"She used to work at the labs. Sacrificed herself for her family and was sent here. That's about all we know."

"Do you know when she arrived here?"

"Six years ago," Caleb replied.

"She's been tested since then. Her data comes up with her changes. Sometimes it's just her, sometimes with others."

The fur on Caleb's body bristled. "We knew something was going on," he said to Tilon.

"She gave you this?" Argo asked, pointing at the map.

Tilon nodded, then shook his head.

"Well, which is it?"

"She gave me a version of this when she first appointed me as mission leader. The one I have here we've found and put together along the way."

"She dictates where you scout, right? Has inside information. Knows where the danger is coming from. Doesn't like being challenged. Gives her a sense of power. How am I doing?"

"Spot on," Caleb said.

"Here are the areas I've found, and the ones missing from your map." They compared the two side by side. "How many of you are there?"

"Close to two hundred," Tilon said, his eyes flickering from the map to the text flashing on the monitors.

"There are more of us, scattered throughout the island. The other groups are a lot less friendly than you lot, and that's saying something."

"Did you kill some of theirs too?" Tilon grunted, shutting Argo up.

"How many groups?" Caleb interjected, not willing to stop the information from flowing.

"At least two. And a handful of ferals."

"You've done a lot more exploring than we have."

Tilon let out a growl and stormed out of the room, one fist clenched as tightly as his jaw, the other gripping his spear for balance.

This is so much bigger than we thought.

Caleb stepped back, trying to give himself room to think as he plodded through the room.

"Wait." Argo's voice pulled him back. "There's more."

Caleb sighed and followed Argo to a half-sized fridge full of vials. Saliva, blood and faecal samples lined the shelves in neat rows. Each one was labelled with a series of numbers printed along the side. He squatted down to examine them through the safety of the glass. Thousands of questions ran through his mind. Was no one out there looking for hundreds of missing people?

These facilities were more advanced than anything he'd seen with Delia. Far enough away to stay unnoticed, but close enough for hybrids to be captured, experimented on and disposed of. Delia wasn't just ignoring the truth; she was part of it. He was angry, but nowhere near as angry as he imagined Tilon was. What would Winson think?

His fists clenched against the concrete, veins protruding against his skin. How could she do this to him, to all of them? Sit by while people were stolen, used and left to die?

When he opened his eyes, a label caught his attention.

FAE-SPR-023.

The numbers looked familiar. His stomach twisted as he remembered the broken crate he had seen in the forest before he had been taken in by Delia and Jan. The bloated body stared at him accusingly. It had said "023" as well. *Could this be the year they were shipped?* He'd seen similar numbers scratched into crates back at Delia's compound. Different numbers. *Different years.*

He opened the fridge. Chilled air brushed his face as he lifted one of the vials. Deep red liquid swirled inside. Who was this? Someone who had been taken in the last raid? Brought back here to be poked and prodded? Sedated and drained? Some poor hybrid who had been used to plot data against others back at camp.

Caleb placed the vial back. His eyes scanned the rows of bodily fluids lined neatly in rows.

No.

He reached toward the back, a slightly off-colour label striking out at him like a beacon.

LUC-SER-023.

Lucia.

Heat rolled through his body, a wave of nausea threatening to spill over.

"What is it?" Argo asked, looking over his shoulder at the vial.

"The girl. This is …" Caleb's clothes felt too hot. Too tight. His skin crawled and a scream caught in his throat.

"Caleb. What girl?" Tilon questioned, stalking back into the room.

"There was a girl, the night Argo and I were taken. Her name was Lucia. Her dad introduced me. I thought she … I thought she died. Her eyes …" Lucia's face flashed before him, the shock of it making him fumble the vial.

He pulled himself up short, his mouth pulling against his canine teeth.

Breathe.

Tilon and Argo watched him, waiting to see what he would do next.

"This is it," Caleb said, steel in his voice.

"This is what?" Argo asked.

"Proof. Proof of what they are using us for, how they are keeping tabs. If we got this back to camp or brought others here …" He stopped, staring at the vial, not sure he could believe it. He gripped the beaker tightly in his fist.

"Hey!" Argo's voice cut through his rage. "We don't know what's in those. There are gloves for that shit."

Caleb wasn't listening. He was fixated on the dark ooze moving slowly within the container, spots of black circling through the liquid. Reality caught up to him, knocking the breath from his lungs.

She hadn't died that night. She had been here the whole time.

Until they took her – again.

LUC-SER-023.

Caleb didn't want to be right, but he knew this blood was poisoned, whether from whatever was injected into the subject or whatever had happened afterwards. The world needed to know about this. The people responsible had to be stopped.

Caleb frowned down at Lucia's blood. Determined to know more, he made his way to the monitors and hit the spacebar.

He was greeted by a beep and an error message flashing across the screen. Lines of numbers and text shifted, scrolling up only to reveal more gibberish.

He hit it again. Same result.

"Just give me a fucking search bar," he yelled at the machine.

"Easy," Argo said. He and Tilon pressed in behind Caleb. "You need to click into it."

The text vanished, replaced by a dialog box displaying the word "Search".

"Thanks," Caleb muttered, fighting his growing anxiety.

The cursor flashed, waiting. He typed "LUC-SER-023". The letters blinked back at him from the screen.

Caleb hit enter. The system came to life, filling with reports and data sets pertaining to a woman he wished he knew.

Each entry confirmed the truth he had been desperate to uncover and the truth he had been trying to avoid. The real consequences of these experiments. One word stood out, pulsing in a harsh red.

Lucia De La Courte: Deceased.

His stomach dropped, the cursor hovering over the attachment icon next to the death notice.

The click of the mouse sounded like thunder in his ears.

A series of whooshing sounds accompanied documents opening in rapid succession. Each one confirmed the pieces he had put together over the last few weeks. He wished he could undo it all: hitting enter, taking the vial, the entire expedition, waking up in a goddamn fucking box in the middle of nowhere. Everything.

A sharp gasp escaped his lips. A grainy image filled the screen. Lucia was tied to a hospital bed, her veins unnaturally engorged against her dark skin. Her long torso was arching off the mattress, her muscles strained.

This was the moment of her death. He could feel it. The light in her eyes had dimmed. Nothing but a grainy, black-and-white snapshot of a life lost.

"Why am I here, Caleb?" Her voice echoed in his head, sending a shiver down his spine.

"No," he choked out at the screen, gripping the edges of the table so hard his knuckles turned white.

"I'm sorry," Argo offered from behind him.

"Me too," Tilon said, his own voice defeated.

"How many of these files have you searched?" Caleb asked.

"Not enough." Argo couldn't hide his shame. "I was scared, man. I'm still scared."

Waves of anger and sadness fought for Caleb's attention. The young woman's eyes were open, slitted with black against stark white, blood appearing to be making its way out of each socket. Her long, beautiful, curly hair had matted around her face, framing it as she convulsed for the camera. Caleb gulped, his eyes making their way to her mouth. White foam mixed with darkened blood dribbled down Lucia's front.

He turned from the screen, shielding himself from the horror, shaking, unable to get the image out of his head. His body was fighting for control; he wasn't sure if he was about to shift or faint. Either way, he needed to get a grip.

Tears ran down his face as he let himself drop to his knees.

"Mum."

***

"Mum?" Caleb's voice sang through the house, bouncing up and down the halls with gradual impatience. The house staff had been sent away, and it was so close to dinner time. He was starving. Who was going to serve him? He giggled to himself

at the thought of being waited on hand and foot, a life he was already getting used to.

His parents had become more and more preoccupied over the course of several months. Caleb would have felt neglected if it weren't for the cooks, the tutors, the tennis coach ... He had plenty of people at his disposal.

It was all to keep him away from kids his own age. His father refused to let him bring anyone home – except for Argo. For some reason, his dad liked Argo.

Mr Markus was always around.

Caleb didn't mind. He lived in his own little bubble. He would've liked it more if their house had a fast-food chain inside, like a kid he had seen in his mum's favourite movie, but he guessed he couldn't have everything.

"Mum!"

He was getting angry now, his feet stomping up the hallway. Who was going to make his dinner? This wouldn't have been a problem if there was a burger joint in the house.

A sudden, piercing alarm shattered the quiet. It grew louder, closer. Something was terribly wrong.

"Mum?" This time, the question was quiet, anxious.

People were barging into the house, forcing their way through the front door with a solid boom. Uniformed bodies pushed past Caleb in a hurry as if they owned the place and knew exactly where they were going.

Caleb froze. His throat tightened, breath caught in his chest. More sirens blared outside. He gulped, forcing himself to move. Step by step, he backed down the hall toward the door of what would soon become his father's study.

The room was a mess. His father's massive desk had been shoved aside; the once neatly stacked papers and reports scattered. A medical monitor lay shattered on the floor and safety glass splintered in every direction.

Time slowed. Colour drained from his world.

All Caleb could hear were his father's ragged sobs and the pounding of his own heartbeat. Paramedics flanked his mother's still body. Needles pierced bulging blue veins, her skin a ghostly white.

His father reached out, fingers trembling, as if touching her would change something. John's fingertips hit blood. His mother's back had arched, a gaping wound in the centre of her chest. She looked like she had shrunk and then expanded, causing her body to fold in on itself. Blood trickled steadily from her glazed-over eyes; a pale foam continued to froth out of her mouth as the body convulsed.

Cold understanding washed over Caleb.

His mother was gone.

"Come here, son." His father's voice held more warmth than Caleb had heard in years. John's eyes shone with tears, barely held at bay.

All Caleb could feel in the moment was anger, hot and heavy. Had his father done this? He was here, with her, desperately trying to keep her blood on the inside of her body. He had locked him out, again.

This was his fault.

"No." The word came out shakier than he intended. If his father had reached for him again, he might have faltered. But John let his hand drop, defeated. The paramedics wrapped up his mother's body and called the time of death.

Police pushed their way inside and approached his father.

A middle-aged cop stepped in front of Caleb. He was slightly overweight, a smattering of white in his hair and beard. "Wait, son. I have a few questions if that's alright." His eyes were kind and grey, but they also wouldn't take no for an answer.

Caleb tried anyway. "No."

The cop's eyebrows lifted, but after a pause, he nodded. "Alright, kid. I'll find you later."

***

"Caleb?"

Caleb stood and forced himself to refocus on the photo. The presence at his side was warm. He couldn't look away, though every part of him screamed to run.

"Hey ... guys?" Argo called to the group, not leaving Caleb's side.

"He told me it was a fit." Caleb forced out the words, his throat dry like sandpaper. He gripped at his arms, his nails puncturing the skin, forcing their way into the soft flesh. Anything to bring him back to the present. "I believed him. He fucking told me ..." He couldn't find his voice, fighting for air, a lump of dread blocking his airway. His father hadn't just torn people from their families – he had shattered Caleb's home long before his mother died. The truth was crushing him.

He felt the blood pool slowly against his fingers. His breaths grew sharp and fast. Every second Lucia's lifeless eyes stared back at him, the betrayal hit him again.

Argo's hand landed on his shoulder, a firm tug meant to pull him away from the screen.

"Don't touch me." Caleb's voice dropped to a dangerous growl, vibrating through the room. His glare snapped to Argo. "Did you know?" Spittle flew from his lips.

Argo lifted his hands in surrender. "No, Caleb, I swear. Not this. Not until I got here. Not until I saw ..."

"Saw what!"

"Saw your name."

Caleb stopped in his tracks. His name, listed with the others on the night of the party. Was there more here? Is it possible the those that had been tasked to watch them had samples for each new hybrid that was dropped? Something to test against their ongoing changes when the raids occurred. He was furious; he felt his back broaden and muscles pulse, his skin ready to tear into his wolf form as he struggled to get his temper under control.

The rest of their group hung back at the door. Caleb had heard them come forward even as blood throbbed in his skull. He gripped at his skin, unable to let go. The group was quiet; even Ethan hadn't dared to say a word. Caleb looked at him, the child clinging to Ava's leg. He wasn't much older than the boy when he found his mother murdered. His vision flickered, threads of red and black threatening to push him over the edge.

"Control yourself." Tilon's voice sounded distant, though he stood right beside him.

"Is this how he shifts?" Argo asked, his voice dripping with worry. The larger man was beside him again, a firm hand pressing against his back. "This is what I was trying to tell you months ago. Whatever this is—"

"Not a great time for an 'I told you so'," Winson scoffed, only to be hushed by someone next to him.

Argo tried again. "Caleb."

He leaned over the monitor, broad frame blocking everything else. Caleb forced himself to stand, inching toward the screen.

Argo waited. Patient.

The tears no longer mattered. The anger had drained from his body, leaving nothing but the final memory of his mother.

"I remember her. Lying there. I ... I believed him," Caleb stammered.

"You were a kid," Argo said.

Caleb stared at the screen. Lucia's dead eyes looked back at him accusingly.

He swallowed; his mouth felt too full, too full of spit and teeth. His body was too hot, his skin crawling like thousands of insects had gotten underneath it. Caleb wanted to rip it off. He never wanted to feel this way again. He wanted to clamber back into a crate and throw himself into the rapids, willing the damn thing to fall over the edge.

Argo gripped him. "Look at me."

Caleb couldn't.

He collapsed, folding in on himself, a panicked shell of the man he wanted to be. All of this had been happening for so fucking long, and he hadn't even known. A strangled sound escaped him. Argo moved without hesitation, lowering himself to the ground, curling his big body around Caleb's and refusing to let go.

"Give them some room," Sythe said quietly. Caleb barely heard the shuffling of feet as the group backed away.

"Mum." Caleb sobbed into the dirt, rocking against Argo. His friend pulled him closer, arms locked tight around him, steady and unyielding.

"I've got you," Argo murmured.

No one spoke. Caleb let his grief spill, the weight of his emotions held steady by his friend. Eventually, he stilled. The tears stopped, and his body slumped forward.

"You good?" Argo asked, helping Caleb into a sitting position.

"I think so."

"All those hovering out there can come back now," Argo called towards the door.

Grace and Berrum poked their heads into the room, their noses twitching before entering but keeping their distance. Ava and Ethan were next, followed by Tilon, Winson and Sythe.

Caleb forced himself to sit, fighting his desire to crawl in on himself once more. Argo moved from behind him, letting him hold his own weight. He would thank him later. Right now, he couldn't bear to look at him. Instead, he waved Ethan over. The child's eyes flicked to the blood drying on Caleb's palm.

"It's okay, love," Ava said before Ethan knelt in front of him, holding a small pot of cream.

"Here," Ethan said, offering the salve awkwardly.

Caleb reached for his hand. The boy flinched, then hesitated before offering his own smaller hand to help pull him up.

"I'm sorry, Ethan." He couldn't take his eyes off the child, knowing fresh tears shone in his own. "I'm sorry you ended up here. I'm sorry you have to see all of this."

"It's okay ..." Ethan hesitated. His lips trembled, betraying his distress. "I want to go home."

Caleb stood, pulling the boy into his side.

"We all do, kid. I promise I'll try."

"Me too," Argo said.

"And I," Ava added.

"We'll get you home," Tilon said, resolved.

Caleb turned to Argo, refusing to let go of Ethan, who clung to him, small hands gripping tightly around his middle.

"What else do you know?" Tilon asked loud enough for the group to hear.

Time is Running Out

Chapter Twenty-Four

They were still being followed; Caleb could hear their pursuer on the outskirts of the camp. Tilon had warned against a confrontation in case there were more waiting for a signal to attack. He, Winson and Sythe took it in turns to run security watching for the suspected threat. The scouts were tasked with scouring through the camp's resources – protein bars, bottled water and crates of medicines – to create meals and pack what they could into their bags. Ava hunted for clues among the storage crates and paperwork left behind while Ethan slept.

Caleb and Argo spent the afternoon working through the labels. Each had a set of initials, a species code and a year just like Lucia's. They typed each code onto the screen waiting impatiently for the new horrors to show up. Caleb had pages filled with tiny, scrawled data sets and equations that made little sense to either of them. They took turns running the numbers and calling out their findings. These samples were most definitely from their drop. Caleb recognised some of the guests from the night of the party.

Several hybrids had two or three vials lined together in the specimen fridge. Their blood or urine samples changed colour and consistency from their control to their recapture, the blood getting darker and thicker, or lighter and watery. Argo found a microscope, and they had tried to place a few drops onto a glass slide but neither of them had a clue what they were seeing.

The more they searched, the clearer the picture became. Some of the experiment files included photos and reports from the facility they found themselves in now. Most of those had the same finality as Lucia's report, ending with the word "Deceased".

"How do you think they got all this stuff in here? And the other camps?" Caleb asked as they worked.

"From what I can tell, this place is huge. It took me a over a week to make it further inland. The clickers on the coastline were relentless. They're fucking everywhere out there, man. The ocean runs as far as the eye can see, not another island in sight. If they are going for subtlety, I would say they get in by boat, maybe even a submarine if they have the money for it." Argo was making notes from the screen.

Winson and Sythe stepped into the space, offering a protein bar to each of them.

"Have you ever heard a boat?" Caleb asked.

Winson shook his head. "We've heard choppers before." He was still standoffish with Argo, making sure to keep his distance when in the same room.

"Has anyone tried to take one?" Caleb asked.

"It's normally a warning for clickers being let into the camp, or soldiers coming to take us away. It's a sign for us to prepare for a raid."

"I think they tried, once. Once was enough," Sythe offered.

"What happened?" Argo asked.

"The group who tried were killed. No questions asked. Scared everyone enough not to try it again."

"And Delia?"

"Happened before my time, man. Sorry." Sythe shrugged.

Caleb sighed, forgetting the protein bar.

One thing at a time.

*****

Tilon came into the room, checking on their progress during his watch break. Argo pulled out more rough maps he had drawn on paper bark while scouting the surrounding areas. Tilon, surprised and impressed, warmed to him once he learned Argo was a cadet. Argo had used his training well, marking the bases he'd uncovered. This was the first one with signs of life. The others he had found looked to be of similar structure but dismantled and small. Each had something left behind, the teams not quite covering their tracks.

Tilon urged them to rest and reminded them that they would need to move soon. They refused, needing to memorise and take down as much information as possible before they set off again.

"There is enough here to prove we're onto something," Caleb said when the three of them huddled around the bench.

"The threat is still out there, Caleb. Not to mention Delia, Jan and her hunters. They would have noticed by now. If she is as involved as we suspect, there is a very real chance she knows this place exists."

Caleb paused to listen. Their stalker had stopped moving but the presence was still on the periphery. "We haven't gotten through all the vials yet."

"We're going to have to make a plan on the information we have. If you won't rest, you have time for a couple more but then we move."

"What's next?" Argo turned to Tilon, asking him directly.

"We have two options. Both come with risk," Tilon replied. "We go back, confront Delia and our hybrid siblings, or—"

"We go further into the woods," Caleb confirmed.

Tilon nodded. "We try and find one of them, capture them. Ask them how they come and go, where this information is stored and sent. How much time they spend here."

"Their direct reporting lines. Their bases." Argo continued the train of thought.

"How to get back to the mainland and stop this at the source," Caleb finished, leaving out the part about wanting to find his father and pin him to the ground in wolf form.

Caleb knelt before the fridge; they were close to the last row of vials. He ran his fingers across them, looking for another set, someone who had more than one entry, before his exploration stopped. His hand caught on a single tube, the label making him stop in his tracks.

"Argo?"

"What?"

"Did you look at all of these, before we got here?"

"Not the way we are now, why?"

Caleb pulled the vial from the fridge, holding it in front of their eyes. CAL-CAN-023.

"Because it looks like this is mine." He blinked down at his label. The blood was healthy – deep red and flowing.

Argo took the container from his hand with care. Caleb let it go without a fight.

"I'll take this one," Argo said, walking back to the monitor and typing in the code.

"Hang on a sec." Caleb returned to the fridge. He was missing someone. Someone more important than himself or Argo. Someone who hadn't changed at all. He pulled out the sheet of vials, glass clinking as he shuffled through them. His fingers moved quickly. Argo called him back to the screen, but Caleb wasn't listening. He had to find Ethan. If the boy was an experiment, whatever they had spliced him with hadn't taken at all, and Caleb needed to know why.

Vials clattered to the ground, the glass thick enough to keep them intact. Ethan wasn't there. There was no "ETH" in sight. Was he part of a control group? Someone with unaltered genetics for the hybrids to be tested against? He hadn't been in the forest long before Caleb had found him. He should have been in the same drop.

"Caleb, please."

Argo had moved from the screen, and Caleb looked up to see an image of himself asleep in his luxurious home suite, his father's hands on him. A drip was tied to his bed post and attached to his arm.

Caleb let himself be led away, barely hearing the soft chime of vials being placed back in the fridge.

"What is this?"

"It's your file," Argo said, examining the screen. Caleb caught sight of the vial Argo was holding – his own, the label bolded in the centre.

ARG-CAN-023.

"And this is yours," Caleb said, focusing on the vial in Argo's hands.

Argo's voice faltered. "Yeah. I think whatever happened to you, happened to me as well. Only, I can't control it like you do."

"I don't have control over this. None of us do!"

"Maybe not, but I bet you haven't woken up to the blood of a bunch of recruits, or a dozen dead clickers in a rage you can't control."

"You almost had it. When you shifted yesterday." Caleb left out the fact that Argo had killed one of them. "You're not bad."

Argo paused, meeting his stare. He breathed deeply and faced back towards the screen. "Come on, you need to see this. I'm right here."

Reluctantly, Caleb gazed at the monitor, unable to let the point drop. He had spent enough time jealous of Argo for no good reason. "You have never let me down. Even when you should have left me to my own selfish devices."

"I'm dangerous, Caleb."

"Yes. You are." Tilon's words were clipped from the other side of the room where he was committing Argo's maps to memory, the owl watching them all on the bench. "But now that we know what you're capable of, Winson, Sythe and I have discussed ways of putting you down."

"No one is putting him down," Caleb huffed.

Tilon kept his gaze on Argo. "Keep trying to control it, and if you don't ..." His ears twitched as he bent back over the maps. "I'll do what needs to be done."

Caleb braced himself before reading his file. Colour drained from his face as an image of his younger self appeared. Argo hit the right arrow. Another photo – maybe a year before the last. Argo kept going, and with each click, Caleb grew younger and smaller. Frame by frame, he shrank, always lying in the same position. The same drip. The same injections.

He snarled when his mother appeared in one of the photos. It must have been shortly before she died. Her face was twisted in rage. He could hear her screaming in his head. Someone held her back, arms wrapped tightly around her middle, pulling her away out of the frame. The grainy quality of the image made it hard to tell who was holding her, but she was fighting them, reaching for Caleb on the bed.

Caleb's hands gripped the top of the monitor, knuckles white. He was ready to tear the piece-of-shit computer from the desk and smash it. His vial shattered against the ground. Argo caught him from behind as he struggled, blood seeping from the broken glass at his feet.

"Dammit, Caleb!" Argo sputtered, struggling to hold on.

It was too late. Caleb was shifting, his fear for his future and fury for his past overtaking him. His mother had been ripped from her life; his own had been planned, stolen from him, year by year. His father had never cared.

"That bastard," Caleb growled at the screen, straining against Argo's grip. He felt his friend's body react, his breath hot against Caleb's skin.

"We're a pack." The thought echoed through his mind like a cruel joke. It was as if his friend could reach him during the shift.

Caleb broke free. He wanted to run. Wanted to fight. He needed the fury building up inside of him to let loose, to show his father what he really caused out here away from the safety of his lab.

"Come on, Argo." Caleb's voice came out as a rough bark. "Let's see who's stronger now."

"No, Caleb! I can't control it. You and your friends will end up fucking dead. Don't you understand that?"

Caleb didn't care. He wanted to taste the adrenaline and blood, feel something other than white-hot anger.

Argo's body responded to the challenge.

Tilon clambered from the bench, putting himself between the two snarling, shifting animals. He faltered, bringing his crutch up in front of him as a weapon.

Caleb laughed, a ragged, guttural sound.

"What is happening in here?" Winson's voice cut through the growls. He stopped short when Caleb glared at him, chest heaving.

"Shit," the lizard muttered, backing away. He turned, calling out to the others. "Move! Get away from them!"

"Argo could kill him," Tilon objected from somewhere in the distance. His voice barely reached Caleb through the thick haze in his head.

"I'm doing my best not to," Argo said, struggling.

Sythe stepped into the room, pulling Tilon away. Caleb and Argo still writhed against their changing bodies. "You're not ready, boss. We agreed – you will fall in from the back if and when the time comes. But this ... this is Caleb's fight. Now go!"

Good. They should run. Caleb's shift settled and he fixated on Argo.

"Caleb, please," Argo warned, his voice strained.

He dropped Caleb's arms. His limbs stretched, growing longer, thinner, stronger.

Caleb was similarly too far gone. His clothes tore. Fur covered his body and he dropped to all fours.

Murder gleamed in his eyes.

"Tilon!" Argo shouted in a final attempt to save them all. "Run!"

"GO!" Tilon's voice rang out, followed by scrambling footsteps.

Argo collapsed, the last trace of his humanity bleeding from him.

A wolfish grin spread across Caleb's face, his animal instincts taking over.

Argo and Caleb glowered at each other, teeth bared, waiting for the other to make the first move. Caleb looked small against the giant tan-and-white beast that Argo had morphed into, his canine form carrying remnants of blood from his past fight. When they moved, they moved together, circling like vultures, an animalistic understanding of what was about to happen playing subconsciously in their minds. Argo dropped to his haunches, muscles straining for release seconds before he pounced. Caleb's smaller grey form darted to the side, his size affording more agility than the bigger creature. Using speed to his advantage, the smaller wolf lashed out as his friend's white paws hit the ground. Caleb leapt on Argo's back, his claws punching into his flesh, growling and snapping.

Teeth met fur. A howl shot skyward, raw and furious. Caleb tasted blood. The metallic tang hit his throat like fire, stopping him in his tracks. Argo roared as he bucked, throwing Caleb off. The force sent him skidding into the side of the building with a clang.

Fuck.

"I warned you." Argo's distorted voice rasped through Caleb's skull.

He can hear me? Caleb thought.

"You ... shouldn't ... have ... pushed," Argo snarled, turning his body to face him head on. Caleb saw the blood dripping from the bigger wolf's neck before he ran for him, jaws open.

Caleb tried to dodge the large beast, but Argo anticipated the move, jerking his head to snap at him as he jumped. Caleb howled, Argo's teeth ripping at his fur, missing his skin.

"Argo, shit. It's me. I didn't think about what I was doing."

"You n-never ... do." Argo's giant paws hit the ground deliberately as he stalked his friend.

Caleb moved backwards, trying to pull the larger wolf away from the rest of the group. He would have to rely on his speed and size to get through this fight.

Tilon's voice broke his concentration. "Get back," he yelled. Both hybrids turned to see Ethan shaking at their leader's side. Caleb hadn't pulled the bigger wolf far enough away yet.

"Look at me! You don't want them. I challenged you. Not them."

The group watched from the far end of the camp. Argo's eyes homed in on the boy.

He turned, faster than Caleb thought possible.

"NO!" Caleb screamed in his mind. *"Argo! This is my fight! You don't want him!"*

Tilon yanked Ethan behind him, standing firm against the charging wolf, spear in hand ready to attack. Argo was too far gone. Caleb felt his hunger for blood, his anger and jealousy at the boy who hadn't been changed.

"Argo. Stop!"

This time, there were no scientists working under his father's evil guise; there were no genetically enhanced clickers to focus on. There were only his friends, and he had pushed Argo away the second he got overwhelmed. Just like he always did. Except this time, it wasn't a boxing ring or a playground fight. He had put his friends' lives on the line for his own selfish needs. And Argo was headed straight for the only good thing to come from these fucking woods.

What have I done?

Argo's paws pounded across the ground, gaining on the group. Sythe and Winson gripped their spears, stepping in front of Tilon who urged the boy further back with Ava and the scouts. Ethan wasn't moving.

No, he thought again, the vision of his mother flashing in his mind.

Ethan would not be a part of this. He refused. The child wasn't even in the systems they had searched. There was no reason for him to suffer.

Caleb's body surged forward, his feet hitting the ground with force, each leap closing the distance between them within seconds. Ethan's eyes were wide, terror written across his face as his body failed to move. The group stood braced, the three warriors holding their weapons at the ready. Caleb wouldn't let it get to that point.

He had started this.

"Argo! Stop!"

"You did this to me!" Argo growled, turning to snap toward Caleb, his teeth flashing before he changed direction and jumped towards him.

Their bodies collided. Caleb yowled, winded from the contact.

"Argo, please." He sounded pathetic and he knew it.

Argo paused, glaring at him, chest heaving.

"The boy shouldn't be here."

He turned back, leaning down on his haunches, the power building momentum in an instant.

Caleb ran forward, desperate to catch Argo before leapt.

"You will not touch him!" Caleb commanded, gnashing his jaws. He pushed the order out with every fibre of his being, forcing his will into Argo's mind. The larger wolf stopped short, a snarl rumbling up his throat as they fell apart.

"He ... shouldn't ... be here!" Argo growled, refocusing on the boy.

The larger wolf leapt again, this time his body twisting in the air, turning back towards his friends. Caleb launched to intercept the strike. He clamped his jaws around Argo's ankle, teeth sinking into muscle. Argo crashed to the ground with a thud, sending leaves flying as they skidded closer to the others. He whined, struggling to stand, his wound bleeding.

"You're lucky I didn't hit the vein, you colossal twat," Caleb thought, pushing the words into Argo's mind. He panted, standing over the fallen hybrid, who couldn't seem to move on the injured leg. *"Stay down."*

He looked into Argo's eyes, watching for a sign of movement. The wolf avoided the gaze, letting his body fall back into the dirt.

"I can't ... control it." The sorrow of the words hit Caleb like a brick.

His throat swelled, a force of air pushing through his vocal cords only to be huffed out in an exasperated breath. He stole a glance at his pack, Sythe and Winson still at the ready with their spears. He looked back down at Argo's wolf form, tucking his snout under his friend's head, nuzzling into his bloody fur.

"You just did."

Argo whined. A cry that broke his heart.

Caleb padded towards Ethan on all fours, something he wasn't sure he would ever get used to. The kid had reminded him what he was fighting for. He vowed to never let his anger take control again. Ava tensed beside Ethan, watching Caleb warily.

"It's alright," Caleb thought, unsure if his telepathy extended beyond Argo or if it only worked on those who were able to shift.

Ava's hand reached for Sythe's spear, which the hybrid gave up reluctantly.

"He won't hurt me. He said it's alright," Ethan said bravely, holding one foot behind him just in case he needed to run.

Caleb's head tilted despite himself. *"You can hear me?"*

"Yeah. I can hear you." The boy took two small steps towards him, nodding. Uneasy glances passed between the others.

"Um. What's he saying?" Winson asked, his voice high with disbelief.

Caleb sat back on his haunches, letting the kid decide the next move. Ethan walked towards him and extended a hand. Slowly, his fingers brushed through the dirty but soft fur on Caleb's head.

Caleb's breath hitched at the touch. Warmth spread through him, sinking deep into his skin. He stiffened, and Ethan ripped his hand back.

"Come back, sorry. It's okay, just weird to be pet, is all." Caleb let out a coughing laugh.

Ethan hesitated, then reached out again, scratching behind Caleb's ear.

Good lord, that felt good.

Caleb's leg twitched, lifting slightly, twisting to replicate the boy's scratching motion.

Laughter broke out around them.

He was no better than a damn dog.

Ethan's giggles wormed their way into his heart, and Caleb nuzzled into the boy's hand, hoping for another scratch.

Another whine from Argo drew Caleb's attention. His friend had given up on his endeavour to stand. His body started to shift back.

Caleb wanted to go to him, to offer reassurance, but he couldn't bring himself to leave Ethan's side.

"Why can't you change?" Ethan asked innocently.

Caleb's ears twitched as a sudden roar boomed across the sky. In the heat of the fight, he'd stopped listening for their pursuers, let alone Jan. He had heard nothing but his own idiot need for blood during the fight. He had missed the advancing movement of Delia's hunters. They didn't have a day; they didn't have minutes. Jan's giant form thundered through the trees.

Fight or Flight

Chapter Twenty-Five

Ava acted quickly, Sythe and Winson still watching Argo like a hawk. She threw herself towards the new threat, the spear in her hands shaking with every step. Caleb saw Jan; his heart thudded in his chest as he placed himself in front of the boy. Argo was weak and Tilon was still injured. His muscles loosened, too fatigued from the fight to keep up his shift. He wouldn't let it happen – he was stronger in wolf form.

Fear and anger, he thought, letting the memories of his previous battle with Jan fill him with terror. The anger had been simmering in him since he'd arrived. Now he needed to find the balance. Caleb braced, the shift settling back into the beast he needed to be. He was prepared to protect who he could. They had left the safety of their camp because of him, and he wouldn't let them pay the price. Not now.

Jan crashed through the trees, raising his snout to the sky, the call erupting from his jaw. It sounded like he was alerting others close by rather than a call of rage. Caleb's ears raised to catch the response. Wind rustled through the trees, leaves moving with the force of bodies coming from every direction.

"We're surrounded." He pushed the thought toward Ethan, urging him to voice the warning.

"Argo, get up!" Caleb had no idea if his command would reach him. Argo lay sprawled, too injured to fight. His body was dirtied and bloodied again. *"Heal faster."*

Jan raised a paw, sunlight glaring off the black tips of his claws, which looked ready to rip through whatever they came down upon. The bear struck with brutal speed, his blow aimed at Ava. She screamed; the cry shattered all hope they would make it through this attack. Grey flesh tore, thick layers of skin splitting open, causing Ava to gasp. Blood pooled at the wound, dripping down her body, coagulating as it met the air. To Caleb's surprise, she laughed. Gripping the shaft of her spear, she struggled to stand, legs trembling under the weight of her injuries. He had never seen anyone look so determined fight. Hatred burned in her eyes.

"I'm thick-skinned, Jan, or had you forgotten?"

The ground shook as Jan dropped to all fours, the mutant bear's eyes fixed on her. His lips curled to show a row of teeth that could rip her apart in an instant. Caleb caught a flash of red through the bear's eyes before they settled into their natural black.

"Argo, now would be good. This bastard could turn feral any second."

His friend groaned in response, his leg crusting over as the blood dried. Caleb wished like hell his own body would heal the same way because he was about to do something really, really dumb.

Pushing off the ground, he sprinted towards the massive, mutated bear. Winson and Sythe flanked him, their movements in sync. Ava had stepped back out of Jan's way after his heavy swipe.

Think fast. Brute force wouldn't work. Jan was too big.

"Round him up." Argo's voice was faint in Caleb's mind. He stole a glance at his friend, who was struggling to shift. He hoped Argo would have control. They would need him, but what was the cost?

More movement pattered through the trees. They would be physically surrounded in seconds. He could smell them now – Delia's hunters. He hadn't met them as a group before, had only ever seen them training close to Delia's quarters. The tall, powerful creatures moved with effortless grace, their bodies creating a wall as they surrounded them.

Caleb sprinted around Jan, forcing the bear's head to whip back and forth, trying to track him. Jan growled, swiping frantically at Winson and Sythe as they jabbed at him with their spears. The sharp tips barely scratched his weathered fur.

"Enough."

All heads turned.

Delia stepped into the commotion.

Jan immediately retracted his claws and stood to attention. The snarl vanished from his lips.

Good pet, Caleb thought mockingly, his breath heavy.

"I don't like the cat's hold on him." Argo's thought played in his head. He breathing was evening out but he still didn't have the energy to stand.

Delia reached out, her fingers closing around Caleb's jaw. He fought the urge to snap at her.

"Be careful, wolf." Her voice dripped with condescension. "Stay too long as a pup, and you might never change back."

A low rumble made its way up his throat, ready to let her know just what he thought of her advice. The hunters pressed inward, at least a dozen of them, their presence threatening to finish what Jan had started on Delia's behalf. Caleb sniffed, picking up on their unfamiliar scent masked beneath musty earth from the days trekking through the forest growth.

Caleb's back arched involuntarily, his body seeming to react to Delia's presence. He tried to focus and stop his muscles shifting back. He was tired and he didn't know how much longer he could hold it. *Just a little more.* His skin tightened and expanded before settling back into place. The effort caused him to whine pathetically. Delia's hand still held the base of his mouth in a tight grip.

"Why do you keep us here!" he screamed internally.

"Because it's safer for us."

"Did you just—"

"Yes, Caleb. I have been at this a lot longer than you. Now, shift." The weight of her hand was heavy on his fur. He reacted to the command.

Can she really—

He didn't have time to question it. A yelp escaped him as muscle and bone shrank and shifted under his skin. It felt like fire and ice were fighting for a place in his veins; he was paralysed by the pain of his rapidly changing body. It was over as fast as it had begun, leaving him panting against the dust.

"What the fuck was that?" he said breathily. Ava ran to his side, her hands roaming his body with a mother's touch, her own skin having pulled itself back together in rapid time.

"You're alright," she offered, finally resting her hand on his back.

"C ... ant," he panted, the horror of being made to shift scaring him more than anything over the last few weeks.

"Aye, ye can." Ava's hand was warm, kind.

"You betrayed us!" Tilon yelled, followed by the clash of spears pushing their wounded leader back.

"You're the reason we're being taken!" Winson screamed toward the group. Another crash, followed by a struggle. Caleb tried to concentrate on the sound of Winson's slippery body fighting for freedom against the hunters' arms.

"I suggest you all settle down," Delia said calmly, turning her gaze back to Caleb and Ava. "You're outnumbered and outskilled here."

Ava pressed against Caleb's body, wordlessly pulling his attention back to her. He was shaking, fighting tears, before noticing the deep red stain on her side.

"You're still bleeding," he said.

"I'll be alright. I heal faster than your friend over there."

"How did she do that?"

"Can we get on with it, Delia?" one of the hunters asked, their voice like smoke, cutting off almost as soon as it began, as if it were never there to begin with.

"And he wanted to lead them?" another of the armed hybrids scoffed. "He hasn't a damn clue what he's up against."

"Easy now," Ava said, helping Caleb sit upright, handing him yet another set of clothing.

Tilon emerged through the wall of hunters, Winson and Sythe doing their best to hold him upright. His wound had reopened; clear plasma and blood mottled the fur at his side.

He must have taken another hit when he tried to break through.

With a grunt, Tilon leant against his spear, pushing the other two away from him.

"Where are Ethan and the scouts?" Caleb coughed.

"They're okay. Caught. But safe for now."

Caleb nodded, shrugging Ava off, and stood on wobbly legs. He pulled air into his lungs, tasting the blood in the breeze. His eyes met Delia's as he took a step towards her.

Her hunters followed his movements with hands on their weapons. Jan looked like he would kill Caleb then and there.

"Let him come," Delia said, standing straight and unmoving. Her long black tail swished, betraying her irritation. Her upper lip curled into a smirk, exposing thin, pointed teeth.

"Enough now." She caught his eye, watching his movements carefully. "Give it up. This isn't a game for you anymore. It never was. Your father is playing with real people, real lives. And there is nothing for us wherever you think you're going."

"You said we had a choice."

"You still don't get it, do you? This is the best option for you. This island is full of dangers, and outside of it, there are more. Your father put you in here … with us, or don't you remember that? I cannot protect you if you continue these foolish attempts at escape."

"You are denying these people their freedom," he huffed back.

"There is no freedom, Caleb." Her jaw tightened. "This has been happening long before you started giving a damn. I'm the one who's protected these people. Not you. Don't you dare think you are the protector of this pack. The ferals, the rebellions – no one has come for us. Not in the way you want them to.

"And why? We are damaged goods. You're here now only because your father finally decided to see what his good-for-nothing son could do. Your arrogance has poisoned this pack and now some of you want to leave again." She sighed. "I have tried, Caleb. And I have lost. Now I do what I can to offer a peaceful life to those who want it."

"Doesn't seem all that peaceful," Winson scoffed, his arm being held by one of the hunters.

Delia stood her ground as Caleb leaned down into her face. The hunters around her tensed; she held a hand out, stopping their advance. Jan was close by, but Caleb wasn't ready to risk another fight with the bear.

"Tell them what you're hiding, Delia." His voice was cold, his gaze locked on hers. "It's time to tell them."

She bristled, the fur along her spine standing on end. "You have no idea what you are—"

"Enough of the lies, cat!" Caleb yelled.

She looked at him defiantly, narrowing her eyes.

"They need to hear everything you've been keeping from them. Everything you've been too chickenshit to admit since the moment I got here."

"Back up, boy."

Caleb caught two of the hunters press forward in his peripheral vision.

"I can handle the wolf," she hissed, her spittle landing on his face.

"You sneak off for days at a time; you hold council with hybrids we barely ever see. You use Jan as your spy – he's your eyes, right? You've got the biggest threat in here wrapped around your little fucked-up finger. He can't talk; he can't tell us what's really going on," Caleb spat in accusation. "There is more to you than people know. Those of us here have figured that out. You talk about poisoning the pack, but you've taken away their hope."

His team had gone silent, the tension between the groups palpable. Delia stood rigid, unreadable. She looked like she was about to bite back, opening her mouth to respond.

Then the silence was broken by a low, rhythmic whirring.

Caleb's head snapped up. The others heard it too.

A chopper?

They all turned as one, scanning the sky. The sound drew closer, the thwack of the blades pounding in time with Caleb's heartbeat. People. People were coming. If he could get to them, he could get to the vehicle. They could fly out, get help. *How hard can it be to fly?* Maybe they could overpower the pilot, force them to fly to the mainland.

He took off, spinning on his heel, momentarily forgetting he was human and unable to turn with the grace of his canine body.

"No!" Ava and Delia called out together. Their voices barely registered over the pounding in his skull.

He paused, torn between instinct and reason.

This was their ticket out.

He had to take the risk. For Ethan. For the future.

The scouts had returned through the trees, their small frames heaving with the effort of catching their breath. "Raid!" they yelled. The rapid whirr of the blades intensified, the trees whipping around them in the wind. Caleb groaned as dirt and rocks battered him from all directions before the air stilled and the blades slowed. It wasn't far ahead; he could still make a break for it.

"How can there be a raid? We are days away from camp!" Sythe questioned, unable to hide his panic.

"They are here for us," Delia said, oddly calm.

"Do we fight?" Argo was standing now. He'd managed to cover himself with his ripped shorts, barely. His scarred, now heavily furred chest looked broad and menacing as he crossed his arms.

"Who are you?" Delia asked.

"Later, puss-in-boots. Do. We. Fight?" Argo's usually playful tone had dropped.

Delia's small ears twitched back against her head. The whirring was closer, the wind slowing as the helicopter prepared for landing.

"Yeah, Argo. We fight." Caleb nodded at the bigger man. "Aim for the pilot. Capture, not kill. It's time we get out of here."

***

Caleb barely heard the shouts of protest from Delia as he and Argo ran in the direction of the machine. His ears twitched, picking up on the location of the new arrivals. Two voices were muffled by the whirring of blades as it descended. One was deeper, vaguely familiar, the other more feminine and distorted. *The pilot*, Caleb thought. He caught the scent of mottled fur and dirt.

Shit.

"Clickers," Caleb warned.

"If I shift, I can kill them before you even get there," Argo panted, keeping pace.

"If you shift, you might kill everything, including me and whoever's with them."

"I'm trying, man."

"We can't risk it," Caleb said, bursting through the trees into harsh sunlight. He gasped at the brightness, momentarily blinded after their time shielded by a darkened canopy.

"What the—" Argo raised an arm to shield his face.

"Hello, boys."

"You!" Caleb snarled, making to run at the Shepherd. Argo's grip held him back.

"I know you!" Argo said, incredulous.

"You both do, in one way or another."

"Who is this guy?" Caleb spat.

"Oh, just a friend of your father's, son. Good to see you, Argo."

Caleb struggled against Argo. "I'll kill my father the second I get my hands on him."

"Such a temper." The man's voice lifted in amusement, white teeth flashing a Cheshire-cat grin. "You wouldn't want me to let Kajia off her leash, now, would you?" The two clickers flanking him sat at attention, waiting for his command.

"Let me rip him apart." Caleb tried to break free again. He was sick of being held back all the time. He wanted to go home, and he wanted to go now. Argo's grip remained firm. Caleb's ear picked up on the rest of the group moving toward them.

The Shepherd, two clickers and a pilot. Between his party and Delia's hunters, they could overpower them easily. Let Delia show her true colours one way or the other.

"Good boy," the man said to Argo, whose knuckles had gone white from holding Caleb in place.

"He's dangerous," Argo muttered. "Not to mention the fucking clickers."

"Clickers?" The man laughed. "Suppose that's as good a name as any. I think of them more like hybrid bounty hunters. They track you down, bring you back. Dead or alive, depends on the day."

The creatures beside him growled in unison. Caleb felt Argo bristle.

"Feeling's mutual," Argo scoffed. "I've killed plenty of them."

"Yes, interesting. You're both ... interesting cases. In fact, you're why I'm here. This time, anyway. I hear you're causing some trouble."

"What are you talking about?" Caleb still fought against Argo's grip.

Delia had made her way through the trees, her movements graceful, making it look as if she were gliding through the space rather than walking. Her hunters followed in slow pursuit while the rest of his own party were surrounded in the middle of their march.

The Shepherd ignored Caleb's question and turned to Delia. "Ahh, there she is! My girl. How's that beautiful purr, my love?"

Caleb stumbled back as the newcomer shoved him aside with surprising strength, pushing him backwards into Argo's chest.

"You ... bitch!?" Caleb tore free from Argo's grasp. "You're STILL working with them!"

How dare she talk to him about his father then waltz up to this guy with literal monsters on a fucking leash? Rage burned through him. He wanted to scream.

She *had* been a part of this all along.

"I wouldn't get any closer if I were you," the Shepherd teased. His clickers were standing at his side, teeth bared.

"Caleb, please." Delia's words wavered beneath a desperate attempt to smile at the intruding force.

He held his fists tight, nails digging into the palms of his hands. He took several sharp and uneven breaths. She eyed him cautiously, placing a small, clawed hand on his chest. His body broadened, muscles pulling taut, expanding beneath his skin. His rage fuelled his desire to change, needing to be more powerful than the threat in front of him. He could give in, let it take over, rip her throat out—

No.

He was better than that. He forced himself to breathe. The tension he was holding eased slightly.

"Don't touch me," he spat.

"Thank you," she said before pushing him out of her way to close the gap between herself and their new guest.

"Sweet Delia." The man opened his arms as if to embrace her.

Caleb watched her steps slow, hesitation creeping into her movements. The man wrapped his arms around her petite frame, holding her close. A rough squeeze nearly pulled her off balance.

"See?" he chided, condescension thick in his tone. "We can all be friends now, can't we?"

The clickers grumbled, shifting uneasily.

"Let's take a look, shall we, pet?"

Delia winced, tilting her head to expose the back of her neck. The Shepherd freed his hand from one of the leashes, trusting the clickers to stay still. Caleb hoped their training was enough.

A small beep sounded. A flash of red lit up Delia's skin.

"Hmm, no new changes. Good," he said. Caleb watched Delia shudder, unmoving as the Shepherd checked the screen of his device. A nod of approval followed as the scanner was placed back into his coat. "Turn around. Hold out your arm."

Delia did so obediently, looking small against his big frame. Worry flickered in her eyes. She stared at the ground and winced as the needle plunged into her vein, a long pull of blood being drawn to then be squirted unceremoniously back into a test tube, labelled and pocketed. Her soldiers turned away from the scene, watching Caleb's friends in the middle of their circle. They rolled up their sleeves, like they were next.

"What the fuck," Argo whispered under his breath.

Caleb fought with the need to take over, to run towards the helicopter sitting so close. He could almost taste freedom. There was only one pilot who hadn't moved since turning off the machine. He could make a break for it.

An image of Lilah flashed through his mind. The last time one of them tried to take on anything by themselves, they had been killed.

Caleb doubted Argo would last long in a fight without turning, which may be the worst thing that could happen to them all. Tilon didn't look like he would be able to stand much longer, let alone swing a spear. He would have to bide his time. Take it all in, get them back to the main camp, use what they knew to convince others to join their cause. To build their own force to fight back. They just had to make sure they made it out of here alive first.

Delia's hunters broke formation one at a time, lining up to have their own necks scanned while the others held his friends.

"Stay there, pet, we're not done," the Shepherd said to Delia while checking the others.

Caleb braced. One of the hunters held Ethan. The boy looked tiny against the blackened skin of the beast behind him. His wide eyes stayed frozen on the clickers, fear rooting him in place.

Fuck. This.

"Argo?" Caleb called out, testing his telepathic abilities again. *"Come on, man. I can't do this alone. Not against so many of them."* His friend didn't respond.

Dammit. "Ethan?"

Nothing.

I swear, if this guy goes to stick a needle in the kid, I'll make a break for it. Clickers be damned.

"Oh yes, more fur, yet your humanity still seems intact." The Shepherd took his large thumb and placed the tip against his tongue before holding it to the new wound.

"What are you doing?" Caleb's voice came out weaker than he wanted. His stomach churned.

"Patience, boy – you're next."

"Fuck you." Caleb spat.

"Stop, Caleb," Argo said weakly.

The man laughed, the sound rolling from his belly. "I'm glad he gave you a playmate in here. You two are very interesting indeed."

"Who the fuck are you? Delia?" Caleb's patience snapped, his words sharp with accusation.

Delia stood rigid in the man's grasp, his hand pressing against the back of her neck. She cringed, jaw taut, fists clenched. The hair along her spine bristled and her tail flicked. He was drawing it out, taking his time, a smile on his lips.

The clickers sat, watching the group. Their leashes had fallen to the ground.

"Thank you, pet," the intruder said, moving away from her. She drew her hand to the back of her neck, rubbing where he had touched her.

"Tell me, how are they?" Delia said, her authority seeping back into her voice. "I've kept my side of the deal as always, Shepherd. Now, tell me."

Delia had taken a step towards him, seemingly unfazed by the clickers snarling at his side. She moved past the beasts, her hands reaching out to tug on the intruder's jacket. Her eyes had grown wide, looking up him with desperate hope.

Tilon, Sythe and Winson pressed forward, moving closer to the conversations. The hunters eyeing them with disdain. Ava followed their lead, pulling Ethan then the scouts up beside her. Regardless of the lingering threat, Caleb was thankful to have them close again.

"What the hell is happening?" Caleb asked, eyeing Kajia.

"I don't know," Argo said flatly, "but it looks like we underestimated how deeply Delia was involved in all this."

"The microchip?"

Tilon nodded, Sythe having shushed them from behind.

The Shepherd turned to look at Delia, the gleam in his eye predatory. She was obviously desperate; the hold he had over her laced the air with tension.

"They are fine, pet. For the most part. Looked after as promised, or didn't you trust us?"

Caleb's eyes screwed up, his brow furrowing as he took in what was happening.

"And Elia? She ...?"

"She made it through. Yes."

"Fredrick?"

"Not so fortunate, I'm afraid. The last raid was unsuccessful, you see. No new specimens to examine. Tut, tut. You must do better. Even if you do have John's pet causing havoc."

Caleb stiffened at the mention of his father.

"What did you do to him?" Delia shrieked.

The Shepherd held her in place, his fingers digging into her.

"Just a little accident, my love. He'll be fine, as long as you meet your next quota."

"When?"

"Now, now. Where is the fun in that?"

This is sick.

Delia was a pawn, being played like the rest of them. Only this time, they had her children. His mind flashed to the picture on the wall of her office. They must have been teenagers by now. Did she mention their names? If they were holding them hostage for compliance ...

Damn, he thought, the need to hate her conflicting with sympathy and sorrow. His mother had tried to save him too. He remembers the image of her being pulled back out of the frame while his father supposedly read him to sleep.

"You bastard!" Delia shrieked. "You promised you would keep them safe; you said if I helped you, they would be left alone to live their lives without this ... this bullshit! Those were the terms!"

The man scoffed and stepped closer, gripping her jaw. His knuckles whitened as he applied pressure. "The terms were compliance, dear. And yet – you keep fighting us."

"There are other groups out here! Why do you keep coming for mine?"

"Oh, we have other allies, pet, don't you worry. You just happen to be my favourite. Besides, you have the boy." The Shepherd looked up, meeting Caleb's eyes with a wicked smile. "I am sure your son will make a full recovery in time," he said, his attention back on Delia, letting her go. Wetness darkened the fur around her eyes. "Must be off. A new shipment will arrive in the coming weeks. Half of the last one turned up dead – bad formula. Not quite right. We needed to try again. Do better, dear. Don't fail me again, or who knows ... Fredrick may not be so lucky."

Caleb couldn't stand still. Who was to say the other hybrids would even believe him when he begged for them to join him? Delia had them under her rule for so long; they trusted her and it was clear she would go to any lengths to get information about her family. How could he compete?

"Wait! Where are you going?" He yanked free from Argo's grip and ran toward the man, only to be met by his snapping clickers.

"Heel!" the Shepherd's voice boomed. The two beasts at his side responded immediately, sitting back on their long limbs like well-trained dogs.

"I suggest that you don't do that again. They don't always listen." The man let his gaze drag over Caleb's body, slow and deliberate, as if committing him to memory. Caleb fought the urge to recoil. "I'll let your father know you live; he will be ever so pleased. You too, boy." He nodded towards Argo. The man turned, no longer interested in their entourage, the blades of the machine slowly starting to turn as the engine engaged. "Delia, always a pleasure."

Shouts erupted from the hunters. Caleb turned to see Sythe charging past him, spear in hand, advancing on the Shepherd.

"Sythe, don't!" Delia screamed in protest, but the brave, stupid hybrid didn't stop. His feet pounded along the ground, gaining distance by the second. Winson dashed around the opposite side. The colour drained from Caleb's face. *Shit.* It hadn't even occurred to him that someone else might make the suicidal run for the helicopter. It was always going to be him making the bold move. Sythe was running straight for it. Caleb let his adrenaline seep into his muscles, feeling himself broaden.

"We need more allies, Caleb. We can't," Argo said next to him.

"What the hell are you talking about? We could overpower them." A spear prodded his back, a warning from one of the hunters.

"Best if you don't make more of a scene." Her voice was soft and haunting.

"Fuck this." Caleb bristled, but Tilon's paw clamped onto him and Argo gripped his other arm.

"Stop." Tilon panted, leaning on him once he had stopped in his tracks.

"We'll get the chopper!" Winson shouted over the roaring wind as the helicopter blades picked up speed.

Dread seeped into Caleb's bones. His friend was running straight into danger, and he couldn't move. His feet refused to obey.

"We'll never make it," Argo whispered. "This is insane," he cried, ripping himself free of his friends' grasp. "They will die out there alone."

"You'll die now if you chase after them, foolish dog." Another spear jabbed him in the back. He stopped shifting, defeated, settling back into his skin.

"I'm sorry. Caleb, Argo and the child need to stay. It's better for us all," Delia said, stepping towards them. Ava, Grace and Berrum were pushed further into the circle of hunters holding Ethan between them.

"What's happening?" Ethan asked shakily.

"Stupidity and death," Delia said sadly, reaching out for the child.

The owl flew overhead, crying out above Winson as he and Sythe ran toward the whirring blades, the Shepherd not far in front.

The owl is going to watch them die; we all are.

"How could you let this happen!" Caleb turned on Delia, cut off by Jan's bestial roar.

The Shepherd hesitated at the noise.

Just long enough for Sythe to strike.

He lunged, his spear missing by a hairsbreadth. The Shepherd grinned, teeth flashing in amusement as he released the leads to his beasts.

Sythe's screams filled the air, his agony underscored by the deep, reverberating laughter of the Shepherd. Caleb winced, his body leaden as the clickers ripped Sythe apart.

A metallic tang permeated Caleb's nose. Deep gashes in Sythe's flesh turned into red rivers across the forest floor, his coloured fur now stained with his own entrails. His eyes glazed over as he tried one final thrust at the animals. The tip caught one in their underbelly. The clicker snarled, swiping the offending spear away before its sharpened fangs clenched down on its prey, a sickening crunch sounding as teeth met bone. Sythe stilled. The clickers fed, momentarily forgetting the rest of the group.

Winson had made it to the aircraft, the blades continuing to increase in speed. Argo's hold on Caleb changed, his hands no longer restrictive but offering comfort, pulling him towards his chest to watch the fight unfolding. The hunters' eyes and spears moved with them.

"Relax. You've got us," Argo said, pushing the spear away from his back.

Caleb's eyes grew wide, unable to look away from Winson. His ear twitched as he picked up more and more of the conversation taking place. He saw the scaled outline of the lizard hybrid launching upwards towards the open door and gasped as a gun was pointed directly at him.

"No, Winson," Caleb whispered under his breath.

"Prepare to move," Delia ordered one of the hunters.

"No," Ava said defiantly.

"Excuse me?"

"You watch. Watch as two of the people you swore to protect die because you were unable to lead us all to safety." Ava's voice was laden with steel. Her eyes bored into Delia.

"You don't understand—"

"You better feckin' believe I do, lassie. You're not the only one with children back home. Only, I had to let mine go. And I hope they are okay, I really do. But you let hundreds of us be slaughtered for the chance of one more look. So, you watch. And then you tell me it's worth it."

Caleb witnessed the fight fall out of Delia, the feline hybrid drawing her hand downward, a silent command to the hunters to drop their weapons.

"Ava … I didn't—"

"Hush." Caleb strained his ears, desperately searching for Winson's voice amongst the whir, his gaze fixed on the pilot of the craft. The weapon shook in their hand.

"She doesn't want to shoot him," Caleb said as he caught Winson's pleading, asking the pilot to take them with her, leave the Shepherd.

"Please, we have a child here," Winson begged.

"Let me go," Caleb urged, bouncing on the balls of his feet, muscles bunching underneath his skin.

"You will be killed. Just like Sythe," Delia called, eyeing Argo's movements.

"I can't," the pilot whispered, voice trembling as much as the gun in their grip.

They fired.

The shot rang out, deafening. The bullet missed, vanishing into the trees, and the pilot winced at the recoil, her eyes wide with shock. Winson mirrored the expression, looking like he didn't believe he was still alive.

He regained his posture, gripping the side of the helicopter and reaching in to grab the pilot. A yelp escaped Winson's lips as his body was gripped roughly from behind.

"I'm going," Caleb said. "You coming?" he asked Argo.

"Caleb ... I need you safe," Delia tried.

"Then stop us. Or prove you're on our side. Get your hunters to watch out for the fucking clickers. I'm going in."

Caleb's steps were determined and cautious. The hunters parted, allowing him to leave the circle. This fight may have been over, but they didn't have to lose anyone else in the process. The Shepherd and his helicopter would be back; another raid would happen and next time, Caleb vowed they would be ready.

Winson's body flew through the air as the Shepherd flung him roughly to the ground. The man who had caused them so much grief clambered on, screaming something unintelligible at the pilot. Caleb could only assume it was a command to fly. Nausea crept up his throat. There was no sign of the clickers.

Seconds ago, they had devoured one of his only allies. How long until it was his turn?

Caleb heard their growls. Attempting to scramble upright, he'd forgone his spear for speed, hoping he would be able to shift in time to fight. But there was no way he could take them alone.

"Inside, now!" The creatures slunk past the Shepherd, their mouths still bloodied. Winson was retreating, the hybrid's breathing heavy as he was pushed back by the blades of the helicopter.

Wind whipped against Caleb's skin as he reached for Winson. The lizard hybrid found his arms and gripped for dear life for a sweet, short second before he turned to find what remained of Sythe.

"Winson," Ava said gently.

"Leave him," Caleb said, ushering her back. "Just for a minute."

Winson's body trembled with heaving sobs as he knelt over his fallen friend.

Pick a Side

Chapter Twenty-Six

Winson rounded on the group, his tail whipping out behind him before placing himself on all fours and scuttling with incredible speed towards them. The owl called out, following his charge. His lizard body slithered up to Delia, his fury radiating outward as he hissed down into her face.

"You. Did. Thisssss." His tongue flicked out at the final word. Three of Delia's hunters broke formation to move behind their leader. Spear tips pointed at Winson's throat.

"Stand down," Tilon said, taking charge. "All of you." His disciplined demeanour fought its way through a simmering anger that radiated off the tiger hybrid. Delia nodded.

"What do we do now?" Berrum asked, watching the helicopter get further away.

"Tie her up?" Grace suggested. Jan growled, towering above them, reaching his paw down to push Winson away from Delia.

"You've been helping her this whole time and you're seconds away from annihilating us all. Bugger off," Winson snapped.

"Tie her up," Caleb confirmed. "We won't hurt her, but she doesn't deserve to be free." He put himself between the bear and Winson.

"Like hell," one of the hunters said, turning her spear towards Caleb.

Delia was looking mournfully at Sythe's body, her eyes flashing towards Ava before shaking her head and holding her hands out. "It's okay."

Tilon placed Delia's hands behind her back, tying them together with foraged vines. Her hunters seethed and Jan growled, leaning on all fours, looking like he was ready to charge.

Caleb needed a second to think.

Delia obviously had a reason to buy into his father's experiments. He didn't know what he would do if he were in her position. She really did believe she was doing the best she could, for all parties. She had barely said a word since Sythe had died, since the Shepherd had gotten away. He didn't trust her and her crew didn't trust them, the groups keeping a safe distance from one another at the command of their leaders. Something in her had changed; Caleb only hoped it would be enough.

Tilon grunted and ordered them forward. The dark rings under his eyes made him look tired and gaunt. His brow furrowed as he led them back to the campground. Generators hummed, flooding the space with a bright, unnatural light.

Caleb and Ethan lit a fire, its glow lighting up their faces as the sun set. He was worried about the boy. He was as mute as Delia after witnessing a second member of their camp torn apart in front of his eyes. He hadn't let go of Caleb since they started the trek back.

"Here," Caleb said, holding Ethan. The kid clung to him, his nails scraping as he gripped at Caleb's shirt. "It's okay. We've got you." Argo lifted his arm in silent invitation. Ethan hesitated and his eyes flickered to Caleb, who gave him nod, hoping to convey that it was safe to trust the bigger man. Ethan relaxed against Argo's side. They sat in silence, staring into the flames. Caleb thought about Sythe, about how not long ago he had taught him the ways of the hybrids.

Caleb held Ethan's hand as Tilon tied Delia to the trunk of a tree. Jan watched close by, ever watchful.

"Do you think Tilon is going to speak or just stare at her?" Argo asked, poking Caleb in the ribs.

"Ow, you dick," Caleb cussed.

"Dick is a bad word," Ethan chimed in.

Argo snorted. "Wise kid. You're right. I used to get in trouble for saying it too." He winked. Caleb swore his old friend was going to stick his tongue out at him before Ethan cut him off.

"Mum always told me not to say bad things."

"He's right, ye know," Ava said, plonking herself down next to the boy, handing him one of the food bars.

They looked on as Tilon continued to stare at Delia, the smaller feline doing her best to match his gaze. The big cat now paced in front of her; it felt like an eternity had passed without words between the two, his glare never wavering in intensity. She was clearly exhausted, they all were, but Caleb still couldn't figure out why Jan was leaving them be. She had heard Caleb, in wolf form. *Could they communicate?* The memory of his eyes flashing red sent a shiver through him.

Delia had barely spoken since the helicopter had left Sythe's dead body in its wake. Neither had Winson. The lizard-like companion had moved into the second metallic shelter, unable to be around any of them as he grieved the loss of his friend. The owl watched over them from the bench.

Caleb sighed, taking in the outline of Winson's curled-up form barely visible in the dark of a corner. His stomach lurched, whether from hunger or sympathy, he wasn't sure, but he felt for the guy. Winson had been wary at first, but he was good people. Or lizard, he supposed.

He just wanted to help, wanted to go back to a world where none of them were caught up in this mess.

A tired, familiar anger rose once more in the centre of his gut, the fire moving around his body as he longed to take over from Tilon, to knock some sense into him and Delia both. But he wasn't ready yet. He wasn't the one putting their plans into action; he still needed the guidance.

One day.

"We should do something," Caleb said before he could think of the implications.

"Nay, lad. She'll talk," Ava said offhandedly.

"What makes you so sure?"

"Mother's instinct."

Caleb looked at her, gulping down the words that fought to come out of his mouth.

Ava smiled at him sadly. "Aye."

"How many?" The words hung in the air. Caleb watched Ava's eyes water, but she was too stubborn to let the tears fall. She lifted her chin, taking a deep breath.

"Two. Not sure where they are now. I been here too long. They'd be almost grown, I suppose. Not much younger 'an you."

"I'm so sorry, Ava."

"Don't be, lad. Not your fault."

"What if it is?"

"Listen, boy. You aren't your father's choices. No matter what anyone else believes."

Caleb swallowed hard, fighting the guilt.

Ava continued to speak to him softly, her solid figure shuffling over to take his free hand. "Too often we carry the burden of our elders into our own lives, already struggling to make up for their sins. I promise ye, lad. It's never worth it."

Caleb nodded at her sadly. Argo squeezed his leg, firm but gentle, matching Ava's touch for a second.

"She's right, mate. What my dad did, what your dad did – we can't make up for it, but we can try to fix it."

"I'm so ... angry."

"Good," Argo said. "Use it, and I'll use mine. We will get out of here and find them. Stop them experimenting on anyone else. You and me, brother."

Caleb lifted his head, catching Argo's nod. His jaw tightened with determination. He returned the gesture, though he wasn't nearly as confident they'd make it through the night, let alone long enough to get back home and finish this.

Tilon came over to them and dropped down. Ava handed him a bar, which he accepted without a word, unwrapping the dry morsel as he continued to glare at Delia.

"So ... ahh, she's been working with them, huh?" Argo asked. Caleb rolled his eyes at his attempt at starting conversation.

Tilon grunted, mouth full, crumbs trailing down his fur. His paws were becoming more animalistic by the day. Caleb sighed, resting his head against the trunk behind him. The owl cooed overhead, then fluttered down to stand in front of Delia, hopping up to her feet. They watched silently. *She must be able to talk to the bird, if it was once human. Could she speak to the ferals too?*

"The ferals!" Caleb exclaimed and shot upright.

"Not worth it, boy," Tilon warned.

"You don't even know what I was going to say."

"Sure I do, kid. You were going to say, if we can speak to them, we can control them. If we can control them, we can build our own army. If we can build our own army, we can build a chance to stop this from happening ever again." He looked up at him, gaze stern and unwavering. "Am I close?"

Caleb hesitated, mouth slightly agape. "Spot on, really."

"How do you control beasts in the wild?" Tilon asked. "You don't. And you're not meant to. Man and beast were never meant to live as one. That's part of the reason we're dying. Animals rule their own kingdoms and have their own natural order. It's no different here, kid. When we stop being men, we become beasts."

"Some more than others," Ava interjected.

"The number of new, live hybrids has slowed and new experiments ... well, you've seen how a few of those turn out. There is only a handful who survive each drop. Delia and I, Sythe ..." Tilon closed his eyes to breathe deeply before continuing. "We're different from those who came before us. You and Argo, you're different again." He rubbed a hand over his face. "The only thing we know for sure is that no one is immune to the beast inside them. One day, it will take over. We fight it as long as we can, but once we lose, we turn one way or another. It's a matter of time."

"You're wrong," Caleb said, frowning at the ground. "We're more than just beasts. Those of us who have been lucky enough to survive, we're evolving, in ways we didn't think possible. The owl. Ethan. Neither of them is feral."

"We don't even know if the child has been injected."

Ethan huffed between Caleb and Argo but remained quiet.

"And Jan? You've been saying he is on the cusp for what ... years?" Caleb looked to the bear, who eyed him curiously. "What if he can control it, and the others haven't been strong enough?"

"Maybe I've been wrong," Tilon said, hanging his head. "I don't know anymore."

Caleb stared, struggling to keep his mouth from falling open. This was the most disheartened he had seen the warrior. He looked like he had caved in on himself, as though he were suddenly half of the man, or beast, that he had claimed to be only hours before. Beyond them, Caleb saw movement. Winson shifted from his curled-up form, equipment rattling as he stood and walked outside. Argo stood to follow, gently pushing Ethan back into Caleb's side.

"Where are you going?"

Argo's eyes widened, and he looked at him in surprise.

"How did you do that? We haven't shifted."

Caleb tilted his head towards the taller lad. Winson continued into the trees where the helicopter had departed. Back towards what was left of his companion.

"So you're, just, what? In my head now?"

"And you in mine. Brother."

Argo exhaled sharply, glancing back at Delia. She was still fixated on the bird. *"What about her?"*

"What about her? Eventually, she'll have to talk. There is another raid coming, remember? Where do you think Winson is going?"

"To bury his friend."

Caleb smiled sadly. *"I told you. You aren't bad, Argo."*

Argo shrugged. *"Like I said ... I'm trying."*

"I'll talk to Delia. Go," Caleb thought after him, turning his attention back to the captive.

"Stay with Ava, okay?" Caleb asked Ethan, who nodded as he stood. "Sit down, big fella." He patted Tilon on the arm before focusing his gaze on their camp leader. He had no idea where to start.

The owl hooted at him from its place in front of Delia, calling him over. Jan moved to watch his every step, the giant bear looming over the rest of the group. He dipped his head in a subtle nod. For the first time, it was as if the beast was truly seeing him as something other than a threat. Jan lifted his massive forearm and slowly extended a claw, pointing at Delia while keeping his gaze locked on Caleb.

"Yeah, I'm going."

Jan's giant shoulders shrugged as he dropped his arm. He bared his teeth. Whether it was a grin or a warning, Caleb couldn't tell. What he did know was that those teeth were enormous and too close for comfort.

Ethan shuffled over from Ava's side to stand next to Jan. He padded from foot to foot, not quite looking him in the eye.

"What is it, kiddo?"

"You should take her some food," Ethan suggested. Caleb looked at Jan for confirmation. The bear grunted. *Will I be able to hear your thoughts someday? You must have seen it.* Delia had heard his thoughts before. How long had she been able to do that? Had she known they planned to leave? He grabbed some water and protein bars from the box beside the fire and walked over to her.

The hunters turned towards him as he approached. The group had kept to themselves milling around the second metal structure since they arrived. One of them sighed before they all ignored him once more.

"Hungry?"

"What were you talking about?" Delia asked, turning her head up to look at him.

"You've been here the whole time; we haven't exactly been quiet."

"I meant you and Argo."

"How did you know?" Caleb asked, exasperated.

"You're not subtle, you know."

"I don't—"

"How did you know May and I were communicating?"

"Who the hell is May?" He shot the owl a look. She had hopped over to join them, pecking at one of the bars.

"She's been here a long time, watching over new hybrids from afar. Guiding the lost to the camp. I suspect she was one of the first."

Caleb tilted his head. "But Winson didn't know it – her – when she showed up the first time."

"I'm not surprised. We found Winson quickly after he was dropped here. He was scared, but he didn't need the help ..." Delia trailed off, still watching the bird.

"She didn't turn feral?"

"Observant." Caleb could hear the smirk in her voice.

"Alright. Remember, you're the one tied up."

She chuckled, the sound oddly light in the darkness.

Caleb looked down at her for a moment before dropping to his haunches to face her eye to eye. "I don't know what to make of you."

"And I you, wolf."

"I don't really know what to make of me either," he admitted, sitting down to share her tree. The rough bark pressed against his back, splintering beneath his weight.

May tore into one of the bars, picking out the smaller nuts bit by bit. He supposed May's journey was exactly where he might end up. He could only hope he would be able to guide rather than giving in to the temptations of bloodlust when he shifted permanently.

He unwrapped the other bar and held it up to Delia's lips. She shook her head at it. Shrugging, he took a bite, struggling not to cough as the dryness hit his throat. How could a nonperishable taste so awful?

He opened the water and gulped it down before pouring a capful for the bird, then offering some to Delia.

"Please," she said, prompting him to place the second bottle to her lips, the slight trickle of liquid running down her furred face catching his eye. Her head tilted up, cutting off the flow. Caleb wiped her chin without thinking, his hands gentle so as not to harm her delicate features.

Delia's eyes never left his. She was strong but scared; her vertical pupils caught the moonlight, reflecting it like stars. Caleb let her go, sitting back down. He needed to know if there was anything else she was keeping from them – all except Jan, he suspected. The bear watched them with such intensity Caleb could feel it from across the camp.

They sat in silence for a time, watching the flicker of their fire falter. Winson and Argo had come back; their bodies were blackened with dirt and blood. They retreated in silence to separate structures, both looking smaller than when they had left.

"You were so angry. When you found out who my father was ..." Caleb started, picking up Argo's soft snores in the background, their gentle rumbles tickling his inner ear.

"I was. I still am. But I acknowledge you are not him."

"Did you ever hear about me? Argo? What he was doing to us?"

"No, Caleb. I was never kept that well informed," she replied.

Caleb nodded, glancing over at Tilon and Ava sitting together near the fire, their wounds dressed and healing, Ethan leaning against their healer's good side. Tilon was watching him as intently as Jan was. The scouts had made their way to Delia's hunters, their heads bowed in conversation.

"I've spent so long in silence; it's difficult to undo years of ..."

"Deceit?" Caleb offered.

"I care for these people. Just like you do, albeit differently," she replied.

"Why was it so important, keeping me caged with you?"

"Once I knew who you were, I thought ..." She closed her eyes and sighed, leaning her head against the tree. "I thought you would be my family's ticket to safety."

Caleb swallowed.

"If I had you in my camp, I could finally free them from this mess. I could give John and Markus what they wanted: tabs on you. On their latest success." Her head fell to her chest, her eyes watering.

"You need to let us in, Delia. We have to be in this together or it will never work."

Delia lifted her head, turning towards Ava and Ethan sitting by the fire. The boy was listening to her speak.

Caleb took a breath in before speaking again. "You're hurting them all, not just me."

"I see that now."

"Good."

Caleb reached around the back of the tree, looking for the twine binding Delia's hands, only to find the restraints already in tatters. Tiny scraps of fibre lay scattered around the trunk. Delia moved her hands into her lap.

"That bloody bird," he muttered.

"May," Delia corrected, amused.

"Surprised Tilon hasn't hung you out to dry yet."

"Caleb."

His name on her lips stopped him short. The power she held over the camp was working its way into his being. He tilted his head towards her.

"Yes?"

She sighed deeply. "I thought I was doing the right thing."

"For who?" He tried to keep the judgement and resentment out of his voice.

"For all of us. What started out as a selfish need for news of my family turned into a desire to protect us all. Hard to balance when I knew it would be the end of me, not to mention my kids if I stopped complying."

"You're still here," Caleb said, leaning forward.

"They very likely don't suspect I've changed my ways. Six years is a long time."

"But they will."

"There is a raid coming. We only have weeks. The sooner we prepare our people and put a plan together, the better."

"How can we trust that you want what's best for all of us?"

"I do. Caleb, I never lied when I said Jan and I built the camp to protect those we could."

"You're letting them die—"

"Not everyone wants to be the hero. Some simply want to live in peace. But I shouldn't have taken away their choice. I should have been more upfront about the others and the ferals, and the Shepherd, although, I am still not sure what good that would have done."

Tilon looked up, catching his eye. Caleb waved him over.

"It's time to tell us everything, Delia."

Caleb stood and offered her his hand.

***

"I keep the hybrids in the camp. Report changes. Don't offer resistance to the raids. Don't let anyone know I'm involved."

"In exchange, they gave you news of your children and your husband."

"In exchange, they gave me my life. They gave me an identity I could be proud of. A leader. There, I was small; here, I have power. People listen to me, followed my commands. They want my help, my compassion. Each new hybrid we found, we gave a home. I kept them from the dangers of the woods, the clickers, the militants. I did this to keep my people safe. The news of my children keeps me going ... Kept me going."

Delia turned to Tilon. He crossed his arms over his chest, not saying a word. "I'm sorry, Theodore. I should have listened."

Tilon didn't budge.

"What about the boy that died? If you had made a break for it before now, maybe that wouldn't have happened. Maybe ..." Caleb grew quiet.

"You would never have been here," Tilon finished for him.

"It's getting worse. Ethan ... we shouldn't be here, let alone a child."

"I cannot change the past, and I know you're angry, but neither can you. Let me be here now."

"We can't take them on without the power of the camp. Your lack of resistance will give us the element of surprise," Tilon said, his arms crossed over his chest.

"It's time to use your influence for good," Caleb added.

"Okay," she said, nodding.

"When is the next raid?"

"Weeks. The helicopter was an anomaly. They come by foot, set up camps. There are bases scattered around the hybrid camps."

"What are we waiting for?" Caleb exclaimed.

"No time," Tilon said.

"He's right," Delia agreed. "Six years and we haven't been able to map everything. There are too many dangers out there. Now there are rivalries and experiment zones complete with guards and automatic weapon stores. If they are coming for us, we need to meet them on our turf. News of your survival and success with shifting will reach your father and they'll be desperate for more. Like it or not, they'll come for you, and Argo."

"What if they are waiting for us, back at that camp?" Caleb asked.

"My hunters haven't found signs of life in the known bunker locations in some time. If there are soldiers here, they are further away than we are. Our resources are there; we know those grounds."

Tilon nodded. "It's our best bet."

"I have a bad feeling about this," Caleb said, running a hand through his hair, surprised at its length and softness. More of him had changed. He would have to get to a river soon to see the damage.

Caleb looked over to Ethan, who had fallen asleep by the fire. May stood watch in the trees above the boy.

"Aiel is there," Ava said softly, her eyes meeting Delia's.

Delia softened. "She is. And we both know you're stronger together."

"What's your plan?" Tilon asked Delia stiffly.

"My hunters and I will move out at dawn. We can look out for any clickers or signs of life. You'll follow the next day. My hunters are fast and strong, and Jan scares anything in a five-mile radius. Your journey back should be uneventful. Rest only when you need to and meet us three days from now."

"Why should we trust you not to set up an ambush for our arrival?"

Delia rounded on their pack leader, her gaze steely with determination. "Because you will not survive this war without me or my influence. Something our friend here has reminded me of all too often."

"And if you're met with trouble?" Ava asked.

"One of the hunters will double back to warn you."

"Six hours," Tilon said. "That's your head start. I will not wait a full day. There is no time to waste."

"Agreed," Delia stated.

"I'm coming with you," Caleb interjected.

"Not this time," Delia offered gently. "I need to talk to them first, let them know I am on your side. We will heal together. I need you to trust me."

"Forgive me if the trust isn't all that forthcoming."

"You were going to undo my binding. Back at the tree. That was a start."

Ava placed a hand on his arm, then on Tilon's. "Get some sleep. Sunup is only in a few hours. I'll keep watch on 'er."

"Do you trust her?" Caleb asked Ava.

"Aye. I trust she will do the right thing."

"How can you be so sure?" Tilon commented gruffly.

"Because, if I don't get to see my wife again, I'll go after her myself."

An Exercise of Trust

Chapter Twenty-Seven

Tilon and Delia were deep in discussion by the time Caleb woke. Their conversation seemed much more amicable than the previous night. Delia's hands were moving emphatically as the big hybrid nodded down at her, his brows furrowed in concentration as she talked. Caleb was sure he would be able to pick up their conversation if he focused, but he was doing his best not to invade with his newfound telepathic abilities ... as much as someone who could hear telepathic thoughts on occasion could. Both of them looked healthier than the previous day; Tilon's wound had healed considerably, a dry scab now holding firm over his side.

He watched them with interest, noticing Jan doing the same. The bear was not subtle, hovering near the pair. Caleb wondered if Delia was feeding him thoughts, holding two conversations at once. Would he be able to do that one day?

A deep, earthy aroma suddenly filled Caleb's senses. It couldn't be, could it? His mouth watered, desire over taking his mind. It was close, and intoxicating. He'd been thinking about it since that morning with Ava and Aiel. His skin rippled in anticipation of his friend's next word.

"Coffee?" Argo asked, offering a metal camp mug filled with steaming black liquid.

Caleb could have kissed him. The caffeine addiction that once fuelled his young adult life screamed at him to take the cup and down its contents.

"Oh ... my ... g—" Caleb reached out, his body shaking with anticipation.

The first sip was pure, scalding heaven. Caleb was instantly transported back to his own kitchen, the coffee carafe steaming next to a plate of equally delicious pastries. The thought filled him with nostalgia and longing for home, where the kitchen staff had the best coffee beans ready for him every morning.

"Oh man, that's good."

"Do you need a moment?" Argo asked, teasing. "It's just dirty bean juice." He took a careful sip of his own cup, then winced. "Argh, tastes like shit."

"Tastes divine. Where did you find it?" Caleb said, savouring the heat, ignoring the jest.

"In one of the crates. Whoever was staying here had a bunch of the stuff. They ain't gonna need it anymore, are they? It's awful but it's better than nothing. Hell, I miss good coffee." Argo stared down into his cup, frowning.

"What do you think they're talking about?" Caleb asked, taking a more cautious sip.

"You aren't listening?" Argo quipped.

"I'm uh ... trying not to."

"But you want me to tell you?"

"It's not like I'm the one listening in. You are."

Argo scoffed. *"You're not going to like it."*

"Tell me anyway," Caleb thought back defiantly.

"That's kinda neat," Argo said. Caleb clenched his jaw, his free hand flexing with frustrated energy, waiting for the other wolf hybrid to get to the point.

"Argo!"

"Alright! Calm your tits. Delia has been explaining more of her involvement to Tilon ... Theodore, I guess. Your papi – stand-up guy, by the way—"

Caleb growled involuntarily.

"He's been bribing a bunch of the main players here, not just her. There is another known camp apparently, same size if not bigger than this one. Delia has been instructed not to interact and to keep us away from each other. A turf war within an experiment. Your dad, and mine, I suppose, keep everyone in check."

Caleb rubbed the bridge of his nose. "Go on."

"Delia and a couple of others who have since passed were sort of placed here from the facilities because they knew too much. She was given power to lead. She was drip-fed information in exchange for compliance and allowing hybrids to be captured, experimented on and in some cases ... taken."

"We know all this. What else?"

"Delia said that there were people who used to volunteer; they were excited to be part of these groups. Could see the money machine, building the U.S. forces' next secret weapon. That was until they started changing too much, you know, the shit that's happening to us. Growing fur, teeth—"

"Turning feral."

"Or straight up dying," Argo said bluntly. "Then it became about infecting those that had been involved, so they couldn't talk. The stuff we saw back home, the new recruits – it didn't matter that the hybrids were becoming more animal than man. They were more powerful, they could see and hear better, they were faster. Even if only for the short term—"

"They had their weapons," Caleb interjected again.

"You want to tell the story or ..."

"Sorry."

Argo huffed. "The experiments aren't working, not completely. Delia has been told to watch out for a sign that things have taken a turn. No one knows what that sign is ... but I can guess."

"Subtle, Dad."

"Right? Anyway, she said they want more, always more. More sacrifices, more hybrids found from the drops, more data compiled in places like these." He gestured around him. "It's amped up, but I suspect she's told you that already."

"How does she even know all this? Half of it happened while she's been here."

"She's smart, man, I dunno what to tell you. Those reports she's keeping may not just be about us. Those hunters were a new breed. Another experiment, offcuts, gifted to her for her own forces. All this shit is wild."

Argo stopped talking, his head turning towards the bigger group. Caleb looked over to see Tilon and Delia watching them intently. Maybe they were listening to their conversation now, not the other way around.

"Go on," Caleb said, still holding Delia's glare at the intrusion.

"Some of them fought the extent of the experiments," Argo continued. "Some of them didn't, but it has been going on for so long that it's just a way of life."

"What happened to those that didn't?"

"Like I said, normal hostage bullshit. Kids turned up hurt, wives turned up dead, mothers were put on life support, people were stripped of wealth. Ain't nothing like someone's family being fucked with to make someone else bend over, ya know?"

Caleb didn't know, but he nodded slowly anyway.

"You could have just joined the conversation if you were so curious," Delia said, making them both jump. By the time she reached them, the steel was back in her spine; the weakness from the night before was gone.

The rest of their camp had begun to stir, dawn starting to brighten the sky. More coffee was brewed over the fire.

"Yeah, I'm gonna need more than that," Argo drawled. Caleb could feel his friend's annoyance radiating from his increasingly furred body.

The last couple of days must have gotten to him.

"*I heard that,*" Argo thought back.

"Cool it," Caleb said out loud. "You haven't exactly been a walk in the park either."

Argo grumbled but remained quiet.

"We'll be moving out soon. You will follow this afternoon as discussed. It's a two-and-a-half-day trek. We'll do our best to reach the main camp in two. You will need to move as quickly – take turns carrying the child. We will clear the path. There will be very little time to rest before this next raid, and you two need training. Controlling your shifts will be vital for our success."

The colour drained from Argo's face.

"Tilon has told me about your bloodlust, Mr Kan. I have no doubt my hunters can help you control it. We trained Jan when he lost his humanity."

Caleb raised his eyebrows. "He won't turn feral?"

She smiled at him in response and made to turn away.

"Wait."

She stopped to give him her attention.

"What are we really up against?"

Delia looked at him, the subtle movement of her eyes betraying the pain she kept hidden from them all. He watched her jaw tense as she forced her resolve back into her body.

Caleb refused to look away. "We need to know."

"Very well," she said, steeling herself. "When I was sent away from the laboratory I was working in, the experiments had started to ramp up. My husband and I were approached to take part in a more ... practical way."

"Meaning—"

"They wanted my whole family, injected with the same feline DNA. They wanted to see if they could invoke sharper senses, agility, unquestionable loyalty to those that fed them, so to speak. I refused to give them my family."

"How does that help us?" Argo asked.

"Because you need to know who these people are. They promised to provide for my husband and children if I agreed to do this – their every whim taken care of."

"Where is the money coming from?" Caleb asked.

"You would be surprised how much debt a country will go into to remain a military power," Delia said sadly. "For the next year, I was experimented on and informed of places like this island, where the bodies would be sent. By then, people had started to be taken without their consent. I was powerless to stop it."

"How big is this thing?" Caleb asked.

"Global."

He gulped.

"Things changed when I started to evolve, to become more ... cat than human. It was clear I wasn't fit for the public eye anymore. So, they gave me a choice: be sent to an experimentation zone or voluntary euthanasia."

"That seems extreme," Argo scoffed.

"I had become a liability. The success of my evolution had been celebrated … but I changed too much. They sold the idea of human hybrids, not animals themselves."

"They didn't wait to see how far your changes would go." Tilon grunted the statement.

"Why would they? They had the proof they wanted, the funding for more experimentation. They wanted—"

"Weapons."

"Once they had secured their funding, the evidence against them needed to be destroyed. But if I chose to leave, I would be given the tools I needed to keep watch. There wasn't enough money yet to kit their islands out with surveillance. Very few people knew about these places. The technology wasn't quite there. Still isn't, by the looks of things. But they weren't going to stop; they needed eyes and ears on the ground."

"Your father is insane," Tilon said in disgust.

"Caleb's dad isn't the only one to blame," Argo muttered.

"And many others," Delia said before he could lament further, her voice full of sorrow. "We were part of the elite – the privileged few who knew about the experiments, though not what they were truly trying to achieve."

The rest of Delia's group looked ready to move. Her hunters were still with Winson and May, mapping out their route in the dirt. Ethan and Ava were rummaging through the remaining food stores, splitting the resources between the two parties. The scouts looked to have stacked a canvas bag full of firewood by the camp's entryway, flitting in and out of the trees.

"You need to move; we need to get the camp ready for the raid. We're losing daylight," Tilon said, looking over to their group awaiting instruction.

"You want to go home as much as the rest of us," Caleb said gently, still focused on Delia.

"I would do nearly anything to see them again. I thought I had to settle for the snippets of their lives. I had to let that be enough. I can only hope they survived okay without me."

"The sooner we get back to the mainland, the sooner we can find out," Caleb said with determination.

"I'm afraid that still may be a fair way away. Gregorio will send his troops; he is expecting a larger quota than normal given my recent failure," Delia said. "A larger quota means more soldiers."

"Gregorio?" Caleb asked. "That's the Shepherd!?"

"That's such a villain name." Argo scoffed.

Caleb slapped him. "Be serious for one second, would you?"

Delia ignored them both. "None of us can change what has happened here, or our part in it, whether big or small. But we can try to affect what happens next."

Winson joined them, May perched on the lizard's shoulder.

Traitor, Caleb thought, eyeing the bird who refused his own arm weeks beforehand.

"They're ready to go," Winson said, his voice void of emotion. "The route should take you two days. We've split the supplies; you have enough food and water to see you through."

"We'll follow at dusk," Tilon chimed in.

Delia gave Winson a nod and made her way to her hunters. Several of them were sporting canvas bags. Jan stood watching, waiting for the order to move out.

"See you soon," Delia said, before ushering her group through the trees.

Don't sell us out, Caleb thought, closing his eyes and turning to the rest of his pack.

"What now?" Argo asked, turning to Winson and Tilon, who shared a look.

"You two need to learn how to fight. Without the claws." Winson threw Caleb a spear.

Training Season

Chapter Twenty-Eight

Wind stung Caleb's face as he and Argo tore through the trees at high speed. Their human bodies lacked the agility of their animal counterparts. Tilon and Winson had cleared an arena in the centre of their temporary lodgings, allowing the two men to practise what Argo complained were outdated cadet drills.

Sweat dampened Caleb's palms, his body's first response when trying to cool down, a trait unchanged in either state. Ethan, Berrum and Grace were cheering from the sidelines, watching the two wolf hybrids grapple with each other in their human forms. Argo obviously had the upper hand with his prior training.

"If you want to survive battle, you need to survive the woods," Winson had chimed in through a sly grin. It was the first time he had shown any emotion since they buried Sythe the night before. The distraction was good for their instructor, but Caleb wished it wasn't so painful. His muscles were screaming at him.

"I think we have done okay so far, wouldn't you say?" Argo panted, his tongue lolling out of his mouth – a phenomenon that amused Winson to no end.

"Tilon and I might not always be around to save you," Winson grunted.

"Okay, okay, sorry. What's next, boss?"

Winson smiled before catching himself, quickly masking it with his usual stern expression. Caleb could see he was growing fond of the big oaf.

"These," Winson said, pulling two long, crude spears from behind a tree.

Argo nearly jumped out of his skin with excitement, rushing to grab the longer of the two weapons. "Finally!"

"Don't get too excited," Caleb muttered, nodding at Winson as he took his own spear.

The length was stripped of its bark, smoothed out by rock to the best of Winson's ability, a slight bump creating a groove where his hand fit. The blade had been chiselled to a perfect peak. Argo had already broken away, jabbing and lunging wildly, nearly toppling over with an overly enthusiastic thrust.

"Idiot is going to get himself killed," Winson said, loud enough for the group to hear.

"Not if he turns and just eats them," Ethan offered, making Berrum and Grace stiffen.

"Ethan!" Caleb scolded.

"What? It's true," the boy said, huffing and folding his arms.

"That's enough now," Ava chided. "You three need to rest. We'll be walking all night, you know."

The three of their smallest members groaned.

"Off with ye." Ava tutted, shooing them into camp cots. "You should rest too, won't do ye no good to come against a clicker with one too many knocks to the head, now, will it?"

"Yes Mum," Caleb said sarcastically, rolling his eyes.

Ava raised an eyebrow, making him regret his sass.

Tilon stepped in. "Pick up your spears, boys. We'll run through the basics, but Ava's right. We do need a break before we move out. There'll be no stopping tonight."

Caleb was paired with Winson, the lizard taking it relatively easy on him while showing him the best ways to parry from a distance before striking with his blade up close. He hissed as Winson nicked his side.

"Dammit!" He threw his spear to the ground.

"You're getting better," Winson offered. May, watching from a tree above them, barked out a laugh.

"Can't I just learn to shift on cue? I am so much more effective as a wolf," Caleb whined.

"More shifts mean more changes, remember? We don't know when they're going to stop for you. Your wolf is an asset, but one that should be preserved," Winson said, his voice firm. "Pick that up, that's enough for now." He pointed to the fallen weapon.

"Yes!" Argo roared, dancing around a fallen Tilon who looked unimpressed at being pressed down into the dirt.

"Beginner's luck," the feline hybrid huffed.

"You know what they say about old cats and new tricks." Argo offered his hand toward Tilon, beaming.

"That's dogs, you fool," their leader grumbled, accepting the hand.

Winson's smile faded. Caleb caught him looking towards the woods.

"Hey," Caleb started. Winson turned back to him, holding his hand out for the spear. "You okay?"

"Argo's good," Winson replied, ignoring the question. "May even be better as a human."

"Winson." Caleb wasn't backing down. "Talk to me."

"Argo hasn't been the only one who couldn't control it," he said, eyes not moving off Argo as he continued his training.

"You?"

Winson shook his head. "Sythe. He didn't shift like you do. That seems to be new. But he changed quickly, alongside Tilon. Tilon had control, discipline. Sythe didn't – not at first, not for a long time."

"Do you think Argo can be trained to turn without, you know, turning?"

"I don't know." Winson's voice dropped, sadness and doubt creeping in. "Come on. Eat, try to sleep for an hour or two. We don't have much longer before sundown. We're going to need that night vision of yours. Come on, big fella," he called out to Argo, who hadn't stopped his victory dance.

***

They gathered as dusk settled over their camp. Purples and blues mixed with the melancholy of twilight. They were heading into a battle with not enough time to prepare. Caleb wondered how Delia and her hunters were faring. He had to trust that she would rally their hybrids enough to trust him when they reached the compound in a couple of days.

Tilon took his place at the head of the group, waiting impatiently for Winson to arrive, the lizard having spent their last few hours at Sythe's grave. He came through the trees with Argo at his side, the big man's hand patting the lizard hybrid on the back.

"Let's go," Ethan called, not understanding the delay. Ava pulled the boy close and shushed him gently.

"We ready?" Tilon asked Winson directly.

"Yeah boss. We're ready."

"Caleb and I will take the lead. Winson will follow behind with Ava and Ethan. Berrum, Grace, same rules as before, scout ahead and alert us of danger. I don't expect there to be trouble if Delia has kept her word. Argo, take the rear. You've proven yourself with a spear – keep your eyes and ears peeled for danger and yell out if we need to stop. Agreed?"

Caleb grabbed his spear, taking his position next to Tilon, his eyes glowing in the dark. He leant into his wolven vision, watching the outline of critters rustle through the brush.

"Let's move," Tilon ordered. Ava and the scouts shouldered their packs, and they walked back into the trees as one.

***

Caleb strained against the night, forcing his senses to focus on movement up ahead. His concentration was consistently broken by the members of their group: the light footwork of their scouts, running ahead in either direction; the heavy footfalls of Ava as she carried Ethan on her back when he had fallen asleep; the rapid rustling of game rushing away from them at every turn. It all vied for his attention. He shook his head, staring straight ahead into the darkness, and grumbled under his breath.

"Try to focus on Jan," Tilon offered, keeping pace beside him. "He's the loudest."

"Not always," Caleb huffed. He caught Tilon smirk. "What?"

"I can hear him, is all. We're making good time."

Caleb groaned and tried again, swearing when he heard the scouts coming back to the pack and confirming the way forward was clear.

"When you trust your safety with your pack, it becomes easier to block us out. You know our scents, the patterns of how we move. Search for something outside those patterns. When you find it, focus."

Caleb fought the urge to close his eyes the way Sythe had taught him to use his nose. He needed to be able to do this at a moment's notice. Who knew what sort of force the Shepherd was going to send? He forced his breathing to slow, focusing on the sound of his heartbeat while the group moved behind him. Berrum and Grace split again, moving into the darkness. He trusted them, and their light patter. They would be back in a few minutes.

A thud sounded in his ear, louder than their footsteps, followed by a second and a third. It was heavy and even, keeping almost the same pace as them.

"I found him!" Caleb yelled, earning him a shush from Winson and Ava.

Ethan stirred. "Are we there yet?" the boy asked sleepily.

"Was wondering that myself." Argo's thought jerked Caleb from seeking out Jan's whereabouts.

"Hey! I was busy up here."

"Yeah, well, it's bloody boring back here."

Caleb sighed and refocused on Jan.

"Fine."

Tilon was cradling Ethan against his chest when morning broke. He turned to their group and called a break. Ava sighed in relief, sitting with a thud and resting her back against a tree. She pulled bars of oats and dried fruit from her pack and handed them out. Argo slumped dramatically next to Ava, sucking on a canteen of water like his life depended on it.

"Cadets have gone soft," Tilon grunted.

Argo waved his hand, still pulling at the clean, clear liquid before Caleb swiped it from his hands.

"Save some for the rest of us."

He held his arms out for the boy, handing Ethan the water. He drank gratefully, then hurried off with Grace who had spotted some berry bushes.

"Not the red ones!" Caleb called out after them.

"How long, boss?" Winson asked.

"Couple of hours. We'll go when the sun passes the centre of the sky. We should be there this time tomorrow if we can give up a couple hours of sleep."

"That will give Delia enough time?" Caleb asked.

"It will have to," Tilon said without emotion.

"Sleep. I'll watch over the kid," Winson offered. Ava and Argo were already snoring.

***

The fences of their compound were a sight for sore eyes. Caleb and Tilon whistled the group to attention before taking the lead through its gates. Edgar and Missy stood to the side of the entryway waving them in.

"Delia is waiting for you," Edgar said, stretching his long neck.

"We're finally fighting back," Missy added, sounding pleased and giving the group a smile. "Head on in."

Dozens of eyes turned towards them as they entered the central pit.

"Woah," Argo stammered, having never seen the main camp before. "This is insane. I mean that in a good way. No, really, you did all this?"

"Come." Tilon waved them over to the entryway of Delia's home. Two of her hunters were stationed outside the path.

"Good time," one of them said to Tilon.

"Had to make sure you kept your word," Winson grumbled in return.

"Ava." Aiel's voice broke, her tear-streaked face smiling at her partner from across the fire.

Ava dropped Ethan's hand and ran into her lover's embrace, their lips pressing together, saying everything that words couldn't.

"Leave them be," Caleb said, holding his arm out to the boy. "Let's go see what's next."

Feral

Chapter Twenty-Nine

Delia looked up from her desk when they arrived, her hunters stepping aside so they could enter the crowded room. Her walls had been stripped of the reports and photos Caleb had seen just a few weeks beforehand. In their place were a series of maps taking up the entire wall, variations of the same terrain, down to the torn parchment he and Tilon had left behind before venturing out on their own.

"Good, you're here."

"Did you find any trouble?" Tilon asked. Winson broke off to compare the maps. Berrum and Grace had taken Ethan and left them to break the news of their late friend.

"A couple of clickers. One will be on the spit shortly. We will mourn our fallen friends this evening and gather those we can for briefing."

"What's all this?" Winson called, pointing towards rough circles on each of the maps.

"Suspected locations of others. Red for hybrids, blue for bunkers. These are only the ones I know of. I assume there are more that will need to be flushed out. I have sent several of the hunters to check the bunkers. If they are clear, we will be raided from the sea. Gives us more time."

"And if they find recruits?" Tilon queried.

Delia fixed a firm gaze on him. "Capture for questioning. If we can find out where we will be hit, we can prepare."

Caleb only counted five hunters in the room with them running through reports. "Where are the others?"

The small feline hybrid moved to stand by Winson, pointing up at a red circle. "This used to be a hybrid group. They split from us a while ago, amicably, preferring their own company. I've sent three here, and another group to the east. They haven't been so friendly, but if they hear we are ready to fight back, they may be convinced to join us."

"What about training?" Winson asked.

"Fienna and Neith will start instruction in the morning," Delia said, nodding towards two of her hunters.

"So, they do have names," Argo thought, raising his eyebrows approvingly.

"Argo!" Caleb turned to Delia. "What can we do?"

"Clean yourselves up and do another sweep of the camp for any devices. Jan and I looked but we can't get everywhere. Between you, you should be done by nightfall. Be back at the firepits for supper."

Caleb looked to Tilon for confirmation. He nodded and walked them out.

"Come on, lads. We stink," Winson said, leading them towards the lake.

***

By the time twilight hit, Argo, Tilon, Caleb and Winson had completed two sweeps of the grounds, unable to find any more trackers. The smell of roasting meat had started to permeate the air, and hybrids were making their way to the central pits for the evening's ceremony. Caleb's mouth watered at the thought of clicker fat dripping onto hot coals. His stomach growled with such ferocity that it made Argo jump.

"Easy there, tiger," he said, widening his eyes and glancing towards Tilon. "No offence."

Tilon grunted and made his way forward to Delia.

"Considering he doesn't agree with her methods, he sure does follow her around a lot," Argo grumbled.

"They are eerily similar when it comes to a common cause, though," Winson offered as he approached the pits.

Caleb stopped, observing the gathering crowd. The hair on his arms raised before the fur that had started growing along his spine followed suit. Something was off here. He sniffed, picking up on the scent of new hybrids, eyes locking onto a pair who were glaring daggers at each other. The two of them were seated opposite one another, off the side of the main fire.

Must have come from one of the other groups.

Fear settled in Caleb's stomach. What was he doing? All of these people were about to go to war, and for what? For him. And his strong-headed ideals. Who did he think he was? His hands twitched, an electric tingling tickling his skin. He started to pant heavily.

Argo moved in front of him, blocking him from the rest of the group. "What's going on?"

"What if I can't do this, Argo? What if I really am all talk? I ... I haven't been good for much outside of all this."

"You really can't see your own worth, can you?" Argo said, taking Caleb's jaw in his hand and tilting his head up to look at him. "You've given these people something to hope for, something to fight for."

Caleb jerked his head out of Argo's grasp. "You weren't here before. They didn't want to change, they didn't want me to intervene – what if I've done nothing except ruin their future?"

"Fear and hope are powerful things. Often one feeds into the other without you realising. Tonight, they will come to realise you have been fighting for them since you arrived, even if that wasn't your intent to begin with. Look out there and tell me this isn't for every single one of them. For Ethan. To stop this before it gets any worse."

Caleb slumped, taking a step back from his friend.

"For what it's worth, I'm glad we're here, that you found me. I could never have forgiven myself if the last time I saw you was the night our lives were stolen from us."

"This is bigger than us." Caleb's voice quavered.

"I know, Caleb. Fear and hope. Let's use them wisely."

He nodded, his stomach growling.

Argo laughed, breaking the tension. "Go get some food."

Caleb smiled, patting Argo on the arm before turning towards the fire. He still had a funny feeling about the new arrivals.

How many of us are there?

He had barely made it to the fires before sparks shot into the air. The two hybrids that had caught his attention were squaring up to one another. Caleb braced himself and he saw Winson tensed. Argo had gone off ahead, nowhere in sight.

Caleb scanned the area for an authority figure. Delia? Tilon? Neither was around; they were still off planning what they would say to the group.

Dammit.

It looked like the younger newbie had pissed off an old veteran. The two creatures circled each other around the flames.

What the hell do I do?

The smaller of the two had beady black eyes, homed in on their target. Long, yellowed nails twitched, sharp enough to take out an eye. They screeched.

Caleb couldn't tell what they had been spliced with, but whatever it was, they weren't backing down. The elder hissed, standing his ground and radiating fury, his rough, leathery body glinting in the light of the fire. Golden-brown scales reflected the light in a thousand different places.

"Ssssimmer down."

The voice wormed into Caleb's head. Had the older man even spoken aloud? A serpent of some sort.

Ahh shit.

The smaller creature lunged. A piercing scream escaped their lips as they swiped dirty nails through the air. The serpent hybrid narrowed his eyes, dodging with ease, moving faster than Caleb expected.

Caleb hadn't seen either of these creatures before. The snake hybrid looked a decade or two older than the main group.

Shouting erupted around them. Grievances spilled into the open as others joined in, voices rising over the crackling fire. Nails jabbed into chests. Fists flew. The noise could have woken the dead.

Caleb's head pounded with the noise, his ears picking up on the hurried movements around them. If his father's recruits were out there, there was no way they weren't hearing the commotion.

May called overhead, panicked as she circled the fighting hybrids. The restlessness of the group and sense of danger triggered Caleb's instincts. The urge to shift, to control, to end this before anyone got hurt, surged through him.

He leant into the power rolling through him, allowing his body to thicken and move. Fur raced down his limbs, the tendons of his arms stretching and contracting. He shook his head, his neck cracking as it lengthened. His vision sharpened, his world shifting into greys and blues, vivid with the heat signals and auras of those around him.

Argo, Ava and Aiel had come running. Caleb caught their wide-eyed stares as his body changed. He locked eyes with Argo. The last thing they needed was for him to shift here. Caleb tried to send a message through his mind, but the whirlwind of bodies made it impossible to focus.

He pushed every fibre of concentration he had into the shift, willing his body to work with him as he pictured the image of himself he wished to portray to the group. His spine cracked, his torso contracting into powerful muscle as he remained on his hind legs. Larger, more powerful, but still able to communicate.

He felt his bones break, only to be reformed within seconds. He stretched tall, thinking of every bad werewolf movie he had ever seen.

You've got this!

His torso broadened, coarse fur rippling across his muscles as he dropped to all fours.

Ahh, too much too fast. Dang it.

He felt muscle and sinew tighten and mould to his new body, more power running through him by the second. Then, suddenly, it stopped.

"Enough!" The command was strong, the word echoing through the trees, causing all eyes to turn to him. He had no idea if he had said it aloud or in his head. But it had worked. Caleb growled, prowling between the hybrids who had started the fight. He stalked the younger of the two.

"What is your name?" Caleb sent the thought out to them. They would not have been much younger than him, maybe twenty, barely able to think for themselves out here.

Their eyes darted around, body tensing and letting go as if they themselves were mid-shift, unable to control it. Caleb urged them to focus, trying to draw their attention, pushing out his thoughts telepathically. The tensing turned to a tremble, as if they'd suddenly caught a chill.

"Jam ... ieee," the hybrid said, staring intently into Caleb's eyes.

Caleb tested the word on his tongue, but it came out as an incoherent snarl. Jamie flinched, their sharp, beady gaze struggling to hold his.

"Jamie," he thought instead, and their head snapped back to attention. Raising his snout, he projected a thought outward. *"Who else can hear me?"*

The voices hit all at once. An influx of noise battered his skull. Fear, anger, despair. It was as if a dam had burst, allowing the group's unspoken needs and panic to wash over him.

Caleb's blood boiled. He couldn't control the incessant chatter he had awakened. He wanted to scream, to silence them just long enough to think.

"Alright! Hush!" He propelled the words from his entire body.

"What now?" The serpent hybrid snickered in front of him, followed by a few other laughs.

Ass.

More laughter. No thought was sacred while shifted. Caleb shook his head, forcing the relentless noise from his mind. He had their attention now; it would do no good to lose it.

"What is going on here?" He directed the thought at Jamie. Their lips curled back, exposing thin, sharp teeth against bleeding gums.

"I ... hate ... this." The words came out disjoined, as if Jamie couldn't hold on to the concept of what was being said. The creature dropped to the ground, convulsing like they were having a fit.

"The twerp tried to attack me. Again! Damn thiiiiiing can't control itself."

"Okay, you don't look to be in danger anymore. Sit down, sir," Caleb thought towards the older hybrid, his eyes not leaving Jamie in front of him.

"We're all in danger," he said before moving away from the fire.

Caleb stiffened, trying to shut out the barrage of voices so he could focus.

What the fuck is happening?

"The hybrid is turning, Caleb. Be careful. A feral's blind devotion to destruction is more dangerous than a clicker." The voice in his head had cut through the murmurs of the crowd. He couldn't tell who had given him the warning.

Feral. Damn.

Caleb was glued to Jamie as they thrashed against the dirt, fur sprouting across their body as they snapped and grew smaller. Their eyes flashed red against black. Dirty white foam spilled from their mouth.

"Stop. This. MONSTER." The thought screamed through his mind.

A real scream followed. Human. Ethan.

Caleb couldn't turn to see where it had come from. His focus remained on the scene before him. His body lowered, tense and ready to pounce.

He crouched on his hind legs, muscles tight, every fibre begging to spring into the fight.

Jamie's hands and feet twisted inward, and they screamed. Fury, fear and pain laced the air.

Caleb saw Ava and Aiel in the distance ushering panicked members of the camp away from the unfolding battle.

Caleb growled, the low vibrations in his throat building. The sounds around him started to clear. He was focused solely on the animal in front of him.

The hybrid's thoughts were full of fear and anger but disjointed, each word lost in heavy static.

"Don't know … happen … arrrrghhh!" Jamie's head lifted towards the sky with a crack; a scream tore out of their mouth, blood and foam spraying from their gums.

They convulsed, struggling to catch their breath. Everything was happening too fast. Thrashing against the ground, Jamie scrambled towards him.

"D … d … die!" the creature spat, snapping at Caleb. He leapt forward before the beast could go after anyone else.

Caleb had only ever seen one creature look like this: Argo, right before they pulled him out of it. He doubted they would be so lucky now. He finally knew what Jamie had been spliced with. It was an animal he'd only ever seen in documentaries.

A motherfucking honey badger. Aggressive fighters who don't back down.

For fuck's sake.

"You'll have to kill it." Delia's voice bit into his thoughts. His concentration wavered at the shock of it.

"You're back!"

"This is your chance, wolf. Show the group what you're made of."

A dozen tiny, pointed teeth punctured his skin. He groaned and snapped, missing Jamie's mottled fur by millimetres.

"Where do the other ferals go?" He twisted, biting back. He didn't want to kill them if he could avoid it. There was already too much death in this camp.

Jamie hissed, bloodied spittle flying as they lunged.

Caleb snarled, teeth sinking into their fur. The familiar metallic tang filled his mouth as he tore off a strip of flesh. A high shriek pierced the air.

The camp fell silent.

The thing that had been human minutes ago wasted no time whipping around, still squealing as it lunged for his throat.

"She's right." This voice was stronger, deeper than anything Caleb had ever heard. It rumbled through him, as if coming from the bottom of someone's soul.

Who was that?

Caleb's paw lifted, shoving the much smaller creature to the ground.

Something shifted inside him. His mind raced with fury, no longer caring if this thing lived or died. It had threatened his home. His people.

Caleb pinned the creature beneath him. His body burnt. Rage coursed through him with every heartbeat.

Then he saw it. Fear.

Jamie's eyes flashed with panic, too human for what Caleb had in store.

"Kill it, boy! It is the only way you get out of this alive." The deep voice uttered a command that had to be obeyed.

Caleb's jaw widened. A growl rumbled from his windpipe. He felt others backing away as he gripped Jamie's neck between his teeth.

Four fangs punctured flesh. Hot blood flooded his mouth.

Jamie squirmed, panicked. Incoherent pleas clawed at Caleb's mind.

He tore, shaking his head from left to right, wrenching flesh and fur apart.

Jamie's throat came free in a tangled mess of meat and sinew. Its body spasmed once, twice, then fell still. Blood pooled beneath them.

Caleb was going to be sick.

Jamie's body cooled beneath his paws. He spat, blood dribbling down his coat as he came to terms with what he had done.

The voices hit him at once. A barrage of affirmations and accusations all at once.

"They are letting a monster lead us!"

"The kid could have escaped!"

"He saved us!"

"Caleb?" That last one was human and soft. A scared child asking for reassurance.

A scream bubbled inside him. He needed them all to shut up. Before he could utter a sound, fatigue slammed into him.

His body dropped and darkness took hold. His eyes closed as one final thought echoed in his mind, spoken by the imposing voice that helped him through his first fight with a feral.

"You did well."

Caleb barely had time to wonder who it belonged to before everything went black.

Animal Instinct

Chapter Thirty

*P*anic held Caleb inside of a dream state, his consciousness fighting for him to wake up from the nightmare. He clawed at his chest, wishing his racing heart would slow. He was surprised to feel his skin, his human skin, marred by new, angry scars from the last few weeks. His throat tightened, airways constricting as he gasped for air. His hands clutched his neck, trying to make room for the oxygen he desperately needed. Sweat slicked his skin, dampening the fine fur growing in uneven patches.

A steady beeping caught his attention. His eyes darted around the room, frantically searching for the source of the noise. The monitor. Its incessant beep, beep, beep tapped out a rhythm, a confirmation that he was still alive.

Still breathing.

He gasped and sucked in sweet air, the taste of chemicals coating his tongue. Where was he?

Shit.

Closing his eyes, he forced himself to breathe slower. In. Out.

Was he naked? His hands roamed over his skin, tracing the damp contours of his torso.

Something tugged at his arm. A sharp sting shot through him as a needle ripped free from his flesh.

"Ow."

Grimacing, he grabbed the remaining tubes with his left hand and yanked. His jaw clenched as he bit back the scream that rose in his throat.

"Ahh, I see you're awake." A familiar voice echoed through the room. Caleb winced at the bright moonlight streaming in through the closed window. The ripples of light and shadow made his head spin.

"Dad?" he cried out, the tears falling freely now. "Dad, why?"

"You're helping me change the world, boy. You all are."

"You're creating monsters and killing us in the process. You need to stop."

"It will never stop, not until we get it right. Just think – the future is now. You wouldn't want your mother's death to be for nothing, would you?"

Caleb strained against the invisible force holding him in place. He felt the growl before he heard it. He grunted as his body began to change. Could his father control his shifts? His glowing blue-and-green eyes locked onto his father across the room. His canines dropped from his gums, sharp and ready. His voice rang out, a raw promise in the dark.

"I will kill you. For her. For everyone you've trapped here. And finally, for me."

Laughter rippled through the air. Dark figures emerged from the shadows. There were dozens of them. Each held a fine needle, aimed at him.

"Sit still, son."

A scream tore from Caleb's throat with such intensity that everyone in the room backed away. Someone bolted for the door, terrified of what he might do next. Caleb growled, attempting to break free. The monitor taped to his arm knocked into his side, causing a commotion. His eyes flung open as he felt claws extend from his fingers, the teeth along the bottom of his gums sharpening into points, fuelled by the fury of his subconscious.

"Leave us." The sound of Delia cut through his rage. Caleb found her voice, focusing on her, controlling his rapid breath. *You're back.* His mouth settled, leaving the two sharpened fangs that had become a permanent fixture, a reminder of what he was capable of, of what he had done.

He was in their medical unit, the monitor attached to him salvaged from the experiment zone days before. Delia had ordered them to take anything of use. The generator must have been moved to this location, unless they had managed to find another on their expeditions to the surrounding bunkers.

"Delia." Her name came out as a whimper. Caleb still didn't know if he could trust her, but she was all they had. She was their link between the agents of the experiments and the hybrids who could take them down. He could die trying, but he would make damn sure he saw his father once more, just long enough to put an end to this once and for all.

Caleb slumped against the wall of the medical structure, the metal cool on his back. He was naked. That much was, unfortunately, true. He didn't have the energy to blush or look away.

He had killed someone. Not a clicker. Not some mindless creature. Jamie had been one of their own. Bile rose in his throat. He was a murderer. He wanted to help them, but instead, he had taken one of them out. Argo had no control over his bloodlust, but Caleb? He knew exactly what he was doing when he tore Jamie's throat from their body.

Delia handed him a blanket. Its scratchy fabric irritated more than comforted, but he wrapped it around his waist anyway.

"Hell," he said, his eyes wet with raw emotion. "Was anyone hurt?" His voice broke.

"Aside from the feral, no." Delia's tone was clipped and careful, as if she expected him to shift again at any moment.

"Jamie – their name was Jamie." Caleb's muscles burned as he leant over, wincing against the pain. Delia moved to his side, gently pushing him down again. "Ethan?"

"He's fine. Shaken but fine. Argo is with him now. Rest," was all she said before leaving the room, a nod directed towards Ava and Aiel who had moved back into the room. Aiel walked up to him, a steaming cup of herbal tea in her hands.

"Here," she said. "It's ginger; it should help with the inflammation."

"Thanks." Caleb sighed, letting the spiced liquid warm his heavy body. He leant back, closing his eyes. "What have I done?"

"What you had to," Aiel said, placing a gentle hand against his face. "Who knows how many you av saved out there. You're a hero, Caleb; don't you forget it. Not for a second."

"I'm no hero."

Aiel reached for the empty cup and nodded towards the bed. "We'll see about that, love. Now, get some sleep."

***

When he woke, he noticed that he had been moved into a fresh crate, the bedroll beneath him softer than those in the medical unit. Strength returned to his limbs, more than he had felt since before the fight. He took in his surroundings. The crate had been scrubbed of any external markings. It smelled of fresh wood, treated with something floral.

It looked as if a majority of their crates had been moved to the pathway where he and Ethan had originally resided. *More open space for the battle to come*, he thought. His crate was situated close to the top of the hill, allowing him a view of those working and training at its base. He groaned, forcing himself to sit, catching a glimpse of Argo sparring with Ethan outside. Groups of other hybrids looked to be following drills from a handful of the hunters. Hybrids of all shapes and sizes had come to train, some with weapons, some with nothing but their bare hands.

"Hi-yah!" Ethan exclaimed with an untrained karate chop.

The sight of the child made Caleb smile. He wished it was him out there, teaching Ethan – not that he had much fighting experience. In fact, he would probably need lessons from the gentle giant himself.

He hated to admit it, but Argo looked like an Adonis, the sun reflecting off hard-earned muscles, every ridge defined like it had been sculpted. He wore his scars with pride, the effects of his uncontrolled shifting enhancing the godlike vison.

Prick, he thought. His own lean body would never look like his friend's broad frame.

Argo raised his head, squinting up the hill, a grin spreading across his face when Caleb waved. *"You're up!"* His friend dropped his practice spear, earning him a quick jab from Ethan before the kid followed suit and spotted him.

"Caleb!" The excitement in Ethan's voice made him smile as they both rushed towards him. They could have been brothers in another life, mops of unwashed sandy hair flying in the wind.

"Oooofffttt," Caleb grunted, thanking the medics who had made the salves and remedies that kept Ethan's full-body slam from hurting as much as it would have days ago.

"Easy, buddy." Argo's arm snaked around the boy and lifted him off effortlessly. He grinned down at Caleb, but there was something else in his gaze, something Caleb couldn't quite read.

"You've been out for days, man," Argo said.

"I wanna see him!" Ethan squirmed in Argo's grip.

"Just be careful, alright? Your brother took a hit a few days ago. You can't go slamming into him again."

"Brother?" Caleb lifted an eyebrow.

"The kid has been switching between calling you his brother and hero since you took care of the feral. Can't shut him up."

Caleb let out a soft chuckle.

"Just how many days have I been out?" he asked Argo while reaching out for the boy, wrapping his arms around him as tight as he could. "You're the best little brother a wolf could ask for."

Ethan beamed, settling beside him and picking at the frayed edges of the blanket. He stuck his tongue out at Argo, who laughed and held his hands up in surrender. Caleb kept his gaze on Argo, waiting for an answer.

"Three. The kid wouldn't leave your side. Delia has been in and out. I should go tell her you're awake; the cat wants a war council. You dreamed of me, by the way." Argo smirked. *"I'm flattered."*

"Fuck off."

Argo winked at him with a grin.

Caleb looked at Ethan, concerned the boy could hear him in human form just as well as he could in wolf form. The child didn't show any sign of understanding.

"The heart wants what the heart wants." Argo turned to leave with a dramatic sweep of his arms, as if he were still dancing with a spear.

"Where are you going?" The sound of his voice caused Ethan to jump. Switching between pack talk and human speech was going to take some getting used to.

"To get Delia and Jan. She said he tried to talk to you during the ... attack." He shot a look towards Ethan, who was doing his best not to look like he was eavesdropping. The slightly tilted head gave him away.

"Ethan, can you hear me?"

Nothing.

"I think it's just in wolf form. He can't seem to hear anyone else, either. You two have a pack bond, I guess."

"I hope so."

"That he can only hear you in wolf form? Heaven forbid the boy hears you thinking about me half naked."

"ARGO!"

"I'm kidding," Argo said, holding his palms up.

A sudden wave of emotion swelled in Caleb's chest. His heart pounded as he pulled Ethan closer. Before he could think, he reached for Argo, beckoning him closer too.

Argo hesitated, staring at Caleb's outstretched hand before placing his own against it. Caleb squeezed, holding on with everything he had, resisting the urge to cry.

Confusion flitted across Argo's face. He leaned back slightly, his body tensing like he wanted to flee from the unexpected affection. But he didn't pull away.

Caleb returned the big wolf's smirk from earlier and tugged him down, the force of the pull making Argo topple on top of him. He winced against the pain but laughed as Argo caught himself before he crushed them both.

Caleb reached for the back of Argo's neck, pulling him close. His scent was familiar now, comforting in a way he hadn't expected. It was hard to remember a time when he couldn't stand this guy for being better than him.

Whatever happened next, they were in this together. Their foreheads met and they both closed their eyes.

"We will fight this together. Brothers."

They stayed like that for a minute, breathing together as one unit.

Argo moved first, and Caleb let his hand drop, smiling at the wetness in Argo's eyes. Not that he'd admit it.

"Come on, kid. Let's get Delia. She will want to see our friend awake and ready to roll." He winked at Caleb again.

"Ass," Caleb thought.

"Again, I can hear you."

***

Delia's visit wasn't nearly as pleasant as the two boys', but it had Caleb on the edge of his seat. He listened attentively as she explained her suspicions for the next raid.

"I haven't received any intel," she said, "and there have been no supply drops. They've gone silent on me."

"What does that mean?"

"It means they don't trust her anymore." The guttural, booming voice he had come to know was Jan's thundered through his head.

"Have you been able to hear me this whole time?"

"Pay attention," the bear scolded.

"He only speaks when he wants to. It's difficult for him, but it's how we can tell he is still one of us," Delia said with a soft smile.

"Took you long enough to hear me, wolf." Jan's voice came with a scoff.

Winson poked his head into the crate with May on his shoulder and Grace and Berrum behind him.

"We're headed out, boss. More hybrids have come in from the west; we're going to need more food before the week is out. Our stores will hold us a while but we're off to catch some fish. Be back by sunset. Good to see you're awake, wolf boy."

"Thanks, Winson," Caleb and Delia said in unison.

Returning to the conversation at hand, Caleb asked, "Have there been any sightings of invaders? Other than the hybrids?"

Delia shook her head. "We knew it was a risk, the pattern changing after Gregorio's last visit. What did he say? Weeks. Which means, what ... we have one, maybe two left?"

"We're not ready," Caleb said to her.

"None of us are," Tilon confirmed, entering the crate.

Caleb rolled his eyes. "How long do you think we have?"

Delia looked worried. "I don't know. My contacts have been radio silent. The hunters have found nothing at their usual sites. What did you find?" she asked turning her attention to Tilon.

"Nothing good. We may have less time than we thought. We've caught two clickers a day out from here. If they have sent their watch dogs in preparation, we don't have long."

Delia blew out a breath. "Damn."

"What?" Caleb asked.

"We've seen this pattern before. Clickers this close likely means days, not weeks."

"Then we best organise our forces," Tilon responded.

Delia looked between them. "No group is to venture too far from the camp. Training is underway for our able-bodied, three times a day. Buddy programs have been set up – no one is to move without a partner at any time. No less than two to a crate, more if they will fit. The hunters are stationed throughout the camp; Missy and Edgar have recruited more guards for the front gate and we have a post set near the lake. When they come, the call will be sounded and we will disperse, ready to fight."

Caleb winced as he made to stand, scratches and bruises still covering most of his body.

Delia sighed and moved to him, removing the blanket from his body to inspect his bandages. "You're healing well," she said, reaching for a damp cloth

Ava had placed beside him earlier. Delia set to unwrapping his wound. The healing process was fast, but not fast enough.

"Another day or two and you will be out of bed."

"We don't have days," Caleb said, letting her hands trail his body, both gentle and clinical at the same time. It was the first time he had allowed her to touch him, no longer fighting a desire to bite and snap at her. She redressed his wounds.

"Just rest, son," Tilon said. "You're right – we don't have days. I can give you a few more hours. Delia, have the hunters meet me in the storage shed once Winson and the scouts return."

Delia nodded and turned to leave.

"Delia," Caleb called after her. "What do you think we're up against?"

"If we're not smart, capture and death."

***

Caleb couldn't rest, but Ava and Aiel seemed to be taking watch, making sure he didn't get up before he had to. They came in throughout the day, wiping the infection away from the wound and applying a thick greenish paste around the edges. The sting of the medicine gave way to welcome coolness. Argo and Ethan stopped by with a plate of meat, the smell making Caleb salivate the second it hit his nose.

He tried to focus on the world around him, eyes closed to heighten his other senses. He could see the camp in his mind, the movements of hybrids both familiar and new, their smells and sounds painting a picture of their new life in his head. Caleb tried to reach out to them through telepathy, their voices having left his head once he had changed back into human form. It was only Argo and Jan who remained, the bear seldom speaking into his mind.

Caleb was dozing off as the air started to cool. A warm hand touched his shoulder lightly. He stirred, looking up at the intrusion.

"It's time to get up, kid," Winson said kindly, offering him a scaled hand.

Tilon had gathered Delia and her hunters by the time Winson and Caleb arrived. Jan stood off to the side, ever watchful.

"Council time?" Argo asked in his head.

Caleb found his friend's face in the sea of hybrids and tilted his head towards the gathering group. Argo stood, touching Ava's arm slightly, indicating it was time to move. They got up together, leaving Ethan with Aiel by the fire. The boy looked like he was babbling away happily at the nurse.

"Alright, love?" Ava asked Caleb as they arrived.

"Yeah, I'm good," he said, starting to believe it.

"Glad you're up and at 'em, sport," Argo said, punching his arm lightly.

"Let's get started," Delia cut through the banter. "Tilon?"

Tilon moved to the head of the group, taking his place beside the smaller feline. Together, they went through the map of their camp and its surrounding areas, pointing out the locations they had scouted over the last few days. The hunters watched intently, nodding or offering comments to share what they had found at the bunkers and suspected hybrid camps. Tilon showed them where they had met the clickers, still unsure which camp the beasts were stalking.

"What's next?" Winson asked.

"We speak to the group. The last few days have been busy; they will continue to be until the raid hits. I don't want us to be caught unaware."

"Our recruits are coming along," one of the hunters offered.

Delia nodded her head in agreeance. "I want a watch at all times. We need to be marching the perimeter. Far enough to show the soldiers who they are messing with, but close enough to alert the group. You need to be able to help one another out there. Those who are still here will continue training." She sighed. "We should have been helping them harness their instincts long before now."

"Dwelling on the past will get us nowhere, love," Ava offered.

"Ava, we will need your medical bay stocked as much as possible. Create a number of caches around our camp, here, here and here," Tilon said, pointing out several map locations. "We will draw the fights into these areas; we know this land better than their recruits and we need to use that to our advantage."

Delia spoke up again. "Grace and Berrum have connected with scouts from another hybrid group. They are likewise small, fast and efficient." Their two runners poked their heads into the group, followed by a group of short, skinny, childlike creatures with long necks and dark fur around their eyes. Their heads were coated in a golden-brown fur. They stood at their full four-foot height and looked seemingly everywhere all at once.

Meercats? No wonder they wanted to keep to themselves.

One of them sneezed, shaking their head dramatically. Grace jumped at the sound before joining the conversation. "We're the fastest runners you have." The larger bodies parted to make way for their smallest members. "We'll run between the pairs and alert the camp as soon as we know of an incoming threat."

Delia turned to Ava. "We need to fill the storerooms as best we can with what we have. I don't want anyone bar our hunters venturing out if we can help it. Tilon, Winson and I will continue to train with those who are able to fight. Any who are unable to join us physically can help with feeding, running and mending. Our weak will be kept safe in my home with Edgar, Missy and their rear guards when the time comes. Now ..." She paused.

"It's time to tell the rest of them what we are up against," Tilon finished.

Caleb's skin tingled. He didn't know whether he wanted to laugh or cry as the plans came together. His lip twitched, and Argo raised an eyebrow at him. May flew overhead, calling softly down to the group.

Winson looked upwards and tilted his head towards the bird. "They're ready for us."

"Then let's go," Delia said, leading the way out to the firepits.

"What about us?" Caleb asked, pointing towards himself and Argo.

"You're coming with me, wolf" Jan said.

Be Prepared

Chapter Thirty-One

Jan led him into the woods, just far enough so they wouldn't be in the way but able to get back quickly if an alert was raised. The trees were dense on the outskirts, hiding them from view of the main compound. Caleb had wanted Argo to come, but Delia insisted he was better off with the others. He would be practising shifts with Jan and Argo was still too unpredictable in his wolven form. His friend needed a team around him to help him to control his emotions or wound him enough to shift back if things got out of hand. Caleb was better with a singular focal point. They would both need to learn for the upcoming battle.

"He has been able to pull himself back are the times someone he loves is at risk of his wrath. But you or Ethan aren't always going to be there to save him," she had said. "You, Caleb, need discipline. Your control is much better, but the noise in your head distracts you. If you want to lead, you are going to need to focus."

"You need to channel your anger into your shift, but don't let it take control." Jan's voice echoed inside Caleb's head, pulling him back to his lesson. The giant bear wielded an unexpected amount of wisdom.

A day of one-on-one training was all it took for Caleb to see that Jan's hardened exterior was a front. He cared deeply for Delia and her people and admitted he hadn't always agreed with the feline's methods, though he understood them.

"What happened to you?" Caleb asked telepathically, struggling to hold on to his wolf body, his muscles fatigued from the practice.

"Focus," Jan scolded. *"Your flank is starting to reform."*

"What?" Caleb moved his head to view his side, pale skin poking through his grey fur.

Jan snorted and lunged forward with a swipe.

Caleb yelped, dodging the bear's extended claw. *"Hey!"*

"Get angry and hold it, you damn dog."

Caleb growled at the insult and ran forward to snap at Jan's arm. *"Bugger off."* Heat radiated from his skin where the overgrown hair crept towards the centre of his exposed side, covering it with fur once more.

Jan stood tall, catching Caleb's head and holding him at a distance. *"Good job, now hold it."*

They had been practising shifting at will. Caleb had gotten better after the fight with Jamie, turning his anger into a tool, funnelling it into his body to expand and contract. He was able to lean into the hot, tingling sensation that made his hair stand on end and stop fighting the movement of his bones as they morphed into place. Now it was about learning to remain a wolf through exhaustion and tuning into the voices he needed rather than being overwhelmed by the noise.

"What if I hurt people … when the time comes?" Caleb asked. *"I've shown I could go either way."*

He could have sworn the bear smiled.

"I think you have proven the opposite."

Caleb tilted his head up at his new and unexpected mentor, causing a deep chuckle to reverberate through his head.

"You're laughing at me?"

Jan dropped to his haunches, moving his large body awkwardly to sit cross-legged on the ground before him. It was odd to see his movements become so human after thinking he would turn feral at any moment.

"When you came here, you wanted to fight. Fight us, fight your father and take on the world. You weren't ready. You've seen what the last decade has done to us; some of us will never get to go home. Our people have tried, been killed and blackmailed into a long-running experiment we never asked to be involved in. It

took someone more stubborn than Delia to convince us we had a chance and make us see hope again."

"I'm still not sure I understand why," Caleb said, sitting.

"Your arrival was the first sign that this has become personal for your father. He is no longer playing with lives of others. He picked someone from his own home. I don't know the relationship you both had on the outside, but he wanted to see what you could do here. That changes things. The raids have increased since you arrived, as have our shift-related deaths. If all of this comes down to your father, it looks like he is trying to keep watch. When they realise Delia isn't feeding them information anymore ... Well."

"We'll be ready for them," Caleb thought, feeling his body relax.

"I can see the fire in her eyes again. The one she had when we were building this place from the ground up. When we were truly helping." He sighed. *"Something in the air has changed. It won't be long now. This time it won't be one of ours being taken away and forced under a microscope."*

Caleb felt his body twinge, the tension releasing from his limbs, lulled with Jan's deep voice and his exhaustion. He knew he would lose his ability to speak to the bear as soon as he let go completely. Jan seemed to be able to force his thoughts into Caleb's head now they were connected, but it didn't work both ways.

"Let it happen," Jan projected at him, his eye closed as he leaned his head back.

"I'll lose you," Caleb thought back. He was less worried about bodily changes each time he shifted – there hadn't been anything new show up in days.

"Don't be stubborn. It'll get us nowhere. We'll work on nonverbal commands once you've rested." The big bear's eye closed seconds before a soft snore whistled out of his mouth.

***

Caleb and Jan spent several days together, Delia's warning of a raid whirring in Caleb's mind during each intense training session. They all knew they were on borrowed time, and the tension seemed to build with each passing day.

He groaned as he woke in their training arena, his body aching and muscles screaming for more rest. They were to train with the others in camp from tomorrow. Caleb flicked his ear, focusing on the sounds around him as soon as he woke.

Everything seems fine. Again.

He could feel Jan's presence a short distance away. He sensed the bear tense, the shuffle of his large feet telling Caleb he had moved further into the forest.

Odd. Big bear is bloody quiet for his size when he wants to be.

He sat, groaning and stretching out his back, the hair on the back of his neck rising. Caleb made his way to their water supply, chilled from the cooling air, and splashed his face. Something snapped behind him, larger than a twig. A branch had come off a tree and fallen to the ground. Caleb froze, droplets dripping from his chin as he focused. He inhaled deeply, trying to pinpoint Jan's location.

He wasn't behind him. Another snap. He turned his head toward the vibration.

He caught a patch of darkened fur stalking him through the trees.

Shit.

Jan had told him they would fight, that his abilities would be tested before they rejoined the group. He thought the mock battles throughout the last few days had covered that. If this was Jan's final test, he needed to shift. Now.

Caleb pooled his mental energy, focusing on the physical shift. He was so damn tired. He thought about Jamie, the fear that not all of them would make it out alive. Of his father, the reason so many people had suffered. Hatred swelled inside him, his limbs reacting to his temper. He funnelled his emotion to each part of his body. The snapping of bones no longer startled him, and the pain had become a dull, familiar ache.

They had experimented with partial shifting. A half-wolf, half-man hybrid gave him the benefit of agility, strength and sharpened claws while still being able to talk to the other hybrids as he learnt to command his pack of fighters. His legs thickened, fur rushing down them; he held them there before they could shrink into their powerful, lean animal form. The thudding of his head followed, forcing him to concentrate on holding parts of his body while allowing others to move into the shape he envisioned. His pelt rolled up his torso, his midsection tightening, his abs locking on tight, furred ridges. The veins along his arms pulsed. His chest broadened into a wide and chiselled bust, soft fur lining every inch of him. Finally, his neck expanded to support his head as it elongated and swelled.

Caleb shook his head as sharp teeth pushed through the bottom of his mouth, the copper tang filling his mouth as his nose morphed into a snout. He cried internally, begging the shift to stop, holding it for a second or two before falling to all fours.

He gritted his teeth against the pain. He couldn't hold it. Caleb yelped as he lost control and he became the wolf.

Fuck!

"Brace," Jan said, his voice filled with menace.

"What?" Caleb retorted in his mind before the dust mites and sweat caught in Jan's fur came closer. The trees rattled around them as the bear advanced. Jan's good eye flashed, its haunting darkness coming straight at him.

He launched sideways. Jan faltered at the sudden movement, stumbling to regain his footing.

"Ha! Ya big brute. Forgot how fast I was, didn't you?" Caleb jumped in triumph like an excited pup. His opponent wasn't amused.

Jan's roar seemed to catch him in a vortex, a whirlwind of sound. Caleb froze as his opponent turned and charged again. The bear's massive arm swung out, claws poised to strike.

He wasn't playing. He wanted to see what Caleb could do.

Fine.

The wolf leapt sideways again, eyes locked on the massive paw tearing through the air. Jan missed, but he was ready for Caleb's ability to dodge quickly. His other paw swung around, reaching for fur. Caleb saw the movement and pushed himself from the ground, teeth bared. His fangs sank into Jan's limp arm before the bear had a chance to move it. The beast roared, for real this time. Caleb held on, sinking his teeth deeper. He snarled against Jan's skin, waiting for the inevitable counterattack.

His triumph didn't last long. Pain and warmth spread across his side as Jan's free hand caught him.

Caleb let himself go limp, a dead weight in the giant's grip. Jan hesitated, a brief pause before his mentor instincts kicked in, checking if he was truly hurt.

Sucker.

Using the bear's own hold for leverage, Caleb kicked off, pushing his momentum outwards, twisting as soon as his feet hit the ground.

He lunged – this time for Jan's throat.

Jan didn't have time to react.

Caleb's front paws slammed into his chest, claws digging into thick fur. He barked, opened his jaw, and rested his teeth gently against Jan's neck.

"Got you."

Jan's breathing had stilled. Caleb could see the beat of his pulse against the side of his neck. The bear dropped his arms. The wolf hybrid retracted his claws and landed gracefully to the ground, watching him with caution.

"Well done," his mentor said, his breath steadying.

"What's wrong? Cat got your tongue?" Caleb laughed internally at his own joke. Jan took a deep breath and closed his eye, as if he were holding back the desire to launch for his student again.

"You're as ready as you are going to be." The words seemed final. *"Shift back when you can. We should get back."*

Caleb lifted his head. Something was wrong.

"Jan?"

He inhaled.

Smoke.

Not the kind that came from roasting tubers or clicker meat over a fire. This wasn't planned. The scent thickened, carried by the wind.

The crackle and snap of burning branches reached his ears.

Delia was right, they weren't coming by air.

On foot?

That would mean the raiders had been in the forest far longer than they'd thought. Had they missed the call? Caleb inhaled again.

Thick, pungent smoke.

"Do you smell that?" Caleb asked, his heartbeat racing.

"Move."

Daddy's Home

Chapter Thirty-Two

Caleb clung to Jan's back as the bear tore through the forest, each step bringing them closer to potential devastation. He was drained, focusing on conserving his energy for the next shift.

Panic rose up his throat. It was never going to be enough time to learn to control his abilities, they had all known that, but he'd had to try. They all did if they wanted a shot at escape.

Caleb's nerves buzzed as dozens of hybrids came into focus. Two of Delia's hunters were rushing outside of the camp walls. They had rough wooden chest plates strapped to the front of their bodies, spears in hand.

Caleb could taste the fear in the air, the wind stinging against his skin.

"Get us inside," he called down to Jan. Smoke was rising from their base.

Jan's breathing was heavy. The bear had slowed his movement, grunting while he searched for the best place to enter.

"There!" Caleb yelled, pointing in front of them.

Dozens of bodies were marching into the camp, all of them dressed in black uniforms. They shuffled in formations, hunting down the hybrids with precision. Caleb's breath caught. They had only ever seen a small handful of soldiers at once, accompanied by Gregorio and his clickers. This was something else entirely.

"Hold steady!" one of the hybrids yelled, ordering a group forward. They were dressed in the same rough armour as the hunters running towards the soldiers. Jan tensed beneath him.

"Wait," Caleb hissed. "We need to see what we're up against. They haven't noticed us yet."

Jan grunted as Caleb pushed himself further up the bear's shoulders.

Hybrids were screaming and running in every direction, climbing over each other to get out of the way or racing into the forest for cover. Others had formed into squads, fighting back with everything they had. Teeth gnashed and claws struck out at the enemy. There were too many soldiers and not enough hybrids.

One of the recruits had Edgar by the neck, a needle pushing into him. The hybrid's body fell to the ground and the soldier placed the guard's hands across his chest. "Bag this one; looks like a fucking llama or something."

The familiar tingling sensation ran through him.

"We need to turn those vials back on them," Caleb said with a growl.

A squeal caught his attention. He turned to witness one of their older hybrids fall in a heap, a soldier holding them, extracting a syringe from their neck.

"Take it," the soldier commanded, another lifting the hybrid with ease and dragging them towards the compound's walls. Caleb watched, heart pounding. The soldier barely spared them a glance, focusing on preparing another vial and vanishing into the fray. His campmate's chest rose and fell – unconscious, not d ead.

This wasn't a raid. This was an onslaught, but they wanted the hybrids alive, as many as they could get.

"Motherfuckers."

He rolled off Jan's back. A soldier had turned towards them. Their eyes widened through their hood at the sight of the mutilated bear, deciding against taking them head-on and turning towards another fighting squad.

Caleb let the adrenaline fuel his shifting muscles, his body responding to his command. Jan dropped to all fours beside him. Jan bared his teeth in a snarl.

A scream tore in the distance and Caleb looked up to see Argo's huge wolf form flinging a grown man into flames that had spread out around them. His friend's training looked to have been successful; he was motivated by the needs of the pack, able to focus on the whole group rather than a need for blood. They had both come a long way in less than a week.

Argo roared. Another soldier hit the flames, their uniform catching, mask filling with smoke. The smell of burning flesh permeated the air seconds before their muffled screams.

"Argo!" he called out through his mind.

"Brother!" The voice inside his mind. Argo's voice had changed – raspy and fuelled with anger and a desire for violence, but it was still him.

"You're okay," Caleb said, relieved. He suspected that Delia had been the one to train him over the last week.

"A little help?" Argo asked as two more uniformed bodied rushed him.

Caleb ran forward, dodging hybrids and soldiers caught in their own battles as he made his way through the grounds.

"Shit," he swore, ducking under an arm holding a vial of oozing yellow liquid that slashed towards him. He snapped at the arm, catching the rough fabric in his teeth. Crunching down, his teeth found flesh, earning him a howl from the body inside the suit. They dropped the vial and Caleb snarled at them.

"Caleb!" Argo called. A third soldier had joined his fight. Argo was large and powerful but against three trained soldiers, he was outmatched. Caleb turned, springing off his own assailant with a backwards kick, and changed path.

His body slammed into one of Argo's foes, the force knocking them to the ground and making another turn towards him. Argo used the distraction to lunge, sinking his teeth into the soldier's neck, their body dropping instantly. Caleb turned to see the person underneath him reach into their pocket and stamped down on their wrist. He lifted his lip, showing his already bloodied teeth, hot saliva dripping downward. Their eyes widened through their mask.

"I'm sorry. I—"

Their pleas were cut off as Argo's head smacked into theirs, knocking them out cold.

"Go, I got them now."

"We need one of them alive, Argo."

"We need for us to be alive first. Go and help the others."

Caleb called out to his pack, watching Argo turn and run further into the camp, lashing out with his jaws to pull soldiers away from hybrids as he made his way through.

"Delia? Ethan?" He couldn't pick up on their scents with so much happening around him.

"Come on, Ethan, please!"

May cried above him, flying towards Delia's home where they had agreed to keep their weaker members.

Panic and sweat filled his nose as a dark shape darted past him. They were small, their movements uncertain, running away from the fight, not towards it.

Caleb crouched low, baring his teeth.

They were still part of this, whether they wanted to be or not.

They stopped.

Caleb turned slowly, every muscle tensed, eyes locked onto theirs.

He knew he looked terrifying with his shining eyes and sharpened teeth ready to draw blood. He advanced, one foot forward head lowered in a snarl, eyes never leaving the masked figure before him. They stumbled, two steps to his one, too afraid to turn and run.

Caleb focused on his vocal cords; he had only had mild success speaking out loud while in wolf form during his time with Jan. He felt his throat expand, the tendons allowing him room to push sound through. He tried to speak, giving way to a threatening rasp.

His prey fell backwards over a tree root, looking up at him in fear. The voices in his head buzzed against his skull, dimming as his focus lay on the human before him. Stalking up to his prey, Caleb pinned them down, his paws holding their chest to the ground. Their body trembled beneath him. The smell of urine, putrid and warm, filled the air. They were scared. Good.

"Who. Are. You?"

Each word burned his throat like razor blades, but the shift had worked. Their fear was worth the pain. They lay stunned. Caleb growled and pressed harder.

"Don't make me ask you again." This came out softer the second time. He could feel the cords in his body fighting against him, ready to snap back into place and leave him with growls and snarls for communication.

May's distressed calls gnawed at him.

The body beneath him shifted. Their hand moved to their pocket.

Caleb pinned the arm under his paw, his jaws snapping down before he could think. His teeth sank into flesh, wrenching the limb away. A syringe tumbled free, its shimmering liquid catching the dim light.

Snarling, Caleb nudged the pocket with his nose, searching for more. The recruit's pocket was full of them.

Caleb looked up as a nearby hybrid yelped with panic, the scream filling his head. One of the raiders had them by the scruff of their neck, their small, partially furred body flailing as a vial was plunged into them. The hybrid stopped fighting. His father's minion dropped them before running further into the camp.

The body underneath him squirmed. Caleb gnashed his teeth in front of his victim's face. Sniffles and choked pleas rushed up at him.

The hybrids needed to turn whatever was in these vials against their captors. Give them a taste of their own medicine.

"Vials, Cal!" Argo's voice sounded in his mind. His thoughts were cut off by a new assailant forcing his friend to fight.

The soldier jabbed upwards in another attempt to stick him with a needle. Caleb caught their arm again; his teeth had broken the skin. They screamed, dropping back to the ground in a whimper.

Caleb forced his vocals to work. "Pocket."

"How can you talk?" They had found their voice, still shaking through their tears, their eyes glistening with moisture beneath the mask.

"Now," Caleb growled, releasing the pressure on their arm slightly. They reached down, fingers trembling as they fumbled with the Velcro strip. It tore slowly, each rip of the fabric grating on his patience. Caleb snarled, his eyes tracking the soldier's movements. They could stick him if they moved fast enough. He couldn't let that happen.

They pulled out several vials, each attached to a quick-release syringe. The thin plastic casing over the needles wouldn't stop an accidental jab if either of them moved suddenly. A desire to rip into the recruit beneath him ran hot through Caleb's body. They were here to capture all of them, weren't they? He could kill this one and be done with it, moving onto the next in a matter of minutes.

You need at least one of them alive; this is the first one we've pinned. Grunts of encouragement and disgruntlement sounded in his head from those that had heard the thought.

"Please," the soldier said, softer now. "I don't even want to be here."

The world around the two of them slowed, questions firing rapidly through Caleb's brain.

What the fuck, Dad? They were recruiting unwilling non-hybrid participants now?

Torn between fighting back and taking a few of the uniforms out or shifting back into human form to get real answers, Caleb had to make a choice and just hope like hell it was the right one.

He let his body relax. The shift happened swiftly, pain barely registering as his bones realigned.

Then he noticed it – another patch of wolf fur remained on his forearm. *Maybe the changes haven't stopped.*

He turned his shining blue-green eyes down at the captive. His furred ear twitched, continuing to take in the sounds of fighting around him.

"Do you have eyes on Delia or the others?" he asked Argo, his gaze unwavering from the masked recruit, who had gone rigid.

"I'm searching, man. These bastards keep on coming."

"I've got one of them. A kid, I think."

Argo's voice went quiet in his mind, his normal chatter turning to animalistic grunts as his friend focused on the fight. They were getting closer.

"You're, uh, naked?" his captive said, still trapped beneath him.

He had been for the better part of his training. Around Jan, it hardly mattered. Shifting back and forth was easier without worrying about his clothes tearing every time. Wind whipped past as another hybrid sprinted away from their pursuer.

The body underneath him bucked.

Shit.

He turned to glare at them, pressing down against their arms, pinning their lower body with his hips. He hadn't let his hand-to-hand combat training slip during his time with Jan. The person under him was outmatched and they knew it. Their body stilled with the pressure.

I need to get their uniform. Turn the needles on these bastards.

"What's in the vials?" he demanded.

"Dude, you're starkers. Can you get off me?"

Caleb held the young soldier still underneath him. "If I do, you'll run."

Another hybrid scream filled the air.

"Give me your uniform," Caleb grunted, letting up. When his captive didn't run, he gave them a little more room.

"What?" they asked, dusting themself off.

"Your gear. Give it to me."

"Why?" They reached and pulled back the hood covering their face, revealing a mess of floppy brown hair, their gender not immediately apparent.

"You're just a kid." Caleb's voice dropped. "Like the rest of us."

"Sod off, I'm no younger than you."

"My friends are dying and I'm losing patience. Give me the suit and I may have a chance to save them ... In turn, I won't shift back into a wolf and tear your arm off. What's in the vials?"

"They're just sedated. To be taken back with us, whoever we can get except you and the other shifter, Argo."

Caleb flinched.

"I told you, I don't want to be here. Your dad is fucked up." The kid sighed. "Look, our only orders were to grab as many hybrids as we could, stick them with this shit and try not to die."

"That last part may be harder for you than you think."

"I'm going to hit you."

"Like hell you are."

The punch knocked Caleb sideways. Before he could react, the kid flipped their position, pinning him to the ground with their thighs. He growled, ready to throw them off.

"Shut up and trust me," they muttered. Everything in Caleb screamed to fight back, but they hadn't tried to hurt him yet. Caleb stilled, focusing on the soldier kneeling over him.

They leaned down next to his ear, putting pressure on his chest. "I'm going to take one of these syringes and release it next to you. Any one of these recruits will think you've been captured. When you feel a tap, play dead."

Caleb nodded, the fabric of their suit brushing against his skin.

He felt the soldier reach for the vial followed by the sound of the plastic cap coming off the tip of the needle. The recruit tapped against his arm. Caleb tried to relax, melting into the ground, keeping one eye open.

He heard the movement around them, gruff voices congratulating the soldier for taking their first hybrid down.

"Don't move," his newfound ally said, releasing the fluid next to him, the hiss of it expelling onto the ground making him shudder. "They're going. Stay down," they warned, climbing off him. Thirty agonising seconds crawled by, the sound of heavy boots fading.

"Here." The kid stripped off their suit, standing in nothing but a sweat-drenched tee. They handed it to Caleb.

It would be a tight fit.

"Argo," Caleb thought. *"Where are you?"* He was met with nothing. A sigh escaped his lips, exhaustion looming beneath the adrenaline.

"Delia! Tilon?" Shit. *"Ethan!"* No one else could hear him in this form.

"Caleb?"

He turned towards the de-robed soldier.

"I want to stay. Help, if I can."

"Why would you help us?"

The young recruit looked at their feet, shuffling before answering.

"My sister … she was taken years ago." They paused, "maybe she's still alive. I enlisted too, to see if she was here. To take her home."

Caleb blinked at them, the information taking him by surprise. "You're going to have to lay low. I don't think they will take kindly to anyone helping us."

"Probably not," they agreed.

"What's her name? Your sister?"

Two soldiers ran past in pursuit of a much faster hybrid not noticing them. The hybrid evading them with ease. Caleb caught a glimpse of tiny teeth as they ran.

"Quick. We'll look for her if we survive this fight. Right now, I need to save as many of the hybrids as I can."

Caleb pulled on the kid's uniform. The fabric clung to his form and the once-familiar smell shea butter mixed with the scared soldiers urine made him want to gag. Soap? The kid was clean before they came out here. The material was hot and heavy but flexible. No wonder they were sweating; wearing layers under this would be a nightmare. The pockets lining each leg pressed against him. If everyone carried as much as this suit held, they could take down the whole camp twice over.

Caleb reached for a vial. The fluoro-yellow liquid caught the light, and his stomach turned. Memories flashed through his mind. The party that had put him here, the thick, viscous poison sinking into Lucia. It seemed like a lifetime ago, back when his only concern had been bedding the girl. Maybe being stranded in the woods hadn't been the worst thing to happen to him after all.

The kid snapped their fingers, waving a hand obnoxiously in front of his face. "Hey, remember me? I'm a sitting duck out here."

Caleb pulled them into a group of nearby trees. He could still hear fighting all around them, the noise of the soldiers blurring with the grunts and growls of the hybrids. Hybrids and soldiers alike had been left in bloodied piles. Death had never been in the plan. "I need to find my friends."

The recruit nodded, slumping down against a trunk, allowing their head to loll to the side. They looked unconscious, with their chest rising and falling slowly.

Neat trick, he thought, dropping to kneel in front of them.

He inhaled deeply, tilting his head slightly, using his senses to get the lay of the fighting. Branches snapped to his side. One of the raiders ran past, dragging an unconscious hybrid in their wake.

Caleb frowned, trying to watch where they were being taken while talking to the kid who apparently wanted to help.

"There are other groups," Caleb said quickly. "Why are you after ours?"

"Yours had a leader working for us already. But news got out that she may be switching sides. The other groups are more dangerous, less organised. I don't think anyone was prepared for you to have a rebellion ready when we came."

Caleb grabbed one of the vials and flicked off the cap. "Will this hurt you?" he asked, rushed as he felt more of his kin panic.

"Come on, dude, I'm helping, aren't I? I can play dead; you don't need to—"

Caleb pressed in on them, leaning in to drive the needle into their exposed skin, the plunger pushing down without a fight. They hit the dirt with a soft thunk.

"Thanks for the help."

"Why?" they rasped.

"The hybrids think you are an enemy right now. If they think you are dead, you may be left alone. I doubt these soldiers will be back, even for one of their own. They haven't proven themselves loyal so far. How did you all get here?"

Blank, glassy eyes stared back at him.

Bugger.

Caleb turned back to the fight, running towards a squealing hybrid. It was the small, weasel-like creature he had seen running from two soldiers earlier. One of the soldiers had been dropped, their wrist exposing dozens of tiny teeth marks.

"Don't even try it! I'll stick you too! I have enough poison for all of you bastards," they said in a high-pitched voice, frantic with fear and fury.

The second soldier yelped as the short hybrid darted forward, fangs first. Caleb caught them from behind, another vial in his hands.

"Easy. It's Caleb," he said, pushing the needle into the recruit's neck. He let the body fall as soon as he felt their weight shift.

"Take the vials," Caleb said. "Stick as many as you can."

Antonia's black eyes flashed, a smile creeping across her face as she reached into the unconscious soldier's pocket and produced a handful of the syringes.

A familiar voice caught his attention.

"You can't have her!"

Shit, Ethan!

The boy's small and determined squeal sounded desperate. Caleb's heart hammered in his chest – the kid was alive and fighting.

Ethan's wail filled him with a mixture of sweet relief and crippling fear. Hot tears touched his eyes seconds before his body reacted with fury.

If he shifted again now, the suit would rip and he would be back at square one. Better for the soldiers to think he was an ally. He ran towards the sound, telling himself to breathe.

Argo and Tilon stood in the thick of the fight, their massive forms towering over smaller soldiers and hybrids alike. Argo looked to have achieved something akin to the half shift Caleb had been trying all week. His broad, furred torso gave way to strong human legs, thick with corded muscle. He had the body of a beast. Black-suited soldiers lay dead or unconscious to the side of them as they took on another small group of his father's recruits.

"No!" Ethan's panicked call alerted him again.

Caleb homed in on the kid's location. He could sense his small body standing in defence of their fallen leader. Argo and Tilon were fine, but the kid was not. Caleb took off in the direction of his young friend's calls.

Careful not to draw suspicion, he made as if to chase down hybrids who had broken free before skirting past them, leading them away from other soldiers. Looks of confusion from his campmates followed him as he made his way to the boy.

Ethan stood in front of an injured Delia, gripping a sharpened stick with shaking hands. A black-clad figure loomed over him.

This cat must have more than nine lives at this point.

Ethan's gaze flickered towards him. He glared, holding his weapon as steady as he could.

"Stay back," he said determinedly, still holding the stick out towards the advancing figure, eyes darting between the two of them.

"Get the kid," a feminine voice hissed from the other suit.

Caleb thanked the stars that they hadn't clocked him as a threat just yet. They would soon enough.

Inhaling, he caught the scent of blood weeping from a deep wound through the thick lining of their get-up.

"Ethan, it's okay," he said.

The boy's grip faltered. The stick nearly slipped from his hands before he steadied himself. "Caleb?" His voice was small, almost innocent. It would have been sweet if it hadn't set the other raider off.

"You!" the soldier yelled, taking their chance and moving for the boy.

"I wouldn't do that," Caleb warned. He let a vial slide down his sleeve, flicking off the stopper as it landed in his palm. He hoped the motion went unnoticed – and that he wouldn't prick himself by accident.

The recruit lunged.

Caleb reached for Ethan just as the boy screamed and shoved the pointed end of the stick toward his attacker. It struck deep, a sharp gasp escaping the soldier as dark liquid spread across their uniform. Ethan yelped and let go, stumbling backward towards Delia, tripping over debris.

Caleb made a move towards the injured figure, kneeling to catch them as they fell. With their weight leaning heavily on his forearm, he placed the tip of the syringe against their neck and plunged. They lost consciousness almost immediately, their weight going slack in his arms. His stomach twisted at the sight of the stick lodged deep in their gut.

"What did you do?" Ethan asked shakily.

"Put them to sleep," Caleb rasped. "Look, buddy, I gotta get back out there. These vials ..." He pulled one from his pocket, holding it up. "They're meant for us. The hybrids. Whatever's in them does ... that." He nodded toward the unconscious body. "Chances are, they have more in their pockets. If you can, both of you" – he glanced at Delia – "arm yourselves. Inject anyone who gets too close. As far as I can tell, it knocks them out."

"Caleb." Delia's voice was quiet.

"Yeah, it's me. You're okay now."

"They surprised us. I got separated from Ava and Aiel while trying to hand over the boy. The hunters fought most of them off. But she ..." Delia paused and flicked her chin out towards the slumped figure. "She broke off and got a hit in. Ethan came with me."

"You're hurt," Caleb said, noticing a trickle of blood on her side, another scratch shining along her jaw.

She nodded. "Move the body over there. Ethan and I should be safe here; the fighting has moved inside the camp and it's slowing. Send surviving hybrids to me, in case they come back. Go. You don't throw away a mission because your leader gets hurt." She winced at the last word.

"Thank you for saving us, Caleb," Ethan said shyly.

"We aren't out of the woods yet," Caleb replied. He nodded towards the body. "Reckon you could put that on?" Delia's lithe body would look out of place in the heavy suit, but it might just help them avoid a second glance.

"I can try," she said, pushing the boy gently to help her towards the body.

"Don't stab yourselves with those vials and stay out of sight. I'll do my best to keep them off your tail."

"Where are you going?" Ethan cried.

"I am going back out there. It's time to see how they like being captured."

***

Caleb moved toward Tilon and Argo, who worked in perfect sync. Bodies piled at their feet. He wondered if this was what it had been like when Tilon and Sythe fought together. The soldiers were dwindling – only a handful were still fighting. Others had fled, were unconscious or dead.

"Hey!" he called.

Both men turned, and Argo took a punch from a stocky recruit who took advantage of the distraction. Snarling, he swung back with full force, knocking them out cold.

Tilon tensed, spear raised, mistaking him for an enemy in the borrowed suit.

Shit. Caleb jumped back, hands up in defence as Tilon's spear tip aimed straight for his midsection.

"Wait a second!"

"Nice try," Tilon growled, closing in with swift precision.

"It's me!" Caleb spat out, dodging the thrust just in time.

Tilon barely hesitated, shifting the weapon smoothly into his other hand to keep momentum. He spun, preparing for another strike.

"Caleb?" Argo asked, his voice rough in his half-hybrid state.

"Obviously."

"It's him."

Tilon relaxed, although his face remained tense.

"Nice work," Caleb offered. "Check their pockets."

"What?" Argo asked, his half-wolf body giving way to his human form.

"How did you fight off the bloodlust?"

"This form is much easier to control – I keep a lot of my human thoughts and I can still hear you in my head."

"I've been trying to reach you!"

"I was a little busy."

Caleb busied himself with the pockets of one of the soldiers, feeling for the syringes inside. "Here." He lifted a handful to show the two hybrids.

"These will put them to sleep, then we tie them up and figure out where the hell they came from."

"There were a lot, Cal," Argo said, fatigue washing over him as he knelt to search a pocket. Tilon simply nodded at him, searching another. There were at least three dozen vials between them.

"Did you leave any of them alive?"

Argo and Tilon shared a look.

"We wanted to capture them, not kill them," Caleb growled.

"It was a little hard when they were coming at us," Argo argued.

"Fine. Help me with this thing, would you?" Caleb pointed to the hood, which was becoming suffocatingly hot. Argo's body was behind him in an instant, loosening and freeing him from the hood so he could see.

"Sure," Argo said gently, handing the hood back to him. "In case you need it again."

"We all need them."

"What?" Argo asked.

"He's right," Tilon agreed.

"This is how we beat them at their own game. The soldiers left me alone in this get-up. If we want to capture them, we need to look like them."

"Good idea." Winson came up to them, a bloody stump where his tail had been. Caleb tried not to gag as the flesh attempted to knit itself together in rapid time. Sinew and scale healing at rapid speed, the colouring slightly paler than the rest of his friend's body.

"Are you okay, man?" Caleb questioned.

Winson gripped his shoulder. "Never better. They've called a retreat. It looks like they weren't ready for us to put up such a fight. When they realised they were dying, their leaders pulled them back."

"Are you sure they're gone?" Caleb asked.

"It could be a ploy," Tilon started. "There is a chance some of them are hiding in plain sight, pretending to be injured or dead to take us when we least expect it. We need to check. See how many we have living, or dead."

"Retreat or not, they know we are fighting. It is only a matter of time before they return."

***

The others had donned the black suits quickly, leaving their heads exposed while they caught the attention of the hybrids. Between them, they had forty vials – enough to get some answers or take some of the soldiers down with them.

"Hey," Caleb called out to a couple of hunters walking back towards the main camp. They turned and made their way towards the group. "Do you think you could spread the word that we're in uniform and not a threat?" he asked them. "I would hate to be killed for trying to help, ya know?"

Both hunters nodded, taking a moment to take the group in. "We'll do our best, but you will need to put those masks on if you want to be believed."

Caleb grimaced at the incoming stench of someone else's sweat before fastening the headpiece.

"Let's split up. Winson and I will take the left, Tilon and Argo the right. Check the soldiers. If any are still breathing, stick them with the vials."

"And the dead?" Argo asked.

"The hunters can help us move the bodies into piles. Dead into one, unconscious captives in another. Report to Delia, see where we can place them, ready for when they wake."

The hunters nodded with a grunt.

"And what about us?" Neith queried, joining their group with Fienna and another male hunter.

"Do the same with the hybrids. We need to know who we've lost."

"May?" Winson asked, looking to the bird perched atop him. The owl trilled and flew into the camp.

"Move out," Caleb said, not missing a huff from Tilon at the command.

***

Their hybrids looked worse for wear – gashes, bruises and fallen limbs littered their path. Their compound was in total disarray. The able-bodied were moving slowly to pick up the pieces.

Ava and Aiel stumbled out of the debris, Ava sporting a new, bleeding limp. Caleb caught Aiel's gaze as she did her best to support her thick-skinned partner, tears trapped behind her eyes.

He reached for her hand as he passed. "Hey. She'll be okay," he whispered, the others turning to see what had stopped him.

"You don't know that," Aiel sniffed.

"Aye, he bloody does," Ava huffed, shuffling towards their medical supplies.

Ethan and Delia made their way back to them once the commotion had died down. Between them they counted a dozen hybrids missing and a handful of suited bodies captured. Their forms were rigid with unconsciousness.

"It looks like they took some of the equipment too," Winson commented.

Ethan made his way into Caleb's arms, leaning into him heavily. The poor kid was exhausted.

"It's not over yet, little guy."

"I know," Ethan said, not moving his arms from around Caleb's waist.

"I gotta keep working, kiddo. Stay here, get some rest." He turned to Delia. "You got him?"

She nodded. "This isn't the end of it."

"Do you think they will take time to prepare? Give us the same courtesy?"

"I think we have all learnt that this runs much deeper than we initially thought. I wouldn't be surprised if they were back sooner than we would hope, with forces we can't withstand."

"I agree," Caleb said. "We need more bodies; we need stronger bodies."

The group turned to Delia.

"This attack didn't follow the pattern. I don't think we can rely on the past moving forward. We need to adapt. These recruits came on foot – they've been watching our patrols, overwhelmed the hunter pairs from all sides."

"They were far enough away for us to not hear them. But they weren't here for long before the attack."

"What makes you say that?" Argo said.

"They smelt like soap." Caleb shrugged. "They couldn't have been roughing it here for too long."

One of the bodies stirred beside them. "Oh no ya don't," Argo said, pressing another vial of liquid into their neck.

"There could be more," Delia said. "Tilon's right. The retreat could be a ploy."

"There was a kid, a young soldier. I sticked them, but they helped me," Caleb offered.

"Helped you how?" Delia asked. The rest of the pack moved in closer to hear.

"They said they didn't want to be here, that their sister was taken. Some of these soldiers might be our allies."

"And we just ... injected them with this shit," Argo said in horror, flicking one of the syringes away.

"You weren't to know," Winson stated, "but it makes sense. Siblings, cousins, people of a similar age catching wind of what is happening. Not all of us volunteered." He shot a look at Delia.

"When do we start the questioning?" Argo asked. Caleb took a moment to turn his head. He surveyed the area. There were dozens of unconscious forms littering the ground. The hunters continued their search, moving around the camp with the efficiency of trained soldiers.

"As soon as possible. If I'm right, we don't have much time." Caleb pinched the bridge of his nose. "Tie up the captives. Let them come to. Tilon, Winson, stay close. Get ready for when they wake. Aiel, how many injured do you have in the medical bay?"

"We're full, lad."

"Aye, Delia's house too," Ava said weakly.

Caleb shuddered, a tingling sensation creeping up the back of his neck.

"What is it?" Argo asked.

"Something feels off. Smells off, too." His ear twitched, catching the sound of water rippling.

Jan's heavy footfalls caused the trees around them to shake. A pained groan sounded as the bear broke into the space.

"Jan!" Delia gasped.

"Move!" Winson pulled Delia out of the way as Jan lost his balance and fell. A massive boom sounded around them.

"Shit, man!" Argo exclaimed, opening his arms to Ethan, whose wide eyes betrayed his terror.

Jan growled, his lips pulling up over his teeth. He tried to get his arms under himself, pushing upwards.

"Stay down," Delia said, putting her hands on his side.

"Look." Caleb pointed towards Jan's back. He could see at least three vials sticking out of his fur.

Aiel rushed toward the bear. "Reach those, will ye? Take them out slowly, they still look half full."

Jan's good eye was crusted over, unable to open from a nasty gash.

"Help me turn him over," Aiel said. Caleb, Tilon and Argo pushed the bear onto his back. The beast was covered in his own sick.

Delia's tears fell. Her tenderness towards her friend filled Caleb with unexpected emotion. The mutated hybrid opened his paw, reaching for her. Delia placed her small hand in his.

With Aiel's help, she pushed Jan upright against a tree, the bear's body slumping forward.

Aiel placed her leathery hand against his neck. "His pulse is too fast. I don't know what was in those vials, but it seems like anyone who doesn't immediately fall unconscious is subject to whatever this is. I'll warm some broth for him, give him something for any nausea. It's best he rests."

Caleb thought he caught the sound of sloshing water again and felt the hair on his arms rise. He frowned. Not everyone was accounted for. There was still another location they could be taken by surprise.

"Tie them up," he said to Tilon, indicating the pile of unconscious soldiers. "Ethan, see if you can help Ava, and be careful."

"Argo, we need to check the lake."

Water Sports

Chapter Thirty-Three

"A little help!" Argo yelled. One of the soldiers had leapt upwards, grabbing onto Argo's leg.

Caleb cursed, running over to knock the recruit off his friend.

The soldier was fast, diving into their pocket and flicking the cap off a syringe with practised speed. Caleb let out a gasp, seeing the needle come towards him. Argo kicked out. A sickening crunch sounded as their attacker's arm was snapped mid-way to finding their target. They screamed, turning on the bigger man, determined to land a hit.

"Go for the back of the knee."

Caleb complied. The recruit yelped and fell into Argo's open chokehold. They lost consciousness quickly, landing on the ground unceremoniously. They stuck them with one of their needles to make sure they wouldn't get up anytime soon.

"Can you sense any more of them?" Argo asked.

Caleb nodded, placing his finger to his lips then his temple, telling Argo to speak telepathically.

"How many?"

"A handful; the retreat has been called. Hush a minute." He moved quickly and quietly down the path to the lake, urging Argo along behind him. *"Stay close to the wall. If they look up, they'll see us. Sheila has them cornered – go."*

A handful of bodies lined the banks. Limbs had been torn; necks had been snapped. Whoever had remained behind to capture their water-based hybrids didn't have nearly as much luck as those on land.

Caleb could make out parts of the soldiers' conversation as they made their way to the bank.

"Move now! If you don't, you will be left the fuck behind." The voice was firm.

"Argo, there." Caleb pointed to a soldier pinned by their alligator hybrid. Sheila's body was broad and scaled, her arms and legs webbed and thick with powerful muscle. She had been here almost as long as Jan and had taken to the water since they set up the camp. Lucky for them, she was terrifying and able to breathe both in and out of their reservoir.

"GO! Get to the pick-up zone," the soldier called out.

He looked up, eyes wide upon seeing Caleb and Argo running towards him. "Tell Murilo and Kan we have eyes on the boys! They're here!"

Caleb's blood ran cold. Sheila croaked, a threatening bark rumbling through her throat, her golden, slitted eye narrowing when she saw them running towards her.

The soldier bucked at her distraction, earning him a growl. Sheila's jaw opened wide, showing long lines of pointed teeth.

"Sheila, stop! We want him alive."

She closed her maw, snapping it next to the soldier's ear, pressing down with her claws to hold him in place. She kept one eye on Caleb and Argo before flicking it to the edge of the bank.

A grey-green lump ending in a trail of red caught his attention, stopping him in his tracks. *Lou*, he thought sadly. He had been introduced to the water-bound hybrid briefly on his first trip to the shore. He and Shiela spent most of their time together. Lou's pointed snout looked as if it had been torn in the fight. Caleb almost felt sorry for the soldier caught fighting in Sheila's natural habitat; if Lou had been killed by his men, their alligator hybrid would be pissed.

"Sheila?" he tried, but she would not be swayed from creating as much terror as possible. "Sheila!"

"Help me!" her captive shouted.

Sheila's eye flicked again. A gasp caught in his throat as he saw a gelatinous body lying face down in the water. The jovial creature he had met during his first few days bobbed gently in the water, floating away with each violent thrash of the soldier.

"Do you want me to grab him? Sheila looks like she's got it covered," Argo said, his arms crossed over his chest. "Should I chase the others?"

Caleb shook his head, trying to focus on the soldier moments away from becoming gator food.

"No." The word came out weaker than he'd intended. "Help me with this," he said, pointing towards the recruit. "Keep him pinned," he told Sheila. Caleb and Argo knelt either side of their captive.

"Help me. I won't do you a lot of good if she kills me, now, will I?" the soldier argued.

"I'm not helping you," he spat with disgust. "You decided to come into my camp and attack my friends, and you want help?"

He stopped splashing. Caleb nodded towards Sheila, her heavy, webbed foot pressing harder into the body beneath her.

"How many of you are still here?" Argo asked.

"None, the retreat has been sounded." His eyes were too focused on the threatening presence of Sheila's jaws.

"Not strictly true; we have a bunch of you tied to a tree as we speak," Argo said, bearing down on their captive and watching his reaction. "Several of you are dead. I can't say I'm sorry about that."

"Why should we stop her from adding you to the pile?" Caleb asked. Shelia's forepaw expanded, giving her more room to press down on the captive. An involuntary noise escaped his throat.

"Okay, look, I don't want to die, but I also don't want the world full of ferals!" His words were coming out in a panicked rush. "The institute is determined to make this experiment work, but to do that they need you, your bodies. They don't want you dead. They sent us here to get those who had changed, more animal than human. Like the thing standing on my arms." Sheila stood unmoved.

"Tell us something I don't know, or I'll let her tear your head off," Caleb offered.

"Fucking hell!" the soldier gasped. "Look, government funding has threatened to dry up unless your parents can provide proof they've had a breakthrough. A decade or so is a long time to wait on results, no matter how much he's managed to change you lot over the years."

"Get to the point," Caleb sniped.

"You're Caleb, right? We've all been briefed on you and Argo. Two hybrids primed from a young age to act differently with the catalysts. The feedback so far is that it's working. Which means the institution wants to start sticking kids from eight or nine with pre-release jabs, let them grow, ready to become just like you as they come of age."

Ethan's age.

"John wants to hold off. Two people isn't enough of a sample size. You and Argo have been under strict control since they first sent hybrids to this island. But global tensions are rising, and the armed forces want an army – now, not in another ten years' time. Which means fast-tracking what happened to you."

Caleb felt his eyes widen. "What does that even mean?"

"It means a breeding program. Kids injected from birth. There is a drive to pay couples to give up their unborn children as we speak."

"That's fucking barbaric."

Sheila snorted, turning towards Caleb.

"Your dad is trying to prove that he needs more time, but also that what he has done for the last decade is working. That he knows enough about each of you to create the hybrids they want. To recruit volunteers, not pay people for their unborn."

"Nice of him to draw a line somewhere," Caleb huffed.

"Kid, your old man is in trouble. This whole operation is about to be in a hell of a lot of debt. And if it doesn't work, thousands of failed hybrids need to be eradicated."

"What do you mean, 'eradicated'?" Argo asked, looking at Caleb.

"Several islands, and a big bang."

Caleb threw his arms upward. "You have got to be kidding me!" He pinched the bridge of his nose, taking a moment to breathe. "Will you run if she lets go?"

"What?"

"Answer the question. Will you run if I ask her to let go?"

"Are you going to kill me?"

"Depends on whether you cooperate."

"I don't have a choice."

"Fine. Sheila, on three, let him up." Caleb looked at the trapped soldier. "And when she does, lose the mask and don't run. She is faster than you think."

He counted to three and Sheila lifted her claws from the soldier. He slipped before scrambling up the side of the bank. Argo followed, keeping their captive within arm's length.

Caleb spoke to Sheila in a hurried whisper. "Check on the others. Bring any bodies you find to the shore. Leave the suits for the clickers, give them a taste of their own damn medicine." Sheila tilted her jaw before sliding back into the water.

Caleb turned towards Argo and the now unmasked soldier. Sweat-soaked, curly black hair gave way to ochre skin and deep brown eyes. Neat stubble lined his strong jaw, his mouth set in a serious line. There was something familiar about the man before him. Had he seen this guy at one of his father's gatherings? Caleb frowned at his face, trying to place him. The soldier looked towards Argo, then back at him.

"If you aren't going to kill me—"

"I'm not sure what we are going to do with you yet," Caleb said. An incessant buzz sounded in his ear, making him wince, his hackles rising along his spine.

"Do you hear that?" Caleb asked Argo, tilting his head toward the sky.

"Hear what?"

***

"What's your name?" Caleb asked the soldier as they walked up the bank. Argo had tied the recruit's hands behind his back with vines from the shore and was leading him toward camp with a pointed stick behind his back.

"Are you going to inject me with that thing?" he asked in response.

"Not yet," Argo mumbled.

"Name's Nadir."

"They aren't coming back for you, are they?" Caleb asked, needing to confirm.

"Anyone who isn't at the pick-up point will be left behind. I was to stay back and make sure we all got on the subs."

"Submarines?"

"Why do you think you haven't found a dock?"

"I thought it was the clickers killing us off."

"They are used to patrol, yes. But there also isn't a way off this island. A new class of weapon has just been introduced to the waters. They aren't tame, but they are highly effective. None of you would make it. Not even your water-bound friends."

"And what will they do when you're not there?"

"Take who they can and assume the rest of us are dead or soon will be. We're expendable, kid."

Argo grunted.

Nadir glanced back at him before continuing. "More so than your hybrids. You offer your father a future, even if it isn't the one he envisioned. We're merely tools for the cause."

"And you're okay with that?"

"Who said I was? My mother tried to leave Murilo's enterprise. I had to see for myself what had become of it."

"Tried?"

"She died, not long after."

"Why join? Were they coming for you next?" Caleb asked, ears pricking up at the noise in the distance.

"I had to know."

"And are you satisfied?" He tried to keep the disdain out of his voice.

"No." The answer was short, dejected.

They crested the ridge, walking through the broken camp to the main firepits where Tilon and Winson had tied their captives: four of them, plus the recruit who helped Caleb, all unconscious.

"Tie him over there." Caleb pointed to a free tree along the line of captives.

Nadir didn't resist as Argo led him over. Tilon walked behind the pair, syringe in hand.

"That's hardly necessary," Nadir tried. Tilon plunged the vial into his skin. The soldier squinted, fighting the inevitable loss of consciousness. "Taylor?" he asked before giving in to the sedative.

Caleb scratched at his head, rubbing against his ear.

"What is it?" Argo whispered.

"You sure you can't hear that?"

Interrogation

Chapter Thirty-Four

Caleb and Tilon stood in front of the first waking captive, arms crossed over their chests. What looked to be a woman in her mid-thirties squinted at them in the sunlight. Letting out a groggy groan, she hung her head before forcing it back upward to glare at the two of them.

"Fucking freaks," she spat coldly. "Gerome, wake up." She kicked the older man tied up beside her.

"We had to hit – Gerome, was it? – with a double dose. I doubt he'll be awake anytime soon," Caleb said.

He knelt to offer the soldier a cup of water, lifting it to her lips. The woman hissed and bucked, knocking the clear liquid all over herself.

"Get away from me."

He felt Tilon's clawed hand pull him away from the thrashing captive. He knelt, flashing his fangs as he leaned close to her face.

"Fuck off, freak."

A glob of spit landed on Tilon's cheek. The hybrid smirked before standing to his full height in front of her. His shadow engulfed the soldiers.

"Where did you come from?"

"My mother and father, same as you. Next question."

"I wouldn't piss him off, lady," Caleb said.

"No one asked you, wonder boy. You're untouchable; why the fuck do you even care what happens to these freaks?"

"I don't know if you've noticed, but I'm one of them," he said, flicking his ear.

"Not according to your father. You weren't to be taken, not yet."

"And where is John? Why didn't he come with you? Or Markus, for that matter."

"Caleb," Tilon bristled. "Not the time."

"You won't get anything from me, asshole."

"No?" Tilon asked, moving forward with rapid speed, kneeling close to the soldier's snarling. Caleb felt her heart rate quicken. The smell of fear rolled off her.

The soldier looked at him, her eyes giving away her fear, before she scowled and pressed her neck against Tilon's mouth.

"I dare you," she said before snapping her jaws shut.

Something sweet and acidic filled her mouth. Tilon's jaw opened.

"Tilon, get back!"

The big cat jumped backward, "what?"

Argo and Winson were walking towards them, ready for the next soldier to wake.

"Something smells off," Caleb said.

The soldier started to convulse, her body jerking against the restraints.

"What the hell?"

The woman's head lolled to the side, foaming bile spilling out of her mouth. A slow trickle of blood dribbled from her ears, dripping down her shoulders. She shuddered, straining against the vines before she stilled.

"Check her pulse," Tilon commanded. Caleb walked forward, keeping his head away from the soldier's mouth. Dead.

"What ... the fuck ... was that?" Caleb asked, wide-eyed.

"Suicide pill," Argo said flatly. "Our dads really have us all on a tightrope right now if it is worth dying over."

"This is fucked."

The remaining captives stirred one by one. Gerome had seen the woman and immediately bitten down on his own pill, followed by another unnamed soldier. The group hadn't had the chance to ask them anything before they died.

"Three down, two to go," Argo said in Caleb's head.

I am not qualified for this, Caleb thought.

"What the hell?" Caleb heard from behind them, a dazed voice adequately conveying the absurdity of the situation.

"Shit," Caleb said.

The young soldier who had helped him during the fight lifted their head groggily.

"Oi! Wolf head, I helped you, and you ... drug me?"

Tilon and Argo turned towards the sound, both snarling at the intrusion, making their way toward the kid.

"Wait!" Caleb yelled. "Just, hold up." He raised his hands in defence. "This is the kid that helped me. They might be our best chance." Tilon stopped his advance.

"Appreciate it. Mind letting me up?" they said.

Caleb knelt to free them from their tree.

"Did you find my sister, dude?"

"Stop calling me dude ... and no, at least I don't think so. But I'm glad you're alive."

The kid rolled their eyes. "Oh shit," they said, looking past the hybrids to stare at the two dead soldiers. "They really chomped down, huh? Mikaela? Damn."

"You knew her?" Caleb tried to gentle his tone despite his annoyance.

"Sorta. We were recruited together, if you could call it that. The brainwashing got to her more than me. It's like a cult, man ... sorry." They paused to stretch. "We all get them. The pills. Some of us are smart enough to take them out," they said, opening their mouth to show the gap where their tooth should have been. "It's full of arsenic or some shit, we don't really get told. Just ... bite down if you get captured. If you reveal our secrets, doom will fall upon you and your family. It's so stupid. I mean, look at all of you. You probably just want to go home. I know I do, and I've only been here a few days."

"Days?" Delia approached, using Ethan as a crutch as she limped. Fienna and Neith were not far behind her.

"No ... shit. You're actually a cat. This stuff is really working? Like, turning you into animals? Say, are you gonna kill me ... or do you think you could back up a bit?"

"This 'stuff'," Delia said, pointedly cutting them off, "has been working for a decade. Now, we wish to stop it." She turned to Caleb. "This is the one who helped you?"

He nodded.

"They're your responsibility."

"Wouldn't be the first time a kid landed in my lap," he said, untying the restraints.

"I'm not a kid and I'm on your side," they grumbled, shaking out their hands before extending one to Delia. "I'm Taylor. Pleased to meet you."

Delia looked at them, eyebrow raised, before offering a slender claw. Her delicate hand was immediately enveloped in human flesh. Taylor's eyes were wide with disbelief at the contact.

"Wow!" they exclaimed while Delia retracted her hand slowly, eyes not leaving their unexpected ally.

"Respectfully, we don't have time for this," she said. "Tell us where you came in and I will send my hunters to inspect the sites."

"There is no second wave."

"And why should I trust you?"

"Delia," Caleb said. "The kid's done nothing but help."

"Where is the pickup point? For the retreat. Maybe we can get there first," Argo offered.

"I wouldn't."

"Why not?" Delia asked, annoyed.

"For starters, you look a little worse for wear. Second, they now know you're willing to fight. We were going to grab you unconscious and take you back to the labs. It's set up like a fuckin' zoo pen. If they don't take these experiments to the next level on their own, someone with more power and more money will."

"And you know this ... how?" Argo asked.

Taylor shrugged. "I'm not great at staying put."

"How are we going with them?" Delia asked Tilon and Caleb, pointing to the unconscious soldiers still tied to the trees.

Caleb glanced over at the captives. "Ethan!" he hissed, catching the boy poking the soldiers with a stick. The boy dropped the implement and ran to the group sheepishly.

"Why are you not in vines?" Ethan asked Taylor.

"Guess they trust me, what about you?"

"I didn't try to take them!" Ethan stated defiantly before narrowing his eyes at their new arrival.

"That's fair," Taylor said, smiling at their youngest member.

"Are you a boy or a girl?" The question fell out of Ethan's mouth. Caleb wasn't sure either; the kid rode the line of androgyny like he had never seen before. He didn't know whether to be appalled by Ethan's inquisitiveness or curious as to the answer.

"Ethan," Delia scolded. "That's not polite, now, is it?"

Taylor chuckled awkwardly. "Both? Neither? I've never really fit."

"What should we call you?" Ethan followed up, his small brow furrowed in confusion.

"Just Taylor is fine. Something neutral if you must." They smiled.

"I don't get it," Ethan said to Caleb loudly enough so the camp could hear.

"Sorry," Caleb said, rubbing the back of his neck.

"You don't have to get it," Argo said gently. "Just respect it. Besides, we have bigger problems right now."

"Have the other two spoken yet?" Delia asked as Winson made his way towards them with May. Caleb turned, frowning. The buzzing was still gnawing at him.

"No," Tilon said. "Argo and Caleb brought that one with them. A sergeant or team lead; he was the last to get sticked."

"Said his name was Nadir," Argo offered.

"Nadir?" Delia said, unbelieving, taking a step towards the floppy-haired captive and pushing him upright.

"My God," she whispered.

***

Delia stood over Nadir, waiting for him to come around, nervously pacing in front of the tree. The remaining captives had stirred and refused to talk, but grudgingly accepted Taylor's offer of water. Their new ally hovered as much as Delia, waiting for their leader to wake.

Once Jan roused, Ava and Aiel were able to guide him to lean outside of the medical bay. Caleb still couldn't get rid of the constant buzzing in his ears and the feeling something was wrong. He had taken off with Argo and Winson to count their survivors. He gasped at the discovery of Edgar and Missy lying with their necks broken among the group of murdered hybrids.

So much for capturing rather than killing us, he thought angrily.

He returned just in time to witness Nadir waking up and sucking in lungfuls of air.

"Nadir?" Delia said softly.

"Delia," Nadir returned a gentle smile accompanying her name. "I'm glad you're alive."

"Your parents. Are they ...?"

Nadir shook his head sadly.

"It's been—"

"Eight years. We've heard about you," Nadir choked. "The bosses are pissed you seemed to have turned your back."

"We know." Caleb frowned, scratching his wolven ear as it twitched again.

Nadir stole a glance at Taylor, his eyes softening. "You made it."

"Do we have more allies amongst you?" Caleb asked.

"Some, like Taylor, I suspect. We were meant to weed them out. Too risky to have sympathisers amongst our recruits. There is a group looking for you; they have been known to try and infiltrate our numbers," Nadir said, not unkindly. "I'm not sure I am an ally, truth be told. I don't think you belong back with us, but you also don't deserve this. The military taking over isn't exactly what John and Markus had planned. They hold some remorse for sending you here, you kn ow."

"I find that hard to believe," Argo scoffed.

"I just don't know what a world looks like with you in it."

"Who's this?" Winson asked, wandering up to the group from the direction of the medical unit.

"Nadir," the soldier offered.

"Friend or foe?"

"Unsure," Caleb said. "Someone tell me you can hear that?"

Winson shook his head and stepped over to the remaining captives, kicking at their feet. "Ready to talk?"

Ignoring Winson, they turned to Nadir. "They are coming back for you, right?"

"No. And it's in our best interest to cooperate," Nadir replied. "Mind taking off the binds? I couldn't run even if I wanted to."

"I don't trust him," Winson said.

"Then trust my survival instincts." He looked at Tilon. "Soldier to soldier."

"Let him up," Delia said. "Them too." She pointed at the last two soldiers.

"I'm not telling you anything," they said, lurching against Argo's attempt to undo their vines.

"Your vials have been destroyed and there is nowhere for you to go. Come, Nadir, we'll fix you a plate."

***

They sat across one another by the fire, the hybrids who had survived the invasion giving Taylor and Nadir a wide berth. The remaining captive, Amabella, had chosen to stay by the trees on the outskirts of the compound. Delia had stationed a pair of hunters to watch over her.

Caleb, Argo and Ava sat close by, listening to the conversation between Delia, Tilon and Nadir. Winson continued to organise relief efforts well into the night.

They would hold a day of remembrance followed by a new age of structured training and scouting missions with the help of Nadir to get off the island.

Argo leant down to whisper in Caleb's ear. "I think you're right."

"Hmm?"

"I can hear it."

Delia shot daggers at them, turning back to Nadir.

"What can you hear?"

"I dunno. A whirring, maybe mechanical. It's a while away. I can't tell if it's just in my head though."

Caleb heard his father's name and tuned back into Delia's conversation.

"The forces want John and Markus to start again. Either abandon this place completely or commit mass genocide. The military is leaning towards the latter. Less mess, less questions – could be played off as a natural disaster. There are people sniffing around, like I said. This way ... there would be very little evidence of foul play."

"Why?" Tilon asked, his arms crossed over his chest.

"They believe John has the technology to create an acceptable army that will enhance our forces. Enough to put the combined United States and Australian forces on the map as a global threat. The clickers, your hunters and now the water-bred weapons prove that experiments can be created in batches, all with similar features and abilities. They could prime a generation of fighters from birth using the same sequence as your two resident wolves." He looked at Caleb and Argo.

"How does that help them if they want an army now?"

"Delia's hunters have been studied alongside her when Gregorio visits. Mass cloning has been attempted with very little success, but enough to provide an enhancement to the front lines while the army is built. Their use of genetic enhancers can speed up the aging process; others are then used to stop it when the young are ready to receive treatment."

"Dad doesn't agree?" Caleb asked.

"No. Your father thinks he can do more, but he needs more time. Always more time. He promised an army of shifters, hybrids with a multitude of abilities to be used in every aspect an army could need. You have them here to varying degrees of success: scouts, fighters, medics. But he's running out of time."

"So why aren't you here to kill us?"

"John and Markus have been given an ultimatum. Another year or so – I am not privy to the specifics. What I do know is the labs are ready. Any of the hybrids captured here that are deemed a successful experiment will be cloned, mass-produced and trained."

"We have to stop them," Caleb murmured.

"Now that I've seen you, I agree," Nadir said, standing and stretching. "I don't know what the answer is, but whatever you're planning, you'll need help."

"And if you want to survive in this place, you're going to need our help," Caleb retorted.

"Touché."

Nadir watched him as his head tilted once more to the sky.

"Caleb. I figured out what that noise is," Argo warned.

Mother. Fucker.

That wasn't just one chopper. It was a whole fleet of them.

"Hey." Nadir had his hand stretched out towards him. "Truce?"

"We're about to find out."

The Last Wave

Chapter Thirty-Five

The approaching thump of the aircraft blades stirred the remaining captive. Amabella yelled towards the sky, screaming for rescue. Hybrids emerged from their crates, bleary-eyed at the commotion. Dawn would be upon them any minute now and tensions were already high.

"Tilon!" Ethan's voice called down from their room at the top of the hill. Caleb spun to see Amabella gripping Tilon around the neck, having straddled his back, jabbing a needle in him. Tilon's body dropped with a heavy thud.

"How did she get a fucking syringe!" Caleb yelled, about to leap forward towards his friend only to find himself held back by Taylor and Nadir. He fought, trying to shake them off, but they were too strong.

"Don't." Taylor's voice came out hushed and hurried. "She doesn't understand."

"And she won't hesitate to hurt you," Nadir added. "They need you alive, not unharmed."

"I'm a fucking wolf, or have you forgotten?"

"Just ... let me try," Nadir said.

Amabella bent down to hook her arms under Tilon, attempting to drag the large hybrid toward the direction of the helicopters.

"Bella." Nadir's voice fought for purchase over the increasing noise.

"Fuck you, traitor," the soldier said, tugging the body weakly, no match for the dead weight. "They are coming for us. Not you. You left your post, and I'll be damned if I am letting you come back all high and mighty like you were the mastermind behind the capture."

Winson and Argo came to stand beside Caleb.

"This isn't going to go anywhere. Let's go," Argo said.

Delia's claw gripped his arm; she allowed her weight to lean on him. The noise was getting closer. If they were going to see what the hell was going on, they needed to move.

"What if Nadir was wrong about another attack?"

"Doesn't smell like soldiers." Argo's voice caught him off guard. He was right; it smelt sick.

Amabella had given up, dropping Tilon's body and turning to run. Taylor held up their hands in front of her. "They aren't here for you."

"No one asked your hybrid-loving ass. Why the fuck are you even here?"

"To stop this!" Taylor screamed at her.

Jan let out a cry, the big bear standing tall and hovering over the campsite. He grunted, ushering able-bodied hybrids forward toward the sound. He was moving slowly, but fast enough to scare Amabella. She was outnumbered and she knew it. Those strong enough to stand suddenly loomed in every direction, a mixture of scales, feathers and fur exposed along human skin. If the government wanted an army, they were looking at it.

"You just fucking wait, they'll be back. They'll come for us. And when they do, I'll be ready to take you down along with them," Amabella screamed, tears falling down her face.

The thunderous whirring of the helicopters was almost above them now. Caleb could hear the whoosh of the canopy fluttering in the fast-moving air.

"They aren't here for you," Caleb said to Amabella, repeating Taylor's sentiment. The soldier looked to the sky, uncertainty painted over her features.

"How the fuck would you know, golden boy?"

"The brief was clear. Those not at the pickup location would be left behind. You're a liability now," Nadir said firmly.

"Fuck you," she grunted, the fight falling out of her voice.

"Should I tie her up again?" Winson asked.

"No need," Nadir asserted. "She'll cooperate. Won't you, soldier?"

"I'm not helping you."

Caleb growled. "From where I stand, you have two options: bite down on your suicide pill or get on board with getting us out of here. All of us."

"You don't really think these freaks deserve to be rescued, right!?" Amabella yelled, looking from Taylor to Nadir.

Caleb felt his hackles rise, his muscles tensing, ready to put this soldier in her place.

"Watch what you're saying," Tilon grunted, forcing his body upright and taking a step towards the soldier. His natural strength was no match for the drug's potency. Still, the large, cat-like hybrid had been weakened. Caleb watched as Tilon launched a groggy and lazy swipe at Amabella. She dodged the attempt with a scowl.

"You're probably going to want to start being nicer to these 'freaks'," Taylor bit back, their voice tight with their own annoyance. "You're in their territory now. The briefs have nothing on the forest. You ever met a clicker in real life?"

"We could send her to the ferals," Ethan suggested, making a couple of the hybrids around him snigger unexpectedly. Argo looked at the boy like he was seriously considering the suggestion.

"No, Argo. We don't even know where they are," Caleb chided, the visible relief on their newest member's face amusingly evident. Silence fell amongst the group as the dirt beneath their feet started to tremble and shake. The chuff and thump of rapidly spinning rotor blades came through in a sudden crescendo of noise. Leaves fluttered with ferocity around them, trees threatening to snap in the onslaught of wind as the aircraft moved overhead. Caleb felt his jaw drop as he looked to the sky.

There must have been over twenty powerful machines creating a flurry of wind and noise. The smaller hybrids dropped to the ground while those standing dug their heels into the dirt as hard as they could, buffeted by clouds of rising dust.

"No!" Amabella's voice rang out with hopelessness as she dropped to her knees, eyes laser-focused on the powerful machines flying overhead with no sign of landing to pick up their fallen recruits. It looked as if it had finally sunk in; she wasn't getting out of here. Not without their help.

Caleb spied crates swinging heavily on powerful chains. Whoever or whatever was inside could be friend or foe – and there was only one way to find out. The trees started to settle, and bodies shuffled around him. He looked over to Argo and nodded.

"Let's go," Caleb said, leaning down on the new but powerful muscle that corded through his legs.

He felt Argo take a similar stance and let his lips twitch into a smile despite the situation they all found themselves in.

Standing once more, Caleb closed his eyes and took a breath. he inhaled long and deep, letting the tension release from his body as the air pushed outwards.

"Let's all go," he corrected, looking at the hybrid army gathered around him.

Caleb offered his hand to Amabella. "Looks like you're with us now," he said.

She allowed herself to be pulled upright, the fight having fallen out of her.

"Okay?" Argo asked.

"Okay." Caleb nodded, encouraging the group forward. They moved as one, a dozen sets of feet at the front, those he had come to know and trust, and those he had come to love without realising it.

Whatever came next, Caleb finally admitted he wasn't alone.

Attempting to venture swiftly, they made their way to the nearest ledge that overlooked a great valley beyond. It was the clearest view of the forest they had, seldom going up there for fear of spies or predators, preferring to stick to the shadows – a time that was now past. The shadows were not home anymore; they never would be again.

Caleb tensed as he counted at least twenty new hybrids swaying in their crates. He knew they would have to hunt, reach or save each and every one of them in the coming weeks.

Without realising, he had started to prepare a search party in his head.

A small, furred hand found its way into his own, shocking Caleb from his thoughts.

Delia squeezed his fingers tight.

The sun cast them all in a glow as it broke on the horizon, the shadows of early morning creating ominous shapes across the landscape. Caleb could only hope it wasn't a sign of what was to come.

Another hand found its way to him. Argo's strong, calloused palm was on his shoulder, his body heat providing a small comfort.

Ethan had stepped in front of the two of them, and they reached for him without thought, pulling the boy close, one hand each on his small chest, feeling the gentle rise and fall of his body.

Whatever happened next, Caleb knew his pack would guide him through. Whatever their future held, he would protect them as best he could. He wasn't alone anymore; perhaps he never was.

A smile touched his lips as more bodies moved in behind them to watch the spectacle. The heavy, drugged steps of Jan thundered as he made his way across the ledge.

Tilon and Winson came into his periphery, Tilon's strong frame and Winson's lithe, scaley form. Their jaws were clenched with determination, staring down the helicopters lowering in practised formation across the forest.

Caleb could feel them mapping out the locations of each crate as they were moved into the trees. Ava had brought their scouts from a mission that seemed so long ago, and Sheila had led those able to leave the water to join them. They were all in this together.

The sky burned with its golden glow, their collective anger rising with the sun. Together, they watched as the first crate was dropped, the solid thump of its base connecting with the ground echoing around them. For better or worse, the next wave had arrived.

Epilogue

Not Just an Experiment

A soft glow emanated from under the office door, the house quiet as a cemetery in the dead of night. The staff had been sent home hours ago. John desperately needed to be by himself before he snapped – again.

He didn't have much time to prove he was ready before they took it all away from him and made it their own. He was the mastermind; this was *his* life's work. He had sent his own damn son into the experiment to prove he was making progress. Only, it had been that progress the governing bodies latched onto. He had already created an army, far off the coast of the country. There must have been close to a thousand of them now in various stages of change. The last batch had shown promise, his labs filled with a dozen bodies that had become stronger with his intervention – warriors. But it would take more than a handful to prove his point.

He needed to move faster.

The questions were piling up. The authorities were breathing down his neck, trying to tie him to disappearances across the globe. They were getting close. Too close. None of that would matter if he could prove his worth. Trouble was, suspicion had moved in-house and there was only so much John could do to stop it. Those who spoke about it were removed without warning or compensation. John didn't have time to coddle them, not anymore. The international powers that wanted his army far outweighed any official investigation by the local police. If John was in their good graces, he couldn't be touched. But their favour was dwindling with each passing day.

John focused on his breathing as he waited for the cameras to activate. He had tried to award the victims of his experiments some shred of privacy. The raids were costly, and the soldiers were dying now that the hybrids had started to push back. He needed more, needed to see what they were doing between raids. He needed to know exactly where they were, at all times. The world wanted an army, and the government demanded proof that they couldn't take his technology, his genetic experimentation, and mass-produce it more efficiently.

It wasn't ready. The damn hybrids were still turning feral. If they needed more than his reports and snapshots, he would give them more.

His stomach churned as he waited for the equipment to be activated. *I had to do it*, he thought, trying to convince himself he hadn't crossed yet another line.

An incessant beeping made him wince, the sheer shrill of it grating his ears until he hit the pager, acknowledging the message. The latest hybrid captives were sedated and ready for testing. The raid had awarded him with several beasts who had nearly completed a full transformation. Not fully animal, not feral, but changed to the point they could be used. Good. He had to find a way to stop them from turning. An army was useless if the transformation couldn't be stopped, and it was still happening. He needed to understand why.

Collateral, he thought. He needed a list of the missing soldiers. Their families would need to be compensated.

He hit the chair heavily, the plush red leather swivelling with his force. His lamp shined a focused light on the latest set of papers from the university, ugly red lines squiggled all over his research. He had been given twelve months to show he could do it, or he would be removed from the project altogether, allowing the big corporations to take over. They would pay him handsomely for his services for the future of the United States Army.

Raking a hand through his hair, John gripped down hard on the official notice.

Lights flickered above him as the newly installed screen burst into life.

This was it; he was going to see it in real time. He had never been to the island himself, outside of choosing the uninhabited landmass more than a decade ago. He had seen snippets of the camps, sent in shipments of seeds and shelter with each raid, making sure they had just enough to survive, but not enough to advance too much.

His heart skipped a beat as he lifted his head to take in the massive wooded area reserved to keep his "dangerous" experiments out of people's homes. He imagined the clickers patrolling the coastline, the underground bunkers holding a handful of soldiers ready for the next raid. There wasn't another island in sight. The mainland would take them days to reach by submarine. Only surfacing to drop new troops on the shore, dipping back under the waves undetected. It was all changing now. This was it. He watched in awe as the cameras rolled over the compound that had taken his experiments years to build, its integrity destroyed by the latest raid. Before John realised it, his head was down, and the tapping of the keyboard filled the room as his initial observations were recorded.

John smiled. They would see this was his project, and he wasn't letting it go without a fight.

The invites were already sent. He could see it now – the proof he needed for more money than he could imagine. He had already accomplished so much. John eyed creatures and people he barely recognised. Everyone in his circles wanted to be rid of someone, bodies donated to the cause in the guise of clinical trials. He didn't need the military to take over, to breed new hybrids into life; he had all the subjects he could ever want.

He thought of the first time an official showed up at his door having caught wind of his research. They wanted in. They foresaw the perfect weapons changing before their very eyes. They needed to get it right, for the world.

John felt his chest swell with a deep sense of pride mottled with shame, the two emotions battling against each other inside of his tired mind.

The air whooshed out of him in a sigh as he stared back at a man he once knew, a man sporting two new eyes full of a fierce fury he had never known before. The camera shook as the wooden crate shifted, holding his only means of visibility of his son.

John stared, waiting for the camera to focus as it got further and further away from the group watching out over a hill, surveying as he sent more souls to take part in his life's work. He couldn't help staring himself, that one brief look allowing him to take in how his son's body had changed into something new, something strong.

He had done that. And he would create more, as many as were demanded of him.

It was working, they would see.

John picked up his phone to tap out Markus's number, sending him the date and time of the meeting the following day. The man had been a dishevelled mess since agreeing to send his own boy off into the wilderness. If only he could see him now. He would. They all would.

Tomorrow.

A smile tugged at his lips. The child he couldn't bear to be around after the death of his wife, the one who had helped him start all this, would be his salvation. They had fallen apart, but he had made him into something he could be proud of. He hoped the kid would be ready for what was coming.

One thought played through his mind over and over as he reached for the light and bathed the room in darkness.

"You look good, son."

THE END

Dedication

To Grandpa Ian Smith

A Simple Gesture

A lot of little learnings
   I missed along the way.
   I never knew how to sit or walk
   and lost the things to say.
   Brought up in social constructs,
   not knowing how to be.
   An answer round the corner
   but unbeknownst to me.
   Then suddenly, something clicked.
   My body, it was wrong.
   Perhaps I wasn't born this way
   and my mind knew all along.
   Discovery came with familial guilt,
   I thought, forever I'd be shunned.
   Instead, was met with faith and love
   and not just from above.
   I questioned almost everything.
   Who I was, and how I am.
   But the day that grandpa shook my hand
   I knew that I could be a man.

About This Book

The concept for ALPHA came to me in a particularly dark and daunting time in my life. The Post-it note where I scribbled down some initial thoughts still sits in my beat-up wallet to this day. I remember very clearly not knowing what to do with my increasing amounts of gender dysphoria, feeling trapped in a body that wasn't mine, all the while the picture of my future getting clearer and clearer in my mind. It was during this time I had started to dabble in the fact maybe I wasn't okay, maybe there was something worth exploring in this feeling of wrongness, the need to tear myself from existence, that maybe not everyone felt this way.

It was also around this time I was relying heavily on Lindsey Stirling's *Artemis* album, ironically named after the Goddess of the hunt. Stirling created music I could see on the page, unfolding with my own story. Nearly every song in this album has a scene in this book, with two reserved for book two. The opening scene of Caleb and his father's soiree was inspired by "Masquerade", and the closing scene can be largely attributed to "Guardian". Where the remainder fall? Let's see if you can pick up on them.

While that note remained in my back pocket for a few years, and I explored creating other fictional works, something told me I couldn't release anything until ALPHA was done. But I wasn't ready. I didn't know everything I would need to make this story what it is: fundamentally a fictionalised mirror of my journey as a transgender man. When I wrote my scrappy note, I was pre-medical transition but exploring gender therapy. I was drinking myself to sleep to make the inner turmoil stop, and walking my days in survival mode. It wasn't until I felt comfortable in my own skin through surgeries and hormone replacement that I could sit down and start exploring these incredibly complex emotions. I had to unwrap the layers of who I have always been but couldn't see in the mirror yet. A lot has changed over the past seven years, and although it wasn't pleasant, I have been grateful for the journey and the pack I have made along the way.

In this book you will find references to hormones, physical and mental changes, found family, unsupportive families, allies, those who don't quite understand but are curious enough to give you the time of day, the wider community, self-discovery, positive parenting (through said found-family elements), corporations who want to put us in a box, corporations who want to use us for marketing and clout and those who will throw us away when administrations change, non-binary identities and there is still more to come.

Ultimately, while this book isn't outwardly a story of human medical transition, I hope my pack feels seen. To those who came before me, Tiffany, Ben and Andrew, thank you for answering my million questions even when we hadn't spoken in years. To my transmasc nibling Rian, we grew up in our transition together and I couldn't be more grateful to have you by my side. To those who came after, Melinda, Steve, K and anyone who has reached out through my personal socials, it was an honour to be the one answering questions this time around. And to those still figuring it out, welcome to the pack.

Acknowledgements

Remember the saying "It takes a village"? Well, writing a book is another one of those things that takes a mountain of people to create a viable product. ALPHA is no exception.

There are so many people to thank here, first and foremost my beautiful wife, copyeditor and proofreader, Rachel (Bella) Marchesi. Outside of the red pen marks, you have held my hand from the very start. Not just this book, but the life we now share. Your curious mind, fierce loyalty and unwavering love have lifted me up and helped me grow strong over the last seven years. For helping me to discover the man I could truly be (and the facetious drawings of Argo and Caleb), thank you.

To my best friend and alpha reader, Nathan, your honest feedback and excitement for this story was infectious.

To Mark Timmony, what can I say? Alpha reader, writing sprint motivator, critical analyser, question answerer 5000 and one of my dearest friends. This book wouldn't have made it without you.

To my developmental editor, Olivia Hofer, you challenged me in a way I didn't expect and made me delve into my "why" to the nth degree. I now know these characters back to front. You took a story idea and made it into something I never thought I could achieve. You are a master at your craft, and I thank you.

To the beta reading team, Esmay, Katherine, Abel and Jym Bobbilton Esquire the 3rd (I told you I would put this in here), your feedback was unanimous, and I thank you for guiding me to change how the ending went down. The book is better for it.

To the ARC team, thank you for being ALPHA's early champions.

To everyone who helped share the cover of ALPHA – that day was so surreal, and you made it a blast, thank you!

To the indie community, readers and writers alike who band together and face the self-published world with such passion, you're all superstars. Special mention to Palmer Pickering, who reminded me to keep the story my own through the extensive editing process. To Helen Rygh-Pedersen, who shared the highs and lows of the self-published world. You have been there since the beginning, and I thank you. To Michael Michel, Bard and Butter's very own hype man. You changed our world, brother. Thank you.

To the other members of the JKLM crew, Justin, Lilli and Marnie Marchesi. Thank you for your love, patience and grace while I figured myself out.

And finally, to you, dear reader, for taking a chance on this book, it means the world.